PRAISE FOR
What You Need

"Deliciously real, modern, hot, and funny."
—*New York Times* bestselling author Katy Evans

"Relentless chemistry and sizzling romance make this book a must read!" —*New York Times* bestselling author Laura Kaye

"This refreshing new series by James is a tender excursion into the lives of an uptight billionaire and a company employee."
—*RT Book Reviews*

"Fun, sweet, and sexy. Lorelei James captures the angst and anticipation of a slow-burn family-run-office romance with engaging characters. . . . Fans of Jaci Burton and Shiloh Walker will enjoy *What You Need*." —Harlequin Junkie

"If you're looking for a quick, sexy read, this one is definitely for you. I can't wait for the next! Well-done, Lorelei James! Very well-done." —The Reading Cafe

"The characters are perfect; the romance is perfect and takes things step by step. Not too rushed, not too slow. . . . This is a series I'll be looking forward to seeing more of soon!"
—Under the Covers

"Lorelei has blown me away with a beautiful romance that is sexy and sweet, and I loved every second of it!"
—Guilty Pleasures Book Reviews

continued . . .

PRAISE FOR THE OTHER NOVELS
OF LORELEI JAMES

All You
Need

THE NEED YOU SERIES

LORELEI JAMES

JOVE
New York

A JOVE BOOK
Published by Berkley
An imprint of Penguin Random House LLC
375 Hudson Street, New York, New York 10014

Copyright © 2017 by LJLA, LLC
Excerpt from *Just What I Needed* copyright © 2016 by LJLA, LLC
Penguin Random House supports copyright. Copyright fuels creativity, encourages
diverse voices, promotes free speech, and creates a vibrant culture. Thank you for buying
an authorized edition of this book and for complying with copyright laws by not
reproducing, scanning, or distributing any part of it in any form without permission.
You are supporting writers and allowing Penguin Random House to continue to
publish books for every reader.

A JOVE BOOK and BERKLEY are registered trademarks and the B colophon
is a trademark of Penguin Random House LLC.

ISBN: 9780451477576

First Edition: April 2017

Printed in the United States of America
1   3   5   7   9   10   8   6   4   2

Cover photo by Claudio Marinesco
Book design by Kelly Lipovich

One

—

ANNIKA

The first time I met professional hockey player Axl Hammerquist, the maître d' busted him banging our waitress in the coat check room.

The second time I met Axl Hammerquist, he insulted me before texting me a half-naked picture of himself.

The third time I met Axl Hammerquist, I caught him doing body shots with two scantily clad blondes.

I did not have high hopes for this meeting.

I considered it a bad sign that I'd literally taken a wrong turn in St. Paul. Even as a Twin Cities native I occasionally got lost. I pulled over and tried not to yell instructions at my Bluetooth on who to call.

My assistant, Deanna, picked up on the second ring. "Annika Lund's office."

"Why hasn't someone invented GPS that takes oral commands? Where I could channel Uhura and set a course by speaking the address into the com instead of having to stop the car and physically type it in?" I complained.

"I love it when you show your inner Trekkie geek, boss. Envision me sitting at my desk making the Vulcan sign for 'live long and prosper.'"

"Envision me attempting a Vulcan mind meld on you instead of asking you to please text me the address again."

"No problem."

After I typed it in, I realized I hadn't been remotely close to where I'd needed to be and the program rerouted me. "Thanks, D."

"Good luck. I have Pilates at six, but I'll be around after that to bail you out of jail."

"Let's hope it doesn't come to that. See you tomorrow."

Once I'd found the place—in a bit of a sketchy neighborhood—I parked. I passed by the sign that was hammered into the strip of grass in front of the ten-story building and that indicated the structure had been zoned as a multiuse space for offices and residences with "retail space coming soon"—*soon* being a relative term.

Inside, the lobby wasn't anything special. A high ceiling that ate up half of the second story. Three seating areas done in gray and teal. Glossy floors sporadically covered by rugs. Nondescript artwork. A receptionist's desk was off to the left and a security guard station blocked the bank of elevators on the right side.

I smiled at the secretary. "Annika Lund here to see Peter Skaarn."

"I'm sorry to say Mr. Skaarn has been detained. Please have a seat in the lobby and I'll let you know when he's free."

I managed a smile and walked to the farthest corner from the desk to brood and look out the windows. *Why couldn't I cool my heels in Peter's reception area?* Maybe I needed this moment to batten down my mental hatches.

Both times I'd said no to aiding Peter's client before . . . I'd ended up saying yes.

Peter would cajole me.

And the hockey pucker would . . .

You know what you'd like him to do to you.

Okay. So maybe I'd been rendered speechless the first time I stood in the shadow of Axl "The Hammer" Hammerquist. The Swedish hockey player redefined *hot*. His handsome, angular face, his wavy hair, his strength and abilities on the ice.

Not even his icy attitude diminished his hotness.

Our first meeting had started out badly. My family had strong-armed me into welcoming Axl and another hockey player to the Twin Cities on behalf of my cousin Jaxson—Axl's former teammate with the Chicago Blackhawks. I hadn't known what to expect beyond that I'd been asked to utilize my Swedish translation skills because of Axl's inability to speak English. I'd even coerced my cousin Dallas into attending the dinner to even up the male-to-female ratio.

So I'd become a tongue-tied twit when Axl approached me at the restaurant.

But his arrogance quickly snapped me out of my *holy shit* silent admiration.

He wasn't interested in conversation.

However, he wasn't interested in drinking either, which I appreciated.

When the waitress arrived to take our order, he mooed at her to indicate what he wanted to order, which caused her to laugh.

He finally asked me a question: could I order him a huge steak dinner and find out if the waitress was single?

The night had gone downhill from there.

Dallas and the other hockey player, Igor, had been cozied up, whispering back and forth somehow despite the language barrier. Meanwhile Axl flirted with our waitress, using sexy smiles, smoldering glances and "accidental" touches. I'd decided to take off when Axl's agent, Peter Skaarn, joined us for coffee and dessert.

I understood why Dallas and Igor had bailed. But Axl had also disappeared.

That was when the situation morphed from irritating to bizarre.

Peter admitted he'd set up the dinner with my mother's assistance—they were old friends from Sweden—because he needed my help. My brother Jensen—a tight end with the Vikings—had contacted Peter's prestigious sports agency about representation. And Peter, who already had a full client list, had agreed to rep Jensen as a favor to my mother. So when she'd bragged that I was the genius in charge of Lund Industries' PR department, Peter suggested that Mom repay the favor by asking (ha! as if she'd given me a choice) me to spearhead a campaign to revamp a client's image.

The client in question? Axl. Who apparently had a reputation as a ladies' man, a bad-boy brawler and a party animal. Last year his vices had affected his career—hence getting traded from the Blackhawks to the Minnesota Wild. Axl needed an image overhaul: from being a *playa* to being a hockey player focused one hundred percent on proving he was an asset to his new team.

Before I could point out my PR experience was in building brands, Axl had sauntered back to the table. His disheveled appearance suggested he'd been either attacked or fucked.

Like any guy would be dumb enough to attack a Nordic giant like "The Hammer."

Our waitress, who'd also been suspiciously absent during that time, had returned equally unkempt and handed Axl the coat check ticket he'd "forgotten"—in her cleavage apparently.

Then the maître d' approached our table and asked us to

leave, pointedly telling Axl the coat check room was a place to hook up coats, not hook up.

Too bad the smug Swede hadn't understood English, because that classy admonishment was the best I'd ever heard.

At that point I'd declined Peter's proposal.

Of course, my mother's machinations and guilt trips knew no bounds.

After her repeated pleas with me to consider my brother's future, the emotional manipulation succeeded and I'd ended up meeting with Peter and Axl in the stands at the Parade Ice Garden, the Wild's alternative practice rink.

And despite mentally preparing myself not to respond to his powerful physical presence, once again lust bombarded me upon seeing Axl in action on the ice. His big, muscled body looked built for speed and aggression, his intensity obvious even in the back row of the arena. The man was mesmerizing.

My attraction to him—completely unwanted—wasn't the norm for me. I went for intellectual guys or arty hipster types. My brothers claimed I chose beta men because as the alpha, I could boss them around. There was some truth to that. They also pointed out a skinny dude would be easier for them to snap like a twig if he wronged me.

Instead of trooping off to the locker room after practice ended, Axl removed his helmet and gloves and scanned the bleachers.

Why did he have to look so damn good soaked in sweat?

Peter hadn't arrived yet and I had felt the weight of Axl's gaze on me. But his handsome face remained stoic, so I couldn't read him.

He towel-dried his hair, right there on the rink—*do not imagine he's wet and naked after exiting the shower*—and tossed the towel aside.

Then he left the ice.

Fifteen minutes later he and Peter walked into the arena.

Peter waved to me—or waved me down.

But Axl snagged a water bottle and scaled the four-plus flights of stairs up to me as if he hadn't just practiced for three hours.

Impressive stamina.

Peter clapped Axl on the back before he sat next to me. "Looking good out there, Axl. I've been here a little while, watching the coaches watching you."

"Thanks." He squirted a stream of water in his mouth. A few droplets spilled out and trickled down to mingle with the beads of sweat dotting his neck.

Stop crushing on him like a teenage girl. Focus. Be the PR professional you are. Besides, he's a jerk. "I'm sorry, Peter. What did you say?"

"That you've agreed to spearhead Axl's PR."

I faced him. "I said I'd look at the packet of media mentions that the Wild PR team provided to see if there's a workable angle."

"Let's get started."

"Right here, right now?" Axl said, glaring at the file folder on Peter's lap. "Can't it wait?"

"I agree with Ax-hell. I haven't had time to look through it and make notes. I can't create a campaign on the fly. This will take planning."

Axl leaned forward. "What's in this for you?"

"My brother gets a top-notch agent."

That surprised him.

I cocked my head. "Speaking of media mentions . . . there was one about your superior stick-handling skills on Twitter this morning. The waitress from the other night gave you high 'service' marks."

"I don't read anything on Twitter."

I shrugged. "Ignoring the things you're caught doing doesn't negate the fact that you did them."

"How would you spin that, Miss PR?"

"I wouldn't try. I believe the whole point of this"—*exercise in futility*—"is to stop you from doing stupid things like banging a waitress in a coat closet."

"I don't need a fucking babysitter, Attila."

"Annika . . . Attila . . . I get it. Funny, puck-head." I addressed Peter in English. "Is that folder filled with incidents like that?"

He sighed. "I honestly don't know."

"Don't you employ a social media person who tracks your clients' online presence?"

"Yes. Some things slipped through. Our newest employee is backtracking and tagging everything and updating files. But that isn't the point." He focused on Axl. "The team's PR person was in touch with me first thing this morning about the tweet, asking if there'd be pictures forthcoming."

"No." Axl squirted another stream of water into his mouth. Then he said, "It doesn't matter. I'm here, practicing my ass off. That's all they need to know."

"Good. The next time you're tempted and think it doesn't matter? Think again. It does. Walk away," Peter said.

"A concept we can all agree on, right?"

Axl's gaze started at my knees and roved up my body, lingering on my chest and my mouth. When our eyes met, his were as smoldering hot as a blue flame, even when his clipped "Stay out of my sex life" was frigid.

I laughed. "That'll be easy, because you won't have one."

"Wanna take bets on that?"

"Enough, Axl. She's here to help you, so you *must* cooperate with her."

"Sounds to me like she's all about helping her brother."

That was when Peter took Axl aside.

I snagged the media reports and scanned them. *You lead a big life, Axl Hammerquist, which is why you're in big trouble.*

I tried to wrap my head around two items on the list that had to be a joke. He'd gotten tossed out of the zoo for trying to climb into the bear cage. And he'd broken his collarbone wresting an alligator.

Before I could read further, Peter interrupted me. "I hate to cut this short, but we have a meeting with a potential sponsor."

"No problem."

"You two should exchange phone numbers," Peter said.

I whipped my phone out and added him as AX-HOLE HAMMERTIME—in all caps—and punched in the number Peter recited. I resisted the urge to send him half a dozen middle finger emojis when I fired off a text.

His text to me? A picture of a bare-chested man who apparently lived in the freakin' gym because he had the buffest chest I'd ever seen. Super-defined pecs. Even the hard nipples were muscled. His bulky biceps and triceps were works of art. I tracked the pic from the washboard abs at the bottom to the sexy grin at the top. No other part of Axl's face was visible, just the angular jawline and lips stretched wide into an "I'm sexy and I'd rock your world" grin.

My gaze snapped to Axl's face and he aimed a smile at me, an identical replica of the one on my phone screen.

He'd sent me a tit pic? God, he was arrogant. But at least he hadn't sent a dick pic.

"You two all squared away with each other?" Peter had asked.

More like we'd squared off against each other. "Yes, I compiled a list of rules for Axl to follow until we meet again."

Peter said, "Hit us with them."

"No nightclubs, no day clubs, no dance clubs. No bars—including titty bars, piano bars, coffee bars and monkey bars. No hookers, no escorts, no meter maids, no waitresses, no baristas. No fucking in public—including coat closets and bathrooms, a town fountain and the ninth hole on the golf course. No fighting, no spitting, no vodka-shooters contest, no public urination. Last, no drag racing, no wrestling—bears or alligators." I paused to take a breath. "That covers all your bad behavior from the last year. Or have I missed something?"

Ooh, Mr. Drool Over My Hot Chest wasn't smiling now.

I looked at Peter. He didn't know what was in the report? My ass. He knew *exactly* what kind of troublemaker his client was. I handed him the folder. "If Ax-wipe can follow those rules? He's back to being golden. Consider that my official PR recommendation."

And until Saturday night I hadn't needed to see Axl. I'd heard from him via text. So the pucktard should've heeded my warning instead of openly defying me and putting on a drunken show—

"Miss Lund?"

I blinked. Whoa. I hadn't meant to drift that far when battening down the hatches. "Yes?"

"Mr. Skaarn is ready for you now."

"Thank you."

At the elevator, the guard didn't stop me. I frowned at him. "Don't you require ID?"

"For anyone else? Yes. But I recognize you from the media. Plus, your mother was here yesterday, and you are the spitting image of her."

Don't remind me. She's the reason I'm in this mess. "Thank you." I turned and walked down the short hallway to the door marked STAIRS.

"Miss Lund? The elevators are right here."

I avoided elevators whenever possible. This did not look to be one of those times. "Sorry. My mind was elsewhere." I poked the up button and the elevator doors opened. Thankfully the car wasn't super small. I hit the button for the tenth floor and started my tried-and-true mental chant before the doors slid shut.

The space is not closing in on you.
The lights will not go out.
The doors will not get stuck.
You will not be trapped.
There is plenty of oxygen in here.
Repeat.

I was still silently chanting when the elevator doors opened.

Peter Skaarn smiled and held out his hand. "Annika. Thank you so much for coming. Sorry for making you wait in the lobby. Floors eight and nine are being remodeled and we can't chance people accidentally wandering around." He kissed both my cheeks. "You look as beautiful as ever."

Flattery isn't going to help your cause, pal. "Thank you."

"Your mother is well?"

"Yes, she is, as you well know, since she was here yesterday, allowing you to try to convince her that I needed to give you another chance. Since clearly you mistakenly believe that your client's reputation is somehow redeemable. Which I now know—firsthand—it is not."

Peter ushered me into the conference room, decorated in the usual Minnesota masculine style I tended to call "North Woods office chic," a hunter green and navy blue color scheme, with hunting and fishing themes, minus actual taxidermy and muskie heads mounted on the wood-paneled walls.

"I understand the situation was distressing. That's why my client would like a chance to apologize and explain."

Just then the enormous leather chair at the head of the conference table slowly spun around, revealing not Adam Levine as I'd hoped, but the blond bruiser and utter bane of my existence the past three weeks.

Aka—the pucktard.

Aka—the Swedish meathead.

Aka—Ax-hole, Ax-hell and half a dozen other names I was too pissed off to think of right then.

The best I could come up with was "You."

And did he act contrite at all? No. He aimed that smarmy grin at me and said, "Attila."

"Axl," Peter warned.

"I was joking," Axl said in Swedish. Then he stood and crossed the room.

I'd spent my life around Minnesota farm boys, born of Scandinavian and German immigrants that generations later were still producing tall, broad, good-sized men. But at six feet five inches and two hundred and some odd pounds of solid muscle, Axl dwarfed most of them. I wasn't a shrimp at five feet eight inches, but even wearing three-inch heels I had to tip my head back to meet his gaze.

"Annika, it is lovely to see you again," he said in that deceptively smooth baritone.

"Shall we sit in the lounge area and keep this meeting informal?" Peter inserted.

As far as I was concerned, it didn't matter where we sat; this would be a short conversation. "Fine."

"Would you care for a drink?" Peter asked me.

"No, thank you." Then I chose the only single seat, leaving them to sit together on the sofa.

After they were situated, Peter said, "Axl has something to say to you."

Axl stretched his arm out across the back of the couch. It spanned the entire length and I couldn't help noticing how the position put his honed biceps on display.

Do not ogle him—that is his MO—he tries to dazzle women with his fantastic physique.

"I am sorry for the distress you had last weekend at the club."

Wow. That could've been just a little less sincere.

Not.

"Remind me again . . . why was I distressed?"

Those eyes, the Siberian blue of a husky, narrowed. "I apologized. Is that not enough?"

And . . . the Iron Princess within me sprang to life, ready to do battle. "That wasn't an apology. Not only did you blatantly ignore my list of instructions, but when I saw you in the club, you became belligerent, like *I* was the problem. And then not only were you grinding on two chicks at one time on the dance floor, but after I pulled you off there with a warning and told you to go home, you defied me yet again. Half an hour later I found you with two different women as their cleavage became your personal vodka shot dispensers! By then you'd drawn a crowd, and phones were already out recording everything. When I attempted to intervene, one of your drunken vodka babes took a swing at me and ended up on the floor. And let's not forget you suggested I could take her place in your threesome."

He gave me a cool smile. "I am sorry you had a hard time grasping our . . . cultural differences."

"Are you freakin' kidding me right now?" I gaped at Peter, who didn't look happy with his client. I shot to my feet. "I'm done."

"Wait. Please." Peter stood too. "I promise I wouldn't have asked you to come here if he was just a drunken discipline problem."

"I don't need this extra headache in my life. Axl's PR problems are best handled by the hockey team's PR department, or a shrink, not someone from the outside."

"So that's it? I didn't think you were the type to give up," Axl mock-chastised me.

"I'm tenacious when I have something worth my time to accomplish. But you've proved time and again that's not the case with you." Leaning in until I had Axl's full attention on my face—not my chest—I patted his massive shoulder. "I can't fix stupid. But here's some free advice. Save your aggression for the ice. Keep your eye on the puck. Keep your dick in your pants. And keep reaching for the stars."

Silence.

"Are you for fucking real?" Axl demanded.

I added, "Oh. And 'Go Wild!' but not literally. Figuratively speaking."

He glared at Peter. "That is exactly why I don't want anyone thinking she's my girlfriend."

"I'm sorry—your what?"

Axl aimed that steely-eyed stare at me. "My girlfriend. Another stupid thing I did Saturday night that I don't remember? I muttered about you being a jealous girlfriend."

My jaw nearly hit the floor. "What is *wrong* with you? Why would you even *say* that?"

He shot to his feet and loomed over me. "Because you *were* acting like a jealous girlfriend, yanking me off the dance floor and chewing my ass about dancing with other women."

"As your PR consultant, I saw you making poor choices, and it was my job to call you out on them!"

"But I couldn't exactly tell people *that,* could I?"

"Unless they spoke Swedish you couldn't tell them anything," I retorted. "So what mysterious 'people' are you talking about?" I paused. "Your little 'honeys' buzzing around and getting buzzed with you?"

Axl's face had gone red.

"Oh, this ought to be pure hockey gold. How'd you drop the puck *this* time?"

"A woman I . . . *met* at the club the previous week was there Saturday night."

Damn him. Did I have to point out he'd violated the rules last weekend too?

"She was one of the ones I was dancing with when you pulled us apart and . . . she became angry when she thought that I hadn't told her I had a girlfriend when I . . . *met* her.

She followed us and recorded you yelling at me after one of the blondes took a swing at you—"

"Because I'm the buzzkill for breaking up your tequila tasting when your agent hired me to improve your image."

God. Could this get any worse? Dallas's warning—*never taunt the universe with that challenge*—popped into my head two seconds before Axl said, "Then she uploaded the videos to YouTube. If you had left me alone and let me do my own thing, none of this would have happened. Which makes it just as much your stupid mistake to fix as it is mine."

"Omigod, you did *not* just say that. This is entirely your fault. And you're right. No one would believe we're together, because I'd never date a serial manwhore."

"Enough." Peter literally stepped between us. "Obviously we have a lot to talk about."

"You know what, Peter? I changed my mind. I will take that drink after all."

Two

AXL

I watched as my "girlfriend" downed a dirty martini in two gulps and wiped her mouth with the back of her hand.

Classy.

"Let's conduct this portion of the conversation at the conference table," Peter said.

I returned to the chair at the head of the table I'd sat in earlier.

She muttered in English, assuming I didn't understand her.

Except I did understand her. In fact, I spoke nearly flawless English. It was hard not to react to some of the crazy stuff that came out of her mouth. Like now, hearing her mutter about finding a crowbar to forcibly remove my ass from the chair.

Go ahead, Princess. I'd like to see you try.

But having her here, skirting me, her sexy ass accentuated by her formfitting skirt, I felt the surreal situation sinking in.

What had I gotten myself into? I'd screwed up Saturday night. I should've stayed in and gotten shit-faced with my buddies Martin and Boris, who lived in my apartment building, instead of heading to the same club I'd overheard Annika saying she planned to visit. After hearing so much about her PR superpowers, I couldn't resist the opportunity to see if she could keep me from getting lit up the one night of the year I pushed my limits of how high I'd blow.

"So here's the situation," Peter said. "Those videos are our golden ticket."

"How do you figure?"

"Because the lovers' spat caught on tape is a precursor for the two of you convincing the world you're a couple. And Axl falling for you means Axl is focused on two things: his hockey career with his new team and his new woman—in that order. It's the feel-good story of the year just waiting to happen."

Even I snorted at that pronouncement.

Annika demanded, "I get why Ax-hell would need to shore up his reputation, but what do I get out of it? Besides *my* reputation being questioned by my family, friends and everyone else I associate with? Because he is nothing like the men I usually date. Nothing."

I imagined the type of men she dated had soft hands and soft heads but a solid bank account.

"It's a three-prong plan, Annika. First, you agreed to do PR because your mother asked you to as a favor to me for taking your brother on as a client. She's on board with this new direction."

"Funny, she did not mention this new direction to me, the person it affects the most. She just assumed I'd go along with it like a dutiful daughter?"

I frowned. Her mother hadn't even asked her? That hardly seemed fair. Or professional for Peter to just expect her to comply with his plan.

"We'll get back to that," Peter assured her. "Second, if Axl's season goes the way we think it'll go, he'll be in high demand socially, and you'll look smart to be half of the 'it' couple in the Twin Cities."

"There's an incentive," she muttered in English.

I had to fight a smile. I sort of hated that she amused the hell out of me.

"Third, he will work tirelessly on any of your LCCO projects. Anytime, anyplace."

My head snapped up at that. "What?"

Peter's eyes flashed a warning at me. "I told you the Lund family is heavily involved in charitable causes. It goes without saying that you'd support Annika, since she will be supporting you."

"Just as long as it doesn't interfere with my hockey schedule. The only reason I considered doing any of this is to clear up some misperceptions about who I am off the ice."

Annika's eyes narrowed. "Misperceptions? The first time I met you 'off the ice,' you banged our waitress between the entrée and the dessert course."

Okay. She had me there. But the woman had smelled like cookies and my sweet tooth had started throbbing.

"You admitted tonight that you hooked up with the amateur videographer you 'met' at the club last week. I did my homework on you. According to what I read and saw online, you haven't been seen with the same woman twice. So, maybe the only person with the skewed perception about you . . . *is* you."

"You told me yourself everything could be spun, Miss PR. I did my homework on you too." From the moment I'd seen the beautiful blonde, I'd imagined her naked and in my arms while I swallowed her cries of pleasure. So I'd purposely presented myself as aloof because I couldn't act on my attraction to her. I'd known Peter planned to show up before the dessert course to ask for her PR help—I just hadn't been looped in on the particulars.

After we'd gotten ejected from the restaurant and Peter had torn into me about my self-destructive behavior, I decided to familiarize myself with the smart, sexy, sassy bombshell. As much as I hated doing an online search for personal information, it was the fastest means to gather data even if it wasn't the most accurate. After poring over pictures captioned by the media as the "Iron Princess" as she was seen with a parade of men over the years, I had proof she had no room to judge me. "Are you involved with every suit who escorts you to the excessive number of charity events you attend? What do you think is the public's perception when your picture is in the newspaper with a different guy week after week?"

That observation took her aback.

Good.

"Here's the difference between us. I don't give a damn how many of those dates you've slept with, because it doesn't matter; I wouldn't call you a slut. Yet you feel entitled to toss out the term 'manwhore' at me. If I'd slept with as many women as I've been accused of, I'd be too damn tired to hold a hockey stick, to say nothing of sustaining the stamina to practice every day and play over eighty games each season. So there *are* misperceptions about me I'd like to change. That's the whole reason I need your help."

A flush crept up her neck. She dipped her chin and her gaze fell to the table, immediately drawing my attention to the long sweep of her eyelashes resting above the razor-sharp edges of her cheekbones.

Contrite wasn't a look I'd expected to see on her, yet there it was.

But was it an act?

Peter cleared his throat. "We've gotten off track."

Annika slowly raised her head. She locked her gaze to mine. Her fiery gaze.

Shit. I'd awakened the beast.

"Actually Axl brought up some things I'd want to discuss with him if I was considering taking him on as a client. I'd still like to go through my questions before I make a final decision."

"Excellent idea," Peter said. "We'll just—"

"Alone," Annika said to him, maintaining eye contact with me.

I envisioned my entrails painting the walls the moment Peter left us alone.

"There's no need to worry about client privilege in this case, Annika, since Axl is my client."

"With all due respect, Peter, if Axl and I are going to convince the world we're in a relationship, we need to be able to speak freely to each other without you running interference."

She had some balls. I'd give her that. I said, "I agree."

"If you'd rather we had this conversation elsewhere . . ."

"No, that's fine. I'll leave you to it. I always have paperwork to catch up on." Peter glanced at his watch. "Axl and I have dinner plans with a sponsor. So no bloodshed." He stood and strode out, closing the door behind him.

Annika reached into her bag and pulled out several file folders before she looked at me. "Maybe this seems—"

I held up my hand. "Before I answer any questions, I want to explain about last weekend, because as Peter said, it is not normal behavior for me."

"Make it snappy. As you can see"—she gestured to the folders—"there's a lot of ground to cover."

"What, exactly, is all that?"

"Data."

I grinned at her. "Attila. I'm touched. You've been studying my hockey stats? How far back does that go? To my youth hockey days in Sweden when I broke all the national records? Impressive for a D-man, isn't it?"

"First of all, I don't give a puck about your impressive lats—I mean stats or whatever."

Lats? Freudian slip, Princess? Do you still have the picture of my bare torso? Because I saw more interest than annoyance in those baby blues after I'd sent it to you.

"Second," she continued, "I really don't need to know what specific bra cup size you prefer in your pack of puck bunnies—"

"Hold up." I refocused. "Where did bra cup size enter this conversation?"

"*D-man* ringing a bell, Ax-hell?"

"You know, Attila, do yourself a favor and buy *Hockey for Dummies* so you have the first clue about the sport your *boyfriend* plays . . . D-man is short for a defenseman, not a bra cup size." My gaze dropped to her chest. I preferred C's anyway.

She blushed. "It sounded sexual and you can't fault me for not knowing much about the sport."

"I can fault you, because your cousin is a hockey player. You've been to Jaxson's games. What position does he play?"

"You are purposely leading me astray so we don't have to discuss this." She waved the folder in the air. "Additional data Peter's assistant sent to me last week that she compiled from social media."

This should be fantastic. "What social media data?"

"Women who claimed they'd 'partied' with 'The Hammer' over the course of the last two seasons in Chicago. By partied, do they mean . . . ?"

"Come on, no euphemisms. Say it."

She rolled her eyes. "Women you pucked."

"The night didn't always end in pucking. And 'partied' is a broad term."

"Then it appears you've *partied* with a lot of broads," she muttered.

"What's the magic number I've supposedly 'partied' with?"

"One hundred and seventy-six."

I laughed.

"I'm serious. That's what it says."

"I was serious earlier about that being impossible."

Annika cocked her head. "No cracks about getting your stick bronzed for reaching that level of studliness—even if it's not true?"

I shook my head. "Never been my goal to be the player with the most notches on my stick. My only goal has been to be the best player I can be. I did what I had to do to get out of the cluster fuck that was Chicago"—*shut your mouth, man*—"so can I tell you why I got hammered last weekend?"

"By all means."

I paused to take a breath, glad she hadn't zeroed in on my Chicago slipup. "I'll summarize for you so I'm not wasting your time. Growing up, as far back as my memory goes, all I cared about was hockey. I lived it, breathed it and was consumed by it. I had that in common with my best friend, Roald. We played in every league in Sweden that would have us. We played internationally. Right after we turned twenty we were scouted by the NHL and invited to Detroit's training camp. A month before we left, Roald crashed his bike and ended up paralyzed from the waist down."

Annika reached over and squeezed my forearm. "That is awful, Axl. I'm so sorry."

"Long story short: I came to the U.S. and lived the dream he couldn't. It took four years of paying my dues in the AHL before I got called up to the Blackhawks. But Roald never knew. He died the summer before. So Saturday night was the sixth anniversary of his accident. Sounds sappy to admit that I feel lucky every day. But on the anniversary of his death, I can't escape the guilt that swamps me. I get drunk to try to forget and do stupid shit I don't remember." Given the last year I'd suffered through in Chicago, I tried harder for that state of oblivion and I found it sooner than I expected. In the morning I'd woken up facedown on the couch in the lobby of my apartment building with no recollection of how I'd gotten there.

"Total asshat behavior, but sadly it's behavior I'm familiar with. I have three brothers and three male cousins."

"I can promise you it won't happen again."

"Until next year."

"Then it won't be *your* problem, will it?"

"I guess not."

She studied me.

"What?"

"Two questions."

"Yes, that was a true story."

She bestowed an evil smirk on me. "Good. So I don't have to be callous and remind you of this awesome opportunity you've earned that your friend never got to experience. And ask if a night filled with booze, bunnies and blackouts is worth losing your life's dream and getting deported back to the land of lutefisk, ABBA and IKEA."

"Please tell me you plan on following up that comment with an evil witch's cackle before you fly away on your broom."

She drilled me in the biceps with her finger. "Consider me your reality check. I may not know a D-man from a goalie, but I did market research. You are twenty-six years old. If you screw this up? You're back to the AHL for good. No other NHL team will pick you up. You'll be too old to be a damn rookie."

"You think I don't know what's at stake here?" I exhaled. "I'm sorry. It's not your fault I made a few bad decisions and I don't want to take my frustration out on you."

"But?" she said with more interest than sarcasm.

"But I'm not convinced a PR scam is in my best interest. That's what this 'girlfriend' angle feels like—as if we're trying to pull one over on the public. Wouldn't it be worse if they found out? Wouldn't it be better if I agreed to stay out of the media spotlight?"

Annika flipped the pen in her hand end over end as she scrutinized me. "For you? No. All your press in the past year has been bad press. The media loves a misbehaving bad-boy athlete. They're content to saddle you with that moniker your entire career. It happened with McEnroe. No one remembers he was a gifted athlete. So I agree with Peter. We need a positive spin for you. One where we can take you from Cassius Clay to Muhammad Ali. He was the same guy. The only thing that changed about him was the public's perception of him."

I looked at her with new admiration. "You're really good at your job, aren't you?"

The compliment startled her. Then she granted me a smile sexy enough to tighten my balls and sweet enough that I wanted to lick her lips to see if they tasted like sugar. "Yes, I am."

Not coy about her skills. I admired them too. "In your professional opinion . . . should we use the 'we're a couple' angle that Peter suggests?"

"It makes the most sense."

"Don't sound so enthused," I said dryly.

"Pulling it off won't be easy," she warned. "There are a lot of people in my life who won't believe that you and I are romantically involved."

Despite my desire not to react with antagonism, I said, "I'm not a troll or a serial killer, Annika. And I have a list of women who'd be happy to tell the world we're coupling."

She raised an eyebrow. "Dude. Think about it. That's *why* you have this problem."

Peter knocked twice and opened the door. He paused, his gaze winging between us. "What's the verdict?"

"Annika was just about to pucker up so I could kiss her to seal the deal."

"Puckered up, clenched up . . . same thing, right?"

I laughed. With her smart mouth and that hot body, she intrigued me as much as she annoyed me. Were her fingers as nimble as her brain?

Our gazes clashed and I could almost read her mind.

I'd take clever and cutting over vapid any day. These next few months with her would be a challenge. And I loved a challenge.

"Happy as I am to see that you two have found your own way to work together, there's one last thing we can all agree on: no one but the three of us needs to know the true nature of your relationship."

"The three of us plus my mother," Annika reminded him.

Why did she sound more resigned about her mother's interference than pissed off about it? That bothered me, but it wasn't a question I'd ask her in front of Peter.

Peter sighed. "So, to keep your personality clashes out of the spotlight, it'd be best if your first few strategy sessions take place somewhere private. Will I need to be there to referee?"

"No. We'll get it figured out," I said.

Three

ANNIKA

It hadn't occurred to me until my assistant, Deanna, tried to corner me first thing the next morning that I hadn't come up with a plausible lie for how things had gone down with Axl last night.

Gone down? Wishful thinking on your part, isn't it? Since you're all talk and no action.

My libido had spent her idle time—which she had a lot of—pouting or trying to convince the rest of my girlie bits that I needed to get naked with Axl ASAP to lend believability to our fake relationship. The rest of me was far from convinced it was a good idea, but I suspected my girlie bits would throw a coup and scream *Yes!* if Axl's boy bits got involved.

For now, I had to focus on the immediate issue: how to assure Deanna I hadn't subjected myself to a lobotomy; I'd just experienced a Grinch moment with a change of heart.

Deanna knew the basics about my meetings with Axl,

which were already slightly fabricated. I'd been asked to serve as Axl's interpreter, and that had led him to ask for my PR advice. I'd kept the specifics about our other private meetings basic. So when she approached me yesterday morning with the exact details of what'd gone down in Flurry Saturday night, I should've suspected social media would be buzzing. But since I'd lived it and hadn't wanted to get sucked into pointless speculation, I'd done the mature thing and avoided it. Now I'd have no choice but to dissect the uploads on a purely professional basis.

So what could I say about my new couplehood with Ax-hell that would pass my assistant's bullshit meter?

Right then a determined rapping sounded on my door and Deanna strode in bearing a bribe, a bag from the Salty Tart Bakery. A bag that contained my favorite breakfast treat—an apple and brown butter scone.

Oh. She was good.

Especially when she nonchalantly asked, "So, how did the meeting go last night after you finally found the place?"

Just come at her strong from the get-go. "D, this cannot go any further than us," I warned her.

"Now I'm too curious to know what happened to be pissed off that you even had to qualify that, boss. Spill it."

I sat back in my chair and told the mother of all lies. "You want the details before or after Axl kissed me?"

"He kissed you? Why?"

"Evidently the big, bad hockey player is seriously crushing on me. Last night he hard-core groveled about being such a drunken ass to me at Flurry last weekend. Then the real kicker? None of this 'hiring me as part of his PR team' was true! He used it as a way to get to know me so he could ask me out on a date. But he realized he'd made a terrible impression on me . . . blah, blah, blah."

"What did you do?"

"I went off on him. Ripped him a new one—not easy to do in Swedish when I was literally spitting mad. One minute we were yelling at each other and the next he was kissing me like I was food, air, sunshine all tied up together and better than hockey." Holy crap, did I suck at this. Who would believe that claptrap? I always felt guilty about lying, so I figured I'd better make it worth it and I tended to overembellish. Case in point: In my head, Ax-hell the smitten Swede had already pinned me to the conference table in Peter's office as he kissed me. I clamped my teeth together so I wouldn't start adding elaborate details to an imaginary situation.

Deanna flat-out gaped at me. "Omigod, Annika, that could only happen to you!"

"Right?"

"No wonder you were in a mood this morning. So, what happens now?"

"He's kind of old-fashioned once he sheds the shackles of hockey player entitlement. He wants us to start a relationship and not sneak around. He's cooking me dinner tonight."

"That must've been some kiss."

Don't respond. You will totally blow this and you've convinced her so far.

She leaned forward. "Come on. You have to give me something juicy."

I imagined Ax-hell's confident grin if I waxed poetic about the wonders of his mouth—because he did have killer lips and a dirty-boy smile that spoke to me on so many levels—all of them wrong. So I decided to knock him down a peg. It wasn't like he'd ever know. "To be honest, I think he might've been nervous, because the kiss was wet and sloppy and utterly lacked finesse. Kind of like an eager puppy licking your face until you have to push it away."

"And yet you're going out with him tonight?"

"I figured it can't get any worse, right?"

She stared at me hard.

Damn it. I'd raised her suspicions by going into too much detail. "Besides, have you seen his slamming body? The man is solid muscle. His biceps are as big as his head! I'm pretty sure the phrase 'rock-hard abs' was coined after seeing him shirtless."

"Not to mention he's been gifted with that bronze-worthy face of a Nordic god." Deanna sighed. "Plus that shaggy, devil-may-care blond mane. Those piercing blue eyes. I am so jealous you're getting a piece of that, A."

Her overly detailed description of Axl's physique bothered me for some idiotic reason. "I'm taking one tiny bite of him at a time because he's worth savoring." Oh, gag. "I'll spare you the particulars to keep your jealousy to a minimum."

"I can't wait to see the two of you beautiful blonds together in person and in the media. I bet you look amazing. And it's so romantic that you speak his native language." She sighed again. "But the language of love doesn't really need words, does it?"

Oh for god's sake. I pointed at the door. "Please get out. You are dripping sap all over my chair."

Deanna laughed and stood. "This is gonna be a total trip."

"What?"

She smirked. "It's too sappy, so I'll spare you." She turned around when she reached the door. "Lennox asked to meet with you at two."

I frowned. "Did she say why she wanted to schedule a meeting?"

"You know how she likes to keep everything that happens in the office by the book."

I adored my sister-in-law, but her insistence on formality bordered on the absurd. She was married to my brother Brady—the CFO of our family company, Lund Industries. She didn't have to schedule an appointment with me. "Thanks, D."

Most days I worked through lunch, preferring to eat at my desk. Deanna sent all the calls to voice mail during her lunch break, so I relished that hour with no interruptions.

I'd started working at Lund Industries—LI—my junior year in high school. But just because my last name was Lund didn't guarantee me a cushy, high-paying job. Especially not at age sixteen. I'd started in the mail sorting and package delivery department. From there I'd moved up to interdepartmental errand girl. The benefit of being everywhere was I saw the inner workings of every department. So I knew that Finance wasn't my thing. Nor was Human Resources. I considered Legal as an option and kicked around the idea of heading to law school after earning my undergrad degree. But I also felt the pull toward marketing and had chosen to intern there after I graduated from college.

Luckily I had a great mentor in Suzanne Jones, who ran the Marketing department. Unlike so many people I crossed paths with, she didn't feel threatened by me because my last name was on the company letterhead. In the ten years she'd headed the department, she'd expanded and redefined Marketing's role in the company. While I admired that, the cleverest marketing gimmick in the world wouldn't achieve the desired effect of increasing sales and visibility if the product wasn't getting into the hands of the right people.

LI's small PR department had always been stuck under the purview of Marketing. I recognized that PR was a vastly underutilized entity. At that time, Bud Tschetter, the head of PR, was one of those old-school guys whose idea of company PR was hosting an annual community golf tournament and distributing money to charitable causes. He had no plan to promote the Lund Industries products—so the Marketing department was equally frustrated with him and his outright refusal to do anything differently.

Fortunately, Bud's second-in-command, Victoria Bass, had

been hired by my cousin Ash, who was on the fast track to the COO position. He enacted major changes at LI, including offering Bud early retirement, splitting PR and Marketing into two different entities and naming Victoria head of PR. PR's focus would be increasing visibility of the vast array of LI products.

But giving back to the community had always been a cornerstone of our business philosophy. So with that in mind, Ash established Lund Cares Community Outreach—LCCO for short. For years, Ash's mother, Priscilla, married to my uncle Monte, president of the LI board of directors; my aunt Edie, married to my uncle Archer, CEO of LI; and my mother had run the Lund Foundation from their homes, so creating one organization with dedicated office space and full-time staff fulfilled another goal.

With Victoria in charge, the scope of the PR department changed drastically. I was still in college when the transformation began. It thrilled me to be a part of it. It really thrilled me when Victoria named me department VP as soon as I received my degree, because I'd truly earned it. And since I'd documented everything from the very beginning, I used that as my thesis project for my MBA—which I received a year after my bachelor's degree.

With the diversity in LI's products and subsidiaries, every day presented a new challenge. I didn't even mind working with my family most days.

Except today I really could've done without my mother's surprise visit.

Selka Jensen Lund swept into my office, coiffed in an ivory-colored linen jacket and matching pants she'd paired with an open-collar silk blouse the same frosty blue as her eyes. She had secured her hair back from her flawless face with a scarf patterned in magenta, pale blue and orange swirls. A thin patent leather belt in orange-and-magenta pumps completed her ensemble.

"Mom, is there ever a time when you don't look like you stepped out of the pages of *Vogue*?" I complained good-naturedly in Swedish. I was the only one of her children who preferred to converse with her regularly in her native tongue.

"Fresh from the bath I wear nothing but water." She'd skirted the desk and angled herself over me to cup my face in her hands. "Come. You need tea."

I didn't bother to buzz Deanna to bring it in. Knowing my mother, she'd already requested it before she waltzed into my office. I followed her to the seating area in the corner and flopped into the club chair. The unladylike move put a tiny wrinkle between her eyes.

Her gaze started at my feet—taking in the tan-colored suede-fringed bootees—and then up to the olive green slim-fit khakis I wore. She scrutinized the pale peach blouse, shirred chiffon from the Empire waist down that hit at hip level, with the upper section composed of delicate lace dotted with tiny, shimmering seed pearls. The three-quarter-length sleeves were sheer on the underside, and the lace pattern trailed down from the shoulders to the bend in the elbows. Her eyes met mine and she smiled. "The hipster chick outfit looks very good on you."

Whew. Mom wasn't ever . . . mean-spirited about my clothing style, but she did consider my appearance a reflection on her. Maybe because everyone went on about how I was her mini-me. Or that we could be sisters. For whatever reason, even at age twenty-eight I held my breath for her approval so I didn't point out that hipster chick and hippie chic weren't interchangeable. "Thank you. I assume you're here to talk about my fake relationship with Axl Hammerquist?"

"I dislike the word *fake*."

I narrowed my eyes at her. "You can't possibly hope it'll turn into a real relationship?"

"No. He is a brute. Not your type at all. I'm concerned that it'll appear as a blatant publicity ploy. So, how are you going to playact this?"

My temper flared. PR was *my* job, not hers. This fake relationship—I'd call it that because that was exactly what it was—would affect me, not her. I had to dig really deep to find a look of confusion that would mask my anger. "Playact this? Didn't you and Peter already decide everything without my agreement?"

She waved her hand as if my concern was no concern of hers.

I loved her. I had to remind myself of that, especially right now when I knew she'd manipulated the hell out of me. Did her sweet baby boy Jensen mean that much more to her than I did? Maybe I sounded like a petulant child, but it didn't feel as if I was out of line. She *was* playing favorites. She'd get precious Jensen what she thought he deserved—even if she had to offer up her only daughter as a pretend girlfriend to a bad-boy hockey player to seal the deal.

But what would be the point of standing up to her and refusing to fulfill this favor? Jensen's last agent was horrible. The only endorsement deals he'd received were borderline pornographic and utterly humiliating. His contract terms sucked. Maybe Peter could propel him to the next level. I'd talked to Jens last week and he was still pumped about Peter signing him as a client.

Yet I knew if Jensen got wind of the crap Mom had pulled, he'd be livid. He'd walk away from Peter's agency, just to prove a point. Then no one would be better off than before this had all started snowballing. I wanted to make sure Jensen had this opportunity. So I'd just suck it up.

"Are you even listening to me?" my mother demanded.

I glanced over at her. "Oh, were you including me in a conversation?"

Sarcasm and sniping are not the way to deal with this.

"Yes. I watched the YouTube videos. You and this Axl . . . so angry with each other."

"If you watched, then you know that my anger was justified."

She shrugged. "So I am here to tell you to let go of it. Call a press conference. Tell the media that you and Axl are working things out behind closed doors and you'd appreciate them respecting your privacy."

"Excuse me?"

Deanna popped in with the tea set.

Mom poured the tea while I stewed over what to say about her suggestion—one I knew she hadn't run past Peter.

She was wrong. She knew nothing about PR.

But her suggestion prompted me to follow my gut about how Axl and I should handle the repair/reveal of our relationship: one hundred percent in the public eye.

Otherwise, what was the point? There was no reason for Axl and me to get to know each other privately. There wasn't an "us" behind closed doors.

That actually lifted a huge weight off my shoulders. "Thanks for the insight, Mom."

She smirked at me from behind the rim of her china cup. "You are welcome. Now, Edie and Priscilla and I were talking . . . and we think you need to consider changing venues for this year's coat drive."

Maybe she had solid reasons, but I wasn't in the mood to hear them today. This was *my* LCCO project. I had the final say, and damn it, she couldn't steamroll me on everything.

"No." I offered her the same type of smile she'd given me. "It's handled."

"Annika—"

I waved her protest off. "Please. Let's *fika* and have no more talk of business, yah?"

Four

AXL

Brutal practice.
   Hard skating.
 Puck-handling drills.
 Three-on-one drills.
 Three-on-three drills.
 Then we suffered through the two-hour endurance workout with cardio, weights and agility training.

 We hit the showers, and I ignored the trash-talking frat-boy antics until I heard my name.

 "Hammerquist didn't invite any of us," Flitte, a four-year veteran forward, complained.

 "That's because none of you bother to speak to him off the ice," Kazakov, our team captain, said. "Most of you don't speak to him on the ice either."

 "Because he doesn't speak English," Dykstrand, another veteran forward, said.

It probably made me a tool not to admit to my teammates that I spoke English. I'd kept up the charade throughout the year and a half I spent with the Chicago Blackhawks. In my defense, I wasn't the only foreign player who feigned English illiteracy. It's surprising what the suits with the power to make or break your career will say right in front of you when they think you can't understand.

"Management has provided a translator," Kazakov reminded him.

"That guy? He's gone as soon as the coaches are done yelling at us. We need a translator down here, after practice. That way we would've known Hammerquist had access to a hot club like Flurry," Flitte said. "I've been trying to get into that club for months."

"Wearing your exclusive Wild team gear doesn't grant immediate access?" Kazakov asked.

McClellan, a fellow D-man, snorted. "You'd think being pro athletes we'd get the VIP treatment. But that club reserves VIP treatment for Vikings and Timberwolves players."

Grumbles followed about the unfairness.

Then Flitte said, "Hey, Kaz, do your Russian thing with Igor. See if he got invited."

I ducked under the spray of water and tuned them out. After I dried off and slipped on a pair of sweats for the drive home, someone said my name. I turned around.

Flitte, Dykstrand and McClellan were standing at the end of the bench.

"So, hey, Axl. Good hustle out there today."

McClellan rolled his eyes. "Great start, Flitte."

"What was wrong with that?"

"A, he can't understand you. B, you're being selfish. Don't just ask him for a favor. Include him." McClellan smiled at me. "You oughta come out with us and have a beer." He mimed drinking.

I said, "Yah."

"Cool." He whapped Flitte on the arm. "See?"

"Fine. I got this. So, after we go out for beers"—he mimed drinking—"then we could go clubbing . . . you know, this"—Flitte threw his arms up and swirled his pelvis in a sad parody of dancing.

"What the hell was this?" Dykstrand mimicked Flitte's lame dance maneuver. "You looked like you just realized you had a dick and you were scared to touch it."

Everyone laughed. I had to pretend to look confused. But I did join in when Flitte shoved Dykstrand into the lockers.

"I don't gotta touch it myself. I've got chicks lined up around the block to touch my dick anytime I want," Flitte said.

McClellan stepped in front of me. "What the two dancing queens are trying to say is call us." Then he wiggled his phone. "Okay?"

"Okay."

"See!" He beamed. "Communication achieved!" Then he faced Kazakov. "If he texts us in Swedish, can our phones translate it?"

"Maybe. Or maybe you should just communicate in emojis. It couldn't be any more confusing than Flitte's attempt with interpretive dance."

After some back-and-forth and lots of laughs and frustration, I ended up with nine of my teammates' numbers in my phone. For the first time in the six weeks I'd been training here, I felt I'd made progress toward being accepted as a team member. I appreciated their efforts, even when I felt guilty because I could've made it a lot easier just by . . . talking to them. It hit me then I needed to find a way to end this English noncomprehension charade.

But all in all, it'd been a good day.

Then I walked out and saw her waiting for me.

I thought I'd at least have time to go home and slip on a Teflon suit before our dinner date.

Although I had to hand it to her, she didn't bother going the discreet route. She'd parked at the back of the Xcel Center, where the players exited. Usually security kept fans, gawkers and the press away from us during practice. How had she received special treatment?

Hello. Look at her. No. Seriously, dude. Fucking look *at her. She's gorgeous. Any straight man would do anything to get closer to her, just in the hopes of seeing her bat those baby blues and gift him with that million-dollar smile.*

Nothing discreet either about driving a Mercedes-Benz C63 AMG. Worth five hundred ninety-two thousand krona—a rich girl's car in any currency.

Behind me I heard, "Who is that?" and "Come to Papa, baby," and "Now, that's the kind of classy babe that I'm talkin' about," and "First time I'd do her *against* that sweet, sweet car. The second time I'd bend her *over* the hood."

I adjusted my equipment bag and started toward her.

Then I heard, "No. Way."

"She's with *him*? How'd he score a chick like her?"

"Wait. I've seen her before."

"Where?"

"Dude. She's the one in the video who chewed his ass."

"Think she's his girlfriend?"

"Yeah. I'm pretty sure she is."

"Why would he cheat on her? She's almost as hot as the car."

"We've gotta find a way to hang with him."

I stopped a meter away from her.

She said, "We have an audience."

"You were as much of a surprise to me as you were to them." I tightened my grip on my strap. "Why are you here?"

"Aw. Listen to you. Is that any way to greet your *girlfriend*?"

My focus briefly landed on her plush lips. "How would you like me to greet you?"

"Not like this," she said in English. "Sometimes when you act so cold, I believe you might actually be part cyborg."

Cold? How about I prove how fast I can heat you up and watch those words evaporate right out of your pretty head?

I don't know what compulsion came over me, but after I dropped my bag, I stepped forward and braced one hand beside her shoulder on the car. Lowering my head, I whispered, "Sexy car, Attila. You know you're here because you're dying to take me for a ride."

"Ego much, Ax-hell?"

"*You* drove to St. Paul. *You're* the one waiting for me. Not ego. Fact." My being this close to her made her antsy. I liked the mix of aggravation and interest pulsing from her. But I wouldn't give her the satisfaction of a fast retreat.

You like the way her hair smells as it flutters across your cheek. It reminds you she's a sexy, sweetly scented woman, not an adversary.

"Here's the deal, puck-face. I'm going to put my hand on your chest, but only to push you back. If you get cutesy in front of your buddies and try anything? I'll knee you in the 'nads so hard your balls will be dangling beside your tonsils."

I laughed. Yeah. There was her adversarial response.

She went still.

I pulled back to look into her eyes. "You want a verbal confirmation that I understand?"

"No. It always surprises me when you laugh. It's like you're human."

"I'm flesh and blood and all man. Any time you want to test that? I'm right here."

We stared at each other. The sudden intensity between us was as powerful as a magnet.

"You are dangerous, aren't you?" she murmured.

It didn't escape my notice that her hand was still pressed against my chest. "I'm thinking that's more of a 'we're dangerous' thing, Annika."

"Guess we'll find out, won't we?"

I was looking forward to that more than I'd admit—especially to her.

"Turn down the smolder. I had a question to ask you and now . . . poof"—she took her hand off my chest and made an exploding motion—"it's gone like dandelion tufts in the wind."

I felt that way sometimes, twisting, drifting, trying to follow her train of thought.

"My mom stopped in to chat with me today."

"Did you give her hell for this relationship idea she and Peter concocted and expected you to agree to without consulting you?"

Annika seemed startled by that. "Why on earth would you care? The change benefits you."

"I loathe manipulative behavior. I can't believe you'd let anyone get away with that."

She briefly glanced away. "You don't know my mother. Anyway, I'd been thinking about this since last night and I've come to the conclusion that Peter is wrong."

"About?"

"About us spending time together."

I scowled at her.

She placed her hand on my sternum and I felt the ripple of her touch down the front side of my body. "I mean about where we spend time together. This relationship is to repair your reputation and put the focus back on your hockey game. So our couplehood needs to unfold in public, not privately."

"That actually makes more sense."

Her eyes locked onto mine. "That video makes us look like a real couple having a huge fight."

I hadn't found the balls to watch it yet. "You watched it?"

"Yeah. Anger is a better angle for us to work from. It's obvious you screwed up and I'm pissed as hell about it. So from here on out? You need to grovel. Hard-core grovel."

I leaned in closer. "You'd like that, wouldn't you, Princess? Me, constantly gazing at you adoringly. Shall I hold your hand while you dab your tears? Or should I be on my knees? Because once I get there . . ." *I wouldn't be using my mouth to grovel.*

She said, "Piss off," without any real malice.

"I can play the 'I'm crazy about her and happy she's giving me a second chance' boyfriend, Annika, but I will not be led around on a leash as if I was a bad dog, understood?"

"Fine. What are your other relationship dos and don'ts?"

"No excessive PDA."

"Dude, even if we were sleeping together, public mauling isn't my scene."

"Mine either."

"Since when?"

"Since always. The list of incidents you read at the practice rink? All hearsay, no proof. The blondes were a fluke. Believe me or don't, but I'm a private guy."

Her suspicion about that confession didn't surprise me. I hated that I deserved it.

"So, what do we tell Peter about this rogue decision to do what we want with our relationship?"

"I don't know. Nothing? Unless he asks. And thank you, for kicking him out last night so you and I could talk without an audience. My dossier of bad behavior—"

She snapped her fingers in my face. "Hey, wait. Now I remember my question. I found a copy of your birth certificate in Peter's file. Why doesn't your team PR list your real name?"

"What real name?"

"Klaus Axl Hammerquist."

I frowned at her.

"Aha!" She poked me in the chest. "I knew it. You're embarrassed that your real name is Klaus."

"Is that why you called me Santa at Flurry last weekend?"

"Yep." Annika smirked. "Clever, huh?"

I smirked back. "I'm happy I'm not Santa—the poor guy only comes once a year. And he limits himself to just good girls."

"Of course you have a crude comeback."

"You'd be disappointed if I didn't. Besides, you're wrong about my name. My name is Axl Hammerquist. I don't have a middle name."

"You're lying."

"Look it up. You probably saw my grandfather's name, Klaus Axl, on the genealogy paperwork Peter asked for, because I don't have an official birth certificate."

Now she seemed really annoyed. Which made no sense.

This is Annika, remember? She can go from smiling to fist-forming mad as fast as her sexy little car goes from zero to sixty.

"One thing I didn't find in the paperwork was the date of the first exhibition game."

"Two weeks. You'll need to be there."

"If your game conflicts with Jensen's football game? Sorry, dude. My little brother's game wins."

She wanted to return to combat mode? I could do that. "The same little brother who signed with my agent? Remind me . . . what was the one main condition for Peter taking him on as a client?" I paused. "You owed him a favor that I'm collecting on. So that means you *will* be in the ice arena, wearing a green jersey with *my* name on the back, and not decked out in purple in your family's skybox."

"What. Ever. Glad we cleared that up." She sidestepped me. "See ya."

"Wait. Did you forget we're having dinner tonight?"

"We *were* having dinner. But there's no reason for it now,

remember? Unless you have a list of the restaurants where the press hangs out?"

"No. You're the Minneapolis native. You should already know that. Besides, PR is your department."

"PR *was* my department. My PR skills have become secondary in this situation. Peter has already pulled the 'you don't need the pesky details about our plans—just do what we say' attitude. Now I'm just a pawn."

"So prove you're a woman." I blocked her in and crowded her against the car door. "Give me that mouth."

She parted her lips and shifted closer. "How about a little slap and tickle instead?"

I caught her wrist before her hand connected.

"How did you—"

"Unparalleled reflexes." I brought her palm to my mouth. "And, Attila, you *did* warn me." Then I slid my mouth down and kissed the base of her hand.

"I didn't think you'd catch that," she retorted. Then she tried to jerk her arm free. "Let go. And get your lips off me. I don't know where all they've been."

That stung. "Low blow."

She studied me for a moment before she murmured, "Sorry. That wasn't nice."

I placed a soft kiss on the inside of her wrist before I released her. "Go on. Rev that engine and spin those tires. You wouldn't have driven it if you hadn't intended to show off."

"The only person I drive this car for is me. And you'll have to step up your flattery if you ever want me to take you for a ride."

Five

—

ANNIKA

I dreamed of Axl.

A week had passed since our bizarre exchange outside the Xcel Center. I still hadn't dissected how we'd become coconspirators or why I liked it.

My dreams of him hadn't been explicit in a sexual sense. But they'd been chock-full of sensuality. Of Axl's hair tickling my neck as he whispered in my ear. Of his iron grip on my wrist as he brushed soft kisses across my collarbones. I'd woken up more puzzled than aroused.

Normally I'd talk to Dallas about it, since she had a foot firmly in the woo-woo world and she nailed dream interpretations. But I'd been avoiding her. With her perception skills, she'd see through the situation with Axl and read me the riot act for capitulating to my mother's demands as usual.

Another fun aspect to this situation was a reminder that it'd been two and a half years since I put my dating life on hold.

I'd gotten so tired of the "meat market" aspect of the clubs I flung myself off the crazy merry-go-round of societal expectations. I could admit I loved to flirt, but it rarely went beyond the sexy banter stage for me lately. For official charity functions I had a couple of platonic pals who liked the limelight—win-win for both of us. But Axl had me all mixed up in ways I hadn't experienced. Hot one minute, cold the next. Oozing sexy appeal and then throwing out back-off, brooding vibes.

I'd managed to shove all that aside and focus on next week's big presentation to a boutique hotel chain about them carrying our newest seven-grain cereal in their restaurants, when Deanna interrupted me.

"There's a man out here who swears he just needs five minutes to touch base with you. Peter Skaarn?"

"That's fine. Send him in." I closed my laptop and crossed over to the lounge area as Peter sauntered in.

He gave my office—which was damn nice by anyone's standards—a cursory look and said, "I'll be brief."

No pleasantries at all? That was weird. "What's up?"

"Apparently I didn't make myself clear about what constitutes a relationship. That means you spend time together. Is it true you and Axl haven't seen each other in a week?"

"We decided it'd be better to launch our public couplehood at the opening of the hockey season."

"We decided," Peter repeated, and shook his head. "That had already been decided and you both agreed to it. Now over a week has passed after major social media buzz and he's had no press at all. Zero."

"Back up. The 'major social media buzz' about what went down in the club? Not the good kind of buzz, Peter. We established that." When he opened his mouth to argue, I held up my hand. "Please do *not* spout the tired line that there's no such thing as bad press. There is bad press or else Axl wouldn't be in this situation, would he?"

Peter studied me without response.

Luckily that was an intimidation trick I'd learned to deal with years ago. I stared right back at him.

The *Jeopardy!* theme song played in my head.

Finally he sighed. "Please tell me that you and Axl have been meeting privately."

"I stopped by to see him after hockey practice. His teammates saw us together. But besides that, I haven't seen or spoken to him. And yes, our opinions on how we spend our limited free time do matter. We feel getting to know each other privately defeats the purpose. Our public relationship is what's important, right?"

His gaze turned shrewd.

Why did I feel as if I'd just left the safety of the shark cage to swim in chum-filled waters?

"I do agree on that point. So as of tonight, we're ramping up your visibility. I'm hosting a cocktail cruise on a Mississippi riverboat. Several potential sponsors will be in attendance. This will be one of my more eclectic groups, not strictly my clients. But the primary objective is that you and Axl will be photographed by as many press and social media outlets as possible."

Hooray. "Axl knows about this?"

"Yes. He's already received his personal visit from me today. He's also been informed that since the two of you are dating, you will act like a couple. That means you arrive together. That means you will stay by each other's side during the party—the entire party—unless one of you ventures to the restroom. Am I making myself clear?"

"Yes, sir."

"Excellent. Axl will pick you up at five. Dress is semiformal."

"Thanks for the heads-up."

"Along those lines . . . Jensen will be in attendance." He

glanced at his watch. "My time is up. I'll let you get back to work. See you tonight."

Thirty seconds after he left, Deanna popped in. "Who was that and what did he want?"

"He's Axl's agent. There's an event tonight that Axl is refusing to attend. Peter asked me to convince Axl to go. Now I have to leave early to get ready."

"The lifestyles of the rich and famous are such a drag."

"Oh, piss off. And could you please bring me some coffee? I'll have to kick it into warp speed to finish this presentation today."

Deanna paused. "I'll bring the coffee. But don't forget you have a final interview in an hour for the graphic artist opening."

"Why do I have to do the final interview? Can't someone else do it?"

"Since Victoria is on maternity leave, you're the big boss. It's why you get paid the big bucks, so stop whining and suck it up. I'll be right back with your warp core fuel."

I laughed. Gotta love an assistant who could shut me down and rev me up at the same time.

An hour later, hopped up on caffeine, I was prepared to meet the prospective employee. So it surprised me when Lennox walked in, looking worried.

"Did our applicant flake out?"

"Not exactly. And normally we wouldn't have this conversation in front of a prospective employee, but . . ."

Another woman entered my office. A woman I recognized.

"This is the 'not exactly' scenario I need to explain. I interviewed Lucille. She's easily the most qualified person. I had no idea that she—"

"Is Jaxson's baby mama and Mimi's mother?" I snapped at Lennox. Then to Lucy I said, "I am not surprised you pulled something like this—"

"Let me finish, Annika," Lennox snapped back.

Lennox rarely got surly with me. And she'd stepped in front of Lucy as if she was protecting her. "Fine. I'll hear you out."

"Lucille has every qualification we require in a graphic designer. She had glowing references from her bosses and her coworkers. Her portfolio is top-notch. So in my opinion, we should not automatically discount her employment because of some family issue that doesn't even affect you directly and, from what I've gleaned, happened several years ago."

I glanced over Lennox's shoulder at Lucy, who was watching me. "Your point is?"

"The Lunds are big on the importance of family. The reason Lucille applied here is the day-care program that Edie enrolled Mimi in over the summer. Mimi loved it—as you know. So I ask you. When was the last time you even had a conversation with Lucille?"

My mind blanked. Had I ever really talked to her? Or was everything I knew about her what I'd heard secondhand or thirdhand? That was when I caught Lucy's gaze. I didn't see smugness or resentment. That allowed me to admit, "To be honest, I don't remember. Probably at least back when Mimi was a baby."

A look of relief crossed Lennox's face. "Then I'm asking you to please talk to her. Interview her honestly. Give her a chance, Annika. I know what it's like when people have preconceived ideas about you and dismiss you out of hand. I know you're not like that."

Lennox excelled at making me see things from a different perspective, and I valued her insight . . . even if she had used a heavy hand this time. "On your way out, will you tell Deanna to hold my calls?"

"Sure thing." Lennox squeezed Lucy's shoulder as she passed by.

After the door closed I met Lucy's eyes again. "First question. Do you go by Lucy or Lucille?"

"Lucy is fine."

"Let's sit at the conference table so I can look through your portfolio." Before I took my seat, I said, "Would you like something to drink? Water? Diet Pepsi?"

"A Diet Pepsi would be great if it's not too much trouble."

I grabbed two cans from the minifridge and sat across from her. "Okay, Lucy. Hit me with your professional stats."

"I graduated from Minneapolis Art Institute. I worked at Smithco until I had Mimi. I didn't work aside from being a mom during her first two years. Then things went . . . south with Jaxson and I had to find a job. I did some freelance stuff that still allowed me to be home full-time. Then the market became flooded with freelancers, so I diversified. I took a few beading and welding classes and started my own handmade jewelry company."

I glanced up from thumbing through her portfolio. "I had no idea. What kind of jewelry?"

Lucy flipped to the back of the book. "Inexpensive bohemian stuff. Some folk art, some pieces using recycled materials. At one time I had an entire line of rings, bracelets, earrings, necklaces and anklets. I had so much fun just creating that I ended up with hundreds of pieces. When my friends convinced me to sell my jewelry at summer fairs and fall festivals, it did pretty well for a while."

"What happened?"

She laughed. "Etsy."

I laughed too. "I can see where that'd be an issue."

"I opened a storefront. In fact, I still have one. But it's not the same. I can spend days creating something unique and upload a picture of it. Within hours it's on a Pinterest board and some other jewelry maker has learned to copycat it and sell it for less. So I ended up going back to work as a graphic artist. Thankfully the print shop that hired me worked around Mimi's preschool schedule."

"You must really enjoy working. Because I know Jaxson pays child support."

Evidently my neutral tone hadn't come across that way, because Lucy got snippy. "I wondered when we'd get to this part of the interview, so fine. Let's just go there and get it out of the way."

I took a drink of my soda.

"Yes, Jaxson pays child support, which I'm sure he complains about at every opportunity to his family, because he complains about it to me and my attorney. And yes, every year after our breakup, I had to take him to court to force him to support his own child."

I'd known about the court appearances, but not the particulars.

"I didn't ask Jaxson to support me. Just Mimi. Not in any lavish fashion either. I wanted him to pay for her health insurance, her food, her clothing and our housing. Since I wasn't working, he didn't have to 'shell out' for day care. He fought me over every dime. We spent more money on lawyers that second year than he did on all the support payments. It was such a waste, but he had it in his head that I was somehow trying to screw him over. Yeah. I was living it up on the five thousand dollars a month that he grudgingly paid me."

My stomach roiled. That was all Jaxson had been paying her? He earned millions a year as a hockey player. And that income didn't come close to what his trust funds paid out as a Lund heir.

She closed her eyes. "It was an ugly situation. Jaxson never wanted to see Mimi during the hockey season. But as soon as it ended, he expected unrestricted rights to her. She was only a baby—she didn't know him because he wasn't around and I was just supposed to hand her over to him? Especially when I knew the first month of his off-season consisted of a twenty-four-hour buffet of sex and booze?"

"Is that why you left him?"

"The truth? He left *me* two weeks after Mimi was born. He just dragged out the actual breakup for another eight months." She looked at me. "After I had Mimi we decided I'd stay in Minneapolis and he'd keep a place in Chicago. He'd fly here when he could, but he never did. I had a six-month-old I'd been raising by myself and I hadn't seen him in two months. The season ended and he was supposed to fly to Minneapolis to see us, but he didn't. Five days passed and I hadn't heard a word from him. It seemed overly dramatic to worry his parents and his brother about his lack of communication, so I bundled up the baby and hopped on a plane to Chicago. I basically walked in on an orgy. A drunken orgy. I came home. Then he showed up in Minneapolis late the next day like everything was great. He didn't even remember I'd come to Chicago or that we'd had a huge fight the day before. I told him we were done."

"Lucy. I—"

"I hate that he's made me out to be some kind of evil hag with an agenda. I know he calls me Lucifer—a name that I had to hear from my daughter." Her chin wobbled. "Yes, I've denied him contact with Mimi and the court system agreed with me after I walked in to find him banging some chick while his daughter had screamed herself hoarse in the next room."

I couldn't even speak.

"I knew Jaxson's reputation when we were together. Hockey players are the worst when it comes to screwing around. I never expected fidelity, nor did I believe his promises that he'd be faithful. But when he broke promises about the care he'd give his child when I entrusted her life with him? That's where I drew the line. If I had to support Mimi one hundred percent by myself to guarantee she'd be safe and happy? I'd do it in a fucking heartbeat and I didn't care who it pissed off. That snapped Jaxson out of it a little. He's slowly building a relationship with his daughter. But it's not there yet."

"Lucy. It's okay. Take a drink. Take a breath."

She nodded.

As she got herself together, my thoughts went from my cousin to Axl.

Hockey players are the worst when it comes to screwing around.

And I'd agreed to fake a relationship with that kind of man?

At least it's not real. At least you're going in with your eyes wide-open.

But what if Lucy was manipulating me? Her story sounded plausible—more plausible than Jaxson's claims that Lucy was a horrible mother and an awful person. Mimi was a sweet, thoughtful, loving, smart little girl. Those traits were learned behavior. Since Lucy had full custody of Mimi, logic dictated she'd learned that behavior from her mother. It'd always been obvious too that Mimi adored her mom. A kid with a crappy home life wouldn't be so eager to leave the luxurious surroundings the Lunds offered.

"I'm sorry," Lucy said softly.

"Don't be. I asked you some questions and you answered them."

"Have I totally blown this chance at this job?"

"No." I closed her portfolio. "But I'd like some time to think it over. Does Edie know you've applied here?"

She shook her head.

"There's no question you're qualified, Lucy. It appears you'd work well with Lennox. I have autonomy over this department, so technically I don't have to ask Brady, Ash and Nolan for permission to hire you."

"But?"

"But I'm weighing the potential repercussions if I *don't* discuss it with them."

"I understand."

I smiled at her and stood. "I promise I won't keep you waiting long."

We walked to the door.

"Thank you, Annika, for listening to me with an open mind."

"Thank Lennox. I know I'll be thanking her for forcing me to see beyond what I thought I knew."

With all the things pinging around in my brain, it'd be pointless to try to refocus on work.

Since family therapy wasn't an option, a dose of retail therapy would have to do.

Six

—

AXL

Practice ran late, so I skipped taking a shower in the locker room.

As I stood under the spray of scalding-hot water in my bathroom, waiting for my overtaxed muscles to stop twitching, my thoughts scrolled back to the surprise of seeing Peter sitting with the coaches in the arena this morning. I hadn't known what to expect when he beckoned me over. I'd foolishly hoped for an *attaboy!* for keeping my focus entirely on training and staying out of trouble the past ten days.

But Peter reamed me, in the seething, quiet way that men in power did so well, about my lack of contact and public appearances with Annika. Apparently no press was worse than bad press in Peter's PR world.

So he was shoving us into the spotlight tonight. He'd given me explicit instructions on the time and place where I needed to show up, in addition to what to wear and how to act. I didn't appreciate a sixty-year-old grandfather telling me about dating protocol.

I'd just slipped on a white dress shirt when I heard, "*Skål*, brosky!" shouted from my living room.

It was an accepted practice in my apartment complex that everyone left their doors unlocked. I'd been living in Snow Village, a gated community composed of three interconnected buildings, since I relocated to the Twin Cities at the end of last season. I'd lived here before during the year I played in the AHL with the Wild's farm team.

Snow Village had earned the name because pro and semi-pro athletes from around the globe in winter sports like hockey, snowboarding, skiing, skating, curling and biathlon rented or sublet apartments here. Martin, the lone American in the compound, lived with Verily, Sweden's reigning snowboarding champion, directly across the hallway from me.

As I finished buttoning my shirt, I caught Martin's reflection next to mine in the mirror as he casually leaned in the doorway behind me.

He whistled. "Donning the monkey suit. What's the occasion?"

"A cocktail party my agent is requiring me to attend."

"That sucks. I wanted to kick your ass at *Resident Evil*."

I shook my head at him. "Dream on."

"It's gonna be boring around here tonight."

"Where's Verily?"

"She left for Canada for a week. Shooting a season's worth of ads for Burton and she's got a line on a heli drop."

"That woman has bigger balls than me," I muttered.

"Me too." Martin tipped up a bottle of Old Style beer and drank. "You going solo tonight?"

"No." I grabbed a tie off the dresser. My throat closed up at the thought of putting it on.

Martin pointed with the beer bottle. "With that shirt it'll look better if you skip the tie."

I lifted my eyebrow as my gaze moved over his dreads, hanging past the shoulders of his DayGlo orange Under Armour T-shirt and the tie-dyed yoga pants I'd bet belonged to Verily.

He laughed. "Trust me."

"Whatever." I slipped on the jacket.

"Too bad you shaved. You could've left the scruff and pulled your hair back in a man bun. Chris Hemsworth meets James Bond. Totally on trend."

"Says the dude wearing flip-flops with socks."

Martin laughed again. "Why are you so tense?"

I slipped my wallet into my interior suit pocket. "I'm not. Terse is my main personality trait."

"True. You give mean-eyed Igor run for money in stoic," he said in a flawless Russian accent.

"He'd hurt you bad if he heard your impression of him." I left the bedroom and cut through the kitchen to the dining room, where I'd plugged in my cell phone.

"Wait. You're nervous about your date with this chick, aren't you?"

I glanced up at him.

"Axl. Dude. I say this as a one hundred percent hetero man in love with a Nordic goddess, but you are freakin' hot, man. You're built like a beast. You've developed that arrogant conquering Viking attitude and were blessed with the looks and brains to back it up. So what's the deal?"

"Besides the fact that she's probably the most beautiful woman I've ever seen? She's smart. Like really smart in that clever way that not everyone gets. She pokes every one of my buttons, and that annoys me as much as I like the fact that she's figured out which buttons to poke." I ran my hand through my hair. "So that's the deal."

"Anything else?"

"And she's rich."

"So you're trying to come up with the best way to propose to her?"

"Fuck off."

Martin laughed. "Kidding. You like her. And you don't want to like her. That's the problem."

I scowled at him.

"Okay. I give. If you don't need dating advice, why'd you text me that you need my help?"

"I need to borrow your car."

"Why?"

"Igor is borrowing the Audi."

He raised both eyebrows. "Repo man come calling for the K-car?"

"No."

"So drive it."

"I'd have to leave it in a public lot."

"So you want to borrow my piece-of-crap Volvo."

"Just for a few hours."

He studied me. Then he laughed. "Man. You are whacked. But all right." He tossed a set of keys in my direction.

I caught them and smiled. "Thanks. I owe you one."

I texted Annika my estimated time of arrival and she replied she'd be waiting in the lobby of her apartment building.

As soon as I pulled into the semicircle in front of the modern brick, steel, stone and glass high-rise building—in the trendiest, most expensive section around Lake Calhoun—a security guard tapped on my window, signaling me to move along.

I wondered if he would've been so quick to send me on my way if I'd been driving something other than a 2002 Volvo with a Thule snowboard rack on the roof.

He did step back when I opened the car door and climbed out.

"Sir, this is private property—"

I managed to skirt the front end of the car before I heard her shout, "It's fine, Rick. He's with me."

Good thing I hadn't tried to speak, because one look at her and my mind went blank.

Annika wore a body-hugging dress that at first appeared to be black, but as she walked closer I could see the fabric shimmering with her movement, revealing the color to be a deep purple with hints of blue. Her long hair had been pinned back on the sides and braided in sections, left in long, flowing curls in the back. She hadn't gone with overly dramatic makeup; she just looked . . . stunning.

My eyes met hers. I reached for her hand and pressed my cheek to hers to murmur, "You are breathtaking."

She flattened her palm on my chest and tipped her head back to smile at me. "There's the ultimate boyfriend's greeting."

I escorted her to the passenger side, and the doorman had already opened the door. I waited for her to lift that imperious brow or say with a sneer, "Nice car," but she said nothing except "Thank you."

She didn't speak until we were on the freeway. "When did you get a personal visit from Peter?"

"Today at practice. How about you?"

"At my office." She paused. "He expects us to spend a lot of time together starting tonight."

"You don't have to sound so thrilled about it," I said.

"Maybe we should have stayed in touch. I have no idea what you've been doing."

My hands tightened on the steering wheel. "There haven't been reports of me 'doing' any random women in bars, have there?"

"We both know that just because images haven't been uploaded to the Internet doesn't mean you haven't been through a dozen women and that many boxes of condoms in the past ten days," she snapped. "How am I supposed to just trust you? I don't even know you. It would be typical of the way things have gone for me today, to show up on that stupid boat—not that I was given a choice but to walk the damn plank—and come face-to-face with some woman you were rocking the bed with last night. I don't relish the idea of pretending to act like a lovesick sop in front of everyone, including my brother. And once again it makes me question why I agreed to be the sacrificial lamb in all this. Well, coerced is more apt."

Epic rant. So epic that she hadn't noticed I'd pulled off the freeway and parked in an empty shopping center parking lot.

Then Annika gaped at me. "What in the hell are we doing here? Are you lost?"

"No. But you seem to be. There's something bubbling beneath the surface that's making you more surly than usual. You prefer to pace when you rant." I shrugged. "This is as good a place as any to do it."

"I don't need to pace. I'm fine. I just had a trying day. And besides, we can't be late for this all-important 'see us perform like love-struck monkeys' cocktail party," she said with total sarcasm.

"Exactly. The boat won't leave without us. We have time." I reached for her hand. On impulse, I kissed her knuckles. "Rant and pace. Scream if you want. There's no one here but me. And when you're done, we'll talk, okay?"

Her eyes narrowed. "You're being strangely agreeable."

"For now." I grinned. "I can be as disagreeable as you prefer later."

She smiled back. "Okay."

As soon as I helped her out, she let fly.

I leaned against the door and watched her. I forced myself to listen to what she was saying, knowing she struggled to get it out in Swedish and it would've been easier for her to express herself in English.

Her unhappiness mostly rested with her family. Her cousin Jaxson. Her mother. Even Jensen. I was a by-product of her anger, not a cause. I let her silence linger for a bit after she finished.

"Here's where I pull the macho, self-involved crap and make it about me."

She spun around, her hands on her hips, her wrap fluttering in the breeze behind her like Superwoman's cape, a gleam in her eyes.

Damn, she was magnificent.

"Well, Axl? Spit it out."

"First of all, I promised you no screwing around. So for the past ten days, I've been training during the day. At night, I've been playing video games with my male buddy Martin, who lives across the hall, or I'm sleeping or I'm watching porn. That's it. No parties. No bars. No wrestling. I kept my word. I need you to keep yours and work on trusting me."

She lowered her arms to her sides. "You're right. I'm sorry I jumped to conclusions."

"As far as Jaxson goes? What his ex told you is probably true. His nickname is 'Action Jaxson' because his number of hookups is legendary. That said, I've also heard he's toned it down."

"So it's a team thing?" She sauntered forward. "Or a guy thing? Do my brothers and cousins know he's looked up to for being 'Action Jaxson'?"

"I don't know the answer to that. And do you really want to ask your brothers and your cousins if they knew how Jaxson had treated his ex and his kid? What if they'd looked the other way?" I shook my head. "Let it go. You can't change the past. You have a chance to help her now. That's all that matters."

Annika placed her palm on my forehead.

"What?"

"I'm worried about you, Axl. You've actually been really nice and helpful. There has to be something wrong with you."

I grabbed her around the hips and tugged her against my body. "Let's hope it's contagious and *you* suddenly become really nice and helpful too."

She laughed.

And when she laughed? Even more magnificent.

We stared at each other. We both knew things were about to change for us in a big way, but neither of us seemed ready for it.

Her gaze fell to my mouth.

I could've kissed her then. Damn it, I wanted to feel her lips beneath mine, to taste her, to test that passion I knew lurked under all that professional polish, but I held off. Too many unresolved things hung between us.

Then her eyes met mine again. "We should go."

"In a minute. There's one other thing you brought up that I've been reluctant to talk about."

"Okay. Yes." She exhaled. "I know it'll be hard for you to admit in public, since you're this hot-looking, beefy, badass, snarly hockey player, but it'll be great publicity—"

"What is hard for me to admit in public?" Wait. Had she called me hot? That was a first.

"You know. Me being the dominant in our relationship. It's only natural that I take charge—eep!"

I yanked her against my body and bent down close enough that we were nose to nose. "Do not even joke about that, Princess. There will be no question in anyone's mind—least of all yours—who's the dominant in our relationship."

She went still.

"Got it?"

She nodded.

I thought I'd scared her. Or maybe I'd been too rough. I'm a big guy—it happens.

Then I realized it wasn't wariness in her eyes, but interest. She liked that show of authority.

Good to know. I filed that nugget away for future reference.

Annika stepped back and adjusted her dress.

"Seriously I want to talk about you helping me out, as a favor to your mother on your brother's behalf . . . and getting nothing in return. You're right." I laid it all out there. "You're an incredibly beautiful woman. Any man would be lucky to date you. Don't think I don't know that. By spending time with me, maybe you're missing out on meeting a guy you could be in a real relationship with."

She blinked at me. "You know I'm about to feel your forehead again, don't you?"

I ignored her comment and kept going. "Peter and your mom offering my volunteer services in exchange for you being seen around town as my girlfriend for months? Lame-ass trade-off for you."

"This does have a point besides pissing me off again, right?"

"Yes. The truth is, you're doing the PR as a benefit for Peter. Keep me in line, I'm no longer a problem client, he can ink endorsement deals for me and if my worth goes up, his cut of my pay gets bigger."

"Slightly convoluted line of thinking, but go on."

"So it's only fair that in exchange for you doing something for him, he does something that benefits *you*. Not your mother. Not your brother." I watched the wheels start spinning in that sharp brain of hers.

"Peter did mention today that there will be an eclectic group at this event, not just athletes."

"He may seem like a low-key guy. But he's a serious power broker." Now wasn't the time to tell her that the only reason Peter had taken me on as a client was that he also represented my father.

Annika started pacing again. Muttering to herself. Then she returned to the car and grabbed her phone.

For a guy who constantly had to be moving, I was strangely

content to rest against the side of the car and watch the play of light and shadows flickering over her face as day dimmed to twilight.

When I heard my phone buzzing on the dash, I figured our grace period had ended and Peter was getting impatient.

Annika looked up at me and grinned. "I know exactly what I want from Peter."

"Good. Because we need to get going."

Once we were back on the road, she said, "How bad do you feel like acting tonight, hockey pucker?"

I sent her a sideways glance. "Why?"

"If Peter is as shrewd as you've indicated, then we'll have to play hardball with him. We'll have to provide a united front. If he doesn't give me what I want . . . well, Axl might just revert to bad-boy behavior, and with the media on board, that wouldn't be good, would it?"

"What kind of bad?"

She thoughtfully tapped her chin. "You getting handsy with other women . . . not an option. I can't physically haul this big, hunky, muscular body of yours around if you drink too much, so that's out."

Had she even realized she'd paid me another compliment?

"So the logical problem is to start some fights."

I grinned. "I'm all over that."

"The most newsworthy one? My brother. But you can't really hurt him," she warned. "It has to be yelling and threats only."

Right. Then we'd titty-slap each other and pull each other's hair. The woman didn't need to tell me how to start a damn fight—or how to end one. "Also if any other pansy-ass guys on this boat check you out? I will go off on them. You look seriously sexy in that dress."

Annika slipped her hand over mine on the gearshift. "I'd expect nothing less from my man."

Seven

ANNIKA

After we parked at the port, Axl kept me close as we strolled down to the dock. Acting proprietary was for show, but it surprised me how much I liked the sensation of his hand on my back.

The boat waiting for us should've been called a yacht.

Peter stood on the boat deck. "What happened to you two? You're almost an hour late."

"Someone got lost." I bumped Axl with my hip, knowing he couldn't understand, since we were speaking English. "But we're here now. Is everyone else on board?"

"Yes. We're ready to shove off. I'll just tell the captain."

"Before we get too deep into introductions to the rest of the passengers, I need a moment of your time."

"Of course. I'll be right back."

I looked at Axl. "You want to stick around? Or act like it doesn't concern you?"

"I'll wait on the other side of the boat. Find me when you're done."

Peter returned quickly and smiled at me. "What's up, Annika? No problems with Axl, I hope."

"Everything is fine with Axl. It's this deal between you and me that's a problem. I mean, let's be honest. This favor is benefiting everyone but me. And who is making the bulk of the sacrifices? Me. What am I getting? Besides months' worth of public deception? Months where if I met a guy who sparked my interest in having a real relationship, I can't date him because I'm stuck in a fake relationship with a guy I barely know."

"Annika—"

"Let me finish. In doing this favor, Jensen gets a kick-ass agent. Axl gets a 'do over' with his reputation and you don't have to deal with a PR problem because I'm babysitting him. So I ask you, where's the benefit to me? Axl's volunteer time for LCCO?" I rolled my eyes. "With one phone call I can have a dozen volunteers. The other perk you mentioned of being seen in all the right social circles with Axl? He won't attend the opera at the Guthrie even if you threaten him. I'm already part of the social circles of the movers and shakers in the Cities. I don't know why that possibility was used as a carrot." I paused. "But there is one thing that would make this all worthwhile to me."

For the first time his eyes flashed impatience. "What?"

"A personal introduction to R Haversman and a chance to pitch the debut line of Lund's high-end boutique-style spa products for their catalogue."

"You're joking, right?"

I stepped closer. "Not even a little bit. Peter, I know you're very good friends with Haversman. You spend a week every summer at his place in Wisconsin and a week every winter skiing at his place in Telluride. If anyone can make this meeting happen . . . it's you. Several of our new products would be a perfect fit. It would be a huge PR coup for me to even get my foot in the door."

"I wish it were as simple as making a phone call, but it is not. Yes, Haversman is my friend, but I've learned it's never wise to use one's friends when it comes to business, especially when it comes to him." He smiled. "I'm sure you understand."

"Of course I understand. I'm glad you cleared up where I stand with you." I walked away and didn't turn around when he called my name.

I stood beside Axl and said, "It's on."

"You're sure you want to do this?"

"It was your idea, dude."

"No, I simply mentioned the inequality in the situation." He stopped a server and snagged two glasses of champagne, handing me one. Touching the rim of his flute to mine, he said, *"Skål."*

"Skål."

We drank. I immediately took another long drink because Peter had sprung for top-shelf bubbly. "So you've changed, your mind about helping me balance the scales?"

He moved in close enough I caught a clean, soapy scent drifting from beneath his collar. Close enough I noticed a tiny spot under his jaw where he'd nicked himself shaving. Both of those things felt intimate and I found myself leaning in. "No, I haven't changed my mind. But causing a scene without being able to blame it on too many of these"—he jiggled his champagne glass—"goes against my nature and how I was raised."

"How you were raised?"

"It's a Swedish thing. It's the way we're *all* raised. Have you heard the term *lagom*?"

I shook my head.

"It means 'just enough not to stand out.' That's our way of life."

I smiled. "My mother doesn't live that way. Evidently that's a tradition she left in Sweden when she moved here, so that's why I've never heard of it."

He laughed softly.

That deep, spontaneous laugh caused my heart to skip a beat. "So the emotionless, unaffected persona you present isn't real? Beneath this icy Nordic demeanor there actually lies emotion and passion?"

The intensity in Axl's eyes sent a new awareness through me. "Do not ever mistake an outer calm for anything except an example of a preference for self-control over hysteria." He lowered his head, brushing his smoothly shaven cheek across my jawline, from my chin up to my temple. In that slow and deliberately sensual movement, the ends of his long hair teased my neck, the musky undertones of his scent filled my lungs and the husky murmur of his voice in my ear created an overwhelming maelstrom of lust. "The only way to recognize passion is to experience it." Soft, warm breath flowed across my ear as he paused, keeping me captivated. "Have you ever experienced body-pounding, mind-scrambling, scream-inducing passion, Annika?"

I swallowed hard. I thought I had. But the confident sexuality oozing from his every carefully chosen word, his erotic touch . . . maybe I hadn't. I tilted my chin up, breaking the connection. "Is this where you offer to show me the passion I've been missing?"

"If I say yes?" He nuzzled my temple.

"I might be tempted to call your bluff."

"You think I'm all talk?"

"Ax-hell," I whispered, "you don't even like me."

I felt him smile against my cheek. "Attila, I like you just fine. But even if I didn't? Passion is passion. I could hate you and still feel passion for you."

"Hate-fucking. That sounds right up our alley."

"I've never seen the appeal . . . until now."

I retreated and drained my champagne. Then I turned away, needing a moment to compose myself. Axl in full-on seduction mode was as shocking as I imagined getting whacked in the back with a hockey stick would feel.

When I checked out the other passengers on this deck, I noticed that the guy directly across from us had a camera draped around his neck. He smirked at me and lifted his glass in a toast.

Damn it. Had he been snapping pictures of that private moment between Axl and me?

I froze.

Exactly. Think about that. There are no private moments between you and Axl, because there is nothing between you but a PR campaign. Don't be such a fucking girl, and get all swoony. Take it as a business opportunity at face value.

I spun around and granted Axl a dazzling smile.

Immediately he became suspicious. "What?"

"Let's mingle."

Axl clasped his big hand over mine and led us up to the second deck.

Peter motioned us over to where he stood with two older men in suits. "I'd like you to meet Brian and Brad Sarducci. They own the Blue Badge Energy Drink Company out of New Jersey. Axl Hammerquist, pro hockey player right here in Minnesota, and Annika Lund, VP at Lund Industries."

We shook hands.

Brian addressed Axl. "Think your team has the stones to beat the Devils this season? We shut you out all three games last year."

Axl blinked.

Shoot. He didn't know Axl couldn't speak English. I faced Axl and translated.

A beat of silence.

Then in a completely even tone Axl said, "Tell him that I will personally guarantee that not only do we have the balls to beat the Devils, but we will humiliate them in front of their fans and make them question their loyalty to a has-been team."

Peter's jaw tightened.

I offered Brian a quick smile. "Axl says last season was last season. He's focused on this team, this year. He looks forward to the challenge each team presents every time he skates onto the ice."

I could have sworn I heard Axl release a tiny snort of derision—but I must've been mistaken.

"Lund Industries," Brad said, giving me a creepy once-over. "You're part of the Lund family that owns the business?"

"Yes, I am."

"And you work in PR?"

"I've worked in most of the departments, starting from the time I was sixteen, but yes, I'm VP of the PR division."

"Huh. So, is it a PR problem that barely anyone outside the Midwest recognizes your little Midwestern company? I'll be honest. I'd never heard of Lund Industries until Peter mentioned it tonight and I took a quick second and looked it up on my phone."

Axl growled. No mistaking it that time. Brad's sneer must've alerted him to the dismissive tone of the conversation.

But I was used to fighting my own battles. "Well, jeepers, Mr. Sardonic, it was thoughtful of you to take precious time away from running your company that's what . . . a few years old? To run a quick check on our *little Midwestern company* that's been in business for one hundred years. I'd believe it was ironic that you've never heard of us, but then again, I don't believe we *are* in the same league, us with our billion-dollar annual sales revenue across the globe. Why, I'll bet you've probably used or eaten items produced by Lund Industries and don't even know it because our product lines are so very diverse. And what is it you manufacture? A single type of energy drink?" I paused. "So, no. I don't believe building our brand at Lund Industries has ever been a problem. Especially not on my watch." I lifted an eyebrow at Peter. "I don't appreciate you wasting my time. And don't waste Axl's—or Jensen's—time with a potential endorsement from them. They both can do better." I walked off.

When I glanced over my shoulder to see if Axl was following me, I saw him pantomime a mike drop.

When he turned around his grin had transformed his entire face from good-looking to double-take, stop-in-your-tracks-and-stare gorgeous.

Sigh. It really was unfair that he had it all.

When he reached me, Mr. No PDA actually hugged me. He bent to whisper, "You left them stunned, Attila."

"Your mike drop was a nice touch."

"Had to show solidarity for my girl."

"Even when you had no idea what I said?"

Axl looked into my eyes. "Especially then."

"Why?"

"Sometimes words aren't necessary."

That whole thinking, breathing thing became way harder than it should have been.

His focus kept shifting to my mouth. His big hand still rested in the middle of my back.

Enough sexual energy sizzled from him that he should've worn placarding denoting:

!DANGER! HIGH VOLTAGE WARNING!

For once, I heeded the risk.

I reached behind me and grabbed his hand, eliminating the potential temptation and possible regret. "Come on. Let's check out the view on the top deck."

There were more people than I expected but none on the highest viewing spot.

I stood on the prow, gazing down the river, both sides of the banks a solid line of lights. The water here seemed calmer than on Lake Minnetonka, where my parents lived. I'd grown up by the water, and being on a boat reminded me how much I missed it.

"Having a *Titanic* moment?" Axl murmured in my ear.

When had he become the Velcro boyfriend? I glanced at him over my shoulder. "No."

"Fair warning, there's a photographer off to the left side snapping pictures of us."

That explained why he'd become glued to my side. "Good to know."

"Did Peter tell you how long this would last?"

"Bored already?" I asked.

"Hungry. Where's the food?"

"There isn't a meal on one of these sunset cruises. But there might be appetizers on the lower deck."

"If I don't eat, me punching someone won't be an act."

"Annika?"

I placed my hand on the railing and turned toward my brother. "Jensen. Hey. What's up?"

Axl moved in behind me—right behind me—and twined his fingers through my other hand as if it was the most natural thing in the world. As if he'd done it a hundred times.

Jensen looked good. It'd been a while since I saw him decked out in a suit outside of the required "dress nice" edict after a football game. Although Jens was the youngest of my brothers, he was the tallest and the broadest. But he had nothing on Axl.

"What are you doing here?" he asked me.

"Peter invited us."

"Who's us?"

"Axl and me. We're dating."

Jensen laughed. "Right. I'll play along. I'm Jensen Lund. Annika's brother. And you are?"

"Axl Hammerquist," I answered.

"There a reason he can't speak for himself?"

The make-my-little-brother-uncomfortable side of me wanted to say, *Axl sprained his tongue during our precruise activities.* But with my luck, the reporter would hear that. "Axl is from Sweden and doesn't speak English."

"That's odd. Seven years' worth of English is required to graduate from secondary school in Sweden. It's why they have the highest ratio of nonnative English speakers in the world."

"How are you pulling that stat out of your ass?" I snapped.

"I dated Elsa Verbeek last year. The Swedish supermodel?"

"Funny, I didn't think conversation was required for the women you date."

"Usually it's not." Jensen folded his arms over his chest and studied Axl. "He's one of Peter's clients. Who does he play for?"

"The Wild."

"Ah. That explains the inability to form coherent sentences in any language."

"Jensen!"

My brother offered Axl his hand. In Swedish he said, "Jensen Lund. Annika's brother."

Axl shook Jensen's hand. Hard. "Axl Hammerquist, Annika's boyfriend. I take it a 'footballer' had choice words about the superiority of that game over hockey?"

"Not yet."

"Bring it. I'll remember to use simple words when explaining game-winning strategy so you don't get confused, since winning seems to be a foreign concept to your team."

"Oh for god's sake, Axl. Really?"

Jensen's face went cold. "How did my sister end up with a guy like you?"

"All thanks to you, my friend."

Please don't go there.

"What the fuck is that supposed to mean?" Jensen demanded.

"It means that after you signed with Peter, Peter asked Mom, who asked me, if I'd act as Axl's interpreter," I interjected. "After a rough start, we realized we had a lot in common and we started seeing each other outside of the times I'm his translator."

Axl smirked. "Yeah, but you still like it rough sometimes, don't you, baby—" Axl didn't have a chance to finish before Jensen lunged at him.

A scuffle ensued . . . after Axl moved me to make sure I was out of the line of fire.

People gathered around to watch. No one interfered, because they weren't dumb enough to get between two pro athletes who were beating the tar out of each other.

It wasn't supposed to happen this way. This was supposed to end with a little chest thumping and macho posturing.

Bull. You grew up in a testosterone-fueled family. This was the only outcome.

I yelled, "Stop it, both of you!"

They didn't stop.

Then Peter showed up and stopped the altercation. He sent his other guests downstairs for more complimentary champagne. Then he tossed a linen napkin at Axl and one at Jensen so they could wipe the blood from their faces.

Axl's bottom lip was split open, swollen and bleeding.

Jensen had a cut above his right eyebrow, also bleeding. Strangely enough, there wasn't any blood—not a drop—on either of their shirts.

"What is wrong with you two?" Peter demanded, glaring at both of them.

Neither Axl nor Jensen said a word.

I didn't know which one I was supposed to go to. It was automatic to go to Jens. I'd been kissing his boo-boos since he was a baby. But Axl . . . he actually looked worse off than Jensen.

"Is either of you seriously injured enough I need to be concerned about missed practices or game times this week?" Peter asked.

Axl shook his head.

Jensen followed suit.

"Stay out of trouble for the next twenty minutes until we get back to the dock."

Peter had taken only a few steps before Axl said to him, "I'm on track because of Annika. You see how easy it is for me to slide off. She deserves more and you damn well know it. So find a way to make it happen."

I released the breath I'd been holding. Thankfully Axl did have some tact—I hadn't been sure he wouldn't level a threat.

Peter said nothing. He just vanished down the stairs.

I walked over to where Jens leaned against the railing. "Lemme see."

"I'm fine. It doesn't need stitches." Jens locked his baby blue gaze on to mine. "What was that last bit the stick-head was babbling about?"

"Just business stuff."

"Involving you?"

I nodded. "It'll get sorted."

"If it doesn't, let me know."

"I will."

"Your boyfriend is an asshole."

I smiled at him. "I know."

"Christ. I will never understand women." He smirked at me. "Go tend to his wounds. I hurt him worse than he hurt me."

Of course *that* was the important thing. Men.

Axl rested against the rail. His eyes were closed. He'd dropped the napkin to the ground so I could see that his lip had stopped bleeding.

"You okay?"

He opened his eyes. "For the record, I didn't hit him back very hard. I wanted to."

"Good to know." I peered closely at his lip. "You need to get ice on that."

"I saw guys pulling cans of beer from a cooler over there."

"Stay put. I'll see what I can find." At the beverage station, I bent over and dug out a cold can from the back of the bin. When I turned around Axl didn't pretend he hadn't been eye-balling my ass.

He didn't offer an apology or an explanation. He just watched me approach with those beautifully assessing eyes.

I pressed the icy-cold can to his mouth.

He hissed out a breath.

"I know you're hungry. Do you want me to track down food for you?"

"No."

"Do you want to sit in a lounge chair?"

"I'm not a goddamn invalid, Annika. I got punched in the mouth. That's it." As soon as he snapped out the words, he said, "That's not what I meant. I meant to say I'm fine. But I'd like it if you stayed up here with me." He paused. "Unless you want to go see if your asshole brother is crying in the bathroom."

"Axl."

"Are all your brothers like him?"

"No. Jensen is actually the sweet one."

"Great."

I laughed.

Axl looked at me.

"What?"

"I like to hear you laugh. Come out to dinner with me tomorrow night."

My belly flipped. I started to ask why but changed it to "okay" instead. "But I have to work a little later than usual."

"I'll pick you up at your office. Text me when you're done."

"Stop talking. You're supposed to be icing this." I rolled the can to find a cooler spot and braced my hand on his chest for balance.

Axl curled his hand around the side of my face.

The heat in his eyes could melt the polar ice caps. I was getting warm in all sorts of places.

"You are extraordinarily beautiful, Annika Lund."

Forget warm. I was downright hot. I managed to say, "Thank you. Now stop talking."

He grinned at me.

Peter tracked us down before we docked. He said, "Annika? A word please."

But Axl spun me around and pressed my back to his front so we both faced Peter. "Speak freely in front of me. There are no secrets between my girlfriend and me now."

Peter laughed. "Be careful what you wish for, eh? Anyway, you drive a hard deal, Miss Lund. I commend you. After seeing your confidence in your role at Lund Industries, I will make the recommendation and the introduction to R Haversman on your behalf. There are two stipulations, though. First, that you cannot tell anyone about this. Any preparation you do must be done with the utmost discretion. And two, you have to trust that I will know the best time to approach him. So not only will you have to be patient, but you will have to be ready at a moment's notice. Can you agree to those terms?"

"Absolutely."

"Good. Then we're square." Peter looked at Axl. "Right, Axl?"

"If she's happy and it's more than she was getting from this deal before, that's all that matters."

"I'll deal with the media blitz that'll be coming your way tomorrow after tonight's events. But I very likely won't know which way to spin it until I see the paper in the morning."

Axl looked at Peter. "Why are you dealing with it? Isn't PR Annika's job?"

Good question.

"No. Annika's job is to be your girlfriend. Any PR coming from her about your relationship is suspect. I'll consult with her when I need to, but the truth is . . . this is what she's supposed to be doing."

Don't fume. You signed on for this. You expected this.

Peter sighed. "Jensen is going to take you home, Annika."

"Okay." I stepped away from Axl. "Keep icing that."

"I will."

"We're still on for dinner tomorrow night?"

"Dinner? Yes. That's a great follow-up to tonight. I'll set up the reservations and make sure the media knows," Peter said.

I took another step back and said, "See you."

Axl didn't say anything, but I felt his gaze on me until I disappeared down the stairs.

Eight

___

ANNIKA

So Peter's press machine had done its job; we'd made the paper.

ROMANTIC NIGHT OUT TURNS
INTO FAMILY FEUD
Mississippi River

A sunset cruise turned into a brawl last night on the privately chartered miniyacht operated by Windstar Corporation. According to reports, approximately seventy-five guests were aboard the boat for a cocktail party hosted by athletic agent Peter Skaarn. The cruise, set to sail at six, was delayed thirty minutes until the last guests arrived, pro hockey player Axl Hammerquist and Lund Industries executive Annika Lund.

*There is truth to the rumors of a romantic rela-
tionship between the bad-boy Swedish hockey player
and the Lund heiress. Photos obtained during the
cruise show the couple holding hands and enjoying
intimate conversation below deck. It was when they
surfaced above deck that the first signs of trouble
appeared. A meeting with an East Coast beverage
company earned a smackdown from the businesswoman nicknamed the Iron Princess, while "The
Hammer" stood beside her in silent support.*

*Afterward on the top deck, the blond couple
once again distanced themselves from other guests
for alone time. But they weren't able to escape the
notice of Jensen "The Rocket" Lund, Vikings tight
end and Annika's younger brother. A heated exchange of words was quickly followed by the footballer and the hockey player coming to blows.*

*No one at the party can confirm the details of
the conversation that led to the fight. Jensen was
escorted below deck by the event host while Annika
and Axl remained on the upper level. Soon after,
the couple was forced to separate and Miss Lund,
who arrived with Mr. Hammerquist, left the party
with her brother, leading to further speculation.*

Directly below the article were four pictures. One of Axl
whispering in my ear when we were drinking champagne.
One of Jensen's arms in full swing with his fist heading toward Axl's face. One of me holding a can to Axl's mouth as
I stared into his eyes. The last one of Axl, leaning over the
deck railing, watching me leave with Jensen.

God. This was . . .

What you signed on for. This is just the beginning.

I closed my eyes. Inhaled. Exhaled. Took myself out of the image and approached this from a PR standpoint.

From the pictures, it did look as if Axl and I were a couple. Goal achieved.

The Axl and Jens fight . . . win-win for everyone actually. Axl cares enough about me to get into fisticuffs with my brother. My little brother lets Axl know he can put him in his place if he crosses a line when it comes to me. I'm clearly torn between family and my new man. Not to mention that the sports fans would line up in defense of their player. So they'd build up the rivalry, which is more press for Axl and Jens, and not necessarily bad press because it's easily managed.

The bit about me being a hard-ass businesswoman? Perfect. I would take that description over the years the media cared more about my fashion sense than my business sense.

I closed my laptop and finished getting ready for work. I took the stairs down to the parking garage and exited into the rush-hour traffic. I hadn't bothered checking to see if reporters lurked around my apartment building, because this was Minneapolis. Yes, we had a newspaper devoted entirely to gossip about city residents that no one outside the city would give a rip about—similar to Page Six in the *New York Post*—but our reporters were hardly the taunting, invasive paparazzi types. For one thing, Minnesotans were by and large too polite to act that way. For another, most of the year it was freakin' cold outside and no reporters wanted to freeze their ass off for a picture where the subject would be unrecognizable bundled up against the elements. In the warmer months, stories about the great outdoor activities the Twin Cities had to offer took precedence, since summer was so fleeting.

I parked in my usual spot in the private section of the underground parking garage and sprinted up the stairs. There was a private elevator—another perk of being an LI executive, bypassing the lobby and the public access elevators—but I never used it.

Deanna was on the phone when I reached the reception desk, but I saw she'd left a cup of coffee on the corner of her desk . . . next to the print edition of the article. I mouthed, *Thank you*, as I sailed past into my office. She'd be in to grill me about it sooner rather than later.

I just hadn't expected my brother to beat her to the punch.

Brady strolled in—without knocking—looking every inch the corporate CFO in his custom-tailored suit, not a dark hair on his head out of place. For years my girlfriends had begged me to set them up with my nerdy-hot-but-doesn't-know-it brother, but I'd always refused. Although he was older, I'd felt more protective of him than of Jensen or even Walker. So it thrilled me that he'd finally come out of his workaholic shell and found Lennox, a woman truly worthy of the kind of love and devotion Brady had to give.

"Morning, bro. I assume you're here as the family rep and not the boss?"

"You would be correct in that assumption."

"Dude, if this is an informal meeting, the least you could've done is brought breakfast. Bagels, croissants, donuts, muffins . . . something."

Brady raised an eyebrow. "You do have an assistant for fetching you those types of things."

I sipped my coffee as I waited to see if Brady would sit down or if he'd pace while he lectured me.

He lowered himself into the chair opposite my desk. "So . . . you're dating a hockey player."

"Yes."

"Which apparently surprised Jensen."

I shrugged. "Jens is in his own little world during football season, Brady. To be honest, he's been in his own little world the last couple of years."

"That is beside the point, Annika. *I* didn't know you and this Axl guy were a couple."

"Wash, rinse, repeat the comment about you being in your own little happily-ever-after world with your wife."

"*My wife* didn't know and she works in your office."

"Deanna knew, so I'm happy to hear she's not gossiping about my personal life." I took another swig of coffee. "In fact, this started after I agreed to meet Axl at Jaxson's request and then Mom got involved."

His gaze turned shrewd. "More details please."

So I filled him in, leaving a few key things out, adding others in.

Brady didn't look convinced. Or happy.

"What?"

"This guy was so smitten with you that he went to the trouble of pretending to want to *hire* you in order to get you to go out on a date with him?"

I sighed. "It's romantic, isn't it?"

"Romantic? Jens said this Axl guy is an asshole."

Of course Brady had talked to Jensen first. "I can't really argue with that."

Not the answer my brother expected. Then he veered in the direction I *had* expected. "Annika. It goes beyond him being an asshole. He gets in fights on and off the ice. Not to mention he's a major player with a reputation—"

"That doesn't even come close to the reputation our cousin 'Action Jaxson' has built over the years," I inserted coolly. "Years in which I thought it was so unfair that Lucy kept Mimi from him. So not only was Jaxson the worst kind of player, but he freakin' lied about what was really going on."

Brady said nothing, but the muscle in his jaw jumped.

"Since Lucy applied for a job here, Lennox probably filled you in, but I doubt Lucy told her all the ugly truths that she told me." I paused. "Brady. Be honest. Did you know any of this?"

"I was aware of Jaxson's reputation and that he went through women like water. All I know about the Mimi situation is what Jaxson told us about Lucy denying him access. If Lucy is telling the truth . . . Jax hid it from us because he knows we would've done something about it. No one in the family would stand for that. Then or now."

Major shit was about to hit the fan, because I intended to hire Lucy.

"The point I'm trying to make, sis, is that Axl and Jaxson are exactly alike."

I shook my head. "Axl owns up to the fact that he screwed up in the past. He's trying to change. He *wants* to change, and that's half the battle."

"That's the kind of man you want to date?" Brady demanded. "A player, with a mean streak, who attacked your brother the first time they met? A guy even *you* admit is an asshole?"

Three raps sounded on my door before it opened. Deanna walked in, carrying a vase filled with white roses. A deliveryman behind her held a vase with red roses in one hand and a vase with peach roses in the other hand. The deliveryman behind him carried in a vase of yellow roses and a vase of orange roses. Yet another delivery guy behind him carried in a vase of fuchsia roses and a vase of dark pink roses. The deliveryman following him brought in a vase of cream roses, the petals tipped in red, and a vase of ivory roses, the petals tipped in tangerine. And Brick, the security guy from the main floor, carried in a vase of pale lavender roses and a vase of blush roses.

Brick grinned at me. "There were so many that they ran out of delivery guys."

"Thanks, Brick. And thank you to the rest of you."

Deanna crossed over to the desk with the bouquet of white roses and handed me a sealed envelope. "This came with it."

Heart racing, I ripped the envelope open.

Before I read the actual words on the card, I noticed they'd been written in Swedish, so I knew this wasn't a PR stunt Peter had cooked up; the flowers had actually come from Axl.

Attila~

I didn't know your favorite color so I covered all my bases. Looking forward to dinner tonight.

A~

Grinning, I let my gaze drift over the beautiful array of blooms filling my office before I met my brother's eyes. "Yes, Brady. He's exactly the kind of man I want to date."

Nine

AXL

Training wasn't any different the day before an exhibition game than if we were preparing for a regular season game.

After I left the ice, swimming in sweat, sore, out of breath, I just wanted to go home and crash for a few hours before my date with Annika.

But the beady-eyed guy whose name I never remembered, with no real power but obviously eager to make a name for himself in the organization, stopped me before I reached the locker room. As far as he knew, I didn't understand English, so his one-sided diatribe made no sense.

"You. They're waiting for you in the conference room." He pointed at my feet. "Take off the skates fast for a change. I ain't got all damn day."

I glared at him with my gloved hands on my hips. Mostly because I was still trying to breathe normally.

"God. I hate when you assholes come to our country and don't learn the language."

I know what you mean, buddy. Few visitors to Sweden bother to learn even the most basic Swedish words.

Kaz stopped behind me. We both spoke Russian—not a fact that we broadcast. Quietly he said, "Bosses want you. Media room. Ditch the gear."

"Thanks." I stripped down. Usually I'd shower first, but since they'd commanded an audience they could deal with my stench.

Six guys were in the room. Seven counting my agent.

He intercepted me before I reached the conference table. For once he didn't look mad. "This is a fishing expedition. More good will come from last night's events than harm. I'll admit on your behalf you're in a relationship with Annika. You exchanged words with Jensen. Things are fine now. I'll assure them you're not reverting to previous behavior. Got it?"

I nodded.

"Last thing. You need to start speaking English. Figure out a way to admit you've improved your language skills. You will be asked to speak at press conferences and it'll go easier all around if you don't need a translator." He smiled. "Although I'll admit Annika showed talent in sugarcoating your response last night."

"Maybe she should be my official translator."

"Maybe she's the first one you should come clean with. You heard her put those blowhards in their places last night. I've heard her knock you down a peg or ten. This deception will bring out her snarling beast and she'll paint vivid images of what you can do with your deception. All suggestions will be anatomically impossible, so you'd better have a plan on how to calm her down."

I'd been thinking nonstop about the very explicit ways to keep her mouth occupied.

Peter got right in my face. "Keep those thoughts PG, son."

When I imagined her, XXX thoughts were the rule.

"Come on. Let's get this over with."

The meeting lasted less than ten minutes.

The team's PR department saw more benefits in the tussle with Jensen Lund than drawbacks. I'd expected looks of envy when my personal involvement with Annika became public. I hadn't expected to see expressions of outright shock, and that annoyed the fuck out of me. Because a brawling hockey player like me was supposed to end up with the bar wenches and not the princess? I'd left feeling more insulted than warranted, probably.

None of the guys had cleared out of the locker room as I'd hoped.

A gangly kid I'd never seen before stood beside Flitte, shuffling his feet.

"Hammerquist, we're gonna fix the language barrier between us, since the media reports you're getting into all sorts of fun and we want a piece of it."

The half dozen or so teammates behind him nodded.

"So I hired Relf here"—he clapped the gangly kid on the shoulder hard enough to move him forward—"to translate. Relf attends the U of M, but he's from Sweden. Crazy, huh?" He nudged Relf. "Go on. Start translating that. And it'd better be word for word. No bullshit."

Relf translated, but his voice shook pretty hard. He didn't need an audience for this.

"Tell them it's standard procedure for us to sync our language styles so translating is more effective and we'll need a few minutes to talk alone."

After he relayed that, I took him to the other side of the locker bay. "Are you being forced into this, Relf?"

"Ah, no. Yes. Maybe. Look, I was in the Scandinavian cultural center when two guys from the Gophers hockey team chased me down. And I'll admit, I ran. When they caught me they said they knew I was Swedish and I'd been . . . uh . . . *chosen* to be a translator. Then they brought me here, where I've been waiting to translate for you." His eyes darted to the guys behind us. "That's all I'm really here for, right?"

"Right."

"And no offense, but you're from Sweden and you don't speak English at all?"

I sighed. "I'm fluent in English. I've kept that to myself for my own reasons. These guys are the first teammates who have pushed the issue. So you'll translate. Everyone will be happy. Now, are you really okay with it?"

He shrugged. "I can't miss classes or anything. But outside of that, it's cool." He looked at me. "Most of the students here are from Norway, so it's good to hear the home language."

"I'll get you a ticket to the exhibition game tomorrow night."

His eyes lit up. "That'd be awesome."

"Let's figure out what my teammates want to know."

Flitte grinned at us when we returned. "All right! First question: Did you really punch Jensen Lund in the face last night?"

The questions didn't get more complex than that.

Was I really nailing Annika Lund?

When I wrestled an alligator, had I really bitten the ears off before I broke its neck? I lied about that one and said yes.

Had I really killed a bear with my bare hands? I suspected these guys had seen way too many episodes of *Vikings*.

They demanded that I come out and drink with them right then. For three seconds, I considered canceling my date. I should seize the chance to bond with my teammates off the ice. But I made the right PR move and said no, citing plans with Annika, but promised we would go out soon for team drinks.

They showered me with packages of condoms. All of which I tossed into my equipment bag. Wouldn't want to be wasteful.

By the time I left the arena and dropped Relf off on campus, I realized I hadn't checked my messages to see what time I needed to pick Annika up. I saw one message she'd sent hours ago.

AL: Thank you for the roses. Every color is gorgeous, so I have no favorites. I have a minor issue to deal with that'll get me out of the office earlier than I'd planned. So I'll meet you at the restaurant since Peter indicated we have an open reservation. Seven?

ME: C U then.

AL: English? Have you been drinking? ☺

Shit. Lucky thing I'd kept it short.

I raced into my apartment and jumped into the shower. Still dripping wet after I shaved, I wrapped a towel around my waist and stepped into my bedroom.

Martin and Boris both were stretched out on my bed.

"Christ. What the hell, guys?"

"We saw you run into your place like a serial killer was after you."

"So you planned to . . . what? Beat him to death with pillows when he came out of the bathroom?"

"Nah. We figured you were good. So, what's doin', man?" Martin asked.

"I have a date. And I'm late."

"Another one? Same chick?"

"Yes, the same chick who is my girlfriend."

"How did I not know this happened?" Boris asked.

"It's recent. I'm guessing it was a pretty rockin' date if she got the GF letters after her name last night." Martin held his fist up for a bump. Boris missed.

"Dude. How many bowls you smoke today?" Martin asked.

"Less than two."

Unreal. "Get off my bed."

"No prob." Martin bounced to his feet. "You want us to smooth out the wrinkles in the covers in case you bring her here and get some action later?"

"Get. Out."

"What are you wearing for your date?"

"I could figure it out if you'd get the hell out of my room," I snapped.

"Clothing. That easy," Boris said, sitting up. "Parachute pants and biceps cuffs."

"What the eff, Boris?" Martin said.

"His nickname Hammer-time, right? Wear Hammer-time clothes."

"You definitely smoked more than two bowls today, huh, my Finnish friend?" Martin pulled Boris to his feet and pushed him out the door. "Ax-man, wear the dark gray pin-striped suit with the light gray shirt. Go with a plain tie. No funky pattern. Have it match the shirt more than the suit and don't go with anything really dark like black."

"What about shoes?" I said snidely.

"Oxblood-colored oxfords." He grinned. "You're welcome. And drive the damn K-car. Impress this girl."

"It'll impress her more if I'm not late."

It was ridiculous being nervous for this dinner date.

Because it's not a date. It's a PR push to capitalize on last night's events.

Why didn't it feel like Annika and I were just following an agenda?

Because you aren't. Sending her eleven dozen roses might've been over-the-top.

That was what made it fun. No way was she expecting that. Especially not from me.

When the voice in my head wouldn't pipe down, I cranked up the stereo. Nothing like Swedish thrash metal to drown out all internal noise.

As I leaned against the building, it felt less like a date. Not that I could remember the last time I'd done the "pick a night, pick a restaurant, pick her up at her place" kind of date.

You're more the "pick up the chick and bang her in the bar" type.

When had I turned into such a pussy, second-guessing everything about myself?

I glanced up and saw Annika sashaying toward me with that long-legged, loose-hipped stride only the most confident women could pull off.

Annika had every reason to be confident. She was so smoking hot her stilettos should've left scorch marks on the pavement. The slinky black cocktail dress hugged her curvy body from her shoulders to her knees. She'd swept her hair to the side in a loose braid and nestled a rose behind her ear the exact same shade as her deep red lipstick.

I started toward her, pausing at the curb to watch the woman literally stop traffic.

This was so not a PR thing anymore.

I'd lasted one damn day before she snared me in her web.

"You're scowling at me," she said, drawing my attention back to her.

"Not scowling." I pressed my hand into the small of her back, bringing her body against mine as I brushed my cheeks to hers. "I'm concentrating on coming up with a compliment that isn't too boring or too lewd."

Annika tilted her head back to look at me. "Just for fun, let's hear the lewd one."

"You are immeasurably fuckable in that dress."

Her eyes never left mine. "Axl. The way you growled that wasn't lewd at all. It was sexy."

"I'll try harder next time."

Laughing, she reached up and ran her thumb across my lower lip. "It's still swollen." She smirked. "No kissing for us tonight."

"It'd be worth the pain."

The whisper-soft brush of her mouth over that spot didn't count as a kiss, but my lips tingled anyway. "Let's revisit that idea after dinner."

Peter had chosen a farm-to-table restaurant focused on Scandinavian cuisine. "Have you eaten here?" I asked her.

"No. But it is highly rated." Before she could give the staff her name, the woman said, "Right this way, Miss Lund."

After we were seated at a cozy table in the back, I said, "I'm surprised Peter didn't insist on a spot in front of the windows."

When the server came, Annika said to me, "Trust me to order your beer?"

"Sure."

Annika said, "We'll both have a Leinenkugel Sunset Wheat."

I didn't bother to look at the menu, although I had checked it out online.

Annika giggled from behind her menu.

Such a rare, carefree sound coming from her. "What's so funny?"

"My mom is always whipping up 'fusion' dishes and now we'll have to stop making fun of her because Swedish-American fusion is a real thing." Annika rattled off two choices that fell under a "bizarre" heading as far as my palate was concerned.

"I'll skip those. Other options?"

She read me the entire menu without complaint. Stopping to discuss certain aspects of each dish. After she finished, she said, "Does any of this sound like what you'd eat at home?"

"Not even close."

Our beers were delivered.

I asked Annika to order the braised lamb and roasted root vegetables for me. She chose buttered noodles and breaded eel for herself.

I raised my beer mug to hers. *"Skål."*

"Skål."

Annika set down her beer mug and studied the tablecloth before she glanced up at me. "I hate this part."

"What part?"

"The 'I don't really know you and I don't really know what to ask you to get to know you' part of a real date. It's always awkward. And that doesn't take into account the awkwardness of us pretending to be something we're not."

I rested my forearms on the table. "If I hadn't been an . . . ax-hole the first night we met and asked you out on a date, what would you have said?"

Annika tilted her head. "Depends on whether you would've had a quickie with the waitress."

"No quickie."

She continued to study me. "I'll be honest. I don't know if I can pretend that meeting was anything besides a disaster."

"You're probably right." I took a long swallow of beer. "I can't wrap my head around all the things you do to help your family."

"I'm supposed to say no when they request a favor from me?"

"Yes."

"Axl—"

"I will not be another person in your life who takes advantage of you. If you don't want to play the part of my girlfriend, then we'll go to Peter's house directly after dinner and tell him you're done. And then we will go to your mother's house—"

"Stop." She reached over and squeezed my hand. "It wasn't my intent to turn this dinner date into a shit show."

"What can I do to make this date less awkward?"

"Don't look at the waitress like you're eyeing the dessert cart?"

Such a flip answer. One that I deserved. "I haven't noticed any woman but you since the moment you crossed the street." I turned her hand and kissed the inside of her wrist, then her palm before I closed her fingers into a loose fist. I brushed my mouth across her knuckles and the back of her hand. "You scare me, Annika Lund."

"Why?"

"Because you're outrageously beautiful, extraordinarily smart, ridiculously clever, utterly devoted to your family and so fucking sexy I fear you might ruin me for all other women."

Her eyes softened. "Totally scored extra charm points for that, Axl."

"It's all true. So hit me with the getting-to-know-you questions." I'd expected the basics. Then again, this was Annika. I took a big swig of beer.

"How old were you when you lost your virginity?"

She'd almost caught me in a spit-take. "You're kidding."

"Nope. A few vague-ish details of that time would be helpful."

"Why?"

"Because of your reputation with the ladies."

If she'd intended to throw me off guard, she'd succeeded. "I was fourteen. The woman was older . . . nineteen, I think. She believed I was older because of my size."

Annika lifted both her eyebrows, and damn it if I didn't blush.

"The overall size of my *body*, Miss Dirty Mind. Anyway, I'd been watching porn a lot that year, so I faked my way through the first time. She taught me the rest. She disappeared when she learned how young I was. What about you?"

"I was eighteen. He was the head lifeguard at the pool where I taught swimming lessons. We flirted and messed around all summer, but he wouldn't touch me until I was of legal age. We were together three weeks until I started college."

"Did you break his heart?"

"No. But he didn't break mine either, so that was a plus." She smirked at me. "Did you know that I'm two years older than you?"

A small knot tightened in my gut. I wondered how much of my bio she'd read. "I have a weakness for older women." I could see the wheels churning. "Why are you so geared up to ask questions?"

"PR habit. I don't like surprises. Plus, I'm nosy."

Peter's voice popped into my head, reminding me to come clean about the language issue—or lack of issue.

"But it's not the things listed on a bio that interest me," she continued. "It's the obscure life stuff. Like what was your favorite candy when you were a child?"

"I've never been a fan of Swedish fish," I said dryly. "I guess it was probably Salt-Skallar."

"Why?"

Because my dad had shown up out of the blue and taken me to a football game. He'd bought that candy for himself, so I'd gotten the same kind. "I don't remember. What about you?"

Annika made a face. "I ate six boxes of sour Skittles I'd liberated from Jensen's Halloween candy stash when I was eight. I puked my guts out and haven't been able to stomach them since. Getting sick served me right for stealing from my little brother and I never did that again either."

"'A thief with a conscience is a thief no more' lesson learned in young Annika's life?"

"Yes. What was your most memorable life lesson?"

"Never skate on thin ice."

"Funny. So at age seventeen, favorite way to spend your day?"

"Playing hockey," I said automatically.

She seemed skeptical. "You'd rather be on the ice than anywhere else?"

"Back then? Yes."

"Now?"

"Now . . . I'd spend the day in bed."

"Sleeping?"

I granted her a lustful look. "Want to come over on my next day off and I'll show you all the fun, dirty things we can do in a bed besides sleep?"

She opened her mouth.

That was when the food arrived.

My meal was delicious. I noticed that Annika kept pushing hers around on the plate. "Problem?" I asked.

She sighed. "I'm not a super-adventurous eater. Everyone in my family gives me crap about it. This is . . . weird. The noodles are good. But the eel?" She flicked a chunk with her fork. "Do Scandinavian people still eat eel?"

I kept a straight face. "Historically we ate a lot of eel because we were limited to what the sea's bounty produced. Let me try a bite."

"Have at it."

"No, Annika. Be adventurous. Feed it to me."

She speared a noodle, then a piece of eel, then another noodle, dipping the bottom of the fork in a pool of sauce before holding it across the table.

I leaned in, watching her eyes watching my mouth as my lips closed around the fork.

"Well?" she said huskily.

"I'm not sure. I need another taste."

This time she teased me, touching the tines of the fork to my bottom lip and then slightly pulling back. "Say please."

"Please."

"Open wide."

"An-ni-ka."

She slipped the fork between my lips, waiting until my mouth closed before she slowly pulled back. "You have the hottest voice, Axl. My heart races when you use that 'don't fuck with me' tone."

I swallowed and took a long drink of my beer, never taking my eyes off hers. "And yet when I use that 'don't fuck with me' tone, you don't pay it any mind. In fact . . ." I reached out and twined a hank of her hair around my finger. "You tend to go out of your way to mess with me. Why is that?"

"Because messing with you and seeing that fire in your eyes makes me feel like I'm doing something naughty."

Now we were at the getting-to-know-you part that I understood.

"Maybe you've already figured this out, but I'm the good girl who follows the rules. Who always does what's expected of her. What's asked of her."

"I did notice that . . . except I didn't believe it."

"You'd be the first."

An awkward silence settled between us after the server picked up the dishes.

Screw this. Time to go on the offensive. I picked up her hand. "What's the one thing you wish you were better at?"

"Skiing."

"Downhill? Or water?"

"Downhill. I've taken lessons numerous times, but I haven't improved much. I end up skiing by myself because everyone in my family is awesome at it."

"Have you ever tried snowboarding?"

"That would be worse. I'll bet you're an expert at both."

"Winters are long in Sweden." I cocked my head at her. "What's the scariest thing that ever happened to you?"

"My brother Brady went missing for twelve hours when we were kids and the police were convinced he'd gone swimming alone and drowned. I was terrified I'd never see him again. That day seemed nine years long." She looked away for a moment and I knew she hadn't been totally honest. Not that I doubted her brother's disappearance had terrified her, but it wasn't what still put the fear in her eyes. "What about you?"

"My friends Roald, Mikel and I were playing hockey on a lake by Mikel's house. The ice had started to thin and thaw in spots—not that we were aware of it until it was too late and Mikel went through the ice."

Annika gasped. "Omigod. You weren't joking about 'skating on thin ice' being a life lesson. What happened?"

"Roald and I got ahold of the back of Mikel's jacket and kept him from sinking into the water. Hockey gear weighs a lot. Wet hockey gear . . . Anyway, we laid our sticks across the hole so Mikel had something to hold on to. I stretched across the ice on my belly behind him, holding his jacket. Roald ran up to the house in his hockey skates to get help.

"The entire time we were out there waiting, all I could hear was the cracking and shifting of the ice. I decided if I died in a cold-water grave, I'd come back as a ghost. A really mean ghost who'd scare kids away from the lake."

"Everything turned out okay?"

"Mostly. I had frostbite on my face from crying." I felt my neck heat from that admission. "Mikel . . . the doctors had to amputate both his pinkie toes. After that, I only played hockey on dedicated outdoor rinks."

"I can't say as I blame you. Yikes."

My lips curled into a sheepish smile. "And that's when the dinner date conversation took a turn for the worse."

She laughed softly. "I know what you were trying to do, though. Make me answer the same type of questions I asked you."

"You're better at it than I am."

"What was your next question going to be?"

"What you'd do if I kissed you."

She reached down for her purse and pulled out a round container. "First I'd pop a mint so I don't have fried eel breath." She held the container across the table. "Want one?"

"Sure."

"Besides. That really wasn't your question," she mock-chastised. "Try again."

It was my question. As she'd been talking I became obsessed with her mouth. "Name two things that you think people assume about you when they look at you that are actually true. And one thing that isn't true."

Annika grinned. "You're getting the hang of this. That is an awesome question, Axl. Okay. First, blondes do have more fun—totally true. Second, I spend a ridiculous amount on clothing, shoes and personal care—also true. Your turn."

"First, I play hockey because I get paid to be aggressive—true. Second, I'm an asshole—feel free to chime in and disagree."

She laughed. "Not touching that one. What's the one assumption that you think people make that isn't true?"

"That I'm nothing but a dumb jock. You?"

"I'm successful in my family's company because of my last name, not because I worked hard."

The server showed up with a tray of desserts. Annika ordered a mini-princess cake and coffee. "This was actually a pretty good date."

I threaded my fingers through hers. "What would have made it better?"

She shrugged. "Normal food."

"What's Annika's definition of normal food?"

"Meat loaf and mashed potatoes. A BLT. Breakfast food. Salads."

"We'll go to a place that serves Annika food next time we go out for dinner."

"That's sweet. But it wouldn't be fun if you couldn't eat. I bet you follow a special diet during the season."

"Just a balance of protein and carbs with vegetables and starches. If I eat like shit, I play like shit."

"Are you excited for the exhibition game tomorrow night?"

"Nervous. This is a new team for me with new expectations. I feel strong."

"You look strong."

I glanced up at her. "You've been sneaking into practices?"

"No. But you are a super-big guy. I don't have to watch you lift weights to know you could probably heft a Volvo over your head."

"A Volvo? Really?"

Annika snickered. "Come on. That was funny. And you want to know what else is funny? I thought you'd say the misperception about you is that you based your hairstyle on Prince Charming from *Shrek 2.*"

"Excuse me?"

"In that first scene where Charming slowly takes off his knight's helmet—I'm guessing it's very similar to when you take off your hockey headgear—and he shakes his head . . . There's a collective *aah* as everyone admires his flowing hair? Yours is about the same length and the same color."

I didn't bother to mask my look of horror. "What the hell, Attila? I don't swing my hair around like some vain cartoon character."

"That's why I said 'misperception,' Ax-hole. But it'd be really hot if you did it one time during the season."

I leveled her with my most menacing glower. "Fuck. No."

"Please? Just for me? Ooh, and what about skating around shirtless while you did it?"

"You do realize it's freakin' cold down there, because it's, oh . . . *ice*, right?"

"I know. We could turn it into a fund-raiser. Pay a little extra, come to the game early and see the hockey hottie warming up. Are his muscles twitching and quivering from excitement for the game? Or from the extreme cold?"

"Maybe they're twitching from extreme anger." I eyed her empty beer mug. "We had the same amount of booze, so I know you're not drunk."

"I'd want to be stone-cold sober if I ever got you half-naked."

I leaned far enough forward that I could wrap my hand around the back of her neck and pulled her in so we were almost mouth-to-mouth. "You don't need to go to all that trouble of setting the scene if you want me half-naked. All you have to do is ask. Throw in a please? And I'll bare all."

"God, I'd love to see that."

"What has gotten into you?"

"You've given me some pretty rockin' compliments tonight. I can't do the same?"

Maybe it made me a pussy to ask, but I had to know. "So none of that hair-tossing, bare-chested, muscles-quivering hockey hottie stuff was Annika from PR talking?"

"No." Her mint-scented breath teased my lips; I could actually taste it. "It was Annika the woman who's spent a vast amount of time thinking about you talking."

"It's good we're in a public place."

"Why?"

Because if we were alone I'd prop you up on the table and make you my dessert.

She touched the side of my face. "I like you. Yet I still think you're an ass. It's weird."

"I like you. You're not boring." I grinned. "Plus, you have an ass that I'd like to sink my teeth into."

She pushed away from me. "We were having such a nice moment and you had to ruin it."

"You brought up my ass first."

"I said you *were* an ass. Big difference."

But she wasn't really mad.

The mini-princess cake arrived. The dome-shaped top was wholly meringue. "I'll share," she offered.

"No, thanks. My sweet tooth gets me in trouble."

"So I do want to talk about the schedule. It's a little confusing to me. Exhibition game tomorrow night. Then there's another one out of town next week?"

"All the teams have to travel at least once preseason. Our first game of the regular season isn't at home. In fact, our first two games aren't at home. We don't play at home until two weeks from Friday night."

Annika sucked the meringue off her fork and I had to look at my coffee cup to restrain myself.

"Are you busy a week from Saturday during the day?"

"We leave early Saturday night to fly to Edmonton for the Sunday night game. Which means an early practice. Why?"

"I'm organizing donations for the Lund Cares Community Outreach coat drive that Saturday and I could use help."

"This is part of the charity deal I agreed to?"

"It is. This is the actual working part. Sorting, hanging."

I frowned. "You do that? You don't have employees—"

"Do the dirty work and then I sweep in, wearing my mink coat and tiara, for a fab PR moment on the day the less fortunate souls show up to choose their free winter wear?"

One day I might use my brain before I opened my mouth. "I'm an ass for assuming. Sorry."

"This project is volunteer-driven. So naturally it's hard to find people who want to spend their weekend off helping out for free."

"I'll round you up some kick-ass volunteers."

Annika looked up and smiled. "Super."

After we finished, the server told Annika the check had been taken care of. There wasn't a reason for us to linger in the restaurant, but I didn't want to walk her to her car and end this date.

We paused outside the restaurant and headed to the parking lot. Once the sun had gone down, it had become downright cold and Annika hadn't worn a jacket.

I unbuttoned my suit coat and shrugged out of it, then draped it around her shoulders. "Maybe we should make sure *you* get a coat at the coat drive, yah?"

She smirked.

"What?"

"That's the first time you sounded like my mother."

"Because I worry that you're cold?" I tugged her braid from beneath the jacket collar and pulled the coat more tightly around her.

"No. When you said 'yah.' She says it all the time." She glanced up at me. "Why is it so easy to talk to you? I don't struggle to find the right Swedish words. Don't you think that's odd?"

"No. You're basically a native speaker."

"But don't you—"

I kissed her. A gentle press of my lips to hers, letting them linger as I learned the shape of her mouth.

I ended the kiss before it really got started. At her soft moan of protest, I dragged my lips across her jawbone to her ear. "That is as much as I'm willing to let the public see. Anything else doesn't belong to them, Annika."

"Who knew you had a chivalrous streak?"

"That's what this is?" I mock-gasped. "It is curable, right?"

She head-butted my chest.

"Come on. I have something for you and then we're calling it a night."

"You bought me a present?"

I noticed she'd parked just three spaces down from me. I stopped behind my Audi and popped the trunk. "It's just a team jersey."

"Axl. You're not supposed to tell me!"

"I didn't want you to get your hopes up that it was jewelry." I snagged the plastic bag.

"Thank you." She slipped free from my suit jacket and handed it back to me. "You look immensely fuckable yourself, so you should definitely wear this suit to the press conference after the game."

"Thank you."

Annika kissed my cheeks. "I'm freezing my ass off. See you tomorrow night."

Ten

ANNIKA

Exhibition game night.

I'd been to so many pro sporting events over the years I could've been one of those people who affected an air of boredom. But I was genuinely excited. I loved watching live sports. Being part of the crowd's excitement. Feeling camaraderie with thousands of others over this one thing.

There was nothing like it in the world.

This was a new experience for me. In all the years I'd been around athletes, I'd never actually dated one. Not in high school or college. It hadn't been a rebellious choice; I'd just naturally gravitated toward men involved in more intellectual pursuits. Guys who used brains instead of brawn.

So showing up to the Xcel Center, wearing a team jersey with HAMMERQUIST on the back, was pretty awesome. Although when I made my way to the section that the players had reserved for family and friends, I had a sudden, rare bout of shyness.

At Jensen's games I was in familiar territory, surrounded by the Lund collective. Even at Jaxson's games my aunt and uncle always had a skybox or the stadium's equivalent, no matter which city the Blackhawks were playing in. Now I had to wonder if they'd purposely isolated themselves from the group section so they wouldn't have to see the sheer number of their son's female groupies.

Except I wasn't going to worry about that now. I wouldn't even have to deal with it tomorrow afternoon at the barbecue Walker was hosting, since my aunt and uncle were in Chicago for Jaxson's exhibition game tonight.

I hadn't asked Axl if he had plans tomorrow. I didn't want it to be weird if I invited him to a family function, since we'd agreed that spending time together privately was a waste of time without PR benefits.

But doesn't your family believe you're truly dating Axl? Then wouldn't they expect you'd want to introduce him to them?

This fake-relationship stuff turned out to be way harder to pull off than I'd imagined.

I stopped at the top of the stairs and scanned the seating section below me.

"Can I help you find your seat?"

I glanced up at the security guard and showed him my ticket. "I'm in the right place?"

"Yes, ma'am. Twelve rows down, right behind the glass."

"Thank you."

The arena hadn't started to fill up yet. But from what I'd heard, there wouldn't be much of a crowd. Exhibition games were more for the media than the fans. A chance to meet the new team, catch up on the hockey gossip including recent trades, review last year's stats and this year's predictions. This was the only time every player was interviewed during a press conference. I'd been shocked to read that Igor, the Russian hockey player recently traded from Chicago at the same time as Axl, was an up-and-coming hotshot goalie. Plus, Igor wasn't his first name. His last name was Igorsky—no first name listed beyond the initial S.

Five rows behind me was an entire section of puck bunnies. So when I heard, "Hey, isn't she the one in that video . . . ?" I considered putting on my earmuffs to drown them out. And it was freakin' cold down here, this close to the ice.

"Ignore them," a voice to the left of me said.

I faced a brunette with a sweet smile who wore a heavy coat and gloves. "Thanks. I wondered if it was too soon to pull out the earmuffs."

She laughed. "Never." She offered her hand. "I'm Leah. I'm with . . ." She turned around so I could read the name on the back of her coat: VANDERHAL.

"Nice to meet you. I'm—"

"Annika Lund."

That took me aback.

She laughed again. "Sorry. It's just you are an interesting piece of news in the Wild team world, Annika. Not only are you 'The Rocket's' sister—and you know how this town feels about its football team and players—but you're 'Stonewall' Jaxson's cousin, so you probably own a closetful of Black-hawks jerseys. Now you've been seen across town cuddling up with Axl Hammerquist, and here you are, wearing his jersey."

The paper this morning had a short article on our quiet, romantic, intimate night out—complete with pictures. A shot of me feeding Axl a bite of my food and one of him bundling me up in his suit jacket.

"I guess all of that is news."

"It's the best kind of news if you can actually tame 'The Hammer' and encourage him to focus on getting the job done on the ice," she added.

"No pressure."

Another laugh. "Something tells me you'll handle the pressure—and Axl—just fine."

I imagined the glint in Axl's eyes if I ever used the word *handle* around him. "So, confession time for me, Leah. I've never dated a pro athlete."

"But you're familiar with the game and the unspoken requirements about going off on the refs about shitty calls, yeah? Booing the opposing players if they're called for a penalty. You boo louder if you see the penalty and the refs somehow miss it."

"Got it. What else?"

"Just because we're sitting close doesn't mean we exist for the players. When they're on the ice, they don't give a damn what happens on the other side of the glass. So even if some douchebag from the Blackhawks"—she gave me a cheeky grin—"has your man pressed up against the glass right in front of you? And he's bleeding, struggling and fighting? He doesn't see you. So don't take it personally."

"This has been an issue?"

"Not for me. But for some new girlfriends, yeah. They jump up in the stands and shake their tits, and then get pissed when their efforts to get noticed are wasted. It's a stupid vanity thing." She jerked her thumb at the bunnies behind us. "They're totally clueless about it. The guys who notice them aren't on the ice. And the reason they're not on the ice?"

"Because they're gawking around the arena instead of paying attention to the game," I said.

"Exactly."

"Thanks for the insight, Leah."

"No problem."

A shadow fell across us. We both looked up to see a red-faced young man clutching a bucket of popcorn.

"Please excuse me for a moment. My seat is down there."

We both stood and the gangly kid shuffled past. He left a

seat between us. He stared at the empty rink and began to eat his popcorn.

I turned toward Leah. "Do you travel to the away games?"

"It depends. My husband, Linc, has been with other teams and I have friends in those cities. But traveling is stressful for him. Especially those long stretches. We miss each other, but I have my own life. I'm not just a hockey wife. Not that there's anything wrong with it. Bunny lives for being the leader of the WAGs."

"Bunny?"

"Ironic, isn't it? Especially when she was a puck bunny who actually scored a player for more than one night. Fair warning: she'll be here later. Prepare yourself to be interviewed to see if you're worthy of the inner circle."

"And if I'm deemed worthy but decide that it's not for me?"

She laughed. "I'd like to see the look on Bunny's face if you declined the golden ticket. I don't believe that's ever happened."

"Well, some *bunny* will be very disappointed when she learns that I'm not one to play follow-the-leader or follow someone else's rules." I flashed my teeth with a wide grin. "I'm used to being in charge in my day job. That doesn't just go away when I slip off the heels and set down my laptop case."

Leah leaned over and addressed the gangly kid. "Mind sharing that popcorn with me later? Because this is gonna get interesting."

His eyes widened and he stammered, "S-sure. Would you care for some now?"

"No. Later is fine."

I saw his gaze go to the name on my back and then he looked at me curiously. "You are Axl's girlfriend, yah?"

"Yes. You know him?" I asked his name—Relf—and we chatted a bit longer.

It wasn't until I turned back to Leah and she said, "It's so cool that you can communicate with Axl in his own language," that I realized I'd been speaking Swedish with Relf. The switchover had become automatic, even more so with Axl than with my mother.

Fans started to arrive. I had butterflies in my stomach. This game was important to Axl and I wished I could talk to him, even briefly, to gauge his mood.

I asked Leah, "Do you ever see Linc before a game?"

"You mean, like visit him in the locker room?"

I nodded.

"No. He's a need-to-be-in-my-own-head guy before he hits the ice."

Just then Peter showed up. He stood two rows down in front of the still-empty seats. "Annika. I'm glad you're here early. Axl would like to see you."

Guess that answered that about my boyfriend's expectations.

I followed Peter through a maze. A security guard blocked access where the hallway split into two sections. He studied Peter's all-access pass. My lack of a lanyard earned me a scowl. "Without a pass she ain't allowed back there."

"It's an exhibition game. Her pass isn't ready yet."

"Don't care."

"Look, I understand you're just trying to do your job, but 'The Hammer' wants a minute with her. She won't venture into the locker room; they'll stay in the hallway. I promise."

"Fine. *You* go fetch him. *She* stays here."

"Thank you."

Peter disappeared.

Was I supposed to make small talk with this guy? I knew most of the security guards who worked the section of the Metrodome where the Lund skybox had been located. Before I opened my mouth, Axl barreled around the corner.

My first thought was: *That was fast.*

My second thought was: *Holy fucking shit.*

Axl wasn't completely suited up. He wore black thermal underpieces that molded to his body as if he had been vacuum-sealed into them.

My hands went all grabby. My fingers itched to touch every ripple and bulge. Every deep-cut muscle and groove.

"Annika," he said on a half growl. After I tore my focus away from his chest and arms, it traveled up the thick column of his neck and over that divot in his strong chin—*Do not stop to stare at that sexy mouth*—and finally met his eyes.

Lust was too tame a word for what I felt when our gazes connected.

I remained rooted to the spot, the need to go to him so powerful that I feared it.

But I wanted it.

Peter walked past me—I think.

Then in a nearly indecipherable, guttural tone, Axl said, "Come. Here."

I shook my head and said, "Back up. At least ten steps."

"Why?"

"So no one can see when I throw myself at you."

His eyes went hotter yet.

I launched myself at him.

He caught me, spun me until my back hit the wall and his mouth landed on mine.

My entire body began to tingle from the first touch of his lips. The kiss was hard. Hungry. More than a little desperate.

His tongue sought mine. Every swirl, every lick, every deep suck was a revelation. A glimpse into this man's passion. A glorious awakening into my own untapped physical desires. I knew, without a doubt, that he could fulfill every one.

I thrust my hands into his hair and pulled, because I needed something to hold on to.

That earned me a groan.

When the kiss's intensity tested the limits of sustainability, he kicked it down a notch.

Axl realigned our lips, slowing the greedy, panting, open-mouthed ravenousness. He gave me sweetness. Softness. A gentle sweep of his warm flesh against mine as our mouths clung to each other's.

I forced myself to break the kiss entirely and rested my forehead on his shoulder.

He nuzzled my neck, his breathing equally erratic. "I needed to see you."

"Just think . . . we should've been doing that all along."

"Yes." He planted kisses up my jawline to my ear. "We need to make up for lost time."

"God, it makes me hot when you whisper in my ear like that."

"I want to feel you burn, Annika."

"Axl."

"I want your mouth frantic on mine. Like it was."

Then he kissed me again.

His tongue rubbed and stroked as he pressed the lower half of his body into mine, pinning me to the wall, freeing his hands. They circled my rib cage and slid up, his palms cupping the weight of my breasts as his thumbs found my nipples.

Yes. Even through the heavy jersey fabric, I felt the warmth of his touch. The power in his big hands. The regret in his entire body when he said, "But I have to go."

"I know."

"I want to see you after the press conference. Will you wait for me?"

"Yes."

Axl tipped my chin up and stared into my eyes. "Will you come home with me tonight?"

"I'll think about it."

He frowned.

"I'm not playing games. We've known each other for a

month, but we've only been on two official dates. This chemistry between us is . . . daunting. My strong attraction to you has taken me by surprise."

"Why?"

"It's uncharted territory for me, but it's not for you."

The muscle in his jaw ticced, but he said nothing.

"This isn't a discussion we need to have now." I kissed that rigid jaw and those tight lips until he yielded to me. A few flirty sugar bites and he was smiling again when he set me down.

"Pound some faces into the boards tonight, Ax-kicker."

He laughed. "I like that one." He disappeared down the hallway.

Peter had waited for me by the exit. "Things are going well?"

Maybe he hadn't seen that knockout kiss. "I guess . . . ? I didn't try to punch him during our dinner date."

"The pictures I saw online gave the impression that you two were very cozy. So good job. Axl must really be on his best behavior."

"Or maybe I am."

He smiled. "After the game ends, I'll meet you back here and we'll head to the press conference."

Half an hour passed before the teams took the ice.

I avoided conversation with Leah and Relf, mostly because I didn't want to expose my ignorance.

I had attended Jaxson's hockey games, but the truth was . . . I hadn't paid much attention to the actual games. We always sat up above the crowd of true fans. I ate nachos. Drank beer. Messed around on my phone. Talked to my family members. Cheered at the appropriate times. I'd admit to bloodthirst—interested only when guys beat the crap out of each other. But taking time to learn the actual mechanics of the game?

Nope. I didn't have a freakin' clue.

It wasn't as if I didn't care about sports at all. I loved football. I could talk about football all damn day. I hadn't achieved expert level like my brothers and my dad, but I could keep up. I caught penalties on the field before the ref called them. I knew the positions of the defensive and the offensive players. I'd even memorized some crucial stats. I knew team rosters; I recognized names from the past twenty years and some from before I'd been born. Football made sense to me.

Hockey . . . not so much.

So I'd secretly bought four different books on hockey after Axl accused me of ignorance, figuring one of them would provide me with the information that would allow me to converse somewhat intelligently about the game that ruled my fake boyfriend's life.

Wrong.

What I'd taken away from my hockey homework? I'd never, ever figure out what icing was.

A breakaway isn't always a good thing—a two-man breakaway is preferable, so I didn't even understand why a breakaway was a "thing."

Left wing, right wing and the center were forwards who were considered offensive players . . . except when they weren't.

The two guys in the back were the defensemen, or the D-men, as Axl called them. That, I found out, was the position Axl played. And like their name implied, they were defensive players . . . until they played offense.

The only clear position was the goalie. I kind of equated him with the kicker in football because how many times had the kicker been the one who'd blown the game? Same thing with the goalie who let that puck slide through.

A shoot-out involved no guns whatsoever. Glad the book cleared that up for me. But it wasn't like there weren't winter sports that didn't feature a demanding physical activity and a firearm—uh, *hello*? Biathlon.

Hockey puns were still way better than football puns.

Any form of puck was my new favorite word.

Through the first two periods I paid attention to when Axl jumped the barrier and went in and out of the game.

And given the opportunity to watch the man in action? I couldn't look at anyone else. If the puck changed directions, he skated backward and he didn't even have to watch where he was going!

So cool.

I wished I'd listened during my cousin Nolan and my uncle Monte's detailed discussions about hockey strategies so I had some frame of reference.

At the start of the third period the score was tied 1-to-1. Then Flitte took off down the center of the ice basically by himself—a breakaway?—and slapped a shot in. I stood up and cheered.

Before I sat back down, a woman with teased blond hair and a pair of breasts resembling overfilled water balloons stopped in front of me. She scratched her cheek with a blood-colored talon as she took my measure.

Evidently I posed no threat, because she smiled and offered her hand. "I'm Bunny Ducheneaux. Head of the Wild WAGs."

I shook her hand. She had a firm grip, which bordered on pain on account of the rings she wore on every finger and even her thumb. "Annika."

"Peter said you were in this section. Of course I recognized you right away, since you and 'The Hammer' are in the papers everywhere I look."

Was that jealousy?

"I'm supposed to give you a personal invite to our cocktail party on Monday night. My husband, Ron, and I host. Coach and his wife will be there, so you can almost say it's . . . mandatory."

"Will Axl get the information as far as time and place and attire before Monday? Or is that something I should be writing down?"

"You don't trust him?" she cooed cattily.

"With party details? Hardly. He is a man. When do they pay attention to anything?"

She laughed. "You are so right. The party will be held at the Minnesota Club. Sixish to eight. Semiformal or whatever."

"Thank you. I'm familiar with the Minnesota Club. We hold corporate events there all the time."

Bunny had already tuned me out and peered over my shoulder. "Leah."

"Bunny. You're looking tan."

"Two glorious weeks in the Virgin Islands is the best way to keep that golden glow."

"I imagine it is. I'm jealous. I've never been there."

"You must have Linc take you off-season. And if he doesn't? That's what girlfriends are for."

Leah laughed. "Looking forward to catching up with you at the party Monday night. It's been too long."

"Yes, it has." Bunny flitted off.

After I sat down, Leah leaned in. "Here's a warning. Semiformal in Bunny's world means no ball gowns. But don't make the mistake of showing up in anything less than what others would consider formal."

"Thank you for the clarification, Leah."

"No problem."

So my focus was totally gone for the rest of the game as I mentally tried on and discarded a dozen different outfits.

The buzzer sounded, yanking me out of my virtual closet. The Wild had won 2-to-1.

Relf sidestepped me with a mumbled good-bye.

Leah smiled and said, "See you Monday night."

"You're not going to the press conference?"

"No. It's tedious. But you should go."

"Do any of the . . . WAGs go?"

She smirked. "Once. Have fun."

I wasn't sure why Axl insisted I attend.

Live and learn.

Eleven

AXL

We lined up and did the skate across—"Better luck next time, suckers"—with the opposing team. But at that point, unless the teams were notoriously fierce rivals, all most players could think of was ditching the equipment and hitting the showers.

The coaches—and Jakob, my translator—were waiting as we skated off the ice.

"Flitte, McClellan, Igorsky, Dykstrand, Sundstrom, Vanderhal, Masters, Irving, Ducheneaux, Hammerquist. You're in the second flight. Press conference in twenty. You know the drill. Line up outside. You'll be called up in that order. Keep it brief. Now ain't the time to practice your comedy routine. Exit the room as soon as you're done."

Jakob translated and followed me into the locker room but waited in the media area.

There wasn't much chatter. The first flight of players for

the press conference hit the showers. When it was my turn, I ducked under the lukewarm spray and stayed there for several long breaths, asking myself if I had the balls to go through with this.

But it was time. Better to deal with the backlash shit storm now than a few months in.

One towel tied around my hips, I grabbed another as I passed by the rack. Jakob briefly stepped into my line of sight and tapped his watch.

My belly roiled as I slipped on the suit I'd worn last night. My hair was still wet—nothing I could do about that. With one minute to spare, Jakob and I walked down the hallway. I took a deep breath. "I need you to follow my lead tonight."

He stopped and faced me. "You speak English."

"Yes."

"Why hide it?"

"I've had my reasons. Pay attention to the questions, okay? If I look at you, that means I want you to translate what was said. I'll do that at least a couple of times."

He crossed his arms over his chest. "So it doesn't look like you became fluent overnight, because that is freakin' impossible."

"Exactly. It also means that you won't be out of a job this season."

Peter turned the corner. I'd never seen him smile so big. He thrust out his hand. "You crushed it, Axl. I knew you had it in you."

"Thanks. I felt good."

Peter looked at Jakob, then back at me. "It's smart that you're dealing with this on a night you're golden with club management. I promised to pass on Pam in PR's suggested high points to you. You're happy to be working with the coaching staff. Grateful for the opportunity to skate with such amazing teammates who've made you feel welcome. Thanks to all the fans who came out tonight to support the team in the preseason."

Nothing new there.

"Questions?"

I shook my head and reached for the water bottle that one of the junior coaches held out to me.

"You're last, so they'll ask about Annika. Keep it brief. Keep it positive. And keep it vague so you keep them interested." He clapped me on the shoulder. "Good luck."

I'll need it.

Peter stepped behind the configuration of lighting equipment and took a seat on the outside of the middle row. Annika sat next to him. I'd never been the guy who'd gotten off seeing chicks wearing my team jersey, but I'd wanted to roar with possession when I saw her with my name spread across her back.

The reporters' questions were basic, and the rotation of players into the hot seat at the table up front went fairly fast. Coach sat in the middle, with Kazakov on his right side.

After Ducheneaux exited his seat, Kaz nodded at me.

I walked up the middle aisle, my hand tightening on the plastic water bottle, and fought the panicked feeling I hadn't had in a long time that I couldn't do this.

Flashbulbs popped and clicked as I sat beside Coach. He didn't smile. He just inclined his head, and a chair appeared for Jakob at the end of the table. Kazakov stared straight ahead too.

My palms were damp and sticky with sweat. My mouth was as dry as sawdust.

Coach introduced his support staff and thanked the media for coming before he handed the microphone over to our team captain. Immediately Kazakov spoke of new blood revitalizing the team and of the organization's confidence that I would thrive here. Then he said, "Let's open it up to questions."

The reporter said, "What's the biggest difference you've noticed playing for this team?"

Coach nodded to Jakob. But Jakob passed me the microphone.

I smiled at the journalist. "I've been working on English skills, so practice patience with me."

Laughter rippled through the room.

"Everything is different since coming to Minnesota. The biggest change is I'm playing *with* this team, not *for* this team."

That caused a ripple of reaction throughout the media. A novice English language speaker wouldn't have picked up on the subtle distinction between "for" and "with"—so I'd just blown it.

Fuck it.

"There's no comparison to the level of training, coaching skills and support the staff provides to all team members. The focus on strength and agility isn't about benefiting one particular player, but how it benefits the entire team. I'm thrilled I've been given a chance to meet the coaching staff's expectations for this season, because the players here have set the bar very high."

Every hand in the room shot up. Coach started pointing at people.

Did early stats matter as a precursor to how my season would play out?

Any lingering effects from my broken collarbone from almost two years ago?

Had the coaches for this team taught me to temper my aggression to avoid excessive third-period penalties like last year?

Who taught me the tricks to self-translate from Swedish to English more quickly? Did it work for written translation?

Then came the question I'd been waiting for.

"You've been romantically linked with Annika Lund. How does this relationship affect your game?"

"Positively, if tonight is any indication. No time in the sin bin at all."

More laughter.

"Has she had any impact on your decision to speak on your own in public without a translator?"

"No. This is all on me."

"Are there any more questions about hockey?" Coach said testily.

A reporter in front raised her hand. "Talk a little about the next exhibition game. What will you do differently?"

As Coach answered the question, I looked around the room. Two assistant coaches stood in back. When our eyes met, they glared at me. Same with Pam from PR. A couple of journalists were openly studying me like I was a specimen they wanted to rip open and examine. Peter had a small wrinkle in his brow.

Next to him, Annika had slumped into her chair, her arms folded across her chest, her head down so far her hair obscured her face. Was she hiding from everyone in the room, or just from me?

I stared at her and silently willed her to look at me.

When she did . . . my stomach bottomed out. I didn't see fury. Or hurt. Or emotion of any kind. Her beautiful face was a blank mask. She held my gaze for longer than I expected. In fact, I was the first one to look away.

Then the press conference ended and I saw her trying to sneak out. I caught Peter's attention and mouthed, *Stop Annika from leaving*, before I was swarmed.

My translator came to my rescue. "Okay, guys. 'The Hammer' has had enough. Save some questions for next time."

I raced out the door I'd seen Annika and Peter use. It opened into a hallway and at the end was an exit sign.

The door crashed into the side of the building. She stopped pacing and turned her fiery glare on me. For a second, I feared the fury rolling off her could torch my clothes, melt my bones and turn me to ash.

Peter pushed himself off the car he'd been resting against. "I mentioned this to her, but I don't know if she heard me, so I'll say it to you. A big fight in the parking lot is not the kind of press you need. She has a right to be angry, but she'd better rein it in fast." He walked away with a long backward glance at us.

I kept a slow—but steady—pace as I crossed the parking lot toward her.

At five meters, she held up her hand. "That's close enough."

"I want to talk, not have to yell."

"Too bad. Because all I want to do is yell at you. And if you get any closer, I will start channeling Jet Li and rain fists of fury down on your stupid head and throw in some *Kung Fu Panda* moves too, so don't push me, Ax-hole."

"Sorry."

"No. You're. Not."

Just stand here and take it. You deserve it.

"You know what my first thought was when you opened your mouth in that press conference and near perfect English spilled out? That Jensen had been right. I should've known you were lying."

"When did I lie to you?"

"Excuse me?"

I inched forward. "When did I ever tell you that I didn't speak English?" I paused. "*I* didn't."

"Omigod. You are not seriously blaming this on me! Jaxson told me you didn't speak English, you asshat," she hissed, "and why wouldn't I believe him? That's far more plausible than that you would lie to your coaches, your team's organization, your teammates and the media! Who does that?"

"Are you going to allow me a chance to explain?"

"Not tonight. And if I really was your girlfriend and not part of your PR team?" Her smile—half evil/half crazy and downright mean—had me tempted to cover my balls. "I would tear off this jersey and light it on fire."

The dig about being part of my PR team burned my ass worse than the threat to torch my shirt. We'd moved beyond a fake relationship with that kiss and she knew it.

"Anyway. Here's what's going to happen now. I'll walk over, hug you, trying really, really hard not to gut-punch you, while you whisper sorry in my ear. Then we'll act as if we're reluctantly parting ways."

"Annika—"

"No deviations." She plastered on a smile and swung her hips as she headed toward me.

I enfolded her in my arms and pressed my lips to the top of her head. "I'm sorry."

Annika stayed in place for about five seconds before she retreated. Then she turned and walked away without another word or a backward glance.

I returned to the locker room to find it empty. Plopping down on the bench, I let my head fall back against the metal locker. I didn't want to be alone with my thoughts any more than I wanted to be alone.

"Well, you screwed the pooch on that one. I suspected you understood more than you were letting on," Kazakov continued. "But not like this."

"So in addition to my girlfriend being pissed off at me, you're mad at me too."

"Not just me, Axl. The entire team is livid. No one likes looking like a dumb-ass."

"But no one had a problem treating *me* like a dumb-ass

when they assumed I couldn't understand the shit they were saying. Swedish chef? Meatball boy?"

Kaz sighed. "All right. There is that. Not cool."

"If they wanted to communicate with me, they could've asked Jakob, the translator the team assigned me to understand the plays, to hang out after practice. Communication could've gone both ways. Maybe it makes me a dick, but until they've been in a situation where they're in a foreign country on a work visa, deciphering different dialects, accents and slang in a language that is not their native tongue . . . they have no right to judge me on how I chose to deal with it."

"The thing is, I don't disagree with you. My question is, how you gonna fix this with the team?"

"Use stilted English around them and act like I'm not really that fluent? Let them feel as if they're helping me and over the course of the season my command of the language gets better and better?" I offered.

He rolled his eyes. "If you thought that would fly maybe you shouldn't have been so flawless at the press conference."

I tapped my fingers on the bench as I created and discarded scenarios. "How about this? Anyone who wants to take a free shot at me on the ice during practice tomorrow is welcome to."

"Don't make the offer if you think Coach will step in," he warned. "He'll probably suit up and take a whack at you himself."

"I'll take their hits and won't be a whiny-ass fucking pussy about it."

Kazakov pushed himself off the wall. "Lemme talk to Mc-Clellan about your options. He's more reasonable than Flitte."

"No kidding."

He started texting.

While I waited for that fate, I debated on ways to fix things with Annika.

Flowers . . . already did that.

Candy . . . only if I made an effigy of myself that she could whack like a piñata.

Jewelry . . . more lame than candy because then it really would seem like I was trying to buy her off.

So what could I give her that no one else could?

Multiple orgasms until she can't think straight and then she'll forget why she was even mad at you.

I was all over that idea. I'd like nothing better than to be all over her after that knockout good-luck kiss.

"McClellan told me they'd consider it and they want to talk to you in person," Kazakov said, interrupting my progressively dirtier thoughts about Annika. "They're all at The Whistling Pig. Let's go."

M y team's first punishment? The massive hangover the next morning.

The second punishment? I'd paid for the entire bar bill last night.

So having every teammate knock me on my ass during practice twice the next day had actually been the least painful punishment.

By the time practice ended, I'd mustered up the guts to leave Annika four voice mails—not that she'd acknowledged even one of them—before I crawled in bed and crashed.

I woke up hours later when I heard *Grand Theft Auto* blaring from my living room. I scrubbed the sleep from my face as I wandered down the hallway.

Martin and Boris were parked on my couch, controllers in hand, beer bottles on the coffee table.

"How long have you guys been here?" I asked.

Without looking away from the TV, Martin said, "An hour. You were out. Like comatose out."

Still groggy, I stumbled into the kitchen and grabbed a

bottle of water out of the fridge. When I turned around, Martin was just shuffling in.

He froze. "Dude! You're naked!"

Cracking the seal on the bottle, I said, "So?"

"So put on some clothes."

"You Americans have issues with nudity."

"I have an issue getting an eyeful of your junk."

I shrugged. "It's my place. If you don't like it, go home."

Martin debated. Then he walked past me to the refrigerator. He kept the door open for a long time, as if something besides beer, bottled water, sports drinks and tubes of caviar would magically appear. When he finally shut the door, he seemed surprised I'd remained in the kitchen.

"Cheezus," he said on a near shout. "I thought you'd left!"

Martin was a never-ending source of amusement for me. From his insistence on learning—butchering, really—the Swedish language so he could converse with his "ladylove," Verily, in her native tongue, to his philosophical connections between snowboarding and a Zen state, to his daily admission about being high on more than just life, to his refusal to take the name of any religious figure in vain—Cheezus for Jesus and Bubba for Buddha were the funniest ones. I appreciated how he distracted me from brooding by filling dead air with chatter; silence was anathema to him.

"Okay. So, good for you, buddy, that you're a 'show-er' and not a 'grow-er,' but seriously, can you put on some underwear before you sit next to us on the couch?"

"Sure. But you've got it wrong: I'm a show-er *and* a grow-er," I said as I walked past him.

"Not something I need to see!" Martin shouted.

After another hour or so, more people from the apartment complex showed up. My place had become the gathering spot on weekends. I gave Martin credit for that. He thought the world should be one big happy family.

Made me feel like an idiot when I checked my messages every ten minutes because I still hadn't heard from Annika. She could at least acknowledge the fact that I'd tried to get in touch with her.

At one point Martin asked when he'd meet Annika. I hedged. Then Martin answered my internal question about why I hadn't heard from her, reminding me that the Vikings were playing in Tampa Bay on Sunday. I'd bet the entire Lund family had gone there for the game.

That was how I reconciled the lack of communication.

Twelve

ANNIKA

After I returned home from the game, I changed into my workout clothes and hit the gym in my building. No surprise I was the only one using it at eleven o'clock on a Friday night. I ran four miles on the treadmill and did yoga moves as my post stretch and cooldown.

I rinsed off in the shower and opted for a bubble bath. While the tub filled with the hottest water I could stand and my favorite Lush bath bomb, I rummaged for finger foods that would complement the large bottle of peach cider I'd taken from the wine fridge. I needed something sweet to counteract the sour taste the night's final events had left in my mouth.

Then I cranked up Pink, because I needed loud girl anthems to blank my mind. I slipped into heaven—who needs a hot man when you have a hot bath?—indulged in a delicious assortment of cheeses, crackers, preserves and fruit and drank the entire bottle of cider. So when I crawled into bed, my brain was happy to shut down and let me sleep.

The next morning I slept in. I had a few hours to kill before Walker and Trinity's end-of-summer party started. Although we'd had a warm September, now that we'd reached the end of it, it seemed as if summer had ended long ago.

I decided to work on the Haversman idea on my home PC and set the alarm on my phone. I tended to lose track of time when I worked at home, because I didn't have a million interruptions like at the office.

I avoided all media—*hey, take that, Ax-hole; I can drop you like a bad habit anytime I want*—and accomplished way more than I'd expected by the time the timer went off.

I changed into my favorite sundress, a bright yellow one covered in tiny white daisies and black-eyed Susans, and my black flip-flops decorated with yellow daisies. I'd probably overdressed—my family expected to see me slink in wearing yoga pants and a T-shirt because they all knew if I didn't have an official event to attend on the weekend, I reverted to college casual clothing. But I needed to bolster my mood, and a dress the color of sunshine worked for me.

I stopped at Byerly's and picked up the appetizer tray I'd ordered as well as some fun mini-coconut cakes in purple and white. Jensen's game tomorrow was in Tampa Bay and I hadn't heard whether Mom and Dad were hosting game day, which probably meant they were flying to Florida after Walker's shindig.

It was weird to see so many cars parked around Walker's house. It was really weird to see a Bobcat on a trailer parked in his front yard.

My mom must've been lying in wait for me, because she met me at the front door. "You look lovely. How are you today?"

"Fine." I handed her the tray of cakes. "How are you?"

"Are you really fine?"

She'd blocked the door so I couldn't avoid this conversation. I shouldn't be surprised she'd seen the press conference where Axl's English fluency became apparent. "I'm pissed off at him. He lied to me and everyone else and I have a right to my anger. I'll deal with it. Just not today." I offered her a sunny smile that rivaled the color of my dress.

"I do not trust that alligator smile. But it is better than alligator tears, yah?"

"It's crocodile, Mom."

"Yah, whatever."

I stopped in the foyer of Walker's house. Plastic tarps and drop cloths and dust everywhere. Walker hadn't been kidding about starting the remodeling right away. I followed Mom outside to the tent where the food had been set up.

Walker's girlfriend, Trinity, was behind the banquet table, rearranging the paper plates and then the spoons in the chafing dishes.

"Everything looks great, Trinity."

She looked up at me. "You think so? I mean, I know Walker and I probably should've actually grilled our own meat, since this is a barbecue, but I don't think either of us is ready to take on that kind of cooking responsibility. So we had it catered. But now I'm wondering if I should've gone with steak instead of barbecued chicken, and does anyone really even like three-bean salad? It's kind of gross when you think about it. Dumping canned beans in a bowl and then adding vinegar. But my other choice was pea salad, and that's worse. Canned peas and chunks of cheese swimming in mayonnaise? My grandma's sister Erma used to make it, and I always had to eat one bite to be polite . . ."

She kept babbling, which I secretly snickered at because she was hilarious whenever she went off on a tear. Walker wasn't ever too far away from her, especially at family things, since their couplehood was still pretty new. So my smile grew wider on my seeing Walker move in behind Trinity. She hadn't noticed; she'd just kept on rambling. He very calmly cupped his hands around her face and kissed the living hell out of her.

When he released her and said, "Better?" she nodded. And she'd stopped fiddling with everything in sight.

I probably should've given them some privacy, but I was so happy for my brother. Trinity, with her sweet, quirky ways, was exactly the type of woman Walker needed.

Walker kissed her temple and slid his hand around her waist before he faced me. "Hey, sis."

"Hey yourself. Nice spread. Good thing the weather is holding up and we can be outside. You've got some major destruction going on in there."

"Oh, you noticed?" Trinity said dryly.

"This is actually the last week we'll be living here. We'll be at Trinity's place until the house is completely remodeled and her new studio is built."

"How long will that take?"

"All winter. Most of the spring. We're tentatively planning to return the first of June."

I blinked. "That's major remodeling, bro."

He shrugged. "It needs it. We're doing some of the work ourselves. Trinity is designing stained glass windows for the second floor. I'm redoing the staircase. Grandpa said he'd help me make a traditional hand-carved balustrade. So we're adding personal elements to the house."

"That's exciting. I can't wait to see it all take shape."

"Us either. I've compiled pages and pages of drawings already."

Walker looked around. "Where's this new asshole boyfriend I've heard about?"

Trinity elbowed him. "I can see why she wouldn't want to bring him. Sheesh."

"He's in his last week of training before the regular season starts." I smiled. "So, where are you hiding the beer?"

"Cooler by the pool."

And the first person I ran into was my dad.

"There's my knockout girl."

I hugged him before he could hug me. Sometimes a girl just needed a big daddy hug.

As usual, he held on as long as I needed him to. Then he let me go with a kiss on my forehead. "Grab a beer, sweetheart. We're going on walkabout."

Crap. That meant Mom had told him the truth about Axl. I forced a smile. "Sure." But I grabbed a double-sized Lime-A-Rita instead.

We wandered to the other side of the pool. I waved at Brady and Lennox, sitting with my cousins Ash and Dallas. Double crap. I wasn't expecting Dallas to be here.

When she made the "I've got my eyes on you" gesture, I congratulated myself on grabbing a can with twice the amount of booze in it—I'd need it.

"Talk to me about this bullshit relationship." My dad sipped his Old Style beer. "There's no need to put a PR spin on this situation for me."

"I figured."

"Your mother is the love of my life, but when she told me that not only had she signed off on this con game, but she'd initiated it? I could've strangled her."

Oh yeah. Wishing for a triple right about now. Dad never said anything against his beloved.

"So, sweetheart, I have to ask. I've seen you in action at LI. No one railroads you into doing anything. How did this even happen?"

"Uh, you have *met* Mom, right?"

He growled.

Okay. Still not to the joking stage yet. I backtracked and filled in as many details as I suspected my mother had left out.

After a few moments of silent contemplation on his part, he sighed. "It's highly probable that this Peter guy would've signed Jensen without the added incentive of your translation skills."

"I realize that. I suspect Mom did too."

Then Dad half snarled, "So this Peter dickhead wanted both my daughter *and* my wife indebted to him?"

Shit. This was not where I'd expected this conversation to go. My dad was pissed. And jealous. Had I ever seen him in that state? What was I supposed to do?

"Just how much time has your mother spent with this dick-face from her hometown?" he demanded.

"She didn't tell you?"

He crumpled the beer can in his hand. "Would I be asking *you* if she had?"

Totally out of my element here. My dad had just crushed a can in his fist like it was a piece of tinfoil. "I'm aware of two meetings. I've had more dealings with him than she has."

"And yet that statement doesn't make me happy either."

"I met Axl first because of Jaxson. He asked for my help translating for Axl. Then when Peter knew I was in PR, to be completely honest, I think he just wanted my take on Axl's image issues, and Mom volunteered my time. Peter didn't demand it. Mom would want to ensure that Jensen got the best representation, and, well, she's not above using me to do that."

"Christ, Annika, that makes me so mad."

"I could've refused. And this is something I haven't told Mom." I paused and gulped down two mouthfuls of liquid courage. "I said yes because I'm drawn to Axl, okay? I don't know if it's a savior complex that's just appeared. I don't know if it's just physical attraction. But he annoys me and interests me more than any man I've met in a long time."

"Keep going."

"Axl knew that this 'favor' was one-sided. He's the one who encouraged me the night of the sunset cruise to put the screws to Peter and push for something that benefits me. Not Jensen. Not Mom. Not Peter. Not even Axl. Me. Although Axl said he'd back me to the point where he'd revert to bad behavior until Peter relented. So I did some on-the-fly research and found one thing that Peter Skaarn can do that few others can."

"What?"

I moved in closer. "My deal with Peter is this does not get out. You cannot tell anyone at LI about this."

"Done."

I told him about pitching to R Haversman.

He laughed. "You are truly brilliant and a master strategist. I'm so proud of you."

Those words made it all worthwhile. "So I can't blow the pitch session."

"You won't. Now back to Axl. Level with me. It's not all a publicity ploy between you two, is it?"

I shook my head. "After his little reveal last night, I want to get it back to being just about PR because that'll be easier."

"This is the man who sent you eleven dozen roses?"

"Yes."

"And he initiated a fake fight with your brother to push his agent into equalizing the deal for you."

"Yes."

"Sweetheart, this is more than just an image update for him too. Have you talked to him about why he kept that from you?"

"No. I sort of exploded and left. I've been in avoidance mode all day."

"Give him a chance to explain."

My eyes met his. "Will you give Mom a chance to explain?"

He cringed and said, "Ouch. But you're right. I'll deal with it. But she'll also be giving you an overdue apology when I'm done with her." Then he hugged me. "I love you, sweetheart. I'll back you, no matter what. Even if you secretly like this Axl asshole, who I know even without meeting him isn't good enough for you."

"Dad."

"Come on, let's go test Dallas and see if she can read our auras. Think conflicted thoughts. Oh, right, you already are."

He was such a smartass sometimes. I loved that about him.

Mom gave me the stink-eye as Dad and I strolled over to the food line.

I ended up sitting with Dallas, Ash, Brady and Lennox. Our conversation was devoted to the workings of LI until Dallas said, "Enough. The rule is supposed to be no work talk."

"So what would you like to talk about?" Ash asked her.

Dallas went doe-eyed. "Annika's hot hockey hunk."

Ash shook his head. "Nope. You wanna gossip about boy parts, do it elsewhere. There's some stuff I don't want to know."

"I want to know where your sidekick, Nolan, is," I said.

"He went to the exhibition game in Chicago." Ash cocked his head. "Interesting rumor going around LI."

"There are always rumors and I'd get nothing done if I listened to them."

Lennox snorted.

"I heard that Lucy, Mimi's mama, will be working in the PR department."

I pushed my plate back. "You heard right. She was the most qualified applicant and she'll be a great fit for us. Plus, it'll ease her burden as a single parent to have familiar on-site day care for Mimi."

Ash stared at me in that "I'm the Chief Operating Officer" manner that had most LI employees soiling themselves. But

Ash in "I'm the boss" mode didn't scare me as much as when Brady morphed into corporate officer from hell.

"I'm happy to hear that. If I can do anything to help, let me know."

My jaw dropped.

"Not expecting that?"

"No!"

"Lucy got a raw deal. No one from that branch of the family will admit it, least of all Jaxson, even now when he's started to pull his head out of his ass and stepped up to his responsibilities. Mimi is a sweet, smart kid. When Jax sees her once every two weeks in the off-season and maybe once every two months during hockey season? No way can he take credit for it, because Lucy is raising her. He's a damn drive-by parent."

Ash's declaration stunned everyone at the table.

"What? This crap with him has been brushed under the rug for years. Now that it's out in the open, we'll deal with it."

Dallas reached over and squeezed Ash's hand. "And this is why you're the best big brother ever, Ash."

I glanced over at Brady and smiled. Then I realized I hadn't seen my other big brother in a while. "Anyone know where Walker and Trinity went?"

"I saw them head upstairs when I was inside," Lennox said.

"Getting busy during a party." Dallas tsk-tsked. "Let's tell Trinity that's a surefire way to never have to host a Lund gathering again."

"Omigod, no! She will freak out," Lennox said.

"Too late," Ash said. He pointed behind us. "Check it out."

We all turned.

Walker had Trinity pressed against him. He'd bent down so they were forehead to forehead and he was talking to her as she . . . cried.

My stomach did a loop-de-loop. Why was she crying as if her world had ended?

Then we were all on our feet, including Mom and Dad, Aunt Priscilla and Uncle Archer.

Dad said, "Son, is everything all right?"

Trinity faced everyone and tried to wipe her tears, but they just kept coming. "Everything is perfect in my life because of this amazing man . . ." She sniffled. Then she whapped him on the chest. "How could you do this to me at the first party we hosted for your family?"

"Because I wanted them to be a part of it."

"You tell us now, or I will blow a casket," my mother warned.

My dad must've whispered, "Gasket," because she waved him off with annoyance and said, "Yah. Whatever."

Trinity took a deep breath. "Long story short. My grandma Minnie left me her pearls, but my stepmother has kept them locked up since I was a kid. The night I met Walker, I learned that my half sister was engaged and my stepmother promised she could have Grandma's pearls on her wedding day. I demanded them back and she said no. When we ran into my dad and his wife several weeks ago—"

"I cornered her and threatened legal action if she didn't hand them over," Walker inserted.

Trinity was running her fingers over the double strand of pink pearls that circled her neck. "He got them back for me. My grandma would've been tickled that Walker battled my stepmother for them, because she loved a good story and a happy ending."

"And I want to make this our happy beginning." Walker dropped to one knee.

Trinity gasped. "Walker! What are you doing?"

"Exactly what it looks like. Being with you has made me the happiest man alive. I want that happiness every hour of every day for the rest of our lives. You have a shitty family, babe. Marry me. Be part of my family." He shoved his hand in the front pocket of his jeans and pulled out a ring. "Please say yes to being my wife, Trinity Amelia Carlson, because you're already my everything."

Poor Trinity. I almost felt sorry for her because Walker had hit her with a double whammy today—diamonds and pearls.

Dallas leaned her head on my shoulder.

I felt her tears dripping down my arm. I angled my head on top of hers and took her hand.

She whispered, "I want that, Annika."

I whispered back, "Me too."

She sighed. "Her aura is glowing. But so is his."

"Really? I hadn't noticed."

"Speaking of auras . . . yours is conflicted. I'm getting two different tones, some anger, some indecision."

"You're right on both counts."

"Of course I am." She wiggled free and stood in front of me. Her brown eyes were serious and a little sad. "You've been avoiding me. I hate that."

"I know. I'm sorry. It's just . . ."

"I literally see too much. I get it." She raised her hand to silence my protest. "Believe what you want about the woo-woo factor, but I know what I see. Think about how much it sucks for me. So don't avoid me. Say something like 'Thanks for your cosmic concern, but I need a little more time to figure stuff out on my own first.' I'd be good with that."

I hugged her. "I promise."

"Cool beans." Dallas started to walk away. She turned back. "Oh, one other thing you should know about Axl: In addition to speaking English, he's fluent in Russian. Igor told me."

I was pretty sure my aura had gone completely red.

Thirteen

AXL

Sunday afternoon, after I returned home from another especially brutal training session, I cracked open my laptop and checked my email. A news notification popped up and I clicked the link to discover Annika hadn't gone out of town after all: she'd been *out* on the town. The caption read:

> *Annika and Dallas Lund danced the night away in the Koko Club. No sign of Annika's latest squeeze, hockey player Axl Hammerquist, or Drew Cheney, the center for U of M's football team, rumored to be involved with the youngest Lund heiress.*

Apparently she'd been ditching my calls, because she couldn't hear her phone ring over the loud club music.

This ignoring-the-issue bullshit was about to come to a screeching halt.

———————

I showed up at Lund Industries at four thirty on Monday afternoon. I hadn't planned how to get through security, but as luck had it, one of the security guards recognized me.

"You're the guy who's been in the paper with Miss Annika."

"Yes, I am. I'm surprising her with a romantic dinner tonight. She's still here, right? I can just go on up?"

His eyes narrowed. "I'll have to clear it through her assistant."

I leaned in, as if to make a confession. "Look. Last week I sent her eleven dozen roses. I don't know what I was thinking. How am I supposed to top that this week?"

"Yeah, you are screwed."

"So it'd be great if you could cut me a break just this once. Escort me to her floor yourself if you have to. Trust me, I understand about security. We've got guards, such as yourself, posted at three different entrances at the Xcel Center to keep the fans handled. We couldn't do our jobs if security didn't do theirs."

He hitched up his pants. "Tell you what I'll do. I'll call her assistant after I've already sent you up to her floor."

Better than nothing. "I appreciate it."

My heart pounded as I watched the numbers on the elevator panel. I had no idea what floor she even worked on. Tension seized all the muscles in my body and I shifted my head from side to side until I heard the satisfying pop of my neck cracking.

The elevator stopped.

The doors opened and a receptionist's desk was directly across from the elevator. "How may I help you?"

"I have an appointment with Annika. Security called her assistant, so she knows I'm on my way."

She pointed down a hallway. "Last door."

"Thank you."

As I wandered down the wide hallway, I wondered why none of these doors were marked. How were visitors supposed to know where they were going?

Probably not a lot of drop-in visitors.

Behind door number three—another receptionist's desk. The way this woman eyed me with some familiarity meant I'd just met Annika's assistant.

I offered my hand. "Axl Hammerquist. Annika is not expecting me." I flashed my teeth—more in a warning than a smile. "I'll show myself in."

"Uh . . ."

I headed for the door behind her desk. Once I'd entered the office, I slammed the door behind me and stormed toward her.

Annika's jaw hung open for a second before she snapped it shut.

I had my hands on the armrests of her chair, trapping her.

"Axl! You can't just barge in—"

"Apparently I can, because I'm here. So listen up. I get not telling you that I could speak English was an asshole move. I get that you're mad and hurt. I am very sorry for that." I leaned a fraction closer. "But you don't get to ignore me for three fucking days when I reached out to you, Annika."

"I don't need to hear your excuses for lying to me."

"There's a difference between an excuse and an explanation. I am here to apologize."

"I don't care. I am mad at you. That means I *am* entitled to ignore you. So wipe that menacing look off your face and stomp your lumbering self out of my office."

I ground my teeth together and gritted out a guttural "No."

"No? You have no right—"

"Yes, I do."

"Because of this PR b.s.?"

"No. Because of this." I framed her face in my hands, tilted her head back and took her mouth in a blistering kiss.

Annika's protest lasted three seconds before her hands were twisted in my shirt, holding me in place as she kissed me back with equal parts frustration and hunger.

My body went from tight with tension to hard with desire.

Over the sounds of our heavy breathing and the wet connection of our mouths, I heard the office door open.

Go away. I am not done with her.

One of Annika's hands left my shirt. She must've waved her assistant off, because the next thing I heard was the door closing again.

I kissed her with the overwhelming lust she incited in me—a reminder of the passion building between us. Then I slowed to sweeter kisses, until I was able to eke out a few words between the connection and release of our lips. "I'm sorry," I murmured first in English and then in Swedish. "I'm an asshole."

"I knew that."

Her rapid exhalations teased my damp lips.

"God, this mouth of yours." I started to crank the kiss back up to a combustible level.

But she pulled back. "Axl."

I stared into her eyes. Her heavy-lidded gaze ignited my fantasy of sweeping everything off her desk, shoving her skirt up and lowering myself to my knees to offer an apology she'd never forget. "What?"

"My neck is starting to hurt, so can we take it down a notch?"

Immediately my hands fell away and I straightened to standing.

After I helped her up, Annika tilted her head back and our eyes met. "I need to . . ."

I smoothed her staticky hair back into place. "You need to what?"

"I have no idea. I looked at you and my mind went blank."

I grinned.

She slapped her hands on my chest. "Go sit in the conference area and let me regroup."

As soon as I gave her space, she picked up the phone receiver on her desk and poked a button. "Hey. No, I'm fine." Her gaze hooked mine. "Yes, he's unharmed. For now."

You still have some major groveling ahead, so don't get cocky.

"I'll wrap it up tomorrow. Go—if you're done with everything else. See you in the morning." She hung up.

"Your assistant is relieved she doesn't have to call a cleaning crew in to scrub my blood off the walls?"

"At least not yet."

Annika crossed the room toward me, every step a reminder of her confidence. Sexy and powerful—she was exactly the type of woman I stayed away from. Not because her brains and beauty intimidated me, but she could be as addictive as hockey.

You have time in your life for one mistress, not two.

"Let's get right to it. Why did you keep up the lie?" she said in English. "Yes, I understand technically that you didn't lie to me, but we have a saying here that a lie of omission is still . . . a lie."

"When I came to the U.S., the staff at training camp knew I could speak English. But I'd never spoken it as a first language. That was a stressful time. Roald wasn't with me and I didn't know anyone else. I was physically exhausted and afraid I wouldn't make the cut. It ended up I rarely spoke at all."

"So they assumed you were illiterate?"

"Eventually, yes. Hundreds of guys try out and we all look

the same in hockey gear. I wasn't memorable enough in any way apparently."

Annika's gaze roamed my face and neck. "I disagree, but go on."

"I made the AHL farm team. The coach didn't bother to ask about my English skills. He assumed I understood enough to take his direction on the ice and that's all that mattered." I hated talking about this. I had buried the bitterness and the loneliness and concentrated on improving so I could get the fuck out of the minor leagues. "Same situation with the other two farm teams I was part of over the next two years. My listening skills improved my speaking skills. Everywhere I went outside the rink, I only spoke English. That's where the fluency came from, because I didn't have that six years ago. When I finally got the call-up to the big league the end of my third season with the AHL—I didn't see a benefit in inform- ing the new coaching staff."

"Why not?"

"I'd overheard the discussion where they admitted they didn't want to bring me up, but their injured list forced them to fill the roster and they had no choice. They said a bunch of other things about my skills that needed extra work. They wouldn't have spoken so freely if they'd known I could understand. It was professionally beneficial." I paused. "It's fucked-up. I get that. I'm sorry. It snowballed. I thought I was protecting myself, but I can see how it looks like selfish and self-serving behavior."

"It was. So why did you decide to come clean now?"

"Partially Peter's PR plan. Non-English-speaking athletes have a harder time getting endorsements."

Her face shuttered. "Of course. That makes sense."

"But that's not all, Annika."

She looked at me and waited.

"After spending time with you, I hated misleading you. You went out of your way to help me. Do you know how sweet and thoughtful it was that you read me the entire menu the other night?"

Annika blushed.

"I never meant to intentionally hurt you." My eyes searched hers. "Please believe me."

She opened her mouth—probably to argue—but snapped it shut. She closed her eyes and inhaled several deep breaths before she focused on me again. "Total dick move, Axl. Like one of the worst dick moves ever."

"I know."

Annika lowered her chin, watching her fingers fiddle with the pleats on her skirt. "I'm mad. But I'm just as mad at myself as I am at you."

"Why?"

"When we first met, I said some pretty scathing things to you in English because I didn't think you could understand. That is a ridiculous excuse for being mean to someone. I hate mean girls," she said softly. "I've prided myself on how hard I've worked *not* to become one, given all the advantages I've had growing up, so it's jarring to realize I was one to you. I justified it because you were a man and because you wouldn't know the difference."

"Annika—"

"Just let me finish."

"No." I stilled her restless hand and waited until she looked at me. "You are not taking on any guilt for *my* nondisclosure. I've done the same thing. Called someone an idiot or worse in a language I know they can't understand."

"How many languages do you speak?"

"A few."

"Like . . . three or a dozen?"

"I'm fluent in Swedish, Norwegian, Finnish, English and Russian. I can understand French, Spanish, Italian and German, but I don't speak them well."

Those gorgeous blue eyes widened. "How can you know all that?"

"Scandinavian languages are similar. French and Spanish . . ." I shrugged. "Being around it at an early age makes it easier to pick up. Same with German. I've played hockey with Russians since my teens."

"Why would you hide that? I'd be bragging about it to everyone."

I hesitated a beat before I answered, "Warning. Total selfish, puck-head comment coming."

She snickered.

"I'm here to play hockey. I don't want to be the team translator. I've seen it happen with other players and when there's a translation error, the fault falls back on the translator. Which is why I had Peter insist on an outside translator for me. My teammate Jorgen Sundstrom and I speak Finnish. My teammate Olsson and I speak Norwegian. It probably sounds the same to everyone else, but it's not. Kazakov and I were speaking Russian, but that wasn't something we shared beyond the two of us, because he doesn't want to end up a translator either."

"This is so much more complicated than I believed."

"Politics of hockey."

"So, would that be called . . . hol-itics?" she said slyly.

I grinned. "Clever girl. I enjoy American puns. They are not funny in Swedish."

"Lose something in translation, do they?"

"Such a quick mind. I like that about you." Bringing her hand to my mouth, I kissed her wrist. "Now we have to talk about PR things. Honesty is best, yah?"

She smirked. "Yah. Is there something else you've been lying to me about?"

"No. After the press conference, things have improved with my teammates. I feel focused."

"Focused is good."

"And you are a beautiful distraction. The more time we spend together, the easier it'll be to believe that this is real between us." I kissed the inside of her wrist again. "Maybe sometimes I want it to be real."

"Me too."

Her tiny admission that I wasn't alone in this made it harder to do the right thing. "But we have to remember it isn't real."

Annika seemed relieved. "I agree. But I won't lie, Axl. Kissing you is wicked hot. I like that you play the part of a loving boyfriend very well. As long as we can keep the 'only in public' parameters of affection, we can make this PR ploy work."

"So no more asking you to spend the night with me," I said.

"You got caught up in the moment. Dude, that was seriously one lip-burning, brain-scrambling kiss."

I smiled. "That it was."

"No more busting into my office and kissing the hell out of me either. We can flirt and let everyone imagine we are breaking the bedsprings twice a day." She reached over and tugged my hair. "But, Charming, this is all about hockey. I'm happy you're focused. I'm relieved you're being accepted as a team player. With total concentration on your game? Who knows? Maybe you could be the league's leading scorer for this season."

"Leading scorer?" I repeated. "You really don't know anything about hockey, do you?"

"Nope. And boy, oh boy, lucky you gets to teach me, huh?"

I groaned.

"Think of all the hockey puns my clever mind can come up with off the puck." When I didn't clutch my stomach with laughter, she repeated, "Off the cuff? Off the puck? That was puntastic gold."

"Debatable." I stood. "If we leave now we have time to grab food before Bunny's cocktail party."

Her eyes widened. "Shit balls. I forgot about that. I have to go home and change."

I let my gaze travel the length of her, from the fitted cut of her dark red suit jacket, past the plaid skirt clinging to her curvy hips and the high-heeled black boots that ended just above her ankles. "You don't need to change. You always look fantastic."

Annika unfolded from the chair. "Leah warned me this was one fancy-ass party. So I cannot show up in this."

"There's no time to drive all the way over to your place and back to the club."

"Then you're going solo."

I shook my head. "Not possible after the press conference—Peter wants us to step it up this week, and this party is the highest priority."

She hustled over to the desk. "That's not helping, Axl."

"Where's your favorite boutique? Businesswomen like you—I know this from my mother—have the financial means to request private hours and special services. I'm assuming your preferred shop is close by, since I doubt this is the first fashion emergency you've had."

She squinted at me. "That's the first time you've mentioned anyone in your family."

"We don't have time to talk about that now. Call with your clothing requirements so they have options for you when we arrive or else I'm taking you to the party wearing that."

Fourteen

ANNIKA

Axl barging into my office to deal with the fallout from Friday night hadn't been a shocker. I'd expected it . . . earlier in the day.

However, I had been shocked by Axl's reminder we weren't dating. I'd geared myself up to give him the same speech after having time to think this weekend. Now that we were of the same mind, I was relieved he had no issue with a few make-out sessions once in a while—because holy amaze balls, could that man kiss. I'd never been kissed like that and I'd done my share of macking around.

I'd even tried to dissect why Axl's mouth seemed especially attuned to mine. At first I'd chalked it up to experience—tons and tons of practice. Then I went with the location theory. Sweden was cold. That meant lots of fires. Fireplaces were romantic and the perfect place for smooching practice. Nights under the covers, snuggling for warmth, whispering in the dark air so cold you could see your breath. What better way to cut through that chill than by rubbing your lips together? Or for a whole-body warm-up, creating friction beneath the wool blankets and between the flannel sheets. Or better, lying naked in a bed of fur. How decadent would that feel, arching against a hot, hard, insistent body plastered to the front of yours, that heavy male weight pressing your backside into the soft warmth of fur—

"Annika? Do you need help?"

Startled out of my fantasy, I glanced at myself in the dressing room mirror. At least he hadn't asked if I needed help getting it off.

But I'd let him help me with that in a hot minute.

Once my thoughts threw a gutter ball, my mind decided to stay there. I looked over my shoulder. "No. I'm just about done."

I'd dismissed the first dress Elena had shown me as too risqué for this particular party. Dress number two was fine, but did I really need another little black cocktail dress?

Axl had pulled one off the rack and gifted me with a sexy grin when he handed it over. "This one. You look spectacular in red."

Being a total girl, and receiving a compliment like that from a guy like Axl, I hadn't argued. Now as I adjusted the thin straps across the back, I tried to remember when I'd ever worn red around Axl.

"I'm coming in," he announced.

I closed my eyes and groaned. My mother shopped here. Elena would be on the phone first thing talking about Annika's handsy boyfriend sneaking into the dressing room. I was pretty sure this sort of thing was not "done" here.

Elena's dealt in exclusivity. There wasn't signage above the outer door designating what type of retail shop existed within. I'd been coming here since the store opened. Elena adored my mother—and by default that adoration included me. That didn't mean I was exempt from gossip.

The first sign of his presence was his hot breath searing my shoulder. Callused hands gripped my upper arms.

I opened my eyes to see Axl peering down the front of my dress.

"Really? Leering at my boobs?"

"They're popping out, begging me to look."

"Because the top is too small." I sighed. "Or my boobs are too big."

"They're perfect. But they seem strangled by the straps. Do you need me to massage them?"

I slapped his hand. "Now I know why you picked this dress."

"I like to see skin." He kissed my shoulder. "Yours especially."

He's playing a part. Remember that.

"I'm ready for the next one." I reached for the zipper, but Axl's fingers were already there.

"Let me help you." He inched the zipper down. After he finished, he murmured, "Touching you makes me lose my head."

Our eyes met in the mirror. "Since I'm half-undressed, maybe you should return to the main room like a dutiful boyfriend so you're not tempted."

His warm lips traveled the slope of my shoulder, producing a shiver. "Doesn't matter if you're fully clothed or half-naked, Annika. I will always be tempted by you."

Then he was gone.

I locked my legs. No way was I letting him render me weak-kneed.

Elena sailed in. "Zis dress iz ze one you vant, An-nik-a. Timeless. Classic. Perfect for your skin and hair."

I waved off her help because we were on a tight schedule for time.

The dress was a simple sheath style that ended below my knees. A fabric band stretched across my upper arms, giving the appearance of a strapless dress, yet it wasn't. The top accentuated my breasts without being tasteless. The fabric, in an ethereal blue color of an early-morning summer sky, had been pin tucked down the front, creating texture.

It was stunning.

"Well?" Axl said impatiently outside the curtain.

"This one will do."

His expression when I walked out?

Killer.

I'd made the chiseled-jawed Swede's mouth drop.

"I need shoes as well." I wandered over to the shelf and immediately spied the ones I wanted. Modified mules in a pastel floral swirl pattern, with a tiny blue jewel on the toe. A spiky heel of about three inches and the back of the shoe molded around the wearer's heel. "These. Size eight. And this." I grabbed a small 1950s clutch-style purse in a pearly white satin, with a short handle that I could nestle in the crook of my elbow.

Axl leaned against the wall, watching me from beneath hooded eyes. If he were a jungle predator, his tail would be swinging as he waited for the perfect moment to pounce.

Standing, I slipped on the right shoe as I braced my left hand on the wall. "What?"

"You picked that purse. You like white?"

"It goes with pretty much everything." I switched sides and slipped on the other shoe. Oh. Yeah. These were gonna kill my feet all damn night. "Why?"

Axl pushed himself off the wall and pointed to a rack behind the payment area. "The white fur stole."

Elena's eyes lit up. "You vant Annika to try it on?"

"No. We'll take it." He handed her a credit card. "All of it on this."

ALL YOU NEED   153

"Of course, Mr. Hammerquist." Elena handed him the fur.

Axl turned and stalked me until I'd frozen by the shoe display. His voice was a husky rasp when he said, "Lift your hair."

I twisted it with one hand, my eyes never leaving Axl's face as he draped the fur across my shoulders. The tiny button in the front rested directly above the V of my cleavage, and for a man with large fingers he was extraordinarily deft as he fastened it.

He tugged it in place, smoothing my hair back after I'd released it. Then he held my chin. "Beautiful. Now you truly look like a vision from a fairy tale, Princess."

"Thank you. You didn't have to."

"But I wanted to. I've never had a woman to spoil and now I do."

Elena called for him and he turned away.

Staring after him, I silently asked the universe the million-dollar question: *All of this is pretend, right? Cementing our reputation even in front of Elena?*

I heard my cell phone buzz in the dressing room and went in to grab my bag so I could switch purses.

"These items will be delivered to your office tomorrow morning, so leave anything you don't want to take tonight," Axl said.

"Okay. I need three minutes to freshen my makeup and then I swear I'll be ready."

The fur turned my hair staticky, so I plaited it into a quick French braid. My cheeks were flushed—Axl seriously had bought me a freakin' fur?—so no need for blush. I swept on powder, added mascara, eyeliner and a fresh coat of lipstick.

I exited the dressing room. "Done."

"Good. Let's go." Axl reached for my hand.

"Thank you, Elena," I called as Axl pulled me out the door.

On the sidewalk, he said, "Our car is here," and helped me inside.

Glad he hadn't sprung for a limo. That'd be over-the-top.

Says the girl wearing fur.

Axl lifted my hand from the console and kissed the back of my hand. "Why so quiet?"

"Taking a moment to reflect."

He snorted.

"What? I can be introspective."

"You're fretting about me buying the fur and clothes and you're dissecting my motive."

Damn him. "Maybe I am."

"Simple. You're appearing at this party as my girlfriend. If you weren't my girlfriend you wouldn't be attending the party and you wouldn't need appropriate attire, so it is my responsibility to pay for it. And I cannot stress enough how stunning you are."

"Is this how Axl acts in public now that we've dispensed with the sexual temptation?"

He laughed.

"What?"

"There is nothing short of castration or a sex-change operation that will end the sexual heat between us, Annika. We've discussed not *acting* on it."

"How lucky for us we're both so strong-willed. Lesser mortals might be tempted."

He had nothing to say to that.

The car stopped. Axl was out and on my side helping me out almost before the driver reacted.

I'd been to this private club more times than I could count—both growing up and in recent years as a Lund corporate exec, so I hadn't expected the rush of nerves. Axl too had become quiet. Would I see the man he'd described earlier? The one who listened instead of talked?

A tasteful rendering of the Wild logo on the door to one of the smaller event rooms indicated we'd reached the right place. A woman with a clipboard standing just inside the doorway signed us in and then we were on our own.

"What now? Stand here looking stupid until someone comes up and starts talking to us?" Axl said irritably.

"Etiquette dictates we find the hosts of the party first, thank them, exchange chitchat and then we're free to head to the bar and mingle with other guests."

Axl spied Bunny and Ron and beat a path straight to them. They were already talking with another couple. Axl's agitated state increased, so I tried to distract him. I slid my hand up the lapel of his suit coat. "Have you always had such great taste in clothes?"

"I know what I like."

"Axl. This suit you're wearing didn't come off the rack."

"It didn't." He gave me a fast smile. "I learned early on that I'm difficult to fit and I'm picky. My tailor in Stockholm made my first suit when I graduated from secondary school. He's still making my clothes. Now I can afford a better quality of cloth and need many more clothes, not just suits."

"If it's not our newest D-man," a hearty male voice said.

Axl smiled and thrust out his hand. "Ron-Du. Thank you for the invite."

"Glad you could make it. Happy that we don't need a translator." He clapped Axl on the shoulder.

Bunny said, "Annika. Darling, you are ravishing!"

"Thank you. You are very smashing yourself." Bunny looked ready for prom. In the 1990s. Satin dress in a deep green, the bodice covered in sequins and rhinestones. She had a pouf in her skirt and a pouf in her hair. I still didn't have a clue about her age . . . maybe late forties. But for all I knew she could be in her early thirties.

"Annika, this is my husband, Ron."

"Happy to meet you. Thank you for the party."

"It's Bunny's deal. I just put on the monkey suit when she tells me to." He squeezed her shoulder. "My honey Bunny is the original Energizer Bunny. She'll dangle a carrot and rope you into doing stuff."

"If she makes it through the first five games," Bunny said with a condescending smile. "Few do. Love the fur. Wherever did you find it?"

"Crafted from my own two hands. I trapped, gutted and skinned a couple of rabbits that annoyed me—"

"She's joking," Axl interrupted. "We bought it at Elena's."

"Is that in the Mall of America?" Bunny asked.

"Yes, you can't miss it—it's *catty*-corner from the LEGO store," I said with a straight face.

That was when Axl led me away.

"What?"

"Troublemaker."

"Just making conversation."

Three guys approached him from behind. "So, Hammer-quist, is this the hot chick with the hot car?"

"This is my girlfriend, Annika Lund. These guys were salivating over your AMG more than you, so forget their names right after I introduce you to Flitte, Dykstrand and McClellan."

"Hello."

"Did you know he could speak English? I mean you had to, right?"

I glanced at Flitte after that comment and then said to Axl in Swedish, "You are in big trouble for this."

"You have no idea what I've promised them to make up for it."

"See, dumb-ass?" McClellan bumped into Flitte. "I told you she had to speak his language."

They were off.

We cut to the back corner, hoping to find food.

I didn't hide my snicker when I spied the food on the buffet table.

Testily Axl said, "What's so funny?"

"That." I pointed to the relish trays. "Of course Bunny serves *rabbit* food at her event."

That did bring a tiny smile to his face.

Two media reps worked the room, snapping pictures. We posed, but I knew the more intimate ones of us would reach the news outlets.

Leah and Linc were chatting with Coach and his wife—who looked young enough to be a bunny herself.

But after the photo ops, Axl had a hard time deciding which group to join if any, so we sort of stood in the middle, staring at each other.

"I hate this," he said tersely. "So don't try and make me laugh."

"You'd rather I tried to make you mad? Okay. I signed us up for karaoke later."

"Not. In. The. Mood. For. Jokes."

"Lucky for you they didn't hire a clown."

Axl got right in my face and growled, "Do you even listen to me?"

That was when I realized his stomach was growling. I placed my hand on his belly.

Oh, hello, hard six-pack of man flesh. Would you like to get intimately acquainted with my tongue?

"Did you just offer to lick my abs?" he demanded softly.

I'd said that out loud? "No. The acoustics in here are terrible. Good thing we're not singing karaoke. But I do have a solution to your problem. Follow me." I laced our fingers together and took him through a door at the back of the room.

"We're not supposed to be back here," Axl said tersely.

"Relax. We won't get in trouble. I'm a regular here."

"How regular?"

"'Forced Lund family brunch every Sunday with my grand-father when I was growing up' kind of regular. Now there's an LI function at least once a month. We pay hefty dues to be club members, so we utilize the meeting rooms as often as possible."

I led him down the hallway to the main kitchen. It wasn't super busy on a Monday night.

The cook wiped his hands on his apron and came over to greet us. "Miss Annika. You look far too lovely to be traipsing around in my messy kitchen."

"Your kitchen is always spotless, Maxwell, so I'm not worried. However, I am concerned for my hangry boyfriend. We didn't eat before we came. We assumed there'd be food—real food—here, and that is not the case."

"What party?"

"Ducheneaux."

"Eh, finger food. No wonder you're hungry. What can I do for you?"

"Give me free rein in your pantry and prep area so I can fix my man something."

Maxwell grinned and leaned in to kiss my cheek. "Take whatever you need."

I led Axl to a rolling stool and said, "Sit. You, sir, have to hold my fur."

He latched on to my hips. "Annika. You don't have to do this."

"I want to do this for you." I smooched his mouth twice.

"You are a goddess among women," he murmured against my lips. He slipped the stole from my shoulders, sensually trailing the fur down my bare arms.

Don't imagine him teasing your entire naked body with long sweeps of that fur. Or alternating between the soft fur and his rough-skinned hands.

Shaking off that thought, I grabbed four slices of hearty

multigrain bread, tomatoes, brown mustard, mayonnaise, slices of Gouda and Swiss cheese and a tin of caviar. First, I sliced the tomatoes. I debated on toasting the bread.

"How did you know?"

"That you were hangry? Well . . . I think *hangry* pretty much says it all, don't you?"

"No, what ingredients to choose to build a sandwich." He gestured to the cutting board. "That's exactly what I would've ordered in Sweden."

"When my grandpa comes to visit us from Sweden, he complains about the bread in the U.S., so he started baking his own. He insists on making me lunch like this at least once a week."

"Do you ever visit him?"

"I haven't for a few years."

"You should come to Sweden with me. We'll visit him and I'll show you my favorite places."

I pointed my knife at him. "You wouldn't try to trick me into snowboarding or going eel ice fishing?"

Axl laughed. "No, there are plenty of other things we could do."

"Such as?"

"Such as going for a hike."

I shuddered. "Only if we're hiking to a secluded cabin in the woods with modern amenities. I have no qualms admitting I am an *indoor* enthusiast."

He smirked. "I bet after one hiking excursion with me you'd change your mind about all the opportunities the great outdoors offers. In fact, maybe for our date tomorrow night we should hike around one of the ten thousand lakes you Minnesotans brag about. I'd even pack traditional Swedish hiking snacks for you."

"Let me guess: trail mix. But instead of raisins . . . it contains dried lingonberries. Oh, and dried eel."

"You truly are not in tune with my culture," he retorted. "We're much more sophisticated than that."

"My mistake to compare you to Bear Grylls," I muttered.

"Then after the hike, we could gather up leaves . . ."

My mind wandered to Axl dressed in a turtleneck and a fisherman's sweater, a hand-loomed scarf looped around his neck. He'd look like he stepped out of an outdoorsman's catalogue. Then I saw us rolling around in a pile of leaves, laughing and teasing each other before we settled in for a long and steamy kiss. Our faces would be cold, our mouths hot. We'd reluctantly separate after our hands wandered beneath the layers of clothing and our bodies began rocking together. Axl would gather a pile of leaves and twigs and start a fire, wrapping his arms around me as we gazed into the flames. It'd be the most romantic thing ever. If I closed my eyes I could smell the smoke and feel the chill from the autumn air on my cheeks. I could feel Axl's big body sheltering mine . . .

"Annika?"

I opened my eyes and glanced up at him. "Sorry. What did you say?"

"Be adventurous. Take a hike with me tomorrow night."

I wanted to say yes. But given the parameters we'd both agreed to abide by, that wouldn't be beneficial to him PR-wise. "I'm sure that hiking with you in a place where there's not ten feet of snowpack and windchills in the subzero range would be doable . . . but it's not practical." I lowered my gaze to the food I was preparing. "I doubt there'd be any photo ops in the great outdoors. So we'll just stick with an unadventurous date at a bar or restaurant where we're sure to get our picture snapped for the gossip page. That's what all this is about, remember?"

His sudden silence told me that he *had* forgotten.

While it broke me a little to shoot him down after he'd opened up to me about an activity that he enjoyed in his life outside of hockey, one of us had to retain a clear head. Apparently tonight that responsibility fell to me.

I snagged a platter and assembled four open-faced sandwiches. Bread, mustard, four strips of cheese, two slices of tomato with a smear of mayo, then black caviar sprinkled on top and dusted with salt and pepper. It was a knife-and-fork sandwich, so I passed him the utensils and reclaimed my fur.

He cut off a chunk of the sandwich and popped it in his mouth. The fact that he barely slowed down was the best kind of praise. I liked to watch Axl eat. There was something almost sensual about the way he used his knife and fork.

After he finished, he looked chagrined. "I didn't even offer you a bite of one of the four sandwiches, Annika. I'm—"

"I made them all for you. If I would've wanted a bite, Axl, I would've asked. I'm not shy in asking for what I want."

"Good to know." He studied me. "Shall we return to the party?"

"Can we cut out? I'd rather go home."

He seemed relieved we were skipping out. "Of course. I'll call for the car."

Maxwell let us sneak out the back door.

Axl took my hand and we walked to the corner to wait for our ride. Once we were in the car, he kept a constant caress across my knuckles with his thumb. This unconscious sweetness got to me because I wasn't sure he even knew he was doing it.

He's not supposed to be doing it; there's no audience to see it.

That thought dampened my mood.

The car dropped me off inside the parking garage at Lund Industries.

Axl waited as I unlocked my car. "Thank you for making this another amazing night."

"Amazing? Right. I made peasant sandwiches and awkward

conversation; you bought me this gorgeous outfit. Seems a little one-sided."

He curled his hands around my face. "The sandwiches were fit for a king. Sometimes social situations overwhelm me when I remember I'm in a foreign country, speaking a different language, and I long for one thing that reminds me of home. The sandwiches were exactly what I needed. Thank you."

Then he kissed me—just a quick peck on the mouth.

I didn't latch onto him and feed my hunger that wasn't for food.

"Peter wants us out on the town this week and a hike is out, so what's your schedule?"

"I have time for a nooner tomorrow."

Seeing the interest in his eyes provided the tiny ego boost I needed.

"I'd love to take you up on the nooner," he said huskily, "but I have practice during the day and can't take a six-hour lunch break."

Holy buckets. Images flashed of us rolling around in front of my fireplace, food forgotten as we feasted on each other for hours . . . *yes, please*.

"Don't look at me like that. I'm trying really fucking hard to stick to our parameters, Annika."

I placed my hands on his chest and pushed him back. "Then stop tempting me. Call me tomorrow?"

"Count on it."

Fifteen

ANNIKA

"I think I made a huge mistake," I admitted to Dallas on Saturday morning as we prepped the space in the old school gym for our upcoming community coat drive.

"How so?

Just spit it out. "I invited Rausch."

Dallas whirled around so fast she almost knocked me over. "Why would you do that?"

"Because I was mad." At Axl, at myself, at Peter, at my mom. At my brother Walker for being so freakin' romantic. At my brother Brady for putting that satisfied look in Lennox's eyes. At my dad for still getting jealous after being married to Mom for thirty-six years.

"So you just randomly called up Rausch and . . . ?"

"No. I talked to him Saturday night at the bar when you were out dancing. I mentioned this coat drive and the lack of support it seemed to have, and you know Rausch. He had his phone out, checking his schedule. On Monday he asked his admin to organize a companywide, last-minute blitz, which resulted in over two hundred coats and hundreds of pairs of gloves and mittens."

"Which he is personally dropping off?"

"In about ten minutes."

"Annika."

"What?" I bristled. "That was the goal. To get as many donations of gently used coats and winter wear as we could house in this facility. Maybe this year, we won't run out."

Dallas took my hands away from fiddling with the zipper on the coat I'd been hanging up. "The guy never does anything without expecting something in return. And you know he's interested in you. You know this about him. It's why you stopped asking for his help on other charity events."

"Maybe he's changed."

"Or maybe he thinks that this is your way of reaching out to him to rekindle—"

"There is no *rekindling*, because there was no *kindling* between us in the first place! Rausch and I are friends. That's it."

"He's always wanted more than that," Dallas pointed out *again*, as if I'd somehow missed the first three times she'd mentioned it in the last minute.

"Rausch is a total gossip hound. He has to know that I'm involved with Axl."

Dallas's eyes gleamed. "Exactly. He's the type of guy to see this as his chance to finally prove himself to you. Remember last fall? When he declared to your mother that he was in the running for your future husband? Because he'd known you for years, he worked well with you on charitable events and you shared the same philosophy about giving back. Plus, your families were acquainted and he was in your social, intellectual and economic class?"

I'd kinda, sorta, maybe blocked that out. Damn it.

"And Aunt Selka was relentless? Urging you to 'exploit your options' with him? Is that ringing any bells, A?"

I nodded. "But I'd forgotten about it."

"Only because your mother dropped it as soon as Brady and Lennox became a thing."

That hadn't been the only reason she'd let it go. I loved my mother and she meant well, but last fall she'd started grilling my friends about Rausch. Asking if they believed he was a "faithful man" and if he held old-fashioned ideas about a woman's place after marriage. Usually I laughed off her bizarre behavior, but that time it'd reached a critical and embarrassing level because she hadn't bothered doing any of it behind my back. Anytime I ran into her if I was with my friends—boom, there was Mama Lund, forcing them to answer her stupidly endless matchmaking questions. I could've overlooked it once. Maybe even twice. But by the third time, Mom and I had words. She maintained it was her right to gather information since he'd all but offered himself up as a potential mate and she feared that I . . . *preferred fishing in shallow streams and refused to test my bobber in deeper waters* . . . whatever the hell that'd meant.

For me? It meant I stopped asking my friends to hang with me in the skybox the rest of the football season. Then she'd forced me to do something that grated on the very essence of who I was; I'd had to ask Brady to run interference for me. I fought my own battles every day in the Lund corporate world. So it'd really chapped my ass that I'd had to run to my big brother to call off the bulldog that was our mother.

So the question remained, how had I forgotten all that? Because it had ruled my life for several months last year.

"Maybe I'll get lucky and Rausch only agreed to help me because he's found his soul mate and he wants to rub her in my face."

Dallas laughed and patted my cheeks. "You are so cute sometimes."

"Why are you here again? Don't you have to cheer on Saturdays?"

"I quit the squad," she said offhandedly.

"What?"

She started to walk away, but I caught her. When I forced her to face me, she had tears in her eyes.

Dallas never cried. Not because she was tough but because she claimed it attracted too much negative energy. I bent down to peer into her face because I had a solid six inches on her. "What happened?"

"I can't talk about it."

"Tough pom-poms. Tell me."

She shook her head. "Not now, okay? As soon as the dust settles, I'll tell you. For today I need to stay busy doing things that will have a positive impact on the world."

I hugged her hard and whispered, "I am one hundred thousand percent here for you, day or night. Please tell me you know that."

"I do. That's why I'm here. You are a positive influence in my life, A." She wiggled out of my hold. "I'll look for more hangers."

As I watched her walk away, I didn't need her special ability to read auras to notice the serious lack of pep in her step. Her ponytail didn't even bounce.

Ten minutes later I'd made progress on sorting the infant snowsuits into piles from smallest—omigod, could those tiny little puffy suits be any cuter?—to the largest when I heard "Annika" behind me and I screamed.

Another thing I'd forgotten about Rausch: his preference to sneak up on me.

I forced a smile before I faced him. "Sorry, Rausch. You startled me."

"No worries." He wasn't a bad-looking guy. If I met him on the street, I'd describe him as average. Brown hair, brown eyes, slight build . . . that was the extent of it.

Rausch took my hands in his. He studied my face for a beat too long, making it uncomfortable when he finally leaned in and kissed each of my cheeks. "How is it that you get more beautiful every time I see you?"

"You don't see me that often?" I joked.

"It'd be my fondest desire in life to rectify that situation."

Oh boy. He retained his hold on my hands. I hoped since his hands were sweaty maybe it'd seem natural if my hands just slipped free. I tugged.

Rausch held strong. "I've missed you, Annika. The benefit for the Scandinavian Society wasn't the same without you this year."

"That's kind of you to say." *Now let go.*

"I must apologize in advance. I wasn't able to round up any of our employees to volunteer today. So you're stuck with just me." He ripped his gaze from mine and it swept the room. "It appears I'll have you pretty much to myself."

"You're just early, that's all. Dallas is here. And—"

The auditorium door banged open and Jensen strolled in. "Yo, bossy, here's your coffee. And in the future, if you want it hot, don't send me after it. I got freakin' mobbed."

Rausch finally dropped my hands when Jensen thrust a paper cup at me.

"Thank you. But in the future, I suggest you don't wear your team jersey on a coffee run. It's almost like you want to get mobbed." I squinted at the cup, which probably had a dozen phone numbers written on it. I passed it back to him. "I think this one is yours."

Jens shook his head. "Nope. But give that to me before you toss it. There's a couple numbers on there I want to keep, since I ran out of space on my cup."

I sighed. "Jensen, you remember Rausch Johnson."

"Afraid not. I meet a lot of people." He offered his hand. "Jensen Lund."

"We've met a dozen times, Jensen," Rausch said tightly. "I hope getting tackled on a regular basis isn't affecting your memory."

He did *not* just say that to my brother, who would take great pleasure in tackling his scrawny ass to the ground.

I held my breath.

Jensen ignored him and looked at me. "Hey, when's Axl getting here?"

Why did Jens care? "As soon as he's done with practice."

"Cool." Jensen smiled at Rausch. "Do you know Annika's boyfriend, Axl Hammerquist?"

"No. I haven't had the—"

"Great guy. They call him 'The Hammer' and trust me, he's earned it."

And the other cleat officially dropped.

What the hell was Jensen up to?

"Anyway, I'll see you around." Jensen gave Rausch his back. "What's my assignment today?"

"Can you assemble more racks? That way we can organize the new coats that were dropped off this week."

"No problem."

After Jensen ambled away, I faced Rausch. "Did you want to go through your company's donations?"

"Are you helping me? It'll go twice as fast."

He had a point, so I said, "Sure."

The project had reached the overwhelming stage. We had more donations than volunteers. That had been the main reason for calling Rausch on Monday. I'd needed help, not more coats—not that I was complaining. I stared at the massive pile. The donation truck had literally backed up and dumped these out.

Rausch moved to stand beside me—right beside me—so close our shoulders touched. "I say start in the middle and work our way out until there are two piles."

That'd keep us in close contact for a while. I'd just have to move quickly. I pointed behind us. "But we might as well create four piles. Men's, women's, children's, and ones that need cleaning."

"What do you consider too dirty, Annika?"

Omigod. Really? He thought I'd find that double entendre sexy?

You'd find it melt-your-panties sexy if Axl had said that to you.

But that was Axl. Axl could read off the items in his equipment bag and I'd find it mesmerizing.

"Anything obviously stained. Shoot. Maybe we need a fifth pile. For ones that aren't salvageable."

"Once again you get to decide the final fate on what's considered redeemable."

Pretty jagged barb there, buddy.

Rausch attempted conversation as we worked side by side, but he eventually abandoned the effort when my responses were little more than grunts.

When had I picked up Axl's habits?

I could tell Jensen found it amusing.

Dallas took the coats we'd separated and hung them on racks.

After an hour it didn't appear as if we'd made any progress. I pulled my arm behind my back to try to loosen the knot of tension and twisted my head from side to side.

"Are your shoulders sore? Let me help."

The next thing I knew, Rausch had his hands on my shoulders and was giving me a massage.

"You are so tight, Annika."

No, seriously. He was not aiming for sexy banter.

"Does it usually take a long time to loosen you up?"

I glanced over my shoulder when I heard the door open.

Axl strode in and paused, his focus entirely on me.

Several people filed in and spread out behind him.

Either Rausch was stupid or just that oblivious, but he kept going with his "massage."

The ire on Axl's face indicated wrenching me away from Rausch in the most painful way possible was imminent, so I saved him the trouble and jerked free of Rausch's Vulcan death grip.

I heard a snicker and glanced over at Jensen, who stood off to the side, a smug grin on his face.

Then Axl was on me. One brawny arm wrapped around my waist, one hand tugging me back by my ponytail, his mouth hot and possessive on mine.

I managed to take one breath before the onslaught, filling my lungs with his scent—soap, and the underlying tang of sweat, the taste of him filling my mouth—coffee and a hint of wintergreen mint.

His reaction was over-the-top. Way over-the-top.

Like you care. He's kissing you like he owns you. Isn't that what you want?

I had to remember that he was playing a part. The "I'm the super-jealous boyfriend type, so back the fuck off" response to seeing Rausch's hands on me.

Then Axl softened the kiss and his touch, dragging his callused fingers down the side of my face, stopping to cup my cheek and sweep his thumb across my jawbone before he ended the embrace.

In that moment, I almost believed he was staking his claim on me—for my benefit and everyone else's.

Then he said, "I missed you," in English, giving me a reality check. This was all for show.

"Sorry I'm late."

"You're not." I peered around his arm before I met his gaze. "You brought friends?"

"You said you needed help. You ask, I provide. That is one of the many things I do for you."

He'd said that last part in a husky tone that dripped of sexual intimacy.

I wanted to smack him and jump him. Not necessarily in that order.

"Come and meet your volunteers." He pressed his hand into the small of my back, no surprise that it was practically cupping my ass when we reached his friends.

I smiled at Relf. "He roped you into this? And you don't even have to translate?"

Relf blushed. "I am happy to help."

Next a guy with dreads past his shoulders, piercings in his lip, nose and ear, stepped forward. He had a beautiful smile. "Man. You are way too hot for Ax-man."

I laughed. "Thank you. I'm Annika."

"I'm Martin. I live across the hall from Axl."

"Thanks for coming, Martin."

"This is Boris. He is a speed skater from Finland who also lives in my building," Axl said by way of introduction.

Boris, another giant blond, muttered something.

A gorgeous dark-haired man with assessing eyes thrust out his hand. "Kazakov. Team captain. Call me Kaz."

Interesting that he didn't give his first name.

I recognized the last man. Igor.

So did Dallas. She came running at him.

He caught her and held her tightly.

"I tried to stay away, but I don't want to—"

"It's okay," Igor said. He spun around and carried Dallas out.

I looked at Axl. "Seriously? He speaks English too?"

Axl rolled his eyes skyward and whistled.

All of the new helpers snickered.

Jensen wandered over to the group. "Hey. I'm Jensen Lund. Annika's younger brother. Glad you could help out today. It's appreciated."

After the handshakes and "Dude, you're 'The Rocket'" conversations ended, Jensen faced Axl. "Axl, my man! Good to see you!"

"Same."

Then they did some forearm-clutching, half-man-hug shoulder-bump thing that looked painful.

When had I stepped into an alternative dimension where Jensen and Axl were best buds?

"What's the plan, bossy?"

I glared at my brother. "Sort and hang. Sort and pair up."

"Looks like they've paired up again," Kaz said of Igor and Dallas.

"What I need paired up is all of that." I pointed to the mountain of gloves and mittens. "Four piles. Men's, women's, children's and mismatched."

"I am totally game for being the little kitten that pairs all the lost mittens," Martin said with a grin. "And then I can have some pie."

I laughed. "Great. All the rest of this?" I gestured to the various piles. "Needs to be hung up on the appropriate racks."

Relf and Boris separated.

"You still want me building more racks?" Jensen asked me.

"Looks like we'll need them."

"What am I doing?" Axl asked.

"You're helping Annika and Rausch," Jens answered.

I stared at my buttinsky brother. "You're not in charge. I think—"

"I think Jens is right, since I am here to work directly with my girlfriend on a project that means so much to her," Axl said with total sincerity. "So lead the way."

"No, you can do Dallas's job, since she's disappeared with Igor." I was worried about her. Did her quitting the cheer squad have anything to do with the Russian hockey player? "Anyway, the piles are already sorted by gender and size. Keep them that way as you hang them up."

"Is there a gender-neutral pile?"

"No. That's redundant."

"Not having it is shortsighted. Most of the outerwear in Sweden—"

"Well, you're not in Sweden anymore, are you?" Rausch inserted haughtily. "The way Annika has it organized is highly efficient. I suggest skipping the argument and getting straight to work."

"And you are?" Axl asked coolly.

"Rausch Johnson. I've known Annika"—he shot me a look somewhere between smug and lewd—"for at least a decade. We've done more events together than most married couples." Rausch laughed. "For a while, people assumed we were the ultimate power couple. Didn't they, Annika?"

Sixteen

AXL

'd hated that Rausch guy from the moment I saw him with his hands on Annika.

The smarmy fucker had looked down his nose at me like I was a bug and had just kept touching her. Like he had the right to. Like she wanted him to.

Wrong on both accounts.

So I'd broken my no-PDA rule and kissed the hell out of her.

For the past hour I'd had to listen to him stroll down memory lane. He hadn't cared if Annika had taken the journey with him or not. He'd rambled on to goad me into reacting. As much as I fantasized about laying him out cold—hey, the pile of coats *would* cushion his fall—I prided myself on acting unaffected.

When I ran out of room on a rack, I headed to the back to grab another one from Jensen.

"Here. Take this one. It'd be a damn crying shame if you were to hop on it, lose control and mow down that motherfucker Rausch."

"No love lost there, huh?"

"I hate that asshole."

"We've got that in common," I said.

He wrenched hard enough on a screw that he stripped it. He swore and started to get up to search for a replacement.

"I'll get you one. What size?"

"Three-sixteenths. Straight head."

I rummaged in the plastic cup of extras until I found one. I passed it over.

"Thanks."

"So, what's your issue with Little Johnson?"

He snorted. "He's a mouth-breathing waste of air. And a weasel dick. He's had his eye on Annika for years."

My humor dried up. "She ever eye him back?"

"Hell no. He's one of those guys who knows she's focused on her career and thinks if he bides his time, she'll get desperate to have kids and eventually come to him."

"He doesn't seem like Annika's type."

"Annika doesn't have a type. She dates around"—Jensen glared at me—"not to say she sleeps around. She's never been serious about a guy longer than three dates. She claims she gets bored and it's a waste of her time. I call dating Annika ADHD—Another Date Hits Dead End."

I snickered.

"So that's probably why the press is interested in you, because she's not been linked with a 'boyfriend' before. She has been out platonically with Rausch more than any other guy."

"Why is that? He's got money? Power? What?"

"Convenience. He's got money for sure. Power?" Jensen shrugged. "Some. Less than he thinks he has. He's cocky, which

I don't get. He didn't back off when I mentioned her boyfriend before you got here."

My eyes narrowed on him as I tried to figure out his angle on the situation. "You attempted to pound my face in last time we met, Lund. What changed?"

"I still think you're an asshole. But you're the asshole Annika chose, so I'll deal."

"I'm flattered," I said dryly.

"Don't be." He made a stabbing motion at me with the screwdriver. "I will grind you into dust if you fuck her over. Anyway, I overheard Annika and Dallas talking and Rausch is a 'you scratch my back' kind of dude, so for him being here and helping out today, she'll owe him."

"She'll owe him what? A date? The hell that's happening when she's dating me."

"I hear ya. I just wanted you to be aware of it, because Annika will cave the moment Rausch makes the demand. Now after he's seen you two together? It'll happen sooner rather than later."

I rubbed at the sharp pain in my gut. "Or we could beat the piss out of him as a reminder that their friendship is officially over."

Jensen laughed. "I'm in. Except . . . she'd punish *us* for it."

"Unless we make it a blanket party?" I suggested.

"Where's the fun in that if he doesn't know we're the ones beating the fuck out of him?" he said.

"I don't like that he had his hands on her."

"So don't let it happen again."

"Count on it."

I rolled the empty racks back to where I'd been working and resumed the tedious task.

Later Jensen popped his head in and said, "Where are you hiding my sister?"

I glanced up. "I thought she was with you."

"No, I've been by myself the past hour. We're having a late practice now that the U of M game is over and the stadium is clear, so I've gotta run. Tell her I'll see her postgame tomorrow."

"I will. Good luck. Maybe your QB will actually use his head and throw the ball to you so you're using those hands to catch rather than block, yah?"

Jensen smirked at me as he walked backward. "The life of a tight end is always intense."

Martin yelled, "Dude, I know that line! It's from *Repo Man*! You totally have to come over sometime and we can watch it."

I expected Jensen to be arrogant, acting as if he was too good to ever hang out with a snowboarding stoner like Martin. I'd knock him on his ass if he said that to Martin directly. Martin was a loyal friend and a sweet guy with a good heart.

"Sounds like a plan, Martin. Maybe we could get Axl to quit playing with his stick long enough to join us."

I shot him the finger.

"As long as he's wearing pants."

"I don't even want to know what that's about," Jensen said. "See you later, pucker."

The Lunds and their puck puns.

Kaz jogged over. "I've gotta grab my bag before we head out. You about done here?"

"Go on, I'll meet you there. I have to say good-bye to Annika."

"Don't take too long," he warned. "Igor left ten minutes ago."

"With Dallas?"

"Yeah."

So much for Dallas and Annika being together. I wandered through the rest of the building but didn't see her. She wouldn't have just left. "Where's Annika?" I asked Martin.

"Dunno, dude. She went that way." He pointed to a door in the corner that led outside.

"When?"

"A while ago. Relf and Boris are riding with me."

"Is anyone else here?"

"Just you. Later."

The situation made no sense. Annika's purse was still hanging on the back of the chair next to her coat. I pulled out my cell phone and dialed her number. Immediately her phone buzzed in her purse.

Maybe she stepped outside to give Rausch a personal good-bye.

Screw that. More like she'd gotten stuck outside with him.

I stormed over to the door Martin had pointed out, turned the handle and pushed.

The door didn't budge. That was weird. I tried again, putting more muscle into it. Nothing. Was the handle stuck? These old metal doors were solid, but moisture did a number on them. I jiggled the handle, lifted up and pressed down but couldn't get a clicking noise. Pissed off, because I knew I'd seen the door open earlier, I raised my booted foot and kicked it.

It crashed open.

I expected to see daylight. Not darkness.

I peered into the opening. "Hello? Annika?"

That was when I heard sobbing.

It was so dark I didn't just jump in. I pulled out my phone and flipped on the flashlight app.

Sitting at the bottom of the set of stairs, curled into herself, was Annika.

My heart raced and I took the stairs two at a time until I reached her. "Are you okay? Are you hurt?"

She didn't say anything. She didn't move.

I sidestepped her and landed on the concrete in front of her. "Annika. Hey. It's me."

After lifting her head, she launched herself at me, babbling incoherently.

I staggered back a step and shifted her weight. "What happened?"

"Not now. Please get me out of here. Please."

"Okay. We're going. Hang on."

I scaled the steps with her clinging to me like a monkey and didn't stop until I reached the chair where she'd hung her purse. Even after I'd sat down, she didn't let go of me.

Her body shook so hard I feared she was having some sort of a seizure.

Feeling helpless, I just ran my hand up and down her back and pressed my lips against the top of her head, murmuring, "It's okay. You're okay."

Her grip on the back of my shirt loosened and she turned her head away from my neck, inhaling a deep breath and then exhaling. "Thank you for finding me."

"I knew you wouldn't just leave."

"Seems like you're the only one. I thought I'd be . . . locked down there in the dark all weekend and maybe . . ." She started sobbing again. "Sorry."

I realized there was more to this. My hands slid around to frame her face.

She'd closed her eyes and bit her lip to try to keep from audibly sobbing. Her shoulders heaved.

That broke my damn heart. "Annika. Talk to me. I'm right here. We've talked about everything under the sun. You don't have to hide anything from me, okay?" I brushed my lips across her mouth.

She looked at me. "Feeling your lips on my teeth was weird."

I smiled at her. "I know. Now that I have your attention . . ."

"Asshat."

"Tell me what's going on. And how it pertains to what happened today."

Annika dropped her gaze and began fiddling with the collar of my T-shirt. "Do you remember on our first date when you asked what was the scariest thing that ever happened to me?"

"Yes."

"That thing with my brother was scary. But not as scary as when I got locked in the vault at my grandfather's house when I was six."

"Vault. Like . . . bank vault?"

She nodded. "The Lund mansion is one of the ostentatious landmarks of wealth in the Twin Cities. When it was built it had the best of everything—I can't even begin to list all the features. But one of them was a home vault for cash and bonds and jewels and guns. Hidden away in a room, with a locking mechanism. I don't even remember why I was at my grandfather's house. I stumbled into his study and he had the vault open. The lights were on and it looked like an open invitation, especially to a snoopy little girl. So I snuck in and started checking out all the drawers. I don't know how long I'd been in there when someone shut the vault door. The lights went out and I heard the locks click. I immediately started beating on the door, which sounds crazy now because it's reinforced steel, but I thought someone might hear me."

"How long were you trapped in there?"

"I think they said, like seven hours. Anyway, I developed claustrophobia after that. I'm fine in cars because there's more than one way to get out. I hate elevators. And caves. And certain rooms just have that 'you're trapped' vibe. I went on the Haunted House ride at Disneyland and we almost had to leave the entire amusement park because the elevator does actually close in on you."

"I'm sorry." I kissed her forehead. "Any idea who locked you in the vault?"

"Probably my grandfather. He could blame it on any number of issues besides the fact that he was a sadistic bastard who probably thought he was teaching me a lesson not to snoop." She sighed. "Although it did work."

"So, what happened today . . . how did you end up in the old boiler room?"

She frowned. "I needed more plastic bags and Rausch said that's where Dallas had been getting them. The door was ajar and the lights were on. At the bottom of the steps, I knew there wasn't anything down there except for cobwebs and dust. When I started back up the stairs, the door slammed shut and the lights went out."

"Jensen or Dallas wouldn't have played a joke on you, because they know about your claustrophobia issues."

"No one in my family knows I still suffer from it."

"Why haven't you told them?"

"Because it's embarrassing, all right? They knew I had closed-space issues when I was a kid. They assumed—I led them to believe—I outgrew it. So I didn't dare admit that phobia has just gotten worse over the years. I'm a grown woman. I should be able to handle it, not turn into a basket case." She shuddered.

That left that fucker Rausch as the person who'd slammed the door. So obvious after he was the one who'd sent her down there in the first place. Did the dickhead have delusions of somehow rescuing her? Proving to me—and to her—that he knew her fears better than I did?

My phone buzzing in my pocket yanked me out of the fantasy of my strong hands wrapped around his scrawny neck.

Annika tried to scramble off my lap. "Sorry. You'd better get that."

I held her in place. "It'll keep. What are you sorry for?"

"That you had to find me a blubbering mess and then calm me down. I appreciate it. Even when we don't have an audience to witness how devoted we are to each other."

"Because that's all I was concerned with when I couldn't find you—making sure everyone knew how worried I was about you? God fucking forbid I actually care about you, Annika."

"Do you?"

I got right in her face, close enough she could see the mix of emotions in my eyes. "What do you think?"

"I think it's getting harder to separate the PR couple from the real couple."

"Then maybe we should reassess why it's not working. Why it's never really worked."

Her back snapped straight. "Like we ought to throw caution to the wind and be puck buddies for real."

I went still. "Was that sarcastic?"

"Gee, do ya think?" She jabbed her finger into my chest. "You have been all over me this week with the excessive PDA. Acting the part of the possessive boyfriend today in front of Rausch and your friends. I think even you've started to believe it. Then all that touchy-feely, ass-grabbing, kissing stuff reminds you that you've been celibate longer than you've ever had to be in your adult life. You're horny. I'm convenient. And everyone already thinks we're boinking like puck bunnies anyway, so why not make it real, right?"

So tempting to do a slow clap after that indignant speech.

Too bad it was all bullshit.

Annika hated that I'd witnessed her vulnerability and I knew she had a dark moment from her past that put a deep chink in her Iron Princess armor.

No surprise she'd come out swinging at the first person she'd opened up to about it. I snorted. It'd practically taken a damn crowbar to get her to open up. Then she'd turned it on me and hit me in the spot where I was most vulnerable, where she knew I'd strike back at her with equal ferocity if she poked at it. Then I'd leave angry and she'd reset the distance between us.

Not happening.

"Was that necessary? Taking a shot at me? Where you knew it'd cut the deepest?" I asked her.

She blinked at me as if she couldn't believe I'd taken that tack and not attacked her. Then contrition distorted her face and she started to cry again. "I'm sorry. God. That was such a bitchy thing to say."

"Yes, it was."

After she'd stopped crying, she buried her face in my neck. "Don't hate me, Axl. I couldn't stand it if I kept pushing you away and you actually left."

"Give me a little credit. We Swedes are made of sterner stuff than that."

"See? You're so calm and understanding and I'm just a hot and cold pain in the ass."

That was the first time in my life anyone had ever called me "calm and understanding." Sort of pathetic, really. "You're wrong about something. That 'hello, hot stuff' kiss today was for no one's benefit but mine."

"So you weren't jealous when you saw Rausch touching me?"

I sighed. "Okay. I was jealous. Maybe I was showing off a little for my buddies that such a beautiful woman was into me."

Annika smiled against my chest. "The truth comes out."

"It always does."

"Meaning what?"

"Meaning I knew you'd react that way if I kissed you. It's always explosive between us, especially if we haven't seen each other for a couple of days." I brushed my mouth across the top of her head. "So you are going to forgive me for the excessive PDA."

"Cocky much?"

"Tell me I'm wrong." *Because I know you enjoyed the hell out of it.*

"Axl. I can't even think straight when your hands are kneading my ass like that."

I squeezed her firm flesh from side to side. "Have I mentioned a benefit of me being your real boyfriend is I give killer massages?"

"That must've slipped your mind because you were too busy slipping your tongue into my mouth."

"Clever girl."

A few beats passed before she said, "Tell me something."

"Is this another one of your quirky getting-to-know-you questions?"

"No, but it is random."

"Ask me."

"Would you have expected to spend the night with me after your exhibition win if the press conference hadn't happened?"

That was definitely random. But I wouldn't complain that her thoughts had veered toward us and sex. "I didn't expect anything. I would've asked you again. Or maybe I would've had better luck if I'd tried to convince you."

Annika angled back to rest her forearms on my shoulders. "Have I acted like that's all it'd take for me to get naked with you? A few hot make-out sessions?"

"No. But here's a question for you. Would you have made me work for it?" I tilted my head and started pressing open-mouthed kisses to her throat. Even after working in a dusty building all day, she smelled like honey and oranges.

"Of course. That's part of the appeal, isn't it?"

With her? Absolutely. I wouldn't have bothered with anyone else. "You sure that making me work to convince you that I'm worth the risk wouldn't have been punishment for me?"

"Why would I want to punish you, Axl?"

"Because you believe I've never had to work very hard to talk a woman out of her clothes and you wanted to prove you're special and worth the extra effort?"

"Oh, I don't think there was much *talking* done at all with your track record."

I paused, half afraid that my reputation was about to come between us again.

But she surprised me, tilting her head, nudging me to get back to kissing her neck. "Besides, you didn't speak the language, remember?"

I chuckled with relief because maybe this would finally be a nonissue between us. "Body language is international. No translator required."

"Now who's being clever?"

"And my quick comebacks aren't even the best thing I can do with my mouth," I whispered in her ear.

She shivered.

I continued to taste the delicate skin of her neck and slide my hands up and down her back. Slowly. Letting my thumbs graze the sides of her upper body, from the curve of her hips, to the contours of her waist and rib cage, stopping to caress the underswells of her breasts. For the first time . . . ever I wasn't in any hurry. I wanted to savor her reaction to my every touch. To my every kiss. For the first time . . . ever I wanted to focus on giving pleasure rather than receiving it.

But what I wanted didn't matter, because I had to go.

"So, are we okay?" she asked.

"We're better than okay, because we're finally admitting we can't control this thing between us."

Then Annika kissed me. It was a sweet, soul-sustaining kiss that guaranteed I'd be back for more.

"Thank you for being here for me today."

"You're welcome. Can we set aside time to talk about this next week?"

"Yes. I've got a crazy schedule at work, so can we be fluid with the day and time?"

"Sure. Just keep in touch with me."

"I'll text you. Good luck, Ax-hell."

"I'll walk you out."

I could tell she wanted to argue, but she didn't.

There was the sign I'd been looking for that things between us really had changed.

Wednesday night Annika and I met for a cocktail, since she had to work late.

I wasn't sure if Peter had chosen the venue or if she had, but this was one of the trendier places in the Twin Cities. Annika fit the surroundings with her sexy, yet business casual attire and the fact that she turned every damn head when she sauntered in.

Two guys in particular needed their heads snapped off their necks for leering at her tits as if there'd be a test later on her bra cup size.

Annika smoothed her hand across my chest. "Stand down, Thor."

"Thor?"

"Now that I know there is no Santa connection, linking 'The Hammer' and Thor was next." She paused. "Dude, you had to see that one coming."

"I'd expected something less obvious from my clever girl." I directed her to the two stools at the far end of the bar by the windows.

"It is an obvious comparison when you are a supersized version of the actor who plays him." She tilted her head back, and her gaze roamed my face. "Say something sexy with an Aussie accent."

I kissed her nose. "No."

"For future reference, I hate being kissed on the nose."

"For future reference, I hate being called Thor."

"Then it looks like you're stuck with Ax-hell, Ax-hole and asshat," she retorted.

"You're in a mood." I handed her the drink menu.

"It's been a weird day."

"How so?"

"I'll tell you in a minute. Do you already know what you're having?"

"Club soda and lime."

Annika reached over and touched my hand. "Shoot. We should've had a dinner date. You're always hungry, aren't you?"

Her concern—genuine, not adopted—affected me in the same way it had when she made me sandwiches. I'd never let a woman fuss over me, because it'd always felt contrived. But with Annika, her need to nurture and soothe was an innate part of her, albeit a part she only shared with the people closest to her. Somehow I'd landed on that very short list and fuck if I didn't want to stay there.

Screw the "this isn't a real relationship" bullshit conversation we'd been back and forth with.

I wanted it to be real.

She wanted it to be real.

One of us needed to have the balls to act on it and *make* it real.

Since I had a pair, it was time to use them.

"Axl?"

I mentally shook off the fog and looked at her. "Sorry. You worked until fifteen minutes ago. Have you eaten?"

She stammered, "I . . . uh . . . meant to . . ."

The bartender wandered over. "What can I get for you?"

"A food menu, please. A club soda with lime and a Leinenkugel Sunset Wheat."

"You got it."

"Axl. I'm fine."

I curled my right hand around the side of her neck, tipped up that stubborn chin, guaranteeing I had her attention. "Who takes care of Annika when she's so busy taking care of everyone else?"

"I don't need anyone to take care of me," she retorted.

"But what if I want to?" My thumb caressed the vulnerable spot beneath her jawline. "You saw to my needs the other night. Let me see to yours now."

"You don't owe me anything."

"I understand that. So stop arguing. I'm feeding you. Whether it's here or someplace else."

Those vibrant blue eyes softened. "Okay. But I draw the line at you literally feeding me."

My gaze dipped to her mouth. "Finger foods might be fun. All that licking, nibbling, sucking."

"Your hunger seems to be on high tonight."

Our eyes met again.

"Dangerous look in your baby blues," she murmured.

"Does it make you nervous?"

"Yes."

The bartender returned with our drinks and a menu. I snatched it first.

She smirked. "I knew you were hungry."

"Wrong. I'm ordering for you. Consider it a test to see if I've learned anything about you from our previous dates."

Annika kept her gaze on mine as she tipped up the mug and drank. "Wow me."

I leaned in and brushed my lips across hers. Twice.

"What was that for?"

"You had a tiny foam mustache." I teased her mouth with mine once more. "As cute as that looked . . . with the mood I'm in? It might just push me over the edge to watch you licking your lips." I retreated and focused on the menu.

When the bartender returned, I said, "An order of the mushroom and tomato crostini, the potato, feta and arugula tart, the chislic and sweet potato fries basket with the pesto and aioli."

"Coming right up."

I sipped my club soda before my gaze sought hers.

Hard not to feel cocky at the look of surprise on her face. "How'd I do?"

"Besides overordering? Perfect."

"Why don't you look happy about that, Princess?"

"Because it proves you're not as aloof as you pretend to be."

"I pay attention when it matters, whether or not others notice I'm paying attention. And you matter." I reached for her hand. "Tell me about your weird day."

"My mom apologized to me."

I waited for more.

Annika laughed. "If you had any idea how rare an occurrence that is, you'd be looking for cosmic signs the world is about to end."

"She apologized for . . . ?"

"Forcing my involvement with you." She took a delicate sip of beer. "She and my dad have been out of town and so today was the first time I'd seen her since the barbecue. She was entirely sincere too and she didn't qualify her apology, which was also a first. I'm glad she realized what she did was wrong."

"So everything is good?"

"Seems so. It's just all the stuff going on . . . it's hard to keep track of things."

The way she'd said "things" I assumed we were done discussing her family. "Like what kinds of things?"

"Things between us. PR stuff. Real stuff. Conversations get started and dropped. A couple of times you've hinted something big happened in Chicago regarding your career and then you quickly changed the subject. I'd forgotten about it until today when I went back through the media packet Peter gave me; I couldn't find any mention of one specific incident."

"What conclusion did you draw?"

"That whatever happened was important enough to be suppressed from the media." She flashed her teeth at me. "Or you've been feeding me full of shit."

"And if I said it's a little of both?"

"I'd say start talking so I'm not blindsided about this incident like I was about your English language skills. And yes, it is my job to leave no stone unturned."

One step forward and two steps back with her. As far as I knew, there'd been no bad breakup in her past that had scarred her and put her off on serious relationships. So that meant her waffling behavior had to be about me and my reputation. I brought her hand to my mouth and kissed the inside of her wrist. "I thought we were beyond us just being about PR."

"We are. Which is why you shouldn't have any issue telling me what happened in the Windy City last year," Annika retorted sweetly.

I'd known we'd have to talk about it; I'd just hoped for a more private location. Like in bed, where I'd try my damnedest to keep our mouths too occupied to talk at all.

"You're thinking about sex again."

I grinned at her. "It's a constant around you, Princess. Get used to it."

"No more deflecting." She laced our fingers together and set our joined hands on the table. "Please talk to me, Axl."

Her sweetness didn't surprise me. How she knew exactly when I needed it? That surprised me. "First, I'll give you a longer piece of backstory. I came to the U.S. for Detroit's training camp. I ended up with the farm team. I had a decent season but not good enough to get noticed. The next preseason, I attended Minnesota's training camp."

"Wait a minute. This is not your first stint in Minnesota?"

"First *pro* stint. I played for their farm team for a year. I even lived in Snow Village. Anyway, that year was the best I'd ever had. As a team we were in sync, so everyone's stats were amazing. We reached the championship. Three guys got moved up."

"But not you."

"Not me. Postseason Peter suggested that since Minnesota had a 'young' roster, I'd have a better shot in Chicago. I made their AHL team. When the 'hawks had a run of injuries at the end of the season, I finally got the call-up."

"Were you excited?"

"Yes. And no." I looked around and leaned in. "I played above expectations and helped the 'hawks reach the semifinals. They offered me a two-year contract." I stirred my club soda. "I'd finally hit the big league and I knew I'd hate every second of it."

"Axl . . . why?"

I forced a deep breath because talking about this generally sent me into a Hulk-like rage. "At the start of the season with Chicago's farm team, I met a bunny from Stockholm at a party. We started hooking up, but beyond that I really liked her. I was ready to commit to being in a relationship with her. But she . . ." Fuck. I hated to admit this. "She didn't want anyone to know we were together. She was happy sneaking around. She said it made it more exciting. The fact that she demanded that we fuck in public places, where we could get caught, should've been a tip-off. But I was really into her, really into the sex and . . ." I glanced up at Annika. "Sorry if this is more information than you were looking for."

Annika squeezed my hand. "No. I need to hear it. So tell me all of it."

"This went on for a couple of months. I hated sneaking around. I thought she was embarrassed because I played in the AHL, not the NHL, but I was totally off base with that." I laughed bitterly. "She didn't know I spoke English. So I was surprised when I overheard her talking about her husband. Then I found out she wasn't a puck bunny but a coach's wife. Not just any coach either. Not a farm team coach, not 'a' defensive coach for the 'hawks, *the* defensive coach at the time for the 'hawks."

"Oh, shit."

"Yeah. She hadn't told me she was married. I hadn't even rated a lie about them being separated. I confronted her and she laughed. She'd singled me out—the naive, eager, homesick rookie—after she found out her husband had been banging an intern and she wanted revenge. Then, after I was of no use to her, she told her husband about me. He paid me a visit and said he'd do everything in his power to ensure that I never played in the NHL. The only reason I got the call-up at the end of the next season was that he'd been on emergency medical leave. He was livid that I'd been offered a contract. The next season? He made my life hell. My first thought when I broke my collarbone? I wouldn't have to deal with that fucker for four months. How screwed-up is that?"

"Completely whacked. Keep going."

"Then it was the same situation at the start of the second year of the contract. For the first time in my life, playing hockey sucked. I'll admit it wasn't cool to turn to booze and bunnies to mask my frustrations. My behavior off the ice wasn't any worse than my teammates', yet I was publicly singled out. Sounds like a conspiracy theory, but someone in the front office was feeding the media."

Her eyes searched mine. "Why would management purposely seek bad press for you when it would've been easier to buy out your contract, making you another team's problem?"

"Exactly. When Peter stepped in and asked me if I was trying to get traded, it occurred to me that could be my endgame. My bad behavior was the reason the defensive coach gave for trading me. If he had tried to bust me down to the AHL instead of trading me? I would've used my affair with his wife as leverage. Not a proud moment in my life, but I just wanted out of there. And I wasn't the one at fault."

Her shock turned to skepticism. "So all your female conquests and fights off the ice were staged?"

"To a certain extent."

"Why didn't you tell me all this the first time we met? Damn it. This is important PR stuff that could've made a huge difference—"

"It wouldn't have made much of a difference professionally. But personally between us? Maybe you wouldn't have been so quick to judge me as a manwhore if you knew the majority of the women who claimed I'd pucked them were lying because it was a blow to *their* egos to admit nothing happened when they were alone with me."

"That's not fair. There was nothing between us personally at first. So you should have told me all this right away."

"But I didn't trust you then."

That jarred her.

"I had no idea what your angle was. I believed you had to have one, because everyone does. After the thing with Isla— that's her name—I didn't trust anyone." I glanced up at her.

The food arrived. I wasn't sure if it was the best timing or the worst. I half expected Annika to pick at the food and claim she'd lost her appetite. But the exact opposite happened. She ate everything, leading me to believe she'd skipped breakfast and lunch too. Then she ordered pumpkin caramel crème brûlée and coffee.

She finally met my gaze. "I was wrong. You didn't overorder. Obviously I was starved. Thank you."

"My pleasure." I scooted in closer. "What are you thinking about?"

"How stabby I'm feeling toward this Isla woman." She paused and frowned. "And yet how oddly . . . thankful."

That shocked me. "Care to elaborate?"

"She lied to you. She used you. Worst of all, she gave you false hope that there was something more between you to explore long term. You were young, a foreigner, trying to break into one of the most competitive sports in the world, and she had to know her husband would react that way when he found out. If for no other reason than to save face. He didn't know if she told you he has a tiny dick, or if he has erectile dysfunction or he typically lasts twenty seconds. He had to get rid of you. It gives me a sharp pain right here"—she placed her hand over her heart—"that she did that to you. That she thought she had the right to derail your fucking career because she was playing a game. And then for you to get out of a horrible situation, you had to turn into something you're not." She smirked. "Well, maybe an exaggerated version of yourself, but you know what I mean. But all those trials did lead you here, Axl. And I'm happy about that."

Annika rarely reacted the way I expected her to. This? So far down the list of possibilities, I was pretty sure my jaw hung to the floor.

"I understand your trust issues a lot more than I did before, so thank you for telling me."

I wasn't into PDA, but I needed to feel her sweet curves against me and gorge myself on the sweet taste of her. So I merely plucked her up and settled her on my lap to do exactly that. I didn't give a damn if this embrace made the front page of the *Tribune*.

The bartender waited until the kiss ended before he delivered Annika's dessert and coffee. But she wasn't in a hurry to scramble off my lap—a sign I'd gained solid ground with her this time.

Seventeen

ANNIKA

The first home game of the season and the Xcel Center had sold out. The team had to be pumped about that.

I'd managed to decline Bunny's invite for pregame action without offending her, which seemed to be a feat. There were more politics within the WAGs than I wanted to deal with, so I was happy to be in the seats down on the ice next to the boards with the ragtag group of Wild supporters.

During the coat drive on Saturday, I'd noticed the similarities between Axl and Jensen, not just the obvious sports-minded ones. For the little amount of time Axl had lived in Minneapolis, he had accumulated a large circle of friends. He was generous; he'd handed out tickets to people in his apartment complex, plus Relf, plus a guy he'd met at the gym who reminded him of a friend of his in Sweden.

Axl wanted them all to have a good time, so he'd be

surprised—embarrassed, more likely—to see all of his buddies wearing HAMMERQUIST jerseys.

Leah acted a little annoyed that he had his own cheering section. But I wouldn't let anything wreck this night.

Dallas showed up wearing a jersey with Axl's name on the back. Her subdued nature concerned me and it seemed she purposely sat at the end of the row away from me.

I was listening to Martin's girlfriend, Verily, talk about her recent trip to Canada and trying not to peek at the countdown clock every thirty seconds, when someone bumped into me. I turned to see the person hunkered into the seat, the ball cap pulled down low over his forehead. "Jensen?"

"Shh. Trying to stay on the down low here, sis."

He hadn't worn any of his usual purple football team gear. He'd even donned a jacket with the Minnesota hockey team's logo. "The Rocket" would get mobbed if fans knew he was in the arena. "Are you wearing a Hammerquist jersey?"

Jensen gave me a droll stare. "Are you fucking kidding me? If it doesn't have the name Lund on the back? I won't wear it."

Cocky. But he had a right to be.

Martin tapped Jensen on the shoulder. "Hey, dude. Gonna make a suggestion. If you wanna stay incognito? Don't sit by your sister. She's with 'The Hammer,' so you know they're gonna be putting her face on the JumboTron every chance they can."

"Good point."

Jensen ended up sitting as far away from me as Dallas was, but if it allowed him a chance to watch the game in peace, I'd suck it up and sit by Boris, the Finnish speed skater.

The clock read eight minutes before the players took to the ice to warm up, and I was so antsy I couldn't sit still.

That was when Peter showed up at the end of my row.

I jumped up, incredibly happy because Axl wanted to see me. I followed Peter through the maze. But this time, Axl wasn't back in the tunnel; he leaned against the wall behind the security guard.

The guard—his tag read Bernie—looked at me and sighed. "Go on."

Like before, Axl was on me in three short strides. His meaty forearms wrapped around my back as he lifted me off my feet and crushed me to his chest. "I need my good-luck kiss." Then that hungry, skilled, seductive mouth latched onto mine.

God. I so so so loved the way this man kissed me. I twined my arms around his neck and behind his head.

A cheer went up in the arena.

Followed by wolf whistles.

Even through my fog of lust, I heard the arena announcer say, "That, hockey fans, is a kiss done right. Give it up for 'The Hammer' and his lady, Annika, who started out tonight's kiss cam with a bang."

Axl and I both froze. Then he walked us around the corner, blocking us from the camera.

He peered into my face. "Did you tip off the media?"

"No!"

Peter sauntered into view. He wore a smug smile. "I assumed it'd be a repeat of last time. I decided we might as well get some mileage out of it."

Axl growled, "Get out."

Peter held up his hands and disappeared.

"Fuck. I hate this part."

"I know. But it's what we signed on for."

"Like I need a fucking reminder of that. Sometimes I feel like my life isn't my own. That the only good thing in my life isn't private. And the things I want to talk about, I can't."

Cryptic. He was in an odd mood. I kissed his chin. "You can always talk to me. Will I see you after the game?"

His gaze skittered away. "No, sorry. I'll be wiped out. I might have a quick beer with the guys and then go to bed."

Something was . . . off about that. No "I'll text you" or "thanks for the good-luck kiss" or him demanding to know the next time we would see each other. Did he regret telling me about Isla? Come to think of it, he'd acted distant during our quick lunch date yesterday. And he'd hedged about his plans for after tonight's game then too. I said, "Play hard, Hammerquist."

"No other way to play." Then he was gone.

Peter wasn't waiting to escort me back to my seat. He'd gotten what he wanted.

When I returned to the arena, the entire section I'd been sitting in stood up and cheered.

Had I ever blushed that hard?

I slipped on a jacket, gloves and a hat to keep me warm—I'd learned my lesson last time.

The crowd went wild when the Wild players took to the ice.

So many things went on during a hockey game. Promotions, giveaways, contests, blimp drops, kiss cams, dance-offs, rink girls sweeping the ice, network commercial breaks. All the constant bombardment meant I didn't have to try to keep up a conversation with anyone, which was good because I was trying really hard to figure hockey out.

But I loved watching my man skate. God. He was grace and power and pure, raw male aggression. When he knocked the dude from Philly into the boards right in front of me? I might've had a mini-orgasm.

Who would have guessed that a big, surly, hard-hitting guy did it for me?

At the start of the third period, I noticed Martin and Verily had their heads together and were whispering, as if they were trying to have a private conversation. Right in front of me.

My scalp tingled. My ears itched. My senses went on full alert.

And I was utterly powerless to stop myself from dropping

my program on the floor and leaning in so I could hear them. Eavesdropping was the one bad habit in my life I couldn't kick—mostly because I hadn't ever bothered to try, especially after the desire to snoop had been curtailed early on in my life. For the third Lund kid—and the only girl—listening at doorways had been necessary because no one had told me anything. So in my mind, they'd forced me to learn stealth skills. By age ten I could decipher a whispered conversation across a fifty-foot room. This skill had served me very well over the years, professionally and personally.

Immediately I picked up on the fact that Martin and Verily were whispering in Swedish.

Hmm. They really had tried to keep this conversation private. Maybe next time they should try speaking in stoner language. I had a hard time deciphering that one. But to be honest, they weren't doing such a hot job of speaking quietly.

"You think any of the dudes on the hockey team are vegetarian?" Martin asked.

Okay. That was random.

Verily said, "I doubt it with as many calories as they need to eat. A lot of it has to be protein. Why?"

"Axl told me to order pizzas for the after party. I wondered if we oughta order a veggie or two, just to be safe."

I perked up at the words *after party*.

"Oh, right, that thing he's having after the game. Am I invited?"

What thing? The one-beer-with-his-teammates-before-he-goes-to-bed thing?

"I wouldn't go without you. The hockey team and the farm team are both coming. Then he invited everyone in our building so no one complains about the noise," Martin said.

"Smart. But you'd better order a ton of pizzas if that many people are coming."

Axl had kissed the hell out of me in front of the entire stadium and then not a minute later he'd lied to me.

Why?

So what if he didn't tell you about a party? Is he supposed to tell you everything?

No, he didn't have to tell me everything. But it was a problem when he outright lied to me.

This had thrown me for a loop because I thought Axl and I had reached a point of honesty.

Ten million thoughts ran around my head—none of them good—and I didn't pay attention to the rest of the hockey game. When the crowd started cheering, I realized the Wild had won.

Yay.

I glanced over to see that Jensen had already disappeared.

Martin, Verily and the rest of Axl's buddies were gone too.

I turned around and saw Leah gathering her things. I bounded up the steps to her. "Hey. Nice goal that Linc ricocheted in in the second period."

She shrugged. "He scored. That's what matters."

"So, what happens now? Do you wait outside the locker room for Linc to come out?" I was fishing to see if she'd tell me that Linc was headed to Axl's after party.

Leah looked at me strangely. "No. I go home."

"That's it?"

"Well, Linc and I don't ride here together. Sometimes he goes out with the team for a beer after the game. Sometimes he's stuck doing a press conference—I imagine since he scored one of the two goals tonight he'll have to talk about that. As far as waiting for him goes?" Her nose wrinkled. "The last thing I'll ever do on purpose is hang around a stanky-ass locker room where hockey players and their gear are after a game." She shuddered. "Nasty."

"So you're telling me I shouldn't wait?"

"I know this is new for you, but it'll just make you mad to see the puck bunnies trolling for stick outside the locker room. Some of them will be wearing your man's jersey. Some of them will ask your man to sign jerseys, or body parts. Do yourself a favor. Go home and keep your blood pressure down and trust that your man will come home."

"You don't ever worry Linc will be tempted?" I blurted out.

Leah's gaze softened. "No, Annika, I don't. Maybe because Linc is older and closer to retirement. Maybe because hockey is his job but not what defines him. Between us? I'd be more worried about leaving Linc unattended at the concession stand. He would stuff himself with every kind of sweet they have until he went into a diabetic coma. Sugar is his addiction." She smirked. "And me. There isn't a thing those bunnies can offer him that he can't get better at home."

I grinned. "You are awesome."

"I know. You are too. If Axl can't see that from the start? Walk away. Seriously."

When I returned to my seat, I noticed Dallas remained in her seat at the end of the row. I shuffled over and plopped down beside her. "Hey. What's up?"

"Fuck my life, Annika. For reals."

Dallas never said things like that. "Okay, I'm done giving you space, hoping you'll seek me out when you're ready to talk about quitting the squad and whatever else is going on. Spill it."

"I'm in love with Igor. Like hard-core in love where I willingly wear ugly head scarves and learn to make borscht and peasant bread in order to become his ideal woman. Then he'll beg me to marry him and I'll start popping out little hockey players."

My jaw might've hit the floor.

"See? FML."

"When did the Russian-wife-wannabe delusions kick in?" I demanded.

"Right after I started riding Hessian-style."

I took a moment to let my mind unscramble—a process I went through at least once in any prolonged conversation with Dallas. "Okay. Let's break this down. Knowing you, it has to be a body chemistry thing. So say you've been drinking more frequently. Since this is Igor, maybe you've developed an allergy to vodka and it has distorted your vola, making you *think* that's what you want." That sounded plausible, considering I never understood half the metaphysical stuff she talked about. "Can you reset your vola thingy with chanting and incense?"

Dallas gaped at me as if I'd suggested she attach leeches to her eyeballs. "Annika. That makes no sense!"

"But you fantasizing about shucking this life to become the Bride of"—*don't say it*—"Siberia somehow makes perfect sense?"

"Well . . . no. But I did have a cosmic disturbance in my star chart that indicated big life changes ahead for me."

I started my own "Dealing with Dallas" chant inside my head. *You love her. She is who she is; she is* not *you.* "Truth time, D. If a Gypsy fortune-teller would've told you beets and bread lines were your fate for true love, even as little as six weeks ago? You would've been yelling 'Fraud' at her and smashing her crystal ball over her head as you stomped on her tarot cards."

"I know." She sighed and rested her head on my shoulder. "Penises are evil."

Was there a good response to that?

"In Igor's case it's doubly true because . . ."

Start the chant again! Start the chant! You love her. She is who she is; she is not *you.*

". . . his dick is cursed."

That stopped me. "His dick is cursed?"

"Yes."

Don't ask, Annika. Just change the subject. But this entire bizarre conversation was taking my mind off Ax-hole and his secret party, so I kept going. "So, how did Igor's dick get cursed? A jealous pagan deity saw it when Igor was running naked through the forest and he said, 'Whoa. That dick is *way* nicer and bigger than mine. I am totally cursing it.'"

"No. A former Romanian Gypsy lover cursed it."

"Of course. Why didn't I think of that?"

"Because you only see one realm," she said with zero sarcasm.

"What was the curse? Is it, like . . . deformed now?"

Dallas shook her head. "It's addictive. If he has sex with a woman more than once, she becomes obsessed with his dick and won't leave him alone. Which is why he has the 'only one time' rule."

For the love of god. Was she serious with this? "So this ex-girlfriend didn't curse Igor's dick to shrivel up and fall off? Or give him impotency problems? Or change it to a teeny-weenie? He's cursed to a life of one-night stands? Wow. That curse works out pretty great for him. He sleeps with you once and says, 'Ve done getting nakey-nakey. It's zee curse. You vill go now and save yourself from zis addiction.'"

"Igor doesn't talk like that, Annika."

"But he does lie like that, D. And what sucks? He lied to you in the meanest way possible. He used the kind of things you believe in *against* you. What kind of man does that?" I answered my own question. "A douche canoe pucktard who needs his evil penis cursed for reals." The next time I saw Igor? I'd kick his balls into his throat. No one treated my cousin this way. "Well, as long as we're ripping on hockey puckers, Ax-hole is having a secret party tonight."

"He is?" She perked up in her seat. "Are you going?"

"I wasn't invited. He told me we wouldn't see each other after the game because he planned on having a quick beer with the team and then going to bed early, since tomorrow is a travel day for them. But then I overheard Martin and Verily whispering about where the party was being held, about ordering food and how many guys were invited, so I spent the third period of the game wondering what to do. Confront him tonight? Confront him the next time I see him? See if he confesses? See if someone else tells me about the party and listen to his excuses on why he lied about it?"

Dallas gave me a thoughtful look. "The whole hockey team is invited?"

"Yes. Plus guys from the AHL team who are around for tonight's game."

"The party is at Snow Village where Axl lives?"

"I guess it's in a community party room. Why?"

"I say we crash it."

"What? No! That's *not* why I told you about it."

"It's karma, then." She offered me a smile that looked way more sneaky than serene.

"Karma?" That was stretching it, even for Dallas.

"Yes, it solves both of our problems."

"What problem? I don't have a problem."

"Sure, you don't. You're not obsessing about why Axl laid such a hot kiss on you one second and then basically gave you the kiss-off the next."

I groaned. "Fine. Maybe I am *wondering* about this party, but I'm not obsessed with it."

"I'll be obsessed enough for both of us and you can just ride shotgun."

This is crazy. Do not even consider going along even to save her from herself.

"This party is the perfect chance for me to watch Igor covertly."

"Covertly? He'll recognize you!"

"No, he won't." Dallas grinned. "We'll wear disguises."

"Disguises? Crazy talk, D. Listen to yourself."

"We can pull this off."

"How?"

"Guess who still has a key to the theater on Seventh Street." She waggled her eyebrows. "That's where we'll find costumes and makeup . . . everything we need. Come on, A. When was the last time we did something fun?"

It had been ages.

Then she threw down the gauntlet. "If your BFF, Cara, was here? She'd be on board. She'd remind you it's okay to let go of the reins, just roll with it and give that out-of-the-box idea a chance."

Cara would already have the keys in her hand and be hot-footing it out the door.

In the not-too-distant past you would've been right behind her, accepting the challenge.

My head said, *You are not considering this.* My mouth said, "Okay, say I agree. What do you hope to learn about Igor by spying on him?"

"If he ever finished our book club discussion about *Anna Karenina*." She rolled her eyes. "I want to see if he's back to hooking up. He told me last weekend when we were helping with the coat drive that he hasn't been with anyone since the last time we were together."

I remembered that Dallas had said, *I can't stay away from you.* "The last time? Were you with Igor more than once, D?"

She threw up her hands. "Have you even been *listening* to me? Yes. I was with him more than once."

"How many times?"

"Twenty-seven."

"You had sex with him twenty-seven times? You counted?"

"No, I've met with him twenty-seven times. We've had sex more than that. So can you see why I think the Gypsy dick curse is real? I cannot stay away from him. So maybe if I see him with another woman, then that'll break the curse."

I stared at her. Hard.

"Please? I'll never, ever ask you for another favor."

Yeah, I'd heard that one before. "Fine. But two things. First, you do not get to sneak off and have sex with Igor. This is a mission to gather intel only."

Dallas bumped me with her shoulder. "Listen to you, going all Jane Bond."

"Second, under no circumstances do we not leave together."

"Pinkie-swear, cuz. And I have one condition for you." Her eyes searched mine. "You give Axl the benefit of the doubt."

"What?"

"What does it say about the future of your relationship if you don't trust Axl enough to let him hang out with his buddies even for one lousy night?"

My stomach knotted. If Axl's distance the last two days meant he'd reverted to his old ways, I needed to know before I got in any deeper with him. I liked him. A lot. I wasn't supposed to like him. I was supposed to tolerate him until our mutual goals had been achieved.

It's gone way beyond that, hasn't it? Almost from the beginning.

"Annika?" she prompted.

"It says it's better to see with my own eyes than wonder, doesn't it?"

"Not always. Sometimes you've gotta have blind faith." Dallas popped to her feet. "The arena is clear, so the traffic has probably died down. Let's become the two-faced women." She paused. "Wait. That didn't sound right."

"Dallas, nothing about this idea sounds right."

"True. In for a penny, might as well be in for a million more."

After we reached the playhouse and started pawing through the costumes and wigs, I began to lose my nerve. This idea smacked of slightly psycho behavior.

Disguising yourself so you can crash a party and spy on your not-really-a-boyfriend and helping your cousin try to break a Gypsy curse?

Nope. Nothing wrong with that scenario at all.

Sigh.

Well, life was never boring with Dallas.

I'd chosen a brunette wig with an abundance of curls that cascaded past my shoulders. The stage makeup I slathered on my face and neck was two full shades darker than what I usually wore. I darkened my eyebrows, and that changed the color of my eyes from blue to gray. I went heavier on the eyeliner, adding a cat's-eye curl to the ends. I added a smattering of freckles across my nose and cheeks. No blush—I didn't want to draw attention to my cheekbones. I stuck a jewel on the side of my nose for a fake piercing and clipped two silver hoops in the outer corner of my left eyebrow.

"Well?" I faced Dallas. "What do you think?"

"Gypsy whore meets girl next door?" She tugged my sheer blouse down until my nipples nearly saluted the world. "You are completely unrecognizable."

"Lipstick?"

"Nope. Nude lips. Too much color will emphasize your smile—which is killer BT-dubs—and we're trying to avoid familiarity." Dallas pointed at my feet. "No heels. Some type of shoe that doesn't match, I think."

I gasped. "Do not even *joke* about that."

Dallas snickered. "Okay. Am I dry yet?"

I leaned in to check out the "ink" on her right arm. The stickers looked so realistic, I couldn't believe it wasn't a real tattoo sleeve. "Five more minutes before you can slip on the sheer blouse. Let's fix your wig." Dallas wore a chin-length blond wig cut in an asymmetrical bob style. We'd gone the opposite direction for her, lightening the makeup on her face and neck two shades. She wore a nude-colored bustier, a tight denim microminiskirt and bubblegum pink pumps that matched her lipstick. "You look fantastic as a blonde."

"This is gonna be so much fun! I hope there are a lot of people so we can melt into the crowd."

"We went a little overboard for that. Intel gathering only, remember? In. Out. Gone."

I left my car parked at the playhouse and she drove to Snow Village.

As soon as we pulled up and I saw it was a gated community with a guard, I thought we were screwed.

But Dallas merely told me to hush and rolled down the window. She smiled and said, "Hey, Mr. Darrin. How are you tonight?"

He crouched to window level. "Do I know you, sweet thing?"

"No, sir," she drawled. "My name's Abilene, but you know my sister, Dallas. I'm here visiting her. You probably recognized her car."

"I did." He squinted at Dallas. "But I'm sorry if I don't see even a tiny resemblance between you and your sister. Abilene, huh? Your parents have a thing for Texas?"

"You have no idea. My younger sister's name is Killeen. And our brother? Austin."

Maybe Dallas did the TMI thing too.

"Who's your friend?"

"Natasha. She's from Romania. So I'm hoping that she and Igor can communicate, since she doesn't speak English."

"If Igor isn't interested in her, bring her back here. I got some ways to communicate with her that don't need any words at all."

And . . . eww. But I wondered how many times someone had said something like that to Axl.

Dallas laughed. "My sister warned me you were a terrible flirt. Anyway. The Hammer is throwing a party tonight in the community room of his building. Is that still going on or are we too late?"

"It's still going on. Building B. First floor. The double doors around back are where you enter. You might have to walk a ways. It's a little jammed."

"Thanks for the heads-up. Have a great evening, Mr. Darrin."

"You too. Tell that sister of yours hello."

Dallas didn't start snickering until we'd turned the first corner.

"Abilene? Seriously?"

"I panicked, okay? I almost said Galveston because that's the only town that popped into my head."

"You are impressive, though, D. Wow. Fast thinking on the fly."

"Igor lives here, so I've been here a few times. For once in my life sneaking around turned out to be beneficial."

"So my name's Natasha. Am I the brooding type?"

"Brooding, quiet and watchful type. Can I at least have one drink?" Dallas asked. "People get suspicious if you don't drink."

"One drink. And you can carry the same bottle around all night as a prop, you know."

"Why didn't I think of that? Oh, right. Because that is not fun at all." She parked along the road and took out her cell phone. "Selfie time."

I leaned closer and practiced brooding Natasha. When Dallas flipped the image around, I did a double take. The women on the screen did not look like us at all.

"Sending that to you. And we're leaving our phones in the car, right?"

"Right. Come on, Abilene. Let's break a Gypsy curse."

We walked for what seemed like a mile.

"Man. There are a lot of people here. How did he think he'd keep this a secret?"

"I have no idea."

The entrance to the party room had two security guards manning the doors. "Ladies. No cell phones allowed. You'll have to check them here or take them to your vehicle."

"I left mine in my car," Dallas said. "And, darlin', as you can plainly see"—she spun around—"ain't no place to hide one in this outfit."

"I can see that." The guy gave my outfit a once-over. "You hiding anything, sugar?"

"Just my wild streak until I get inside."

He laughed. "Have fun."

The lights inside the party room weren't overly bright. The music wasn't blasting. But there were a ton of people. Men mostly.

A serve-yourself bar had been set up on the end closest to the doors with bottles of basic booze and mixers. Tubs of ice jammed full of beer and soda. There were a few tables on the periphery, but most people stood in the throng in the middle of the room.

A door opened behind the bar. A hockey player—Flitte?— and one of the bunnies I'd seen in the arena seats straightened their clothes as they exited the room. I counted five other doors like that one. All closed.

I headed for the bar and fixed myself a screwdriver. Evidently Dallas had changed her mind and stuck with orange juice.

We hadn't made a plan, but she and I had attended enough parties that we knew how to work a room. Start at the outside of the circle and worm your way in. Meander. Never make it appear you're searching for someone.

So far that hadn't been a problem.

So far I hadn't seen Axl.

Do not imagine him in one of those rooms with an eager puck bunny.

I did see Kaz with his arms around two chicks. Chick one had her hand hooked in the fly of his jeans as she idly caressed the bulge behind the zipper.

"See anything worth losing your wig over yet?" Dallas said behind me.

"No. You?"

"No." She paused. "Did you expect to see an orgy?"

"I guess I didn't rule it out after what Lucy told me."

"Speaking of that . . . you just believed everything she told you?"

I kept my gaze moving through the crowd. "Yes. I'm embarrassed that I had the Lund blinders on as long as I did. I get mad at Jensen for his reputation. Why had I thought Jaxson would be any different? Especially when he's the most self-involved of all of us?"

"But I worry that you're making absolutes about all athletes based on generalizations and hearsay."

I looked at her. Since when did she play devil's advocate? "These absolutes are not based on hearsay. Axl admitted to his manwhore ways. So has Jensen. I promise I'll ask Jax next time I see him."

"So you're here to prove your theory that a leopard can't change its spots?"

No, I'm here because another member of my family needs my help. "No. We're here to break the Gypsy dick curse, remember? Have you seen Igor?"

"Not yet."

"Think he's in one of the closed rooms?"

"Well, hello, ladies."

We turned and faced a young guy, close to Dallas's age. "Great party, isn't it?" Dallas gushed.

"Players know how to party." He lifted his beer and drank. "I'm Cash. I'm part of the team."

I didn't recognize him, but Dallas went with it. "Ooh, you're a hockey player?"

"Yep. Been on skates since I was three."

"Lord, I can't even stand up on a pair. So what position do you play?"

"Center." That was when he admitted he was in the AHL.

I tuned him out and did another sweep of the room. I saw Martin. No Verily, though.

The married guys from the team were here—that was a surprise—and they were arm-wrestling. I snarkily wondered if they'd had to get permission to attend from the WAGs.

Oh yeah? Don't get smug. If that's the case, then at least the WAGs knew about the party your boyfriend was throwing . . . the one you didn't have a clue about.

Trios of bunnies were making the rounds. Others had already found their marks.

I took a couple of sideways steps to see better.

One of the mysterious doors opened and Axl stepped out.

My heart sank. I wanted to be wrong.

He crossed over to where Martin stood.

But I kept my eyes on the door to see who left after he did. I didn't think I'd missed seeing anyone sneak out before him.

I stared at that door so hard my eyes started to burn.

Dallas bumped into me and said, "Oops. I'll catch up with you later, Cash." Then she tried to steer me away.

"Stop it," I hissed. "Axl just left a room, and I'm trying to see which puck bunny is coming out after him."

"Doesn't matter. Move it, because Igor is headed this way."

Eighteen

AXL

'd had one beer, so I knew it wasn't too much alcohol making me see things.

Annika, you little sneak.

What in the hell are you doing here? Dressed like that?

The harem girl outfit showcased her curves. The jewel in her belly ring played peekaboo beneath the flowing folds of her shirt, giving a glimpse of the generous swells of her breasts. I'd never fantasized about being a sheik, but if she had gifted me with a come-hither stare, I would've done anything to have her before me on her knees, those big blue eyes staring up at me. I'd grab a handful of her hair—

"She looks like Romanian fantasy," Boris said beside me as he caught sight of the object of my fixed stare. "Do you know her?"

"Yes. She's not what she appears to be, trust me."

"I will judge for myself. Introduce us."

"No. Stay away from her."

"You do not get to hoard all the women!"

"Boris, dude, there are plenty of other women here. But that brunette is off-limits."

He stormed off.

She still hadn't noticed me yet. Her gaze kept sweeping the crowd, so I knew she was looking for me.

Are you here because you missed me, Princess?

Or because you don't trust me?

Do you blame her?

When she turned back toward the bar, I skirted the edge of the crowd until I came to the door to the supply closet I'd just left. I reached in and flipped on the light. Not ideal, but I'd rather bring her in here to talk than take a chance on what she'd see in one of the other rooms.

I considered how I should play this.

Act like I didn't know who she was and try to pick her up? No.

Ambush her?

That'd work.

The only good thing about this party was I didn't have to act like a host. No one paid attention to me. I preferred to blend, and with this many hockey players and European athletes, it was the one place I didn't stand out.

So I wasn't stopped in my quest to snare my prey. She and a blonde were pretending to be in deep conversation with their backs to the room. Every so often Annika would whirl around as if she felt me closing in, but I made sure she didn't see me.

The instant the blonde stepped to the end of the table to chat with two guys from the farm team, I swooped in.

My body blocked hers from view. I put my mouth on her ear. "Nice try, Attila."

She gasped and tried to spin around, but I had her pinned against the table.

"Did you really think I wouldn't recognize you?"

Anger rolled off her. "Yes."

"Here's what's going to happen. I will direct you exactly where I want you to go. You will not cause a scene."

"You'd hate that more than anything, wouldn't you?"

I sighed and pressed my lips to the back of her head. Yuck. It wasn't her hair and I didn't get a whiff of the usual warm honeyed scent of her skin. "This is between us, no one else."

"Oh, so you're taking me into one of the private sex rooms? Maybe the one that you just came out of?"

"As a matter of fact . . . yes." Curling my hands around her hips, I shifted us sideways and tossed a quick look over my shoulder to make sure no one saw us doing the weird duck walk the fifteen meters to the door. I opened it and shoved us both inside, quickly closing the door behind us.

Immediately I saw Annika's panic set in. I got right in her face to distract her. "You're with me. I won't leave you in here. I made sure the lights were on."

"This is the room you were in before," she stated.

"It's not a room. It's a storage closet. Take a look around."

She did. "What were you doing in here?"

Hiding. "Looking for another garbage can. Why?" My eyes narrowed. "You saw me come out of here. What did you *think* I was doing?"

"I don't know! I thought maybe it was a coat closet or something." She smirked. "You've had an obsession with hanging out in them in the past."

I'd take her pissyness over her panic. "My coat closet days are long gone. So maybe you can explain what you were trying to accomplish showing up in a wig?" I scrutinized her face. "And fake freckles. Really, Annika? Fake freckles were supposed to throw me off?"

"Yes. The push-up bra was a decoy too." She thrust her chest out. "I'd never wear anything like this to the office."

But you could wear something like that to bed . . . for about three seconds before I'd tear it off with my teeth.

"See? You're leering at my boobs." She jabbed her finger into my sternum. "So it is working. Now let me out of here so you can carry on and pretend I'm a woman you actually invited to your stupid secret party."

And . . . there it was.

I curled my hands below her jaw, pressing my thumbs over her lips to stop the flow of chatter. "Listen to me. I didn't want to have this stupid secret party."

"Why did you?"

"The night the team learned I could speak English? They gave me a bunch of penalties. The last one was I had to promise to get the team into the VIP section of Flurry after the first home game of the season." I paused. "That is the last place I ever want to go, especially when they insisted no WAGs. No exceptions. So I lied to my team. I said I called Flurry and I didn't have the clout for the VIP section and they turned me down. I didn't even tell the guys until the team meeting this morning that Flurry was a no-go. I suggested coming here, hoping they'd just tell me to forget it, and of course they didn't, so there you have it."

"You could've just told me all that."

"When? In front of Peter and the damn cameras? And I wouldn't have kept it from you if I'd had a choice. The 'no WAGs' rule for tonight didn't change."

She snorted.

That annoyed me. "Do I look like I'm having fun?"

"You don't look like you're having fun now that I *busted* you throwing a secret party for all your buddies. You might've been having a helluva good time before that, Ax-hole."

"I wasn't." I stepped back and pulled my cell phone out from the inside pocket of my shirt. After I opened the drafts of my e-mail program, I handed it over and said, "Make sure you check the time stamp on that so you know I'm not lying."

"Then maybe I should read it out loud."

"Go ahead."

She turned the phone sideways. "'Annika. I'm sitting in the locker room after the game, wishing I could just call you and explain this. But the fact remains, I lied to you. I swore I wouldn't do it again, and here I am. I'm not having a beer with the team tonight. I'm throwing the team a party. It's the price they demanded for my lie about not speaking English. Not ideal but it is what it is. One of those parameters is no WAGs at the party. Likely you'll hear about it, and then you'll be hurt and pissed off. I won't blame you. Maybe you'll even believe me when I tell you I didn't have a choice. There will be women around. But know that none of them will interest me. Because you interest me. That kiss tonight wasn't supposed to be for anyone but us. I hate that Peter turned it into a public moment. We've been hit-and-miss in the last week. And tonight I missed you. Sounds strange. Maybe you're even rolling your eyes, but I miss those bizarre questions you're so fond of asking. I apologize and I will offer you the same deal I offered my teammates—feel free to slip on a pair of skates and knock me on my ass on the ice. A.'"

She didn't look up from the phone for several long moments. Part of me wondered if she was weighing which body blow would do the most damage.

Annika glanced up. "Thank you. That does help clear things up."

I quietly exhaled.

"I have two things to ask you. First, did you know it was me right away?"

"Yes."

"How?"

"The way you carry yourself and your mannerisms." I let my gaze move across her body from her chest down to her toes and back up. "And that body. Maybe if you had worn something that covered you from the neck down. But the second you gave me your back and I saw your ass and the way you glanced back over your shoulder? I knew."

"I fooled everyone else."

"They don't matter."

"That rumbling-growl thing you do is sexy, but I will not be distracted from this last important thing." She cocked her head. "Does Igor really have a Gypsy curse on his dick or is that a bullshit line he uses to 'hex it and exit'?"

I blinked at her. "I have no idea what you said just now. Maybe try it again in English?"

"I'm serious, Axl. That's what Igor told Dallas. That his ex-girlfriend put a Gypsy curse on his dick and that's why he broke it off with her. Not that he broke off his *dick* with her, but he ended their relationship. And since Dallas is heavily into all that woo-woo stuff like tarot, cosmic signs, reading auras, spinning her chakras, and cleansing her whatever, she takes the Gypsy-curse thing *very* seriously. That is the main reason we're here incognito, not solely because I didn't trust you. Dallas wanted to see if Igor was cursing some other chick with his magic dick, and I couldn't let her come here alone."

I finally knew the definition of dumbfounded. "How much have you been drinking?"

When Annika closed her eyes and balled her fists, I decided I'd asked the wrong question.

"Sorry. It's so unlike you to go off on a rambling stream-of-consciousness rant, and it threw me. To be honest, I don't know about, uh . . . Igor's Gypsy curse. I haven't seen him with any women."

"Is Igor here tonight?"

I brought my hands back around to her face. "Annika. I don't want to talk about Igor anymore."

"What do you want to talk about?"

"I don't want to talk at all." I lowered my mouth to hers

and kissed her, taking my time. Slowly walking her backward until her back was against the wall behind the door. When I shifted my hand to stroke my thumb along the line of her jaw, my knuckles brushed the underside of the wig and I froze for a second. This wasn't the baby-soft silk of her hair drifting over my rougher skin.

"You flinched," she said against my lips.

"I wish I could rip this wig off." I kissed the corner of her mouth, then dead center on her lips. Then the opposite corner.

"You'll have to improvise," she said huskily as she sucked on my bottom lip. "Find another place to put your hands, since you can't run your fingers though my hair."

Screw using my hands. I'd use my mouth.

Palming her hips, I held them against the door as I bent my head to her chest. I pressed openmouthed kisses across the swells of her breasts, which popped over the square neckline of her blouse, back and forth until she started to squirm.

I started to use my tongue. Following the neckline, pushing my tongue into the valley of her cleavage, then taking tiny nips of that abundant flesh. A primal urge rolled through me like thunder, the need to score her skin with my teeth, suck on her until blood rose to the surface of her skin in the shape of my mouth, use the scratchy tip of my chin to mark her as mine.

She'd parted her legs enough that I could slip one thigh between them. I drove my quad up as I reconnected our mouths.

Her little gasp of surprise . . . sweetest damn thing I'd had on my tongue all day.

One of her hands twisted in my hair while the other hand slid up and down my chest from my collarbone to the waistband of my dress pants. She was scraping her nails deep into my skin on one pass, as if trying to tear through my shirt, and then on the next pass up her touch would turn tender, a sensual caress.

Annika began to grind against my thigh. Her kisses grew frenzied. Her fingers were tight on my scalp.

"Axl," she said softly after she'd ripped her mouth away from mine. "Stop. It's too much."

I put my lips on her ear. "Do you really want me to stop? I will. Or are you asking me to stop because you're surprised you forgot you were in a closet and I'm about to get you off when you're fully clothed?"

She groaned. "That one."

"You'll get over it." I rocked my hips closer to hers in short, fast thrusts, focused on giving her this, ignoring how my heart thundered.

Annika pressed her face into my neck and said, "Oh god, oh god, oh god, oh god." In the next moment, her entire body went rigid, and then she began to tremble in the aftermath.

My neck stung from the bite of her teeth. No doubt she'd left a mark. I didn't give a damn. Nor did I care my dick was hard and wasn't guaranteed any release. What a fucking rush that I could send her flying like that.

"Annika."

"Uh . . . Annika's brain has left the building."

I laughed softly. "Good. But it's that sexy mouth of hers I want right now."

She turned her head and looked up at me.

So freakin' weird to know it was her, but to see that beautiful face surrounded by curly brown hair.

She smirked. "You feel like you cheated on me, don't you?"

I smashed my mouth to hers—that was the only response that wouldn't start an argument.

"Now what?" she said, still rubbing her body against mine.

She was killing me. I craved more of this—her curves melting into the harder planes of my body. I forced myself to focus. "We'll have to leave one at a time and hope no one is paying attention."

"You first." She smacked my ass. "If it's not safe for me to come out, warn me."

"How?"

"Slip something under the door. Or make a whippoorwill call."

A whippoorwill call. Where did she come up with this stuff? "You watch too many spy movies." I opened the door and walked out, closing it behind me as if it wasn't odd at all that I'd spent the past fifteen minutes in a closet. I snagged a bottled water out of the ice bucket and realized things had gotten wilder in those fifteen minutes.

More of the guys were lounging at the tables. But without enough chairs, they'd doubled up—with some of the ladies sitting on their laps. Or two ladies sitting on their laps, or guys getting lap dances.

Someone had cranked the music up. Relf was getting his groove on with an English curler.

Flitte and McClellan had skipped the plastic cups and were drinking straight from the bottle of Jameson. Thank god they weren't dancing.

The married guys, the ones I'd been shocked to see show up, were arm-wrestling. The loser had to take a shot of Jäger and then defend a penalty shot against someone shooting rock-hard biscuits at him. I had no idea who'd created the game or who'd had the foresight to bring a bag of biscuits. The players appeared to be having fun. In fact, there was a waiting line to get in on it.

I scanned the room. The number of people in here had easily doubled. My gaze moved to the main doors. Where were the security guys? I started in that direction, only to be stopped by Martin. "Dude. You know how to throw a party."

"First and last. Enjoy it." I made it another ten meters when Igor stopped me.

First thing that popped into my head? Whether his dick was really cursed and deformed.

Thanks for that image, Annika.

"What?"

"Who invited the Flyers?"

I clapped Igor on the back. "Too much *wodka*, my friend. Go to your apartment and sleep it off."

Igor got in my face. "Russian always last man standing at party. Two Flyers are here in corner. With blonde."

The blonde was the one Annika had been talking to earlier. Then my gaze flicked to the two Philly rookies. What. The. Hell. "I don't freakin' know. I'll talk to security."

He snorted. "Do not bother. Women on knees polishing their nightsticks. Even gate guard outside holding his club, waiting his turn."

"So not only is the gate open to the entire city, but anyone can walk into this party." I'd had strict controls in place. Last minute by invitation only. Security at two separate places. No cell phones.

"Dallas."

"What?"

Igor pointed at the blonde. "That is her. He is touching her. He is dead." Then he ran at them, head down. Charging like a bull.

This party had to end now.

Before things got even more out of control.

That was when Bunny and the WAG posse stormed the place, screeching obscenities. A few of the stronger women started pulling the lap-dancing bunnies off men's laps. Kicking over chairs.

The married players continued to arm-wrestle as if their angry wives were not yelling in their ears.

Two guys who'd lost out on their lap dances and were spoiling for a fight noticed Igor whaling on the Flyers players. They jumped in to help.

Kazakov raced over and broke it up, but not before it got bloody.

A heated argument broke out between the ski jumper from Switzerland and Verily. Then between the alpine skiers and speed skaters.

It was like watching a snowball gather momentum. You knew it'd keep getting bigger and bigger and bring more and more people into it, but you had no idea how to stop it.

So I didn't move. I figured I deserved to get steamrolled.

Me and my brilliant fucking ideas.

I thought I'd have control here.

Someone moved in beside me. The brown hair threw me off for a fraction of a second.

"Holy shit. What happened?"

"WAGs waging war. Security is blowing off doing their job to get blown by a puck bunny—I guess they'd be a badge bunny now. Fistfights have broken out. Some people like them"—I leaned closer to her and pointed to Flitte and McClellan—"are just watching it explode while I'm wondering if I'll get kicked out of my apartment."

Annika was quiet for a moment. "There is a bright side, Axl."

"Which is?"

"No one will ever ask you to plan a party again."

I laughed. I faced her and kissed her, taking a moment to rest my forehead to hers. "Escape while you can, Attila."

"Have you seen Dallas? She's my ride."

"I think I saw Igor follow her outside a few minutes ago."

"Okay." She stepped back. "Is there anything I can do for you?"

"Just pick up when I call you. I might be in jail needing you to bail me out."

Nineteen

ANNIKA

Saturday morning I'd gone into the office to catch up on
things I never seemed to have time to finish during the
workweek. I'd shown up in my normal weekend wear: baggy
sweatpants, a long-sleeved T-shirt—Credit Dauphine today,
a nod to my stealth skills last night—and wool socks that I
wore with flip-flops. No makeup, especially nothing on my
eyes. I'd had a slight reaction to the eyeliner Dallas had used
on me. And even after I'd removed it last night, I woke this
morning with red streaks on my eyelids and beneath my lash
lines. And to top off my fashion statement, I'd slicked my hair
back in a retro '80s banana hair clip. My head itched like
crazy after wearing a wig last night. I looked like a refugee,
but I didn't care. Who'd see me?

Note to self: Even thinking those words is akin to daring
fate to see how much it can piss with you.

Around eleven a.m. the text messages on my phone started

to blow up, forcing me to go online to see what the buzz was. First I read the *Twin Cities Daily Reader* headline:

MEMBERS OF THE WILD HAVE A WILD LATE NIGHT IN MINNEAPOLIS

A private party celebrating the first win of the season for the hockey team took a bizarre turn late Friday night, when the police were called to break up numerous fights, including an altercation between pro snowboarder Martin Michaels and hockey player Axl Hammerquist.

I stopped scrolling. What the hell had happened after I left? Axl and Martin had gotten into an actual fight? Martin defined the mellow, stoner, "bitchin' powder, dude" type of athlete. Axl would wipe the floor with him. And they were best buds anyway. I kept scrolling.

Neither man sustained injuries serious enough to require medical attention. Hammerquist admitted to authorities he was solely responsible for hosting the party and "Things got a little out of hand." While Hammerquist confirmed the rumor that two members of the Philadelphia team that had lost earlier in the night to the Wild had crashed the party and that contributed to increased tensions, Hammerquist refused to comment on the identity of the woman he was seen with at the party (see picture) and refused to answer any questions on the status of his relationship with Annika Lund.

I enlarged the image. Someone had taken a shot in the main room when Axl had kissed me.

Oh no. No, no, no, no, no.

Talk about damning. All you could see of me was my profile and curly brown hair and Axl's lips pressed to mine. For once, Axl hadn't thought twice about it. I'd said something to make him smile and he kissed me to show his gratitude and cement our connection.

That was it.

But it was not what it looked like. At all.

It would be so freaking funny that the media were speculating that Axl was cheating on me . . . *with* me . . . except for the fact that the whole point of this PR campaign was to change his image.

To complicate matters even more, there was no way I could come forward and say, *"Well, I knew Axl was lying to me about something, so my cousin and I disguised ourselves and crashed a private party to see if we could catch him lying in the act."*

Not only would my mistrust of Axl look bad, but I'd come across as a total flake. I'd worked hard to build my reputation working for Lund Industries on my own merits outside of being a Lund heiress.

Tempting to beat my head into my desk, but my brain already hurt.

I cleared my browsing history before I shut down my computer. Then I powered off my phone. I'd deal with all that when I got home.

In an effort to curtail the workaholic tendencies that plagued the Lund family, my uncle Archer had recently instituted a lockdown of the executive facilities on the weekends. No access to our private parking garage. That was a huge perk, especially in the winter. It really made me consider if I needed to be in the office at all—which was the whole point.

I took the stairs to the lobby level and exited the main front entrance.

Reporters were lying in wait for me . . . which was a totally new experience. One I never wanted to repeat.

"Miss Lund, will you comment on the picture of your boyfriend kissing another woman?"

Keep walking.

"Just a few hours earlier, 'The Hammer' kissed you and it was broadcast inside the arena on the kiss cam. Did you have a fight after the game?"

Do not respond.

"Are you and 'The Hammer' calling it quits?"

Do not comment.

"Given 'The Hammer's' reputation, were you surprised that he was caught with another woman?"

There is no other woman!

"Miss Lund, care to comment on your appearance today? Is this the look of a brokenhearted and devastated woman?"

That stopped me. I looked up.

Mistake.

Cameras whirred.

Thankfully I was only a few steps from my car.

I hopped in and burned rubber getting away from them.

The first shitty pictures showed up online a few hours later.

Red eyes that looked as if I'd been crying for hours?

Check.

Bag lady clothing and downtrodden appearance?

Check.

Slumped posture as I exited the building?

Check.

Look of utter devastation at the reporters' line of questioning?

Check.

But since I hadn't commented on any of the articles or

answered questions, they couldn't speculate beyond publishing the sad-sack pictures of me.

I'd gotten one text from Axl.

AH: Coach is mad about the party. We're in media blackout until tomorrow's game is over, so this has to be fast. Peter said he can't get in touch with you. I've told him to back off. We will deal with this when I get back. I'll call you as soon as I can. Take care. You are on my mind, Attila. Be strong. And laugh. Between us? It is sort of funny that I'm cheating on you . . . with you ☺

At least Axl and I could both see some of the humor in it . . . for now.

B y Sunday afternoon, I considered pitching my phone off my balcony. It'd probably make a very satisfying crack when it shattered on the pavement below.

But it was the only way Axl and I were keeping in touch. I hated this for him.

Except he was playing great hockey according to the stats I saw—and didn't completely understand—on *SportsCenter*. That forced him into being part of the press conference on Saturday night. He said "no comment" to anything besides a question on hockey. They played tonight in Anaheim, so maybe I'd actually get to talk to him on the phone.

My phone rang. Even before the second set of drumbeats to ABBA's "Does Your Mother Know?"—I knew it was her. Not only because I'd been avoiding my entire family, but because it was game day. "Hey, Mom. Go ahead and put me on speaker. I know you guys are pregaming."

"Are you all right?" she said in English.

"Besides my phone blowing up with messages from snoopy people I haven't heard from in years? Besides the press camping out at LI and snapping pictures of me in my Saturday worst? Besides that? I'm great. Happy that I can get food delivery until this dies down."

"Hiding is not like you, Annika. We send car service to pick you up in your garage and bring you to the game. A hoodie will keep you incongruous."

"You mean . . . inconspicuous."

"Yah. Whatever. You need to be with your family."

"It's Jensen's game day. That's probably where they'll look for me—if any reporters are still on the trail. So I'll pass."

"You are not avoiding us because you are red-eyed monster?"

"No!" Did she mean green-eyed monster?

"Show me. We FaceTime. Now." She held the phone away. "Ward! Which button is for face flipper?"

"Mom! Listen to me. Seriously. I. Am. Fine. I'm not crying. I am not jealous."

She snorted. "Of course you are not boohooing. You and Axl are PR couple, not real couple. But he reverted to bad-boy Axl, making you look like chimp—"

"You mean chump?"

"Yah. Whatever. But I worry you sit home alone, getting angrier with him and turning into red-eyed vengeance-seeking Valkyrie that plots to tear off his twig and berries with your claws and bathe in his blood beneath cheery moon."

Silence.

Then in the background I heard my dad say, "Selka. For the love of Odin, you are banned from watching those Swedish arthouse films. And I'm pretty sure it's *cherry* moon, not cheery moon."

"Have a great game, but I am definitely hanging up now . . ." And I did.

AXL

Jorgen took the seat beside me on the bus. "You all right?" he said in Finnish.

"Tired. Ribs hurt. You?"

"I got clocked in the jaw at some point, so it's sore."

I smirked and turned my head toward him, miming a blow job. "You sure you don't remember how your jaw got *sore*?"

"Piss off."

Jorgen was gay. In the closet. I didn't care how he lived his life. I knew only because he and I had come up through the AHL at the same time and I spoke Finnish, so I'd overheard a conversation he'd assumed was private. He'd gotten transferred to the Wild last season, so during travel days we'd been catching up.

"Still dealing with the fallout from your party?" he asked.

"Hit me in the head with your stick if I ever agree to that again."

"Gladly. So, the brunette?"

"Not a topic of conversation," I snapped.

"The Swede has a temper off the ice. Call the press," he said drolly.

"Fuck off, Finn. Why are you annoying me?"

"I wanted to ask about a guy I met at the party. A fellow Finn. Boris someone. I couldn't tell if he was giving me a . . . signal."

I shrugged. "Could be."

"So he's not in a relationship?"

"Mostly he's in a relationship with pot. He shows up to play video games at my place a lot. You could come hang out and see what's there."

He grinned at me. "Cool. I'll do that. Thanks."

After he left I moved over a seat as a sign that I didn't want anyone to join me.

It'd been a rough couple of days—on the ice and off.

Starting with the game Friday night.

Then the stupid party I'd agreed to afterward.

And my frustration with the situation with Annika. I needed her in my bed. We'd be good together, but I didn't want to screw things up with her, because I really liked her. Not pretend PR liked her, but liked her for real, which for some reason she didn't believe. So by her not trusting me, she'd screwed things up by showing up in that wig. And because I couldn't seem to keep my mouth off her, I'd kissed her, which ended up being a problem.

Everyone had seen me kiss the brunette. No one except Igor had known it was Annika.

Immediately after Annika had left with Dallas, Martin started shit with me about cheating.

By that time the Wild WAGs were yelling at me for throwing a secret party and some bunnies told the wives it wasn't any of their business because they hadn't been invited and the hair pulling started.

The neighbors from the building across from ours had had enough and showed up to shout at us in person.

Verily got in a Danish curler's face; more girl fighting ensued, which gave my teammates wood. So they were pissed off when the skiers from Switzerland tried to break up the girl fight. Insults flew about hockey players being talentless hacks and then it was on. Even the guys from Philly joined in.

Mass fucking chaos.

Right about then Martin sucker-punched me.

I told him to back off and he kept coming. So his second punch earned him a headlock.

That was when the police arrived.

I spent the next two hours sorting things out with the cops. Another hour dealing with the building and the property manager, signing promissory notes for cleanup and damages. By then I had three hours of sleep before I had to get packed to leave for two days on the road. So I'd been so busy dealing with my end of things—from my teammates assuring me it was the best party ever, to Coach informing me I was personally responsible for the full media blackout after the angry WAGs' phone calls, and media attention—that I hadn't considered that pictures of me kissing Annika as a brunette might show up in public.

When Peter had forwarded me the link to the article with the pictures, before Coach had confiscated our phones, Igor had stopped me from beating the hell out of my locker with my fists.

I knew this one would be bad and maybe there'd be no PR solution.

I also knew that getting angry didn't serve any purpose off the ice.

Whole different story during the game.

So at least I had that going for me.

The bus pulled up to the hotel.

Coach stood at the front of the bus before the driver opened the door. "You can pick up your phones when you get your room assignments, ladies."

I didn't pay attention to the people in the lobby until Kaz moved to stand beside me.

"Got yourself a fan club."

"What?"

He angled his head to the left. "Over there."

I looked. AXL spelled out in huge glittery letters. The last sign read, "You're a player—act like one! #noshame #cantcheatifyourenottieddown #practicesexualdiversitywithme"

"I'm not really seeing that."

"Forgiveness is a beautiful thing, isn't it?"

"Fuck off."

Kaz laughed.

I grabbed my key and my cell—dead, of course—and avoided eye contact with the sign holders when I passed by to the elevators.

In the room, after I plugged my phone in, I immediately placed a room service order for poached salmon, a double order of rice, steamed broccoli and sparkling water. Then I showered and dressed in workout clothes, and my food arrived. As I sat on my bed, in my room, eating alone, in silence, I wondered if this was how the next eight months would go. I loved hockey, the games, the practices, but this . . . not so much.

After I finished eating, I stared at Annika's number for several long moments before I called her.

She answered before the second ring. "Axl?"

"Did I wake you?"

"No. I hoped you'd call."

"Need the sound of my voice to lull you to sleep?"

"Yes. Please start explaining all the different penalties in a regulation hockey game, the exceptions and the rare exclusions, because I guarantee that will have me sawing logs like a lumberjack."

I laughed.

"So. I watched the game tonight."

"And?"

"And you won. What else matters?"

"How did we look?"

She sighed. "Dude. You look amazing skating around out there. You know that it gets me hot."

"You never told me that before."

"Yes, I did," she retorted. "Many times. Like when I relayed my fantasy about you skating around without a shirt on?"

"Can you blame me for blocking that out?"

"See? Even when I pay you a compliment, you don't believe it." Another heavy sigh. "So, how *did* you get to be such a stud on blades?"

"My mother was trying to piss my father off." Right after I said that, I wondered if I was more exhausted than I imagined, because I never talked about this.

Annika was quiet for a moment. "I don't want this to sound accusatory. You always say I don't trust you. But there's so much I don't know about you, Axl, that I wish you trusted me enough to tell me." She paused and added, "If you don't want to, that's cool too, no pressure. I just wanted to mention it."

"It would be new territory for me. Talking about my family."

"Not to put you on the spot, but where do you see this going with us? Because if you truly want to build on the publicity stunt and turn it into something real, this is the kind of thing we'd share. And you already know some of this stuff about me. I realize it is not a competition, but if it was? I'd totally be kicking your ass in the family-confession section of the relationship."

She'd just said the perfect thing. "Annika."

"What?"

"I . . ."

"Why are you so hesitant?"

"I'm trying to come up with a way to say I'm so fucking crazy about you without scaring you off."

"You're not scaring me off."

"Remember you said that." I took a deep breath. "So . . . where to start. My parents never married. My mother is this serious architect and somehow she ended up in a romance—affair, whatever—with my father, who was a football—soccer—player. She got pregnant and after she had me they couldn't make it work, because my father never stopped fucking around."

"Whoa. Back up. Your father is a professional soccer player . . . where?"

"He played in Milan. He's retired now and lives in Italy."

"Axl. Your dad is, like . . . famous, isn't he?"

I closed my eyes and stretched my arms above my head. "Yes. He's probably the most famous player in Sweden. He won two World Cups playing for Milan and he won an Olympic gold medal."

"Holy shit. I'm totally Googling him."

I laughed. "What's his last name?"

"It's not Hammerquist, is it?"

"No. This is where all the pawn stuff started. My mother refused to give me his name. I hardly ever saw him until he retired. Even then . . . not that much."

"Makes sense now why you were sympathetic about the situation with Lucy," she murmured.

"So my mother decided when I was three to put me in figure skating lessons. I could only imagine that she did it thinking it'd somehow embarrass my father if I did well at it. But there were two problems with that line of thinking. First, I didn't have his last name. Second, figure skaters and hockey players practice on the same rink at that age."

Annika laughed. "You saw the sticks and realized you could be knocking people down and hitting a puck? From there I'm sure you were all . . . Sign. Me. Up."

"Yes. Except my mother would only let me join hockey if I continued to take figure skating lessons. So I did both for several years."

"That's why you're such a fantastic skater."

"Honestly? Yes."

"Did you compete as a figure skater?"

"Some."

"This is the *lagom* thing, isn't it? Just be honest. You have a shit ton of trophies."

"Yes, I have a shit ton of trophies."

"Do you have any of those onesie leotard things? Because those are smoking hot, especially if they're cut to your navel."

"Even if I did have one, do you think I'd admit it? No freakin' way."

She blew a raspberry at me.

I laughed.

"At least tell me one of the songs you skated to."

"'In the Hall of the Mountain King' by—"

"Grieg. I love that song. It's epic. What about modern songs? Like—"

"You suggest an ABBA tune and I'm hanging up," I warned.

"Dude. Don't get so defensive. I love ABBA. I was going to say The Hives."

"I prefer Swedish thrash metal, but they frowned on that in competition."

"Where are your trophies now?"

"Storage."

"So, your parents . . . are they super proud that you're a pro hockey player?"

I felt my cheeks heat. "No. They're embarrassed that I make my living being a brute. Soccer is refined. So is being an architect."

"No wonder you don't talk about them. They sort of sound like douche canoes."

I chuckled. "What is a douche canoe?"

"Worse than an asshat, but not as bad as a twat waffle."

"You have a way with words, Annika. Talking to you . . . soothes me, if that makes sense."

"It does."

"But it revs me up too."

"You've done that with great success. In a storage closet and you didn't even use your hands, remember?"

"Vividly." I groaned. "Was that two months ago?"

"Feels like it. But it was just two nights ago."

I yawned.

She said, "I heard that."

"Sorry. I'm wiped out."

"Don't apologize. I'm just really glad you called. I miss you. I like talking to you, Axl. Especially when there are no interruptions."

"I like that too. But next time I see you? No talking. No interruptions. And most important. No clothes."

"When did you say you'd be back?"

"Tomorrow. Good night, Annika."

Twenty

ANNIKA

I opted to work from home on Monday. One of the perks of being the boss.

Not that I was truly working.

I had hit the gym for the third day in a row. After showering, I slipped on my favorite baggy fleece sweatpants, a U of M T-shirt and a flannel shirt I'd stolen from Walker. When I had no intention of leaving my house, comfort always won over style.

In an effort to stay offline, I queued up the first season of a TV show I'd wanted to watch but hadn't gotten around to. Nothing like binge-watching TV for total distraction. It also kept me from checking the time on my phone every couple of minutes.

Since Friday night, I'd listened to the phone calls from Brady, Lennox, Dallas, Ash, Nolan. Nothing from Jensen or Jaxson, but like Axl, they were in travel mode. Likewise for

Walker and Trinity. We all knew they'd sneak off and get married and make the announcement after the fact.

The only call I returned was to Dallas, warning her not to breathe a word of our crashing the party in disguises. She argued vehemently about my decision not to make a public statement. She thought the public would find the wig and clandestine meeting in the closet funny and romantic. Maybe people would, but Axl and I needed to talk things through first.

I'd just finished the fourth episode of the show—too bad life's problems weren't as easily solved within a forty-eight-minute time frame—when the doorbell rang.

My pulse spiked and I forced myself not to run. If I checked the peephole and it wasn't Axl on the other side, I would . . .

"Annika. Let me in."

I entered the alarm code, and the locks disengaged. I barely had the door open before Axl was through it, slamming it shut and pushing me up against the wall.

His hands framed my face. "Have you been all right?"

"I'm glad you're here." I wreathed my arms around his neck and locked my eyes with his. "We've spent so much time together over the past month that I miss you when you're not around to drive me crazy—"

Axl covered my lips with his. He fed me long, sweet, slow kisses while his thumbs gently stroked my cheekbones.

When he finally relinquished my mouth, he left me breathless, mindless and completely turned on. "So, what now?"

"We could talk." Axl kissed the corner of my lips. Then my jaw. Then the spot below it on my neck. "We probably need to talk. But all I can think about is taking you to bed and not talking about anything."

A wave of desire washed over me.

"Does that head-to-toe body shiver mean yes?" he murmured.

"Yes."

I felt his exhale—as if he'd been holding his breath—drift across the side of my jaw.

Then his mouth was on mine again. This kiss turned a little more intense as he loomed over me.

My fingers twisted in his hair as his hands journeyed down, stopping to mold his big hands around the weight of my breasts.

Everywhere he touched me, I ached for more.

But he wasn't in a hurry.

Why wasn't he in a hurry?

I wanted to strip him, taste him, feel his every rippling muscle tightening against mine as we moved together in a tangle of arms and legs.

His lips journeyed up to my ear. "You and me." He tugged on my earlobe with his teeth. "Naked. Now."

I shivered at the rasping command in his tone. "Yes."

"For the next two days, I will be all over you." He paused and repeated, "All over you," just in case I hadn't understood the first time.

"As much as you want."

"Annika." Axl trapped my face in his hands and tilted my head back so he could stare into my face.

For just a moment, I let myself get lost in the depths of his glacial blue eyes. Had I ever imagined this hue to be as icy and remote as the water surrounding some far-off fjord? Because right now all I saw was fiery blue—the very hottest and most dangerous part of a flame.

"We'll have time to talk later, but I need you to know this right now. This is not casual."

With that, my massive crush on him veered from like into something more.

"Meaning . . . I shouldn't frantically start shortening my naked-in-bed-with-Axl wish list because I've only got two days to get through it?"

He blinked at me. "How long is the list?"

"I'm pretty sure it's from here to Stockholm long."

His mouth crashed down on mine as he picked me up and crushed me to his chest. In the next moment we were moving toward my bedroom.

Not that he knew where it was.

He hadn't taken off his coat.

Or his snow boots.

I ripped his winter cap off his head and ruffled my fingers through his thick mane.

And the way he kissed me . . . it was like he wasn't thinking of anything else. As if kissing me required all his concentration.

We kept kissing until we literally hit the brick wall at the end of the hallway.

I said, "Oops, we passed my bedroom."

Axl set me down.

I took his hand and we backtracked.

My loft apartment was open concept, high ceilings with metal rafters, exposed brick, lots of windows. My bedroom, decorated entirely in shades of blue from sapphire to a pearly gray, was enormous with a king-sized bed on a platform in the center of the space. Off to the left was a large sitting area that led to a private balcony. I had a few dressers and built-in bookshelves but no closet—instead I'd opted for a walk-in dressing room, accessible behind the sitting area. My master bathroom didn't even have a door, but with long walls blocking the entire thing from view of the bedroom, it afforded me complete privacy and the openness I needed.

But as soon as we entered my bedroom, I had a sudden bout of shyness.

Axl sensed it. I heard the zipper on his coat and then the rustle of cloth as he tossed it aside. Then *thud, thud* as his boots hit the floor. I hoped he didn't get completely naked, because I'd wanted to peel some of his clothes off.

Then that warm mouth was on the side of my neck and his hands were curled around my biceps. "Show me your bedroom."

"Okay." My face was still flushed from kissing him and my mouth seemed extra dry. He kept his hands on my arms as I walked to the sitting area, composed of a love seat and a wingback chair on one side of a wood coffee table with a barrel-shaped tufted velvet chair opposite it. "So this is the sitting area."

"Nice. What's through there?"

"Master bathroom."

"Show me."

The long wall on the left opened up into the main space. A gigantic walk-in shower, a corner garden tub, a double vanity and—

"Is that a sauna?" Axl asked.

"Yes."

"I recognize that it's a top-of-the-line model made in Sweden. How do you like it?"

"I've never used it."

He turned me around. "Why not?"

"Claustrophobia, remember? I know it's a waste, but I'm afraid the door would get stuck if I was here by myself, and that'd be the worst way to die—"

He briefly pressed his lips to mine. "You trust me if you're about to get naked with me, right?"

"Yes."

Another kiss, longer, more seductive. "Don't. Move."

When Axl opened the sauna door and disappeared inside, the scent of cedar drifted out. Pipes started clanking inside the walls and I heard the hiss of water. Then he stepped out, shut the door and grabbed two towels from the top of the cabinet, hanging them on the warmer outside. "Now. Where were we?"

"You were about to take off your shirt."

He did that "I'm so sexy I can reach behind my head and whip off my shirt with one hand" move that was so freaking hot that I would've jumped him if I'd had any breath left in my lungs, but . . . nope.

Seeing Axl Hammerquist shirtless? Pretty much rendered me breathless and speechless.

Seeing Axl Hammerquist shirtless in my bathroom pretty much made my life complete.

I think I whispered, "Seriously?" when I finally picked my jaw up off the tile.

"What?"

I managed to tear my eyes away from the ripped and muscled chest on display. "How am I supposed to compete with that?"

His brow furrowed. "I don't understand."

"Omigod, Axl. You are this perfect masculine specimen that could be featured in an anatomy textbook for what the ultimate male upper body is supposed to look like—"

"So you are impressed?"

"Yes."

"And just think . . . I haven't even taken off my pants yet." I looked up at him. "Cocky much?"

He laughed. "We are getting off track. Come here."

As soon as we were within kissing distance, he kissed me, but he didn't let me touch him. He rekindled the fire between us and with every breath I felt the anticipation and desire build again.

He faced me toward the sauna and said, "Lift your arms." As soon as I did, he removed my shirt.

I closed my eyes as his hands roamed all over my back, from the waistband of my sweats to the band of my bra. Up my spine, across my shoulders and down my arms, his breath was fast and hot in my ear when he pulled me back against his naked chest.

Then his big hands spanned my hips, moving up to circle my ribs and finally higher to cup my breasts. He lazily stroked the lace edge of my bra with the tips of his fingers and then popped the clasp so there was no fabric barrier between my skin and his.

A rough sound rumbled from him when he turned me around. I let my head fall back as he lowered his mouth to mine, loving the brush of his lips and the ends of his hair across my skin. Loving the rougher squeeze of his hands.

"Annika," he said, kissing a path up my throat.

"Mmm?"

"The sauna is ready." He nipped my jawbone. "Are you?"

My eyes flew open.

I was ready. My body certainly was. But that wasn't all we needed. "I forgot to buy—"

"I brought some." He nuzzled my temple. "But if you need more time . . ."

I wasn't super bold when it came to taking the lead with sex, so my heart beat quadruple time when I grabbed his hand. I said, "Check my readiness for yourself," and slipped his fingers beneath the elastic band of my sweatpants.

Axl took it from there.

Next thing I knew, my sweatpants were off, his pants were gone, he had a condom in his hand and we were in the sauna.

I had a panicked moment when Axl closed the door.

Heat billowed around us.

I couldn't breathe.

But it wasn't dark.

Axl set my hands on his chest. "Think about this. Touch me any way you want."

He maneuvered us backward until he sat on the bench and I stood in front of him. He'd slipped the condom on while I was distracted by his chest. Good thing. Because I totally would've been distracted by that bad boy slapping his eight-pack. Holy crap.

Axl pressed his lips on my sternum between my breasts. "Annika. It's fucking killing me not to be inside you."

I placed a knee on either side of his thighs. I locked my gaze to his as I lowered myself over him.

When there was no more space between us, he kissed the hell out of me as he began to move.

The heat, the steam, the slippery glide of our sweat-slicked bodies . . . I felt like I was drowning in him. In this intensity between us. In this intimacy we shared. In this connection I'd never had with another man. And I never wanted to surface from the overwhelming sensations.

I could get addicted to Axl's lips and tongue and teeth on my skin.

Kissing.

Teasing.

Licking.

Biting.

Sucking.

Oh, the sucking. The soft bit of pressure he applied to the hollow beneath my ear as he steadily stroked deeper inside me.

One hand tightly gripping my hair.

His other big hand clamped on to my hip, his thumb gently caressing and alternately pressing into my hip bone.

"Annika," he murmured against my throat, "let me take you there."

"I don't want this to end." I licked a stream of sweat dripping from his temple. "You feel so good."

He groaned. "I cannot last forever."

"We can do this again later, right?"

"As many times as you want," he panted.

I squeezed my legs more tightly around his waist, digging

my heels into the muscles of his ass as he flexed and released with every upward thrust. "Oh. Yes. Please. Don't ever, ever, ever stop doing that."

He didn't.

And I imploded. Exploded. Went supernova. Whatever. Tingling, stinging, throbbing, pulsating—I had it all happening at one time and it was glorious.

That was when Axl reached that blinding peak.

His body, corded with hard muscle, went even more rigid beneath me. His steady movements turned frenzied. He kept me imprisoned against his big body as pleasure shuddered through him. Almost as if he was afraid to let me see how strongly this affected him.

Wrong.

He and I would have a serious talk about that later.

When I wasn't a limp noodle.

Axl tilted my head back and found my mouth. And the kiss he gave me . . . defied description. It made me a little weepy because I knew this had been more than just sex, or us slaking our mutual lust. I could let the moment go without saying anything, which would be easiest, or I could toss out something flip, which he'd probably appreciate, or I could take a real chance. I swallowed hard.

"Axl?"

"Yah?"

"I like you. The more time I spend with you, the more things I learn to like about you. I don't want to screw this up."

He exhaled and slowly ran his hand up my back in a loving gesture that brought more tears to my eyes. "I couldn't have said that any better, Annika." He kissed my temple. "Let's dry off and crawl into bed for a bit. Then we'll talk."

Twenty-one

AXL

I finally got it.

Why guys wanted to be with one woman.

I had found her. Something had just clicked with Annika. A connection. A bridge.

If I was honest, it had been there from the moment we met. It just took a while for the cement to set.

"Axl."

"Hmm?"

"I really, really, really love your body. Like hard-core love."

"You can massage it like this anytime you like."

She wasn't massaging it so much as using my back as her personal canvas as she traced invisible lines, squiggles and circles across the breadth of it. I'd rather have this kind of reverent caress. Massages weren't anything special for me. The way Annika touched me . . . I didn't remember that I'd ever been touched that way.

She pressed a kiss between my shoulder blades. "You are so warm."

"We were just in the sauna."

"That was awesome, by the way."

"Beyond awesome."

She stopped drawing figure eights. "Really?"

I rolled over to bring us face-to-face. "Where's the doubt coming from?"

"From the same place every woman's doubt comes from." She locked her gaze to mine. "Experience. Or lack thereof."

"Or too much?" I said, trying not to sound snappish.

"Maybe." She closed her eyes. "I don't want to do this."

So don't. But I knew this was how she processed and dealt with things. And like it or not, I had to deal with it her way if I wanted to understand her. "Talk to me, Princess."

"You are gorgeous, sexy, athletic and built, Axl. I've never been with a guy like you. You have the kind of experience where I worry I'll never be able to keep up, let alone measure up. And it sucks because I like you. A lot. That was before you rocked my world in the sauna. So I'm glad we got to know each other before we hit the sheets, because I think that gives me an advantage—"

I covered her mouth with mine and kissed her until she slumped back against the mattress. After I ended the kiss, I propped myself on my elbow beside her and draped my leg over hers to keep her in place. "One thing at a time, okay?"

"Okay."

"I'm not an expert at anything except hockey. And some days even that is questionable. I never gave a damn if women talked about me being a stud in bed. To be blunt, I used them as much as they used me." I pushed her hair off her forehead. "You think any of them ever asked me what my favorite candy was when I was eight? You think any of them would've had a second date with me if I had picked them up in a piece-of-shit Volvo the first time?"

Annika laughed.

"None of them would've read me the menu if they thought I couldn't decipher it. None of them would've made me a sandwich that reminded me of home." I leaned down and kissed her very thoroughly. "Annika, you are gorgeous, sexy, and super hot and I've never been with a woman like you. You're giving, thoughtful, funny and kind and I worry I'll never measure up." I rolled on top of her with my knees positioned by her hips and my arms beside her head. "Or do I need to take another stab at proving just how hot and sexy and perfect you are?"

She let her gaze travel down the front of my naked body to my groin. She licked her lips.

"Annika," I growled.

"What? I'm giving the matter serious consideration."

"You do that. I'll do this." I planted kisses down the center of her throat.

"So you missed my bizarre questions, huh?"

I groaned. Maybe I could distract her. I angled my head and ran the tip of my tongue around her right nipple, until the pink tip grew tight. I'd started to suck when Annika pulled my hair in a half-assed attempt to get me to stop. I looked up at her. "Ask your questions. I'll answer them, but I'll be touching you as I do so."

"How am I supposed to concentrate?"

I grinned at her and pulled her nipple deeper into my mouth.

She made a very soft, very feminine sigh and gentled her hold on my hair. "Last night you said your mother and father never married. Do you have brothers or sisters?"

I dragged my lips across the underswell of her breast. Her

skin was so pale here. So soft. So sweet. "My mother married when I was twelve. She and her husband, Lars, had a daughter two years later."

"Do you consider her your sister?"

"Yes." I pressed a kiss to each of her delicate ribs. "I don't know her that well because of our age difference. I finished school at sixteen, started university and traveled Europe playing hockey. Then I came to the U.S., but I do see her when I go home if she's not off performing."

"What's her name?"

"Birget." I slid my hand down the curve of Annika's hip. Her skin was perfectly smooth right here. I wanted to rub my face against—

"What does she perform?"

I looked up at her. "You weren't kidding about the questions."

"Axl." She dragged the tips of her fingers down the side of my face. "I know some things about you, but there is a lot I don't know. Things that are important. You know my family is important to me, so you had to expect I'd want to know more about yours."

I tried not to bristle. Not everyone had a family like hers. Not everyone wanted one. There wasn't anything wrong with being content with the way things were. The last concept would be the hardest for her to understand. Her family talked out issues. Tried to fix things. My family . . . to say they didn't care seemed cold, but it was closer to the truth than saying we brushed issues under the rug.

"Okay, my family. My mother, Malla Hammerquist, is one of Sweden's premier architects. She has an advanced degree in engineering and is a senior project manager at one of the most respected companies in Sweden. She married Lars Kagg. He's a scientist and holds several patents and in his spare time is an adviser to the Nobel Committee. Birget is a child prodigy on the piano. She's studied all over the world, and to be honest, I don't even know if she lives in Stockholm on a regular basis. Then there's my father, Bjorn Landberg, footballer extraordinaire, who, on top of all the records he holds in Sweden in the junior leagues, played for AC Milan and won two World Cups and a bunch of other championships as well as a gold medal in the Olympics. He never married, has no other children, but he did purchase a vineyard in Italy with his millions. Oh, an interesting historical fact about the Landberg family. They are what's referred to as 'unintroduced nobility' in Sweden, meaning they are one of the oldest recorded families in national history, dating back to the 1300s. They are not of noble birth, but they are welcomed at the Swedish Royal Court. So there are no titles in the Landberg family, but my father and his brother, as well as my cousin, have been invited to functions with the King and Queen of Sweden and the royal family on several occasions.

"And then there's me, Annika. 'The Hammer.' I'm a genetic throwback. I'm athletic—but I'm not compactly built like my father. I didn't choose a civilized and beloved sport like soccer. I'm smart—but I'm not brilliant like my mother. Although I managed to earn a mechanical engineering degree, when my hockey career is over I intend to 'waste' it working on cars. I have always been 'out of sight, out of mind' for my parents. They don't think about me, because I've never been a problem. I've been focused on hockey—it's all I've ever cared about because it's been the only constant in my life. They did provide for me. They neither supported my life choices nor denounced them. At least publicly. They've disapproved privately. I do not hear from my mother unless I've done something that has caught her interest on the other side of the world. When the video of the two blondes was posted? She called me and said she was disappointed to see proof that I'd turned out to be exactly like my father. And I can't honestly remember the last time I even saw my father. Does any of this bother me? Not as much as you might think. I don't have the kind of relationship with my family that you do. I worry that will be what bothers you most about this. I don't want you to see me like they do."

When I saw the look of shock on Annika's face, I feared I'd just made a huge mistake. I'd never told anyone this much about my family life and history. Peter knew, of course, but he kept it from being part of my bio. I'd been in one semiserious relationship in college. When my girlfriend found out my father's name, she hounded me to change my name to his so I could reap all the benefits. It took me two months, but I figured out she thought I'd end up with some kind of title, and she'd be a princess if she married me or some stupid thing. After that, I didn't mention it to anyone.

I started to get up from the bed.

But Annika jumped me. "Oh no, Mr. Big Bad Hockey Player. You don't get to tell me that and then do a breakaway. First of all, you should know that nothing you tell me about your family will change how I see *you*."

My gut unclenched a little.

"Second of all, I'm glad you don't go out of your way to try to please them. They are missing out. Doesn't sound like you're missing out on much by doing your own thing."

My eyes searched hers, and the ferocity I saw surprised me. She wasn't saying this because she felt sorry for me.

"Third of all . . ." She whapped me on the chest. "You're an engineer? You didn't think you could've *mentioned* that at some point? Because how is it fair that you're this massively talented hockey star and now I find out you have a damn math brain too?"

Annika Lund, I think I love you.

"Just for that oversight, I oughta make you fix Dallas's car. It is such a piece of junk. After we left the party the other night, I swore we were going to break down on the side of the road."

"I'm not working on cars as in fixing them. I'm working on them as in . . . designing them."

She smirked. "Like Volvos?"

"I interned there for a semester. It's a great company. I own a Volvo." Then I proceeded to tell her everything about the model I owned that was different than what she could buy in the States.

"You are totally a car guy, aren't you?"

"Yes. I try to spend a few weeks of my off-season working at the auto facility my engineering professor's friend owns in Ängelholm."

Her face went somber. "Axl, I've grown up around car guys. My brothers and my cousins are all collectors. So I know more than a little about cars. And I think you're about to tell me that you've actually been inside the Koenigsegg Factory?"

"Not only have I been in the factory? I've worked there. I've seen some of the upcoming designs. And brace yourself, but I own one."

She gasped. "You *own* a Koenigsegg?"

"Yes. A CCX."

"Is it here? In the States?"

"Yes, you were very close to it at the party. It has its own private garage in my apartment complex."

"No offense, because you are a sex god, but I think I just had a mini-orgasm."

I chuckled.

"Those are the sexiest cars in the world."

"I agree. The power is incredible."

"Will you take me for a ride?"

I brought her mouth to mine and kissed her until she was writhing against me. Then I rolled her onto her back. "All this talk of rides . . ." I reached for the box of condoms I'd placed on the bedside table.

"Let me," she said, knocking my hand away and pulling out a package.

I'd braced myself above her, allowing her just enough room to snake her hand between us. When her fingers closed around me with a delicate, but sexy "I want this *now*" tug, I hissed in a breath.

Annika arched up as I drove into her hard.

No rush. Make it last. That's what she wanted last time.

The sting of her fingernails digging into my ass as I moved, the nip of her teeth on my throat, the feel of her fingers in my hair, just about overloaded every pleasure point I possessed and I had to chant *slow, slow, slow* in my head so I didn't go into beast mode on her.

Then she pulled my hair, forcing me to look at her.

"Show me," she said in a husky whisper.

"Show you what?"

"How you got the nickname 'The Hammer.'" She licked my throat. "It's a sturdy bed. I'm a sturdy girl. Give me Hammer-time."

That was when I knew.

I definitely loved this woman.

Twenty-two

ANNIKA

After spending two spectacular days alone with Axl, I was ready to face the world again.

Or I thought I was.

Peter had asked to meet with me at his office. As far as I knew, he hadn't talked to Axl about last weekend's party/other woman incident, which made me think he'd been biding his time, waiting for it to blow over.

I half hoped Peter's summons had to do with the Haversman pitch. I almost had it ready, so even if he said, *You're off on a plane to Tangiers tonight to pitch your proposal*, I'd be fully prepared. But just to be on the safe side, I hired a car service to drive me to Peter's office in St. Paul. I could better use those forty-five minutes working instead of cursing at morning rush-hour traffic.

The main entrance to Lund Industries was busy from five in the morning until seven at night. So walking into a tomblike office building at eight thirty in the morning set me on edge. Why did this new building feel abandoned?

The only good thing about my claustrophobia? I got cardio in every day, as I always took the stairs—even if I had to climb thirty flights. Luckily this jaunt was only to the tenth floor.

Peter's secretary took me to a small conference room. Breakfast pastries were arranged on a beautiful Limoges plate. The secretary also served as barista as she made me a cup of French press coffee and poured the brew into a coffee cup that matched the plate.

Fancy. One didn't pull out the royal table service unless one was trying to impress someone.

Immediately my mother came to mind.

Don't be paranoid. Maybe he set up this super-fancy breakfast as a test to see if I had the social graces required to sit at the same table as R Haversman. Peter wouldn't assume I had the same flawless manners as my mother; he'd prefer to make that determination himself.

So I became conscious of the way I moved, my posture, even the act of sipping my coffee. I limited myself to one small cinnamon and raisin bun that wouldn't flake or crumble or leave an icing trail across my lips, when I'd really craved a chocolate croissant.

Finally Peter appeared. A woman followed on his heels— her body so overly muscular she sort of trot-waddled.

I stood to greet them.

Peter crossed over to me and kissed my cheeks. "Annika. You look lovely this morning. Thank you for coming." He turned toward the woman. "This is my associate, Sally."

I murmured, "Pleased to meet you," and tried not to gawp at her.

We took our seats, the secretary came in and refilled refreshments and I fought the urge to snap that they should just get on with whatever this was because I did not have all day.

Peter gave me an apologetic smile. "Sorry. We're just try-ing to plug in some last-minute data so we can present the most accurate findings."

"I would appreciate your thoroughness if I had any idea why you asked for this meeting."

"Of course. First of all, I owe you an apology. I know you've got years' worth of PR experience, so when you told me that revamping Axl Hammerquist's reputation was a waste of time, I should've listened to you . . . given this last in-cident."

The girlfriend in me wanted to jump to Axl's defense and explain that it had been a misunderstanding—and a funny one at that. The PR side of me balked. Had I really said that about Axl—as a potential client?

"Unfortunately Axl has gone off the grid, so to speak. He hasn't been to his apartment that we know of. The team prac-tices are on full media blackout. They're insisting it's solely so their players can concentrate on hockey."

Wasn't that the end goal? For Axl to be a solid part of the team and keep the focus in the press on hockey?

"Needless to say, Axl isn't returning my calls." Peter paused and I braced myself for his question. "Has he called you in the past few days?"

I shook my head because that wasn't a lie. There'd been no need for him to call since he'd been in my apartment—and my bed. Now, if Peter had asked if Axl had been in contact . . . well . . . we'd had lots of skin-to-skin contact. Same answer if he'd asked if Axl had been in touch . . . because boy howdy, had there been a lot of touching.

"No, I don't suppose he has called you after the pictures of him and the brunette were splashed across the media." Peter sighed. "His disappearing act when he isn't on the ice creates a dilemma for us."

"How so?"

"He needs to make a statement. Those types of things are sent from this office, but I prefer to have the approval and permission of my client beforehand. This time . . ."

"For once a delay has actually benefited us," Sally inserted. "We've been able to choose the best course of action, given we had more data to work with."

"What data?"

"Media approval ratings, fan ratings, sponsor blowback. The biggest one is Axl's stats. His level of play, his ice time, his plus and minus ranges."

I blinked at her. I dealt with statistics, pushes and ratings and click-through percentages every day, but nothing Sally had said made sense. "You're saying his media approval rating . . . ?"

"Can be as important as his game stats. His game stats are substantially better than last year. Since the incident Friday night, his media impact . . ." Sally glanced at Peter.

My stomach churned. "What?"

"His media impact has gone way up, Annika," Peter said softly.

And my stomach completely bottomed out. "It has?"

"I'm sure this is no reflection on you," Sally said.

But I felt a little ripple of smugness from her.

I'd made the mistake of reading a few online articles and the comments about me were so ugly.

His girlfriend was probably a cold bitch and she deserved to get cheated on.

Beautiful women never have to work to get a man; they don't have to try to keep a man either.

If a woman who looks like her, with that kind of money, can't keep a guy from fooling around on her, what hope do the rest of us have?

"Good for Ax-hell that his approval rating has gone up after a cheating scandal."

Peter shook his head. "Not his *approval* rating. His *media* impact. Because of the scandal, more people know his name, which leads to more visibility for him. I mean, it's exactly what we wanted. Since Axl has a game tonight, we want him to focus on that. So we'll release the press announcement tomorrow morning."

I didn't move. There was no discussion of PR possibilities. They'd made the final call. I knew what was coming next.

"The press release will say that Axl Hammerquist is confirming that earlier in the week, Annika Lund ended their relationship."

Absurdity and hysterical laughter warred inside me.

"I assumed you wouldn't mind the agency speaking on your behalf, Annika. Now you're free to move on."

Oh the irony.

Oh the great big ball of irony that had lodged itself in my throat, weighted down my stomach and turned my feet into lead so there was no way I could escape fast enough.

"I will say, you two were very convincing," Sally said.

That jarred me. "Excuse me?"

"I said you two were very—"

"I heard what you said," I snapped. "I just don't remember being consulted about anyone outside the originally agreed-upon parties being given this highly sensitive information." I whirled on Peter. "This is unacceptable."

"Annika," he said calmly. "Sally works for me."

"I don't care. I don't know her, which means I don't have any reason to trust her."

"I trust her," he said softly.

"And you also trusted the Sarduccis and they turned out to be douchebags."

Silence.

I stood and gathered my things. Then I stepped in close to Sally and lowered my voice so she would have to lean in to hear me. "If I hear one fucking word from anyone, *ever*, about this thing between Axl and me initially only being a PR stunt, I will know it came from you. And you can bet your ass at that point, I will come for you."

I stopped in front of Peter. "You breathe one word of this conversation to my mother? And I'll come for you too."

Peter caught me outside his main office door. "I know you're upset. I don't blame you. But the change in your situation with Axl doesn't negate the deal I made with you regarding Haversman." He handed me an envelope. "This will explain it in more detail. Call me when you've had time to process it all."

As soon as he was out of sight, I slipped into the stairwell. I removed my shoes and took the stairs at a run.

The exit from the building was located next to the delivery ramp.

When I turned the corner, my driver was standing off to the side, smoking a cigarette. He immediately put it out and reached the rear car door at the same time as me. "Lund Industries our next stop, Miss Lund?"

"No. Back to my apartment building, through the garage like before."

"Is everything all right?"

"Actually I feel sick and just want to go home."

I pulled executive status and had Deanna deal with the calls from my family as to my whereabouts. I didn't think she'd actually inform them I planned to travel around the world in eighty days via balloon, but it amused me for ten seconds to give her those instructions, if nothing else.

First, I worked out—being angry and trying to keep up

with Axl on a physical level had forced me back into a fitness routine I'd dropped in the past year.

In the mood to cook after hitting the gym, I chose five recipes and ordered the ingredients from my online grocer. Although it'd take two hours for the delivery, I called down to the security desk and talked to Carlos. He was the only guard I trusted to deliver the goods. The other guards were too easily swayed to sneak my family up here, by the promise of free Vikings tickets, which was the Lunds' go-to bribe this time of year.

I'd set Axl's text tone to the most annoying option when we first exchanged numbers. I couldn't remember the last time I'd scowled at my phone when I heard it.

AH: Typing away at the office?

Me: I decided to work from home all week.

AH: Did something happen?

Me: No. I like working in your jersey.

AH: What else are you wearing?

Me: A smile. ☺

AH: You are EVIL, Attila. How am I supposed to nap if I'm thinking of the bottom of my jersey rubbing on my favorite parts of you?

Me: Swedish sweet talker. I'm not wearing it on my head.

AH: Funny, smart girl. I like your brain. And your face. And your mouth. But I really like . . .

**Me: Get some rest. No more texting. Good luck tonight.
I'll be watching, but I'll go to bed right after the game
so you won't have to sneak away and try to call me.**

AH: OK. Good. Miss you later.

I laughed. We texted in English and there wasn't a word
that meant more than "miss you," like there was in Swedish,
so Axl improvised with "miss you later." I wondered if that
was how my mother's odd language mix-ups had originally
started.

As much as I claimed I'd work at home? I didn't. Instead
I brooded.

Twenty-three

AXL

Our team jet had maintenance issues, so we'd ended up spending another night in Calgary. The issues were still ongoing this morning, so we'd had to find a place to rent ice time, since we had a game at home tonight and couldn't miss warm-up. So we'd all stumbled out of bed at the ass crack of eight, shoveled down breakfast and climbed onto a bus to the rink.

Game day practices weren't taxing, but there wasn't much chatter, especially given our win last night. Once we heard the plane was fixed, we were happy to ditch our gear and get back on the bus that whisked us to the airport so we'd be home for a few hours.

Except Coach had laid down the law that none of us actually got to go home. We'd go directly to the arena in St. Paul after landing in Minneapolis. There'd be extra staff for massages and warm-ups. The lounge would serve as a resting and quiet area and then a catered dinner would be available.

This wasn't unusual. Travel delays happened—most often because of weather. It sucked it'd happened today. The earliest I could see Annika was after eleven p.m. I grabbed my phone to text her and saw she'd left me a voice mail. Annika never left me a voice mail.

"Axl, hey, by the time you get out of practice you'll hear the news that you confirmed via press release that I ended our relationship earlier in the week—or however Peter decided to word it. This decision did not come from me, but I knew about it yesterday. Peter decided it'd be best to wait until your game was over to save you additional press. Please don't think this is what I want. That's not the case at all, so don't make any public comments until you talk to Peter and then to me. Also, I didn't tell him that things had changed between us, so be careful when you talk to him. I'll be home, so call me when you get a chance. I miss you."

As soon as I got off the bus, I called Peter. While he spewed bullshit about media statistics, all I could think about was Annika sitting in his office, listening to him telling her how lucky she was that she and I weren't in a real relationship. And how this PR plan had gone better than he'd ever hoped.

Except it hadn't been a sham. It was time to admit I'd fallen for her.

I wasn't giving her up.

But I wasn't sharing this with the world either.

Fucking Peter and his fucking press release.

All because my media recognition stats were on a huge uptick.

What didn't he get about the fact that I didn't care about any of that? I'd never cared.

None of it was quantifiable.

I'd sabotaged my own media stats during my stint in Chicago. But now, when technically neither Annika nor I had done anything wrong, Peter claimed letting the public in on the Axl-kissing-a-brunette-who-was-really-Annika joke would be a huge mistake.

The thing was . . . I didn't disagree with that decision. It'd protect Annika. But Peter's justification for issuing the statement that Annika had initiated the breakup because it might earn me some public sympathy pissed me off. I didn't deserve sympathy—I sure as hell didn't want it. Her professional reputation shouldn't take a hit because of the messed-up situation I'd put her in. Yet announcing Annika had dumped me made sense. She'd retain her "Iron Princess" reputation for taking zero shit from any man—including an infamous bad-boy hockey player.

Regardless of the supposed positive media impact, I still came across as the cheating douchebag who couldn't keep his dick in his pants. Maybe I'd had my share—okay, maybe more than my fair share—of hookups, but I'd never cheated on a woman if we'd agreed to be exclusive.

You're exactly like your father.

I ground my molars together as my mother's chiding voice played through my mind.

No, I'm not.

For the remainder of the season, I would not make any public appearances that were not hockey-related. From what I'd read of my contract, there weren't many required team events. A few skating clinics. A fan appreciation day. If I ended up part of postgame press conferences, I'd talk about hockey. Nothing else. Never a hint that I was anything but a . . . what had Annika called me? Cyborg? I was really, really good at being cold. Aloof. I'd learned from the best.

I'd fall off the radar when I wasn't on the ice. I could spend more time with Annika. I'd rather be with her behind closed doors anyway. Preferably naked. All the freaking time.

As long as Annika was fine with it, as long as she believed I'd be one hundred percent faithful to her, I didn't give a damn about anyone else.

We lost the home game.

I blamed it on not getting a good-luck kiss from Annika. We hockey players are a superstitious bunch.

I'd done nothing of note—good or bad—during the game, so I skipped the press conference.

It was too much to hope for that the media hadn't waited to hound me outside the team exit. So I'd prepared myself by wearing headphones and cranking the tunes to the highest level. That did the trick; I didn't hear a single question as Igor and I made our way through the throng of reporters to the car I'd ordered to take us to Snow Village.

After I ditched my stuff in my apartment, I snagged two plastic cups and a bottle of Rekorderlig strawberry/lime-flavored cider brewed in Sweden that Martin had developed a taste for. I crossed the hallway. Since he never knocked on my door, I didn't bother knocking on his either. I just walked in.

Martin sat in the middle of his sofa, playing *Assassin's Creed*. He didn't even turn around when I shut the door with more force than usual. No pungent scent of weed lingered in the air as I skirted the couch and parked myself in front of him on the coffee table.

"Go away, Axl. I'm still majorly cheesed off at you," he said petulantly, never taking his eyes off the TV screen as his hands maneuvered the controls.

"I get that. But we have to talk about what happened at the party."

"You show up with a hangdog look and a bottle of cider? You think I'm that easily bribed? Wrong. I have principles, man." His eyes finally met mine. "Unlike you."

"It's not what you think."

"I know what I saw."

"You sure?" I twisted the cap off the bottle and poured two cups, handing one to him.

Martin grudgingly set aside his game controller and grabbed the cider. "This doesn't mean we're cool. This only means I'm thirsty."

"Understood. But you'll let me explain?" Knowing Martin, he'd unload his frustration with me first before he'd let me speak.

"Yeah, I'll hear you out. But I gotta say . . . what were you thinking, kissing that chick? And before that I'm not the only one who noticed you two sneaking out of the supply closet separately. So it was more than just a kiss."

He paused, waiting for me to confirm or deny, which I refused to do. Then he drained his cider and held out his cup for more.

"I don't get it, man. You've been happier in the month you've been dating Annika than I've ever seen you. You're way into her. At the coat drive thing I saw that she's got it bad for you too. Why would you eff that up?"

I held his gaze. "I didn't. The chick I kissed was Annika."

Martin snorted. "Dude, I wasn't *that* high. I know what I saw."

"At the game Annika overheard you and Verily talking about the hockey party I was hosting here . . . after I'd told her I didn't have plans postgame. It pissed her off that I'd lied to her. So she and her cousin had the bright idea of disguising themselves and sneaking into the party." I sipped the cider. "Did you see the blonde with Igor? That was Dallas."

"Get the eff out."

"Obviously their disguises worked if you didn't recognize either of them. When I kissed Annika? I didn't think anything of it because it's my natural response around her. There weren't supposed to be cell phones allowed in, but some asshole snapped a picture and sold it. You know the rest of the story, or at least what's in the media."

He blinked at me several times. "You haven't been back here since the morning after the party because there were reporters lurking around."

I scratched my neck. I hadn't shaved in two days and the scruff had started to itch. "The media blitz basically confined Annika to her place, which wasn't fair. That's where I spent the three days before we left town again. So I wasn't around when my agent's PR team released the statement that Annika had called things off. In fact, I came directly here after tonight's game instead of heading to Annika's so I could clear things up with you." I locked my gaze to his. "I'm not a fucking cheater, Martin."

"Dude. I'm like . . . so relieved to hear that. But this is so effed up."

"Tell me about it." I drained my cider. "There are a number of reasons we can't publicly state Annika was the brunette. And the only thing my agent cares about is the buzz surrounding me in the media."

"What do you care about?"

"Her."

Martin bumped my knee with his. "First time I've ever heard you put anything above hockey, brosky."

"Never had a reason to before her."

His eyes narrowed. "Wait. You came here first? You haven't seen Annika since—"

"The breakup story came out? No."

"Get your dumb butt over to her place. Sheesh. What are you doin' here with me?"

"We're friends. Your opinion of me matters, brosky."

He grinned. "I knew there was a sappy side to you, Swede. But we're cool. Now get motoring to your ladylove."

"I will. But I need a couple of favors from you. No one can know that Annika and I are still together."

"I can't keep something like that from Verily."

"I'm not asking you to. I'm asking you to keep it from everyone else. Also, I want Annika to stay at my place some nights, so could you get her clearance at the gate as Verily's cousin? I don't trust that fucker Darrin not to sell me out if I have a frequent female visitor."

"No prob." He swiped the bottle of cider and said, "You're driving, so I'll take this. I suppose you're also here because you want an apology from me for me taking a couple of swings at you?"

"I don't blame you. I might've done the same thing if I saw you kissing a woman besides Verily."

"Verily thought it was so effing hot that I went after you. She jumped me as soon as we left the party house and we ended up doing it under the juniper bushes. So now, every time I smell juniper, I'll think of her mouth—"

I held up my hand. "TMI."

"So I'm sayin' I can't honestly apologize, because I'm not sorry for what I did at the time. You cool with that?"

"Yes." I stood. "As long as you stop sending me 'you cheating fuck-face' texts."

"Those are from Verily. She sneaks my phone sometimes. She'll be glad to hear you're not a cheater eff-face."

"Keep an eye on my place. I don't know when I'll be back."

I packed my biggest suitcase with everything I'd need for an extended stay with Annika before I sent her a short text.

Me: On my way.

We hadn't exchanged keys yet, forcing me to ring the doorbell at midnight.

A couple of minutes passed and I still stood in the hallway. I rang it again.

Finally after a few more minutes the door swung open.

A sleepy Annika, sporting a serious case of bed head, rubbed her eyes as if I were an apparition. "Axl? What are you doing here?"

My gaze had already homed in on the front of her body. Christ. The lace on her skimpy top barely covered her breasts, and the bottom didn't quite reach the boy-short panties hanging low on her hips. Then there were those killer legs. I'd spent hours running my hands and mouth over them—on the inside, the outside, the front, the back. Feeling the power in them as she locked her ankles behind my back while I drove into her.

"Really? You're going to growl at me? Instead of telling me why you just showed up out of the blue?" she demanded.

I slammed the door shut and focused on her eyes as I stalked toward her. "I texted you that I was on my way over."

"Well, I left my phone charging in my office and went to bed as soon as the game ended."

"Did you really think with all that's happened in the past few days that I wouldn't want to see you as soon as possible to make sure you're all right?" Her back hit the wall and I didn't stop moving until our bodies touched. "To prove to you we are very much still together?"

She slid her hands up my chest and looped her arms around my neck. "You didn't even say hello, Ax-hell. You just stormed in and started growling at me."

I lowered my face until our lips almost touched. "I growled at you because seeing your sexy body half-naked renders my brain useless."

"Oh. Good answer."

I took her mouth in a no-holds-barred kiss. Pouring my relief, my gratitude and my lust into every thrust of my tongue, every twirl and lick, every firm brush of our lips as we shifted into a deeper kiss. By the time we eased off to take a breath, I was completely hard.

"That was a heckuva hello," she muttered. "You're forgiven."

"Good." Annika's head fell against the wall and I trailed my lips down the side of her throat. She was warm and smelled like her sheets and the barest hint of her orange blossom perfume. My hands slid around the curves of her hips to cup her ass, pressing her softness into my hardness.

"You're growling again," she murmured in my ear.

"I really like your pajamas." I dragged an openmouthed kiss to the swell of her breast and straight to her nipple. I sucked the rigid tip through the lace and she arched into me on a gasp. "I'd really like to tear them off you."

"Is this how it's going to be every time you return from away games? You barrel in, push me against the wall and kiss me stupid before you rip my clothes off?"

I tilted my head back and looked at her. "Pretty much. You have a problem with that?"

"Not a single one." Then she gifted me with the sexy smile that filled me with fierce pride.

I lifted her up and she wrapped her legs around my waist. I carried her into the living room and set her on the couch before I backtracked to grab the controller for the fireplace and clicked it on.

Her lusty gaze zeroed in on my chest after I whipped off my shirt. "We're doing this here in the living room?"

"Right here on this couch." I dropped to my knees in front of her. "Fucking you by firelight is as romantic as it'll get this time." I let my fingertips skim the insides of her thighs up to the elastic edge of her panties. "Take these off. I missed the taste of you."

Annika shivered. She scraped her fingernails across the bristle on my cheeks. "You'll give me beard burn."

"I promise I'll kiss it and make it better."

After she bared herself to me, I made good on that promise.

Then we were naked on the rug in front of the fireplace, and I rolled the condom on and slammed home with the first thrust.

"God yes," she said, and her body bowed into mine.

Somehow I managed to rein the beast in. Although I stayed buried inside her, I quit moving and gazed down at her face. "You're beautiful." I kissed her cheeks, her temples, the corners of her mouth, the edge of her jaw. "So amazing how you feel hot and tight around me." I nuzzled her neck. "How amazing you make me feel when we're together like this."

"Axl. You don't have to give me pretty words," she said softly.

"I want to." I rested my forehead to hers. "I need to. You have to know that this is it for me. After all that's happened, it's important—"

She slanted her head and fastened her mouth to mine, showing me with her kiss and her gently stroking hands that she did understand. Then she slapped me on the ass. "Talk to me later. Fuck me now."

That was when I knew I was gone for this woman. Utterly, completely, no-going-back, in-love-with-her-forever kind of gone.

After ward, Annika insisted on cooking for me.

She'd slipped on her favorite robe, which I'd admired every time she wore it during our two days together. Amid all the crap that had happened over the past couple of days, she'd managed to obtain an identical man's robe in my size—no easy feat, since the robes were custom-made. Her sweetness and thoughtfulness blew me away. I'd never had a woman so attuned to me.

I sat at the breakfast bar and watched her cook after she'd refused my help.

She whipped up an enormous egg-white omelet loaded with sautéed veggies and served it with crisp bread instead of toast.

We ate in silence. As soon as we were both finished, I forced her to sit as I cleaned up.

"So you're staying here for a few days?" she asked.

"If that's all right?"

"Of course it is. I'm happy you barged in at midnight, Ax-hell."

Now the way she said Ax-hell sounded like a term of endearment rather than an insult. I glanced down as I dried the pan and said, "I missed you. I hated not being here when the shit storm hit." I looked at her. "I'm here now. And I'm not going anywhere."

"Hearing that has made my whole week." She smirked when I lifted my brow. "That and the rockin' sex. Man. I thought multiple orgasms were a myth. I'm so happy to have you prove that wrong."

I laughed. "Anytime."

"What happens now with the PR situation?"

"I'm meeting Peter in the morning before practice. I'll make it clear that my time off the ice is private. Period. And unless the team holds a public event I'm contractually required to attend, no appearances and no interviews. If I have to be part of the postgame press conference, I'll only answer hockey-related questions."

She chewed on her lip. "Are you sure that's wise? Your media impact is the highest it's ever been."

Angrily I slapped my hands on the counter and leaned in. "I don't give a fuck. The media impact went up because of a scandal where I come off looking like a cheating asshole. So

I don't put much faith in a system that glorifies that behavior, or at least forgives it because I'm a pro athlete. It hurt you, and that killed me. The only good thing that'll come out of this is now you and I have an excuse to lock ourselves away and continue building this relationship in private." I paused. "Do you have any objections to that?"

"Of course not." She hopped off the stool and skirted the counter to duck under my arm. "But there are a couple of things I need to point out, strictly from a PR standpoint."

Stay calm and listen. You'll get your turn to make her understand the only two things you give a damn about are playing hockey without distractions . . . and her. "Okay."

"Peter will use your increased media impact to score endorsements for you. This was one of the end goals for you—regardless if you and I became a real couple or if we had stayed strictly PR lovebirds. Please take advantage of that while you can."

"What company is going to hire a guy who's considered a cheater?" I scoffed.

"Historically? Lots of famous guys with reputations as 'ladies' men' endorse personal grooming products like razors, aftershave, cologne, deodorant and body gel. And besides . . . someone has to sell condoms." She slid her hands up my chest. "Why not you? You're hot and sexy. It'd show you're a responsible cheater, even if the perception is you carry an entire box of magnum-sized condoms in your equipment bag 'just in case' you run across another mysterious brunette you wanna bang."

"Jesus, Annika."

She smirked. "Come on, wouldn't that be the ultimate irony? You shilling condoms when you're finally in a monogamous relationship? Dude. You could laugh about that all the way to the bank."

That made me chuckle. "Fine. But what if they surround me with half-naked chicks and they have their hands all over me during the photo shoot? You won't have a problem with that?"

"I won't like it." She briefly closed her eyes. "Okay, I'd freakin' hate it. I'd be jealous as hell." She looked up, her eyes fierce. "But I know you're coming back to me, Axl, because I give you what no other woman ever has." Another pause. "Complete trust, total understanding of the man you are beneath the hockey uniform and a chance to build a future."

Once again, she'd rocked me to the core. What she gave me was everything I'd ever wanted and feared I didn't deserve. "Do you have any idea what it means for me to hear you say that?"

"Yes. Which is why I needed to say it to you so you believe it."

My mouth sought hers and I poured my heart and soul into the kiss.

I eased off and rested my forehead to hers. "Okay. I'll consider endorsements but only if we discuss them first."

"Deal." She nestled the side of her face against my chest and squeezed me tight. "Thank you."

"For?"

"For understanding that I have to put my job first too."

"What are you talking about?"

Annika tipped her head back and studied me. "Peter didn't tell you." She paused. "Of course he didn't tell you, because there'd be no need for you to know."

"Need to know what?"

"When I met with Peter he told me it had to be very clear in the press release that I was the one who ended things between us."

"If this is the sympathy-for-me angle, that's bullshit—"

She briefly pressed her thumbs over my lips. "Listen. I didn't understand either until Peter shared some crucial information with me about Haversman. Apparently cheating is one of Haversman's hot-button issues. When he discovered his first wife cheating on him, he immediately divorced her. It is his personal code that he doesn't do business with men or women with a reputation for philandering. And he considers anyone who stays with a cheater to have a weak character and no backbone."

"You don't find that odd?"

"No. Private companies don't want to do business with individuals who violate their core philosophies—whatever that might be. It happens more often than you think. So even though our couplehood is no longer part of Peter's PR plan for you, he is honoring his agreement to introduce me to Haversman. By having me initiate our breakup, when Haversman starts his background check on me . . ."

"You retain your 'Iron Princess' reputation by kicking me to the curb." At least I'd put that much together on my own. "But what's with the uncertainty in your eyes?"

"That means we have to stay broken up. We can't let this blow over as a misunderstanding and then in a month I've miraculously forgiven you and we reconcile. No one can know we're still in a relationship. We have to hide it." She glanced down. "Do you know how much I hate asking that of you? Especially when I know you went through this with Isla? Especially when I have no idea when I'll get a call from Peter that the meeting with Haversman is a go? It could be next week. It could be in eight months. But this chance to personally pitch to Haversman . . . if I'm successful it could mean jobs and millions of dollars in revenue, so it's not just an ego thing for me."

"Hey. Look at me." I curled my hand beneath her chin,

forcing her to meet my gaze. "Isla set out to deceive me. That is not the case here, Annika. So that is not even a concern. Tell me you understand there aren't any similarities in the situations at all."

"Okay. But it did cross my mind because I worried it would cross yours."

And that's why I love you. "One question. We can't be in public together at all, but we can be together in private as much as we want?"

"Yes. Of course."

"Then I don't see a problem, Annika. Outside this apartment you focus on your job and I focus on hockey. When we're together? We focus on each other. Besides, it gives us the power to reveal our relationship when we're ready."

She looked relieved. "It won't be easy keeping this from my family and friends, because being with you makes me happy and they're bound to notice. Dallas knows about us, but she's trustworthy."

"I stopped at my place to get clothes and clear the air with Martin. Now he knows you're the mysterious brunette I kissed." I brushed my lips across the top of her head. "He's a good guy with a moral compass and I didn't want him believing I'm a cheater."

"Your friendship with him is sweet."

Sweet. I snorted. "And since I want you to stay with me some nights, he's getting a gate pass for you as Verily's cousin. You might have to wear glasses and tuck your hair up in a hat and not act like your beautiful, charming self, but hopefully you'll be undetected."

Her eyes lit up. "Can I have a badass Swedish Valkyrie name?"

"You can have whatever you want, Annika."

"All I want, all I need is you, Axl."

"You've got me." I kissed her. "Let's go to bed."

"You're tired?" she said with surprise.

"Not at all. It's time I showed you all the things we can do in a bed besides sleep. You seemed to have some confusion about that. Maybe it's a cultural thing." I hoisted her over my shoulder and sprinted to her bedroom.

Twenty-four

ANNIKA

Monday morning, the first day back after my week of media avoidance, my primary task was to finish my intra-office memo welcoming Lucy to the PR team. She'd officially started the week before, and the few times I'd checked in she'd received glowing reports from everyone.

During lunch break, my cousin Nolan strolled into my office and deposited himself in the chair in front of my desk. Our female employees called him "The Prince" because he did have a certain regal air about him. If Brady was the nerdy, number-crunching braniac Lund, and my cousin Ash was the Lund with the bulldozer mentality toward anyone who stood between LI and global domination, then Nolan was the charming Lund mogul in the making, whose sharp sense of style was an intentional distraction from his sharp intellect. He was our family's James Bond: dashing, dangerous and sometimes a total dickhead.

"Rough week, I heard," he said to me in greeting.

I shrugged. "Live and learn. I don't imagine you came here to counsel me on the best way to deal with cheating hockey players. Since you've been turning a blind eye to your brother's cheating ways for years."

"And . . . the gloves are off first thing? By all means. Let's get to it." He cracked his knuckles.

I rolled my eyes.

"You hired Lucifer."

"I will tell you exactly once never to use that name when referring to Lucy again, Nolan. It's disrespectful. Don't make me bring this up at the board meeting."

He held up his hands. "So noted."

"Good."

"You hired Lucy without talking to me or my dad or my mom."

"I don't ask their opinions on *any* of my potential hires."

"This is different and you know it."

"She has a solid portfolio and references."

"If I knew that's what you were looking for, I could've had a dozen people for you to interview, Annika."

"Why are you opposed to her working here?"

He leaned forward. "It'll cause tension. It's already caused issues."

"For who? Brady is fine with it. Ash is fine with it. And the CEO hasn't stormed in here and told me to fire her or lose my job."

Nolan scowled. "My dad wouldn't do that."

"Exactly. He hasn't weighed in on this at all. Neither has Aunt Edie. I wouldn't have given her a chance if not for Lennox. I would've had—I did have—the same 'hell no' reaction that we've been conditioned to experience whenever her name has been mentioned." I picked up my can of soda and drank before I continued. "Interviewing her was the first time I'd ever really talked to her. So when have you ever had an honest conversation with her about anything besides her problems with your brother and Mimi?"

Nolan drummed his fingers on the arm of the chair and said nothing.

"Nolan. Whatever you tell me doesn't leave this room. You can joke all you want about me being a gossip hound, but you know it's not true."

"God. Sometimes I hate that you're so damn . . ."

"Earnest? Perfect? Right all the time? Much better qualified than you to take over as CEO someday?"

He snorted. "And once again you strained the bounds of believability with the last one, brat. The truth is, I hate that you're so damn honest, because it forces me to be."

Not always the case on that "honest" thing.

"Don't judge me too harshly," he said with soft sincerity.

I nodded.

"I knew what Jaxson was doing. I knew about the women and the partying. I just didn't know what to do about it." He blew out a breath. "I worshipped him. Sports star, everyone knew his name, getting laid all the time. He was my hero. By the time he met Lucy, he was starting the peak of his career. Jax seemed happy with her. Mom and Dad were too, mostly because they hoped she'd settle him down."

"Did they know about his lifestyle?"

Nolan looked at me. "Yeah. At that time they had a 'boys will be boys' mentality because Jax didn't have responsibilities. That changed when Lucy got pregnant. But I think the more they hounded him to do the right thing, the more Jax resisted. The first time I caught him cheating on Lucy, she was six months pregnant. He gave me some sob story about her cutting him off from sex and him having needs . . ." Nolan briefly closed his eyes. "And I bought it."

"He's your brother. I can understand that you wanted to believe he had a valid reason for doing something so wrong."

"But I had no right to excuse it every time I caught him after that. So after Mimi was born I showed up to help Lucy out whenever I could because it was obvious Jax wasn't stepping up . . . I think Lucy believed that once hockey season ended, Jax would come home and they'd be a family. But it just got worse. We tried—"

"Wait. Who's we?"

"Me. Mom and Dad."

My surprise must've shown.

"You really think we'd let Mimi live in squalor? We could give her a better environment."

Now I was getting a clearer picture. My aunt, uncle and cousin tried to get custody of Mimi—no wonder Lucy fought so hard. I would've too. But it wasn't an indictment of her as a parent; it was their guilt for their son's failings. "Nolan, why wasn't anyone in the Lund family aware you guys were going through this?"

A blockade went up in his eyes. "Because you all are the perfect Lunds—my dad and mom were embarrassed that Jaxson could be that way to his own child. Jaxson was furious we interfered. No one knows he and I didn't speak for a year."

"And none of us noticed?"

He shook his head. "It was easy to lie when Jax lived in Chicago. Eventually we started talking. He and Lucy worked together so he could get to know Mimi. This isn't something Jax has announced publicly, but he went through alcohol treatment."

"Omigod. When?"

"Last summer."

My eyes filled with tears. "Nolan, you should have told me all this sooner."

"Hey, now, brat. None of that. I didn't tell you to make you feel like a shitty cousin. I only told you because I trust you." His eyes turned as hard as stones. "This is not my news or life issue to tell. It's Jax's. He thought about saying something at the confrontation we had with Walker, but that was Walker's deal, and Jax didn't want to make it about him. It's a huge change for all of us. We're still trying to find our way."

"I imagine."

"Anyway, Lucy getting a job here when all this shit is going down with Jax . . . seemed suspicious to us."

"So you drew the short straw to deal with Annika the softhearted, who falls for every sob story that comes down the pike?"

Nolan laughed. "Need I remind you your nickname is the 'Iron Princess'?"

"In the media and in the halls of LI, but not with my family, Nolan."

"I'll remember that if you stop calling me 'The Prince.'"

"Deal."

"I'm also here to tell you I'm glad you're done with that Axl asshole."

But I'm not done. I might never be done with him. "Why?"

"After everything I just told you about Jax, you need more reasons not to get involved with a hockey player?"

Now Nolan's overly jerkish behavior at the family barbecue when he heard Dallas was dating Igor made more sense. But my situation with Axl wasn't part of this conversation and I saw right through his deflection. "Back to the matter at hand. You need to talk to Lucy. Obviously what you decide to tell her isn't my business and I'll never break your trust, but Jax's sobriety affects Mimi just as much as his alcoholism did. If nothing else maybe you could be a bridge for Jax and Lucy to have an honest conversation about it."

Nolan stood. "You're right. God, it actually causes me physical *pain* to say that."

"I'll show you physical pain." I came around the desk and pretended to punch him in the gut.

He hugged me. "Thanks. And when you're ready to jump back in the dating pool, I know a guy who wants your number."

"How about you worry about your dating life, and I'll worry about mine?"

Axl was as stealthy as a bear. Crashing through the forest. At night.

My heart raced, and I couldn't help smiling at his intrusion. I shouldn't have even pretended to be asleep. I could've enjoyed the show of him unbuttoning his shirt and tossing it aside, then pulling his T-shirt over his head, revealing his bare, muscled chest. Next he'd unbuckle his belt. Unbutton and unzip his pants and shove them down his legs. He'd leave his socks on, as his feet were perpetually cold. His underwear . . . they would stay on if he intended to sleep. But they'd be the last thing he'd remove if he planned on giving me a wicked wake-up call.

I heard the rustle of his clothes as he removed them and then the mattress dipped. Axl scooted in behind me, and his boxer briefs brushed the backs of my thighs.

He snaked his fingers beneath the hem of my nightshirt, and his hand drifted up, over the bare skin of my belly, over my rib cage until he could palm my breast. He sighed deeply. Then he nosed aside my hair until he found the spot behind my ear that he could kiss, nuzzle and reclaim as his.

When I started to turn toward him, he gave me a warning growl.

Well, okay, then.

"Annika, give me this first."

I didn't ask for an explanation, because that would force him to put it into words. I knew what he needed, a reminder that this physical reconnection wasn't just about sex. It was

about a familiar body, a familiar scent, warmth and softness.
A welcome touch. A welcome home.

I felt a little cocky that he'd never wanted that or even
needed that until he met me. I knew it'd make him happy
beyond words to come home to his place and find me in
his bed.

Axl sighed again and tangled our legs together. Then he
reached for my right hand, clasped it in his and stretched our
arms above our heads, tucking his biceps under the pillow.

I loved this position with him. It felt lazy and protective
and yet sexy as hell.

He brushed another kiss below my ear. "I missed you."

"I missed you too."

"I'm glad you're here waiting for me, but I am so tired."

"I know. Go to sleep."

"But I also want to pound you into the mattress until you
can't walk," he murmured sleepily.

"Tomorrow."

S weaty and sated, I slumped across Axl's chest and muttered, "Uncle."

He merely grunted.

We'd hardly left his bed the past twenty-four hours after
he'd returned from seven grueling days on the road.

We were five weeks into our "secret" relationship and so
far, so good. When Axl and I were together, we were one
hundred percent focused on each other. It wasn't just mind-
blowingly intense sex—although it was all that—but shutting
out the world allowed us to get to know each other on a deeper
level. We had to figure out how to deal with each other's mood
swings, career disappointments and triumphs. Set boundaries
for individual alone time, as well as admit to jealousy when

I took an afternoon away from him to spend with my family and he needed a break just to chill out with his buddies at Snow Village and play video games. We fought less than we ever had because we figured out it was a waste of energy. With limited time together, it was easier to set priorities.

I loved being with him, whether we were watching TV or cooking or bouncing the bed frame or just talking. I'd never been with a man who showered me with so much uninhibited affection and who was so eager to receive it in return.

The only downside, ironically, was part of the upside—being confined to my place or his place as our relationship blossomed. I know it frustrated him that I couldn't attend home games and give him a good-luck kiss at the arena before he hit the ice. It frustrated me that I couldn't bring him to Lund family gatherings. It frustrated both of us that our outside time was literally spent bundled up, walking through the snow in full winter gear so no one could see our faces. I'd even gotten so desperate for a change of scenery that I'd agreed to hike with him at a nature preserve an hour outside the Cities.

I'd called Peter every couple of weeks just to see if he'd heard anything about the Haversman pitch, but I was still in a holding pattern. He assured me nothing would be scheduled over the holidays, so he'd touch base with me after the first of the year. As much as I'd wanted to know how he'd managed to keep Axl's media impact so high—yes, I was a PR numbers and data geek and Axl was my boyfriend, so I had a vested interest—I couldn't ask without arousing his suspicions. For the first two weeks after our breakup, Axl's hockey jersey had been the number-one seller for the Wild and for all of the NHL's Central Division. He'd also managed to land endorsements for thermal T-shirts, long underwear and aftershave. That ad made me laugh because it looked as if the female model was slapping him across the face as she "applied" the aftershave. Both ads were slated to run on TV through the holidays.

We hadn't discussed the upcoming holidays. The Wild had a home game the Friday night after Thanksgiving. The past two years the Lund family had traveled to Texas to watch the Vikings play the Cowboys on Thanksgiving Day. Then we had a catered meal in my parents' hotel suite when Jens could join us. But this year Brady and Lennox had called dibs on the Lund family cabin in the North Woods for the weekend. Walker and Trinity were staying home because Trinity had three big commissions to finish before Christmas. So if I didn't go to New York with my parents to Jensen's game, they'd be alone, since Jensen usually "dropped in" for dinner and then bailed quickly afterward to hang out with his teammates.

But I didn't want to leave Axl to fend for himself either. What credible excuse could I come up with for staying home alone on a holiday?

Nothing plausible had popped up so far. Maybe I should ask Dallas if she had any ideas . . .

No! Bad idea. You and Dallas wreak havoc when you're together and trying to misdirect people from what you're really doing.

But I needed to figure this out. Axl would be home for four days. Four days when I didn't have to work. Four days when we could decorate for Christmas, snuggle up by the fire, watch TV in the glow of the Christmas tree lights and get our naked sexy times on.

"You all right, beautiful?" Axl murmured in that husky postsex voice. "I can almost hear the gears grinding in that busy head of yours."

"Says the engineer." I lifted myself up and glanced down into his face. God, he was even more gorgeous with his hair all sex-mussed and that satisfied gleam in his eyes.

"Stop looking at me like that unless you want to end up on your back again," he warned.

"But you're so pretty to look at," I cooed, pressing a smacking kiss to his mouth when he immediately scowled.

"I'm not that easily distracted by your flattery. Tell me what's on your mind."

"Thanksgiving. Namely how I'm going to spend it with you without my family becoming suspicious."

Axl twined a loose piece of my hair around his finger. "I'm a selfish asshole, but I don't want to cause problems with your family, Annika."

"And I don't want my man to be alone."

"I'm used to being alone over the holidays, so it wouldn't be anything new for me."

"That's why I'm struggling with this, Axl. I want it to be something new for you—for both of us. A chance for us to start our own Thanksgiving traditions."

A look I hadn't seen before darkened his eyes. "Starting a tradition suggests—"

"Starting a tradition *means*," I corrected, slightly annoyed, "that it's the beginning of something that happens more than one time."

"You see us spending Thanksgiving together next year?"

"I see us spending *every* Thanksgiving together from here on out. Don't you?"

We stared at each other. It didn't escape my notice he hadn't answered me.

"What?" I said softly when that peculiar look flitted through his eyes again.

"I'd love that."

Axl might as well have said, "I love you." Right then I didn't give a damn what my family thought. I was an adult. If I wanted to make other plans, I could and I didn't owe them an explanation.

Then I found myself on my back with two-hundred-odd pounds of hockey player plastered to my front.

Before he spoke, the outer apartment door banged open. Then someone was beating on the bedroom door.

"Hammer-time. Get your lazy ass out here and play *Assassin's Creed* with me. Martin has kicked my butt, so I need to reclaim my manhood and destroy you."

I froze. What the hell was Jensen doing here?

"Be right out," Axl said over his shoulder. Then he kissed me and pushed himself up to his knees. "How do you want me to play this? Tell him I'm sick and that's why I'm in bed at six o'clock at night?"

"Or you could tell him that you have a chick in your room," I retorted.

Axl dropped his hands beside my head and we were nose to nose. "Only if I can tell him that chick is you."

"No."

"So you'll what . . . hide out in here in the closet? Or under the bed?"

"No. I don't understand why my brother is here."

"Jens and Martin hit it off. The three of us hang out. Or he and I hang out sometimes."

I couldn't believe my boyfriend and my youngest brother were pals and Axl hadn't thought to mention it before now. "How long has this been going on?"

He shrugged. "Since the coat drive. Footballer and I have a lot in common. He's a good guy. And I think he's lonely."

I frowned. "But he has us."

"Us as in . . . your two older brothers who are newly married and spend all their free time with their wives, and you, who spends all her free time with me?"

My mouth snapped shut because he had a point. When was the last time I'd called Jensen just to see how he was doing? Or to ask him to come over or go out for food or drinks?

Turned out, I couldn't remember the last time. So much for the caring and involved big sister that I'd considered myself to be.

"He stopped hanging out with his teammates as much," Axl continued, "outside of practice and game time. He shows up here or at Martin's place and I like having him around, okay? He's funny. And we can talk about career stuff that other people don't understand."

I let my fingers trace the hard set to his jaw. "I never realized until right now that you've quietly made it your mission to pick up strays. Igor. Martin. Boris. Relf. Jorgen. Kaz. And now Jensen. While I hate that my brother is considered a stray in need of a pack, I see I was right about you, Ax-hell."

"How so?"

"You have a big heart. Then again, you have room for it in this massive chest of yours. Can I just say I'm as crazy about this big heart of yours as I am about your big c—"

Axl shut me up with a kiss. Then he murmured, "So, what'll it be? Are you hiding under the covers in here or what?"

It occurred to me that my baby bro would not be buddy-buddy with any guy who put me through the wringer like Axl had. Jens would've killed him. So that meant—

"You can come out too, Annika," Jensen said through the door. "I know you're in there."

I let the shock settle in before I whapped Axl on the butt. "You told him!"

"Of course I did."

"Why?"

"A, I didn't want him beating the fuck out of me. B, I didn't want him thinking I was a low-life cheater. C, I didn't want to be checking over my shoulder for the next six months, because I know Jensen is tenacious about bringing the pain when he believes someone has hurt his family. D, he didn't need to question your judgment on top of everything else."

Right then I knew I was so lucky to have found this man.

"I think it hurt him a little that the truth of us maintaining our relationship and keeping it on the down low hadn't come from you." Axl flashed his teeth. "But he loves the fact that he's the only one in your family besides Dallas who knows."

One-upmanship. Jens would love having something to lord over our brothers.

Axl kissed me again. "Get dressed and come out to face the music." He hopped off the bed, ditched the condom and slipped on his sweatpants.

I said, "Wait," when his hand grasped the door handle. "You're going out there like that?"

He raised that haughty eyebrow at me. "Usually I don't bother with the pants."

I threw a pillow at him and he left the room laughing.

Twenty-five

AXL

Coach's Christmas "gift" to us was one of the most torturous practices I'd ever suffered through.

Flitte stretched out on the ice at the end of practice like he was making a snow angel and groaned.

Everyone thought he was being funny, but I suspected he wasn't, so I mustered the energy to skate over and offer him a hand.

"Sweet baby Jesus, Hammer-time, I think I love you."

"Then I expect a kick-ass Christmas present."

When he was upright on his skates, but still bent over with his hands on his knees, I started to get concerned.

"Seriously, man, are you okay?"

"This is why I hate fucking Christmas. Coach does this to us every year on Christmas Eve. Our bodies pay the physical price for three days for one damn day off. A day that I spend sleeping because I'm too freakin' sore to do anything else."

"You don't go home to your family?"

He snorted and finally pushed himself up to standing. "My family sucks. They think because I have a big salary I should spread the love and buy them all a new car or some damn thing. I send 'em each a ham and a gift card to Red Lobster."

I laughed. "I hope they appreciate that. But if you need a place to go after you wake up from the sugarplums dancing in your head, I'm having food and football at my place tomorrow."

"Food as in . . . Swedish meatballs?"

Oh for fuck's sake. "No."

He wrinkled his nose. "I'll pass if it's lutefisk."

"It's chili and it's casual. Drop by anytime between noon and eight."

"Thanks, man. I just might do that. BYOB?"

"If you want. After today's 'gift' I'll limit myself to one beer. I don't need booze to make me wanna puke any more than I do right now."

"No doubt."

We were all moving slow. The saunas were full; so were the whirlpools and even the showers.

I'd intended to just rinse off, but the instant that hot water hit me, I never wanted to move. Or maybe my muscles seized up and I couldn't move.

The family guys had bailed by the time I hobbled into the locker room.

"So, Hammer-time, got all your shopping done?" McClellan asked.

"I guess. No one really to buy for, so it's easy." A lie. I'd rush-ordered Annika's gift right after Thanksgiving when she showed me how much she loved the holidays by spending an entire day decorating my place. I had a Christmas tree overloaded with ornaments, lights strung up on the balcony and around my front door, a holiday blanket for the couch and even a freakin' snowman candy dish—which I'd have to remember to hide tomorrow so I didn't take crap from my teammates about it.

It'd taken Annika two full days to deck out her apartment with her boxes upon boxes of Christmas decorations. She even had holiday-themed tableware she only used the month of December. It seemed she was baking something every other day and I'd added half an hour of cardio into my workout just so I could sample all of her delectable sweets.

I winced as I lowered to the bench to slip on my shoes. Extra cardio was not happening today.

"You're lucky, then," McClellan said. "I thought I was done shopping, right? My girlfriend just texted and reminded me to pick up stocking stuffers. What the hell? Aren't stocking stuffers for kids and you're off the hook with that shit when you stop believing in Santa Claus?"

"I don't know. I'm not really into Christmas." But Annika was. Now that I thought about it . . . she'd hung stockings with both of our names from her mantel. And I'd bet I'd wake up tomorrow morning to find my stocking full of . . . whatever the hell people put in stockings. Which meant I'd have to drag my ass out and brave the crowds now or else Annika's stocking would be empty and she'd be disappointed. Rather than panic, I casually said to McClellan, "What do you buy for your girlfriend's stocking?"

"Hell if I know. Maybe I oughta go to Victoria's Secret and buy panties in every color and style plus some of those sexy garters."

I nodded. That did sound like an excellent idea. One I planned to steal.

The locker door behind us slammed. We both jumped and turned around.

"No, no, no, no, no," Dykstrand said. "The point of a stocking is to fill it with things *she* likes, not things that will benefit you. And it's especially a bad idea if you're dumping out your stockings in front of her family because then you'd really look like a deviant if all you bought her were thongs."

Also a good point—not that I had to worry about the dumping-it-out-in-front-of-family thing. Annika was spending most of Christmas Eve at her parents' house and heading over to the big Lund family gathering at noon tomorrow. We'd carve out time for us in between all that. It bothered her we couldn't be together with her family. But I wouldn't let her back out of the traditions that meant so much to her.

"And how do you know so much about stocking stuffers, Dykstrand?" McClellan demanded.

"Because I used to have a girlfriend, dumb-ass. She was into all the holiday stuff, which meant if I wanted to get laid, I was into it too. So here's some free advice. Put things in her stocking that will mean something to her and not just gift cards, lingerie and candy."

"Like what?" I asked.

"Like socks if her feet are always cold, gloves if her hands are always cold. Nail polish if you know the brand she uses. A minibag of her favorite coffee, or an airplane-sized bottle of seasonal booze. You can put candy in, but make it special candy, something you can't buy for her the rest of the year. A book or a magazine is good. Maybe some small candles. My girl was crazy for those Lush bath bombs, so I put those in. A travel-sized bottle of her favorite perfume. A gift certificate for a massage or a spa day. Jewelry. Frames for pictures of the two of you. Funny, funky, silly trinkets. You know. Stuff that shows her you pay attention to the little things about her."

McClellan and I stared at him with our mouths hanging open.

"What?"

"Dude. You are like ninja good at this stuffer stuff,"

McClellan said in awe. "Why is it that you don't have a girlfriend?"

Dykstrand aimed his gaze at the floor. "She died. Car wreck. Going on four years ago now." He lifted his head and gave McClellan a hard look. "So don't bitch about having to do this, man. I'd give anything to be out fighting the last-minute shoppers and filling my shopping basket with things for Sara."

"I'm sorry. I didn't know."

"It is what it is. But it's why I'm with Flitte in hating Christmas. It reminds me of her. Reminds me of what I lost."

Neither McClellan nor I knew how to respond to that. McClellan just clapped Dykstrand on the shoulder and said, "Thanks, man. I mean it," before he walked out.

Then Dykstrand and I were alone. I groaned like a ninety-year-old man as I pushed myself to my feet.

"I heard you don't have big Christmas plans tomorrow either," Dykstrand said to me.

"I'm planning to make a voodoo doll of Coach and every time I hurt someplace, I'll jab a pin in the same place on him. See how the sadistic jerk likes that."

Dykstrand grinned. "I knew you were slinking off to a voodoo shop when we had that stopover in New Orleans last week."

"Busted." As I buttoned my coat, I said, "Look, if you don't have anything going on tomorrow, swing by my place to watch the games. I'll have food."

His eyes lit up. "Swedish meatballs?"

"You're funny."

"So, are you serving lutefisk?"

"What *is* it with you guys and your obsession with lutefisk? Not every Scandinavian person eats that shit because it's tradition."

"Just yanking your chain, Swede."

I flipped him off.

"Thanks for the invite. If I can haul my ass outta bed tomorrow, I'll show up."

I pulled on my skullcap and gloves, prepping myself to brave the weather and the crowds.

Immediately after I returned to Annika's apartment, I snagged her stocking and filled it; then I shoved it in my bottom dresser drawer. My body ached like on my first day as a rookie at training camp. I popped the maximum amount of anti-inflammatory meds recommended and spent a solid hour in the sauna before I crawled into bed and crashed.

I woke four hours later and felt slightly more human. I dressed and headed to the kitchen to forage. My phone rang right after I'd finished eating and I was surprised to see my mother's name on the caller ID. It would be Christmas morning in Sweden. Well, at least she was getting the obligatory phone call out of the way early. I said, *"God Jul, Mamma."*

"God Jul, Axl. How have you been?"

"It's been a busy hockey season. How are you?"

"Good. I'm traveling a bit more than usual, running oversight on the project in Oslo . . ."

The polite exchange went on and I decided I'd much rather suffer through the Lunds' manner of saying hello—letting Jensen punch me in the face was better than this.

You're just exhausted.

"Axl?"

"Pardon? Bad connection there for a moment."

"I asked what your plans were for today."

"I'm having a few teammates over. We're back on the road the day after Christmas, so it'll be a day of rest for us. How are you and Lars and Birget spending the day?"

"Snowshoeing. It's cold but clear and the snowpack is good."

If I couldn't get Annika on skis or a snowboard, maybe snowshoeing was an option. "I'm sure it will be a fun day."

"I need to get bundled up for our trek. I just wanted to hear you're all right."

"I've never been better. Take care. And merry Christmas."

"To you as well."

I hung up. I stared at my phone for the longest time, feeling guilty because I felt nothing. Even during the time of year when sentimentality is expected—and forgiven if it's out of character—I might as well have been talking to the reservations clerk at a hotel, not the woman who'd given birth to me.

Just then the door opened and Annika burst in, laden with packages, laughing and cursing when she started dropping things. "I swear I'm going to overcome my phobia one of these days and actually use the elevator."

"Is there more in your car?"

"Nope. I got it all in one trip." She looked at me. Her cheeks were red from the cold. Her eyes gleamed with brightness that rivaled the lights on the Christmas tree. The tassel on her Vikings stocking cap was askew. Her hair, full of static, stuck around the fur collar of her coat.

I'd never seen a more beautiful sight in my life.

Hearing Dykstrand's sad history had been on my mind all day. And seeing Annika, I wouldn't waste another moment in letting her know exactly how I felt about her. I marched over to her, curled my hands around her cold cheeks and kissed her. Then I tilted her head back so I could look into her eyes and she could see what was in mine. "I love you. And although I'm sure you felt it from me, I never said it to you. So I'm saying it now. I love you, Annika. From this day on I will make sure I tell you that every day."

Her eyes pooled with tears. "That's a really rockin' Christmas present, Axl."

"That's not your gift."

"But it's exactly what I wanted."

"At least I did one thing right." I kissed her again and then I began unwrapping her.

"I love you too, you know."

I paused in unbuttoning her coat. "I'm a very lucky man."

"Wanna get lucky right now?"

"After we open gifts, yah?"

"Yah. Yay!" She actually bounced with happiness. "I wasn't sure if you were a Christmas Eve gift opener or a Christmas morning gift opener. I was hoping for tonight." She grabbed my hand and tugged me into the living room. She stopped in front of the fireplace. "Hey. Where's my stocking?"

I shrugged. "Santa stopped by to pick it up."

Annika laughed. "I love this side of you."

"What side?"

"The side you show only to me."

We settled on the couch. She carried the presents from beneath the Christmas tree and set them on the coffee table. We'd agreed to limit the number of gifts to each other to three. I handed her the first package—the biggest one.

She didn't waste time; she ripped right through the shimmering foil wrapping paper. She squinted at the package and then at me. "Really?"

"You've been trying to get me to do wicked things to you while you're spread out on your fur coat. I thought an oversized fur blanket would save your coat wear and tear."

"But, Axl. This is mink."

"Look closer. It's mink on one side and fox on the other."

"We are totally breaking this in tonight." She leaned over and kissed me. "Thank you. Now it's your turn. Here." She handed me the largest package.

I tore into it with equal enthusiasm. Inside was a framed picture of my Koenigsegg CCX. But not a photograph. An actual artist's rendering. "Annika. This is amazing."

"I know, right? I contacted the company and talked to the architectural-concept guy. He said there were only three hand-drawn pictures done of this model. One was hanging in the corporate headquarters showroom, one went to the guy who bought the first model and then this one, which just happens to be the exact color of your car. I thought it'd be cool for you to have a reminder of it during all those months you can't drive it."

"It's . . . stunning. Thank you." I grabbed the next package. "For you."

Riiiip. She dumped the envelope on her lap and pulled out the sheet of paper inside. "Omigod. You're not kidding with this, are you? You trust me behind the wheel of your precious car? I really have a full hour of track time? And I can drive it as fast as I want?"

I laughed. "Yes. The only catch is I have to be there with you."

"Yes, yes, yes! I so wish I could rub this in my brothers' faces. Better yet, I wish they could see me behind the wheel of this badass car, because they will be so jealous! Thank you." She plucked up the next box on the table. "This one next."

This box contained an envelope. I opened it and read through it before I glanced up at her. "A weekend at a ski resort in Canada? After the hockey season ends?"

"Yes. The only catch is I have to be there with you," she teased.

"How did you hear about this place?"

"Verily. She said in that part of Canada they'd still have lots of snow and great skiing in late May. I know you miss skiing and can't take a chance you'll hurt yourself during the season."

"I am really looking forward to this. Thank you." I was beyond touched by this thoughtful gift. Both of them really. She got me in ways no one else ever had. I nudged the flat box toward her. "Last one."

Annika took her time opening it, so my heart raced. Finally she popped the lid open. She gasped and her gaze flew to mine. "Axl. This is . . ."

"Let me put it on you." As I removed the necklace, she lifted her hair and half turned away from me. I looped the platinum chain around her neck and fastened it. Then I kissed the side of her neck. "Do you like it?"

"I love it so much I'm finding it hard to speak. When in the world did you have this done?"

I rubbed my thumb over the platinum charm, two *A*'s entwined. One side white diamonds, the other side black diamonds. "I had it designed for you by a jeweler in L.A. right after Thanksgiving. I know we can't be together the way we both want right now, so this is a tangible reminder of us. We both have light and dark sides. There's equal weight to the diamonds because we balance each other out." I kissed her temple.

"You're going to make me cry. It's the most perfect, personal, beautiful thing I've ever been given. Saying thank you doesn't seem like it's enough. I love it." She turned her head and rubbed her cheek along my jaw. "I love you."

"I love you too."

"Now I don't want to give you your last present because it'll seem lame in comparison to this."

I nipped her earlobe. "Gimme."

She reached for the smallest box and tossed it into my lap.

I didn't drag it out. Inside the box was a coin. I lifted it out. "What's this?"

"A coin."

"What kind of coin?"

Annika plucked it out of my fingers. "It's an EKG of my heartbeat. It's on both sides of the coin. I know we can't carry pictures of each other or anything super personal." She fingered the charm on her necklace. "But no one will notice a coin in your pocket. So it's like you're secretly carrying a piece of me with you wherever you go." She ducked her head. "I had this whole 'you own my heart' speech lined up . . ."

I kissed her and retrieved my coin. Against her mouth I said, "Not a lame gift at all, Annika. I love it."

"Stop talking. More kissing."

I smiled. "But I have one more thing to give you."

"You promised you'd stop at three presents, Axl."

"It's not really a present. It's more good news."

"What?"

"My test results came back. All negative."

"That is good news."

"So no more condoms."

"Nope."

"Merry Christmas to us."

Twenty-six

ANNIKA

The only thing I could think of after it happened was how much I hadn't wanted to be there in the first place.

The plane ride had been bumpy.

The cabbie had driven like a maniac.

The fans on the way into the stadium were dickheads.

The box seating area was too small.

I'd bitched because Soldier Field was the last place I wanted to be on a weekend that Axl was home. And it sucked because I couldn't tell anyone that. Nor could I invite him along.

Then to get to the game and find out that not only did the stupid skybox make me claustrophobic, but everyone else in my family had paired up—including Ash, which had shocked the crap out of me—making it clear that I truly was the odd woman out this time.

The only benefit to my sour mood was it created a barrier

around me so everyone left me alone. I sat in the front of the box, closest to the one exit. Sports magazines were scattered across the table and I thumbed through them. I found six ads featuring my sexy boyfriend. One ad in particular annoyed me today, an ad for compression athletic shorts that showed Axl shirtless. The ad itself didn't bother me. It was the fact that I knew Axl was sitting on my couch in a pose exactly like that right now and I wasn't there to enjoy the view. Or him.

Nothing you can do about it. Just concentrate on the game.

The Vikings were having another so-so season that some experts attributed to the suspension of their biggest franchise player. While others speculated that playing at the U of M football stadium and not having home field advantage had thrown them off. The Metrodome was history; it'd been torn down as soon as last season ended. The new stadium would be constructed in less than two years.

But regardless of the team's stats or personnel difficulties, or relocation issues, Jensen was having the best year of his career. He was killing it on the field. That was part of the reason I hadn't wanted to come to the last regular season game in Chicago—the media demand for Jens postgame meant we didn't get to spend any time with him until we returned to Minneapolis. So I really could've been watching the game at home, sitting on Axl's lap, while I got to show off my sports knowledge to him for a change.

I had been paying close attention to the game, but still the play happened so fast I almost missed it.

Almost.

A late hit.

Jensen on the ground.

Not moving.

Then we couldn't see anything because a swarm of medical personnel surrounded him on the field.

They reran the instant replay a few times, but we couldn't be sure if the angle of the camera was wrong.

Or if the angle of his leg was wrong.

When nothing happened for several long minutes, when no one did anything, I grabbed my coat and purse and took off to see what I could find out. I couldn't just sit there in shock and do nothing.

The security guard for our section stopped me.

"I need to get to the locker and media rooms for the visiting team. Is it straight down and over where their tunnel exits?"

"They're not gonna let you in there."

"My brother was just"—*mowed over by one of your cheating players*—"hit on the field, and I need to find out what's going on with him."

His eyes softened. "I saw the hit, child. By the time you get down there, he'll be on his way to the hospital. Can't you call an assistant coach or someone else for information on where they'll be taking him?"

"I . . ." I doubted Dad and Mom had that info. Jensen kept his professional life far removed from his family life. That was why it'd been such a huge deal when he took Mom's advice and met with Peter.

His agent.

That was a way in. I dug out my phone and scrolled through my contacts. I texted him first because I guessed he was already on the phone.

My phone rang a minute later.

"Annika. I have a call in to the team physician. I talked to the assistant physical therapist and he knows Jensen's family is there at the stadium and needs to be brought in for medical decisions."

"Thank you for that. How bad is it?"

"I honestly don't know what they're treating him for."

"Are they taking him to a hospital?"

"I would assume so—"

"Can you clear it for me to be down there with him?"

"I'll try, but there's no guarantee."

I closed my eyes. "I just don't want him to be alone if he's in pain."

"I understand."

"Let them know unless it's an immediate matter of keeping Jens alive? No one makes any other medical decisions without consulting with the Lund family." Money wasn't an issue in getting Jensen the best doctors and treatments in the world.

"I will make that clear to them. I'll keep you updated."

"Thank you." I hustled back into the box. My aunts sat huddled with my mom. Lennox and Trinity sat with Dallas. Walker, Brady, Ash, Nolan, my dad and both my uncles were on their phones. Since it appeared most of them were on hold, I said, "I talked to Peter, Jensen's agent. He's in touch with someone on the medical team, but they don't know anything yet. He'll keep us informed. Have any of you heard anything more?"

"No," Brady said. "Since I work with his trainer, I've got his number. I see he's in the locker room and not on the field, but he's not picking up."

"They're still just tossing around theories on the network," Walker said. "Nobody knows shit."

"The only sure thing is the fucker who made the late hit has been ejected from the game and escorted off the field," Ash said.

I looked over at my dad. His face was drawn tight. I walked over and hugged him hard, pressing my cheek to his chest.

He tightened his arms around me and kissed the top of my head.

My phone buzzed in my back pocket and I stepped back to answer it. "Peter. You have some news, I hope."

"Yes. They're transporting him to University of Chicago

Medical Center." He paused. It was a *hold on because the worst is yet to come* kind of pause. "Annika. He hasn't regained consciousness. They're taking him to the brain trauma and spinal cord injury unit."

Hold your shit together. It means nothing yet. I had to keep reminding myself to remain calm.

"Thank you so much, Peter. From all of us. And we will keep you apprised of the situation."

"If you need anything, call me."

I hung up.

"Well?" my mother demanded.

"They're taking him to University of Chicago Medical Center. To the brain trauma and spinal cord injury unit because he hasn't regained consciousness since the hit."

Complete silence all around me in the box.

Below us the crowd roared because play had resumed on the field as if nothing had happened.

Walker kicked a chair and Trinity twined herself around him.

Lennox already had Brady's face in her hands as she talked him out of a chair-kicking rage because he felt it just as much as Walker and I did.

I was scared and mad and worst of all, I felt like a clear box had been dropped over me; I could see out, they could see in, but I was wholly separate from everyone. Part of the group, and yet alone.

Don't start to panic, because there's not enough air in this imaginary box.

My phone buzzed in my hand.

I glanced down and saw his name pop up on the text message.

AH: I am yours for whatever you need. Call me, my sweet, when you can. I love you.

Don't cry.

But I wanted him here. He deserved to be here more than the one-offs that Nolan, Ash and Dallas had brought along.

"Is that more news from Peter?" my mother asked.

I glanced up. "No. But who's calling the car service—"

"Done," my uncle Monte said. "You all go. We'll catch up."

I rode to the hospital with Mom and Dad, but the drive itself was a blur.

At the hospital Dad took charge. He secured us a private waiting room.

Another two hours passed before we received the first visit from the medical team.

Jensen was conscious.

The concern now was paralysis.

Not a word—*condition*—any of us could wrap our heads around.

Then they'd left us to deal with that without any new information about how Jensen was feeling and what he knew about his medical condition.

My parents' frustration level was a painful thing to watch. Then my dad left without a word to any of us.

Within half an hour of his return, a woman showed up and introduced herself as our personal hospital liaison. She explained everything to us, from the impact of the initial injury, to why the doctors were in this medical holding pattern with any treatment.

Spinal cord contusion.

Three words that strike fear into any tight end player's family.

Jensen had been unconscious for fifty minutes. They'd stabilized him with a neck collar, but they couldn't ask about his range of motion until he'd regained consciousness. Hours later he couldn't feel anything from the waist down.

That was when my mother had lost it.

The rest of us were in a state of shock.

Then our liaison gave us the encouraging news that perhaps the paralysis was temporary, which was why the doctors were waiting it out. And he wasn't on a respirator—another encouraging sign. But in addition to his neck injury, he'd dislocated his kneecap. If the paralysis did wear off, then he could feel what other injuries he might've sustained.

It was all surreal and overwhelming.

Peter started dealing with my father in recommending the top sports medicine doctors in case Jensen needed surgery.

My aunts brought in food.

The hospital found us on-site sleeping accommodations.

Since we'd be here at least a few more days, my uncles and Ash and Nolan returned to Minneapolis to take care of business at LI. My aunts opted to stay for a day or two and help us out so we wouldn't have to leave the hospital.

Twelve hours after the accident happened, we finally got to see him. Two at a time, or in my case one at a time.

Jensen looked pale and broken in that hospital bed. But he was alive and breathing on his own and that was the important thing. We'd deal with the rest one step at a time.

But once I was in his small room, the claustrophobia kicked in. Panic seized my lungs—no air in, no air out. My heart rate quadrupled. Blood pounded in my head, amplifying my fear of being crushed in this small space. I slid to the floor and hugged my knees, eyes closed, trying to shrink inside myself.

That was the last thing I remembered.

A cool hand touched my face. "Annika."

My mom's voice.

I opened my eyes to see her and my dad looming over me. I almost screamed at them to stop crowding me, but I managed to maintain an even tone of voice. "Please give me some space and tell me what happened."

"You passed out."

"Maybe you should tell us why." This came from my father.

I noticed I was lying on a hospital bed in one of the rooms they'd given us for resting. "The stress must've hit me. I was tired and dehydrated."

Dad didn't look like he believed me. But why would he? No one in my family knew I still suffered from claustrophobia—or why. The only person I'd ever told was Axl.

Axl. I hadn't texted him back and I needed to talk to him now more than ever.

"If you're that dehydrated the staff wants to start you on an IV drip."

"No." I sat up. "That's an overreaction. I just need to get some water and fresh air. Some snacks. Then I'll try to sleep for a few hours." I stood. "If I leave, will there be an issue with me getting back up here?"

"I'll check with the nurse. I don't feel comfortable letting you wander around outside by yourself in the middle of the night," my dad said.

"I'll remind you I am an adult, Dad. And it's almost dawn. I'll stay in the designated smoking areas."

My dad's eyebrow winged up. "You won't find fresh air there."

"I doubt I'll find many smokers this time of day either," I said dryly. "I'll be fine. Besides, I'll have my phone." I walked over to Cathy, our hospital liaison. "I need some fresh air and snacks, but I want to make sure I can get back up here."

"Of course." She'd already set up a makeshift desk. She dug a lanyard out of a box on the floor. "This will grant you access to all areas."

"Great. I'm trying to avoid reporters, so is there a designated smoking area or a rooftop garden nearby?"

"Yes, down on the seventh floor there's an outdoor area. The exit is at the east end."

"Accessible by stairs?"

"Yes. Stairs are across from the service elevator. There are beverage and vending machines on every floor, but for more substantial fare you'll have to head to level A."

"Thank you."

Neither Brady nor Walker saw me head down the hallway after I grabbed my jacket and purse out of the waiting room. I booked it down the stairwell, grateful it wasn't cramped. After popping out on floor seven, I found a vending machine and bought a bottle of water and a Red Bull. Then I stepped out into the chilly Chicago predawn.

Despite the cold and the darkness, I took my first full breath since I'd felt the claustrophobia closing in.

In the aftermath of an episode, I always felt ridiculous. Like I should've outgrown this fear. That I would be so ashamed if anyone ever found out I still struggled with this. Then that was followed by belittling myself; once again I'd made the incident more terrifying than it actually was.

I headed to the railing and looked across the Chicago skyline. I felt so . . . lost.

I noticed the gas heating lamps above a few of the seating areas and clicked one on. The chill immediately evaporated. I settled into a chair, pulled out my phone to call Axl. But it would be rude to call him now, especially since he had to be up in a few hours to practice before tonight's game. So I sent him a text message. A really long text message detailing everything that had gone wrong—including the episode of claustrophobia and my worries that my family would figure out what had happened to me.

Or is it more concerning that they don't look beyond the surface with you?

The long, rambling text took me close to half an hour to type. I ended by telling Axl how much I missed him, I loved him and wished him good luck at the game and that I'd be in touch.

I wanted to tell him I needed him here with me. That I hated hiding what we meant to each other. That I'd been wrong to put my career first and us second. But Axl was having an amazing season. His personal life had not been a blip on the radar since our "breakup," and all the media focus was on his game. That was a huge relief to him. In fact, in the past few weeks he hadn't asked even one time if I'd heard anything about the Haversman presentation, when before, he'd asked me about it almost daily. Now it seemed as if he wanted to continue to keep our relationship under wraps . . . at least until the hockey season ended.

Maybe that was the smartest option. Besides, I had other things to worry about now with Jensen's injury.

The second day we got the best news. Jensen's paralysis had been temporary.

But now he needed surgery immediately to repair his kneecap.

The team physicians, some of the players and other medical professionals all weighed in on which orthopedic specialist should perform the surgery, and they narrowed the list to two.

Neither doctor was in Chicago.

They ended up choosing a surgeon in Florida.

We were discussing arrangements when my phone rang. The caller ID read Peter, and I had a moment of panic that maybe something had happened to Axl. Then I remembered that as far as Peter knew—as far as the entire world knew—Axl and I were done.

"Peter? Did you mean to call me?"

"Yes. Do you have a few minutes to talk?"

"Give me one second. It's loud in here." I left the waiting room and walked down the hallway to the stairwell and slipped inside. "What's going on?"

"Remember when I said you had to be ready to pitch to Haversman at a moment's notice?"

"Yes." Then I said, "Why?" even though my stomach was already sinking and I could guess what was coming next.

"If you're serious about this, you have to be in Belize tomorrow."

"What? You're joking."

"No, I am not. Haversman is hosting his annual mixer and this is the only chance you'll have to pitch to him this year. A yacht docks tomorrow night at sunset, picks up all the guests and takes them to his private island. So you have one shot to be on that boat."

"Peter. They're moving Jensen to Florida tomorrow for surgery. I can't just tell my family I'm flying off to Belize to meet with Haversman on his private island."

"You cannot tell them that anyway, Annika. This is a by-invitation-only event. Anyone who talks to the press about this? Banned for life. And since you're taking my invite, you do not want to do that and fuck me over."

Shit. "I . . . can't. Jensen—"

"Will be doped up for the next five days," he inserted. "He won't know if you're out in the waiting room, or in Belize."

Man, he just cut right to the heart of it.

"You're concerned about your family's reaction. If they'll judge you or get angry. But the truth is, you don't *all* need to be there holding Jensen's hand, because he's only got two of them. This is a huge opportunity for you to expand your vision for the company. It's not like you're blowing off your family to party in the Caribbean. Not only can Haversman put this new line of products you're pitching in his magazines, but he can feature it in his hotels—of which there are now twenty-five hundred."

I knew all this. I truly did.

"Tell me you're not dragging your feet because the pitch isn't ready," he said sharply.

"The pitch is perfect," I retorted. "And the only reason I'm hesitating is that my youngest brother is having major fucking surgery away from home, after an event that's been traumatic to my entire family."

Peter sighed. "I get it, Annika. I do. But there's part of you that knows if Brady said he had a major presentation to make on behalf of the company and couldn't be there, he'd get a pass. If you do the same thing, you're shirking your family responsibilities."

I closed my eyes. I hated that he was right, because we both knew it wasn't "my family" he was referring to, just my mother, who'd take issue with it. "How long does this mixer last?"

"Five to seven days. Haversman arranges air transportation for everyone back to Atlanta, since he's fluid with the number of days."

"Have you been to his island?"

"Yes. It's unbelievable. Truly paradise. So you will have time to relax and get to know the other attendees, which is beneficial if Haversman opts not to market-research your product. There are others who might be interested in it."

"Any kinky bondage games that are played? And are all attendees expected to participate?"

Peter laughed. "What an active imagination. Nothing like that. It's all on the up-and-up. The best food, the best booze, the best spa services, all in a relaxed business environment."

How could I say no? I couldn't. "Okay. Count me in. Last couple of questions. Attire? Do I bring him a gift? And is there cell service?"

"Attire is business but island casual. Yes, bring him as unique a gift as you can come up with at this late notice, but nothing your company manufactures. He likes oddities. Of course there's cell service. He's a tech mogul, but the transmissions are monitored fully. If your call abruptly ends, you said something that revealed too much."

"I feel like I should have a sat phone with me and a code word in place in case I need an emergency extraction."

"You'll do fine. Call me tomorrow and let me know you've made your connections to Belize."

I frowned. "Connections?"

"My admin booked your tickets. Check your e-mail. You leave from Minneapolis tomorrow. I assumed you'd need to return here first and get your presentation."

I could be pissy that he'd assumed so much, or I could let it go and save my energy for the battle to come. "Thanks, Peter. I'll keep you updated."

After I hung up I checked the airline schedules. I booked a seat on the next flight from Chicago to Minneapolis, which left in two hours.

Then I looked at my spreadsheet for Axl's schedule. If I was gone the full seven days, I'd get back the day after he started his nine-day stretch of away games.

My heart hurt. I'd miss him like crazy. But maybe hiding our relationship could finally end—I just had to kill on this pitch and make sure our sacrifice was worth it.

I rested my forehead on my knees and gave in to the urge to weep. If I released the tears from my system now, it'd keep me from breaking down in front of my family and all they'd see was the Iron Princess.

Twenty-seven

AXL

In the last three games I'd ended up with thirty stitches.

The team doctors were taking bets on if I'd rip the stitches today or if I'd require a whole new set.

I'd never actually notched ice time in Madison Square Garden—every time the team I played for had a game here, I'd suited up but ended up warming the bench, so maybe I did need a zipper strip to mark the occasion. But then again, it was better to give than to receive and there were a couple of Rangers players I'd be gunning for who decided it'd be funny to taunt me in the press. We'd see who had the last laugh at the end of the third period.

I had one goal.

Two assists.

I spent two minutes in the sin bin—although I probably deserved more.

I'd played one of the most aggressive games of my pro

career. I'd never felt so satisfied at smashing guys into the boards as I did during those sixty minutes.

We beat them 4 to 2.

Since it'd been an early Sunday afternoon game that aired opposite the Super Bowl, there wasn't much media coverage. So that was probably why I noticed him at the press conference.

My father. Sitting in the back row.

I actually said, "What the fuck?" out loud, earning a sharp look from Coach.

I dutifully answered questions about the vast difference in my stats from last year to this year—*all coaching and teamwork*.

My recent string of goals—*adaptability in the face of the opposition's mistakes is a skill learned only through ice time, which I was grateful to have plenty of this season.*

When asked if any incident triggered my more aggressive playing and subsequent injuries, I couldn't answer, *I'm frustrated as fuck because not only haven't I seen my girlfriend for three weeks, but with our travel schedules I've barely talked to her.* Instead I said, *Hockey isn't a sport for pussies. You get hurt, you suck it up, you get your ass back on the ice and take out your pain on your opponents*, and by the buzz in the nearly empty room, I knew I'd just ended my "lie low" media creed for the past months.

My father waited for me outside the locker room. I hadn't seen him in three years. He didn't look all that different. I suppose we looked alike, same longer blond hair and pale blue eyes, although I topped him by ten centimeters and outweighed him by twenty kilograms. He had the once-preferred slight build of a football player. Now the European football players seemed much bigger and more muscular than in days past.

"Father." I offered my hand. "You're looking well."

"Thank you. Interesting game."

Not "Great game" or "You killed it out there" or "I saw you're one of the leading scorers among D-men this season." Just . . . interesting. "You're in the States on business?"

"Yes. Leaving tomorrow."

For once I wished I had to dash off to catch the team plane. But we were staying in New York overnight. "Me as well."

"We should have a drink and catch up. Where are you staying?"

"At the Ritz," I said.

"I'm at the Four Seasons. They have a decent wine list. You should meet me in the bar. Say . . . an hour from now?"

"Two hours would be better for me."

"Great. See you then." He took off, which surprised me. Usually he'd hang around and expect me to introduce him so everyone could kiss his World Cup medal.

Any elation I'd felt over our win had been soured by his presence.

I reminded myself not to give him that kind of power.

Flitte headed toward me. "Who was that guy?"

"My father."

"No kidding. No wonder he looked familiar. You hanging out with him?"

"In a bit. Why?"

"We're in New York, man. We gotta eat pizza."

"Cool. I'm starved. We meeting the team someplace?"

Flitte shook his head. "Just you and me, Hammer-time. They went back to the hotel to watch the football game."

I hadn't really spent any one-on-one time with Flitte. He wasn't as obnoxious without McClellan and Dykstrand egging him on.

"So, does your old man live in New York or something?" Flitte continued with the interrogation as soon as we were sitting inside a pizza parlor.

I shook my head. "He lives in Italy. He's here on business,

I guess. Weird that I ran into him. Or maybe I should say weird that he came to one of my games."

"He's not, like, your biggest fan?" Flitte said.

"Not even close."

"I know how that goes. My old man wanted me to play baseball. He bitched about the price of hockey equipment constantly—'If you'd picked baseball you wouldn't be putting this family in the poorhouse.' So as soon as I was old enough to get a job, I did and I paid for my own equipment. Hockey paid for college." He shoved the last bite of pizza in his mouth and swallowed. "People say you gotta respect your parents, but I say your parents need to respect you too. My dad still says, 'Think of how great a baseball player you could've been if you had put as much effort into that as you did into hockey.'"

"My dad is the same way. Except with football—soccer."

"Screw 'em both. Hockey rules." He held up his beer mug and we toasted.

After we ate, I hailed a cab to the Four Seasons and spotted my dad already seated in the bar.

He gestured to his glass of wine. "Would you like one? It's a decent Argentinian Malbec."

"No, thanks." When the waiter arrived, I ordered a Brooklyn Lager.

My father wrinkled his nose. Another mark against me.

He scrutinized my suit. "Still with Pontus for your wardrobe, I see."

I said nothing. If I defended my tailor, my father would lecture me on the opportunities I was missing out on in Italy by being loyal to a "nobody designer."

"Your mother is well?" he asked.

"Yes, as far as I know. It's hard to keep in touch with the time difference and my travel schedule." *Besides, do you truly give a damn? You've never been her favorite person—and she never asks after you.*

"Do you still go to Sweden after the season ends?"

"Still up in the air for this year. I'm focused on playing and not thinking beyond that."

"I've been keeping up with your games. Decent statistics. I hope that Peter can leverage that during contract negotiations and find you a winning team."

"I have a two-year contract with the Wild."

He waved his hand. "Those contracts are made to be broken. You'd be better off with a more visible team. If you're going to build a reputation as a brawler and a beast—"

"I'm happy to be in Minnesota."

"See? This is what I was trying to get you to avoid, being satisfied with what you have when there's so many other possibilities."

I laughed, but I doubted he noticed the sound had a bitter edge. "Nothing is ever good enough. Is that your philosophy with women too?"

He smirked at me over his wineglass. "Ah. A philosophy we agree on, since you've been through your share of women— or so I've read."

"Don't believe everything you see online."

"But the stats don't lie. You've been distracted by women in some form or other since you reached pro status. I remember those days. So very, very hard—near impossible—to say no to the opportunities women throw at your feet. And even when you're a young man with stamina to spare, or you believe that to be true . . . you find it isn't. You find that when you cut out everything that doesn't matter and focus solely on the sport, it is a game changer."

I'd memorized my father's stats in my childhood and I knew he'd reached his peak performance level when I was age four—so his comment about cutting out everything that didn't matter included me. His son.

He'd played football for six more years after that. Never

at that same level again, but it wasn't because he'd suddenly become an involved father.

How I wished I could tell him the joke was on him. The exact opposite was true for me. I'd found Annika and she provided the focus I needed because I wasn't out looking for something that I already had with her.

I wasn't anything like him. For possibly the first time in my life, I truly believed it.

My phone buzzed. Normally I ignored it in a social situation, but I welcomed the interruption. Especially when I saw it was a text from Annika.

AL: Are you getting stitched up again, Ax-hell?

Me: No. I'm free-bleeding to show them how tough I am. Why?

AL: The front desk put me through to your room and you didn't answer.

I frowned. *Why would she call the hotel?*

Me: Did you try my cell?

AL: No. I hoped the hotel would put the hotshot hockey player and the Midwest heiress who just KILLED her presentation to Haversman in Belize on the same floor . . .

Me: YOU ARE IN NYC RIGHT NOW?

AL: At the Ritz, room 312.

I jumped up so fast I knocked the chair over.
My father looked at me. "Is something wrong?"

"No, everything is finally right. Thanks for the beer."

I was so pumped up that I could've sprinted back to the hotel, but I was beat-up from the game. And I needed to get control of the adrenaline that'd hit me like a shot of nitrous at the starting line or I'd take Annika up against the door like a beast with barely a fucking *hello*.

She'd like that.

No, she'd *love* that.

Later I couldn't remember the cab ride. Or even how much money I threw at the cabbie. I was striding across the pavement, then through the lobby and into the elevator. When the elevator doors opened on the third floor, I sprinted down the hallway.

Then there it was. Room 312.

I knocked, like a hundred times.

Or maybe that was just my heart.

She opened the door and stood in front of me, the wintry gray New York skies a backdrop in the window behind her, and not even that gloom dimmed the pure joy on her face when she looked at me.

I almost fell to my knees in my gratitude for this bond that I'd built with her. Instead I slammed the door shut behind me. But I didn't take a single step toward her.

"Axl? What's wrong?"

"I am trying to do the right thing. Taking a minute to tell you I love you. To tell you I missed you. To tell you that you are the most beautiful sight I've ever seen after not seeing you for three weeks. To tell you that this might be the greatest surprise anyone has ever given me."

"Okay. If that's the right thing, what's the wrong thing?"

"Tearing your clothes off and fucking you against the wall."

Her eyes went hot with lust. "I definitely encourage you to do the wrong thing."

And . . . I was done.

She'd worn a bathrobe, so the tearing-her-clothes-off portion took, like, half a second.

My pants were no match for her greedy hands.

Then I was on her, holding her close. Kissing her. Bracing her against the wall as I did the wrong thing.

Twice.

Turns out two wrongs do make a right.

Later, we were lounging in bed, sated from sex and food—Annika fed both my appetites; she'd ordered just about every item on the room service menu because she knew how starved I was postgame.

I nobly did not press the woman on why she didn't have a single tan line on her beautifully golden body.

We talked about everything.

About my father.

About her presentation to Haversman in Belize. She warned me that until she had actual confirmation about Haversman's intentions regarding the product line, nothing changed with us; we still had to keep our relationship private. What Annika had failed to grasp was that from the very start of this I hadn't minded our relationship wasn't public. I liked that she was mine in all the ways that mattered. Even now when I was more confident in our ability to weather whatever was thrown at us, I wasn't in any hurry to be the focus of media speculation again. Not that I said as much to her, because she might take it the wrong way—meaning the Annika way.

We talked about Jensen's surgery and recovery. Jensen and I kept in touch regularly, so I actually knew more details about his rehab regimen than she did.

The hour got late and I had to be up early. I set the alarm and crawled back into bed with her.

"I missed this," she murmured against my chest.

"Me too."

"How much longer is the regular season?"

"Three months."

"Then when this Haversman stuff is in the bag and you're off the ice, we can have a coming-out party, right?"

"I'm forbidden to throw any more parties, remember?"

She elbowed me. "You know what I mean, Ax-hell."

I kissed the top of her head. "I do. And yes, Attila. We can let the world know." I chuckled. "I have this vision of you blasting Diana Ross's song 'I'm Coming Out' when we make our first official appearance as a couple."

"No. Way. If we're playing a Diana Ross song? Totally going with 'Endless Love.' It fits us."

"That it does."

Twenty-eight

AXL

"Annika is depressed."

Jensen grabbed a handful of popcorn and said, "No shit," before he tossed it in his mouth.

That was his reaction? After I'd debated a week on whether to bring it up? Going behind Annika's back was a last resort, but I'd been worried about her the past few weeks. "Do you know why?"

"Buzz with the Lund Collective," Jensen said, "is that she hasn't even wanted to celebrate the fact that she nailed the pitch to this Haversman dude, and he's going all out with next year's spring catalogue to feature LI's new luxury spa line."

I froze. Annika hadn't said anything to me about Haversman finally making a commitment to picking up her proposed product line. She'd obsessed about it for so long, and it wasn't like her to shrug off a professional win of this magnitude. Plus, this had a significant impact on our relationship—at least the keeping-it-in-the-dark portion. Now we could change that. So why hadn't she shared this major life-altering news with me? It went beyond me being proud of her accomplishment and expecting to celebrate with her.

Maybe she prefers to celebrate with her family.

I told that snarky voice to shut the hell up. Jensen had just told me she wasn't celebrating with her family either . . . which was why he wasn't surprised when I suggested Annika was depressed.

Jensen shifted sideways, repositioning the leg in the brace he'd propped up on the coffee table. "Man, I hate this couch. The cushions don't stay in place."

"You're welcome to return to your two-million-dollar condo and plop your lame ass on your own couch." Jensen had become a regular fixture at my place since his injury and surgery. It helped him to talk about his future in sports with someone who understood that sometimes choices weren't just his to make.

"Nah. I hate that uncomfortable piece of shit, which is why I'm over here. We should get one of those leather pit-style lounge areas for in here. There'd be room for everyone. It'd be wall-to-wall puffy leather like a freakin' cloud."

"Lund. You do realize you don't live here, right?"

He shrugged. "When you pull your head out of your ass and do the right thing by my sister and move in with her, I call dibs on this place."

"Why? Seriously. Your apartment was featured in *Midwest Architectural Digest.*"

"So? The people in my building are dick-holes. I paid almost two million bucks for my apartment and I have to *ask* the resident board's permission before I can get a fucking dog. That's just wrong. This place? So much more my style. People are friendly. Neighborly. I have a lot more in common with Martin and Boris than I do with Duffy and Muffy."

I'd heard the Lunds called eccentric. But after getting to know the megarich Annika and Jensen, eccentric just meant they didn't have to put up with the usual bullshit in life.

"So back to Annika being depressed," Jensen said. "What are you gonna do about it? Because to be blunt, it's mostly your fault."

I couldn't argue with that. "As soon as the season ends, I wanna take her to the Maldives."

"Boring. It's gotta be bigger than that."

"Why?"

Jensen sighed and looked at me. "I'm breaking the rules by telling you this, but you're sort of a clueless fucker and I think you need the help. I don't know if it's a cultural thing or what. Annika is a romantic. She's never been the princess in the tower who needs rescuing, but that doesn't mean she hasn't wanted her very own prince to sweep her off her feet and prove he can be her own true love for the rest of her life. She believes in that because she knows it exists. Our parents have that kind of love. Our brothers have found that kind of love. That's why she's been depressed. She's found her man and she can't share the happiness with anyone in her life who matters to her. She's had to hide her joy for what . . . six months? Maybe she's questioning whether the joy is real."

"It's real."

"Prove it." He held up his hand to forestall my question on asking him how to do that. "Figure it out yourself. But whatever you decide to do? Prove it to her beyond a shadow of a doubt."

How was I supposed to do that? And how soon did this need to happen? We were in the last two weeks of regular season play and I was freakin' exhausted. Although I was having a great year, the team wouldn't have a postseason. The only upside to that? At least I wouldn't have to grow a beard during the playoffs. I hated that tradition.

Jensen said, "Pass the popcorn. Am I kicking your ass at *Madden* or what?"

"Dream on, baller. One game and then we're playing—"

"Broskys!" Martin called out as he barged into my apartment. "I thought I smelled popcorn. Whatcha doin'?"

"About to play *Madden*," Jensen said. "What're you doing? Isn't Verily back in town today?"

Martin grinned. "She got back this morning. I've spent the past six hours reminding my goddess why she misses me. I wore her out." He held his fist out to both of us for a bump. "I'm too stoked to sleep, so here I am."

At least he hadn't said he was "too toked up to sleep." I glanced at the clock. Annika would be off work in half an hour. "Have fun. I'm heading to Annika's."

"I have a can of whipped cream left over if you need it," Martin offered.

"Martin. Remember when we talked about TMI?"

"Yeah, dude. That's my sister," Jensen complained.

Just to be ornery I said, "Annika prefers chocolate syrup to whipped cream anyway."

As soon as Annika came through the door to her apartment, I was there to greet her and sweep her up in my arms.

"Oh. Hi. I wasn't expecting you."

"Why weren't you expecting me?" I crowded her against the wall. "I'm here all the time."

"If you're in town. Which hasn't been all that often lately," she pointed out.

"Then by all means, we should waste time fighting about it when I *am* in town," I said right before I kissed her neck.

"Axl—"

"Bed. Now."

"Can we do this later? I have so much work—"

"The magic is gone." I sighed against her throat. "Seven months into our relationship and you'd rather work than let me show you all the wicked things I want to do to you . . ." I gave her one last kiss before I stepped back. "So, is there something going on at work that you want to talk about?"

Annika snagged my hand. "I'm sorry. No, I don't want to talk about work, Axl. I want you to work me over, work me up—"

I kissed her. And kept kissing her as I backed her down the hallway. First I said, "Shoes," and reclaimed her lips as she ditched her heels. Next I slipped her tweed jacket down her arms and tossed it on the floor. Her ivory silk blouse was next, unbuttoned and fluttering to the carpet. Followed quickly by her tweed skirt. By the time we hit the mattress in her room, a tiny lace thong and matching bra were the only barriers keeping me from feasting on her.

I pushed her onto the bed and rendered the thong useless with a hard tug. I dropped to my knees and set my mouth on her. I was relentless, demanding everything of her even as I gave her everything I had to offer. My sweet, fiery princess unraveled twice. Before she caught her breath, I rolled her over and impaled her. Setting a fast rhythm that had her arching up and meeting me thrust for thrust.

Words weren't necessary between us at this point. I knew her body, her needs, almost better than my own. We reached the tipping point at the same time and I couldn't believe anything in life would ever get better than this.

As soon as I moved, she twined herself around me. "I'm sorry I almost blew that off to work. Thank you for the reminder that the magic isn't gone."

I kissed the top of her head. "So you're not ready to hand me my walking papers?"

Annika bit my chest.

"Ouch."

"Oh, shut it, hockey player. Why would you think I was done with you?"

Because you haven't even mentioned that the main thing keeping us from going public with our relationship is no longer an issue. "Because I wouldn't blame you. I worry about this beautiful butterfly I've trapped in a box. And I know she's claustrophobic, but even then I can't let her go."

"You sweet, sweet man. You get me in every way that's important to me and I've never been happier than I've been with you these past seven months. Do I wish we could go out and see a movie or try a new restaurant? Sometimes. But you are gone a lot, and when you are here, I'm selfish. I get your undivided attention. We don't have people interrupting and asking for your autograph at my dining room table." She ran her finger around the outside of my nipple. "I have all sides of you in private. In public I get Robo Axl. We are much more solid in our relationship now because we had the time and privacy to build it our way—without input from family, friends or colleagues. I never question anymore whether it's real."

"I love you."

"And then there's that. I never get tired of hearing it." She kissed my sternum and placed a string of openmouthed kisses progressively lower down my chest. When she'd positioned herself over my groin, she smirked at me. "Speaking of worked over . . . let's see if there's any magic left in this stick of yours."

Turned out, there was.

Twenty-nine

ANNIKA

The double life I led was getting to me.

I couldn't even have my friends over to get ready for our girls' night out because they'd see Axl's stuff all over my apartment. Then I became petulant when I imagined moving it because I didn't want to move it; Axl's stuff belonged here. With my stuff.

So I'd packed my makeup, outfit and shoes in my suitcase and rolled it to the door. When I bent down to slip on my snow boots, my necklace swung forward. I should probably take it off so I didn't have to answer questions about when and where I'd bought it, and if the white diamond-encrusted *A* on the front entwined with the black diamond-encrusted *A* on the back meant anything special . . .

Tears stung my eyes. I couldn't even wear the beautiful necklace my man had designed for me.

Screw it. I was wearing it.

Besides, I'd be in the line of fire a lot more if they saw my Wild underwear. But it was game night and since I couldn't kiss him good luck in the arena, wearing his number on my ass had become our tradition and I wasn't breaking it even for girls' night out.

We were meeting at Brady and Lennox's place for some food and pregame action before we started barhopping. I would've been content to pick one bar—preferably a sports bar so I could keep an eye on the hockey game—and stay there all night. But this was a belated celebration welcoming Trinity into the family. She and Walker had been married several months, but between the holidays and Jensen's injury, we hadn't thrown her a belated bachelorette party like we had for Lennox.

I wasn't sure who Lennox and Dallas had invited beyond their edict of "no dudes." I had a pang of sympathy for Axl and his promise of "no WAGs" the night of the party from hell.

The car service dropped me off at Brady and Lennox's funky warehouse and I had a funny tickle in my belly when I noticed an actual party bus.

Only one person I knew ever had crazy ideas like that. Cara, who'd instantly become my BFF in third grade when we discovered we had matching Powerpuff Girls backpacks. But she'd moved to Thailand a year and a half ago to become a master chef.

The front door opened. Cara tossed her arms up in the air and called out, "Surprise!"

"Cara? What in the world are you doing here?"

Dallas, Lennox and Trinity spread out in a line beside her.

Lennox said, "You know how your brothers and cousins staged an intervention when one of the Lund boys was being a dumb-ass? Well, we're doing the same thing for you. Annika

Lund, you are the shit, girl! Scoring Haversman as a client! I cannot believe you don't want to shout that accomplishment from the motherfucking rooftops. So guess what? We're doing it for you tonight."

"What? This isn't a belated bachelorette party?"

"Nope. This party is for you," Dallas said. "Congratulations! Come on in and see who's partying with us tonight."

Taken aback, I burst into tears.

After I had hugged Cara a million times, Dallas forced me to do a shot of Kinky.

I sat on the barstool in the kitchen, trying to catch my breath and wrap my head around all this. Everyone was staring at me. "What?"

"Dude. The 'Iron Princess' cries. We just wanted a moment to take in history."

I flipped Dallas off.

Lennox moved to my right side. "I think you know everyone. We put together a fun group of professional women who wouldn't have any problem shouting 'Girl Power!' every time we do a shot in your honor tonight."

I squinted at Cara. "This has to have been your idea."

"Damn straight. Now intro your new posse, A."

New posse. Right. After Cara had moved I'd gone into a friend funk. I missed her like crazy and hadn't seen the need to audition possible new BFFs, so I'd thrown myself into work for the past year and a half. So seeing that the only friends I had here were actual work friends depressed me. The only new friend I'd made was Verily, and Dallas couldn't invite her without explaining how I knew her, which depressed me even more.

Snap out of it. This is a celebration. Act enthusiastic even if you have to fake it.

"From the work side first." I pointed to my assistant. "You

remember Deanna. She still runs my life. You met my sis-in-law Lennox; she's also in PR at LI now." I shook my finger at Lucy. "No hiding behind Lennox tonight. Lucy is in graphic arts at LI. You know Dallas." Then I squinted. "Zosia? What the . . . ? They let you off the boat?"

She laughed.

I hopped off the stool and ran forward to tackle-hug her. "I'm so glad they invited you and that you came, you jerk. I haven't seen you in forever." I faced the group. "This is my cousin Zosia—she's shy. Oh, unless she's got a fishing pole or a net in her hand and then she is mean. She runs Lund Fisheries in Duluth."

"Someone has to crack the fishing line on those guys."

Then Lennox took over intros for me at that point. "On the couch with the gorgeous dreads is my friend Kiley. Next to her is Lola, my former boss at LI and next to her is Sydney, one of my LI coworkers. Trinity? You want to take it from here?"

"Sure. Next to me is my BFF, Gen, who is also a newlywed. Sitting next to her is Betsy. She runs Walker's office. Next to her is Tiffany, whose husband is Walker's partner."

"Hey. I'm preggers, so I'm driving the bus, which means we will stop for as many pee breaks as y'all want."

I looked around the room and got weepy again. "I can't believe all of you are here. Thank you for letting your friends rope you into this."

Lola, the oldest of the group, stood. "When Lennox asked me if I wanted to come, I thought, what the hell? It's a night out drinking with a bunch of hot young girls. Maybe some old dudes will get tired of getting blown off by them, and I'll get lucky for a change."

Everyone laughed.

"But after I've been here and talked with these ladies, half of whom I didn't know before tonight, I gotta say, this is a damn fine group of women. We aren't all executives, but we're all proud of what we do, and it's great to see us celebrating together."

Cara said, "Girl Power!"

"Girl Power!"

Then Cara slapped me on the ass. "Go get ready."

Dallas said, "Cara, go with her and keep her on task." She smirked and handed me an empty shot glass. "After she has another one of these." She filled it with Kinky.

I knocked it back like a pro.

Lennox directed us to the spare bedroom.

Cara carried in our drinks—we were moving on to the margaritas now—and I unfolded my suitcase on the bed. She whistled. "That is a hot outfit."

"Thanks." I'd brought gray leather pants along with a black silk halter. The shirt had no back, which was why the fur stole went so perfectly with it. "I cannot believe you're here! How long are you staying?"

"Just tonight. I leave in the morning."

"What? You came all the way from Bangkok for one night?"

"I've been in L.A. for a week. But I seriously worked seventy hours in that week. The chef is a major twat waffle, but he's also a culinary genius, so it's been fantastic. I had this one night free and thankfully it worked into everyone's schedule."

I hugged her again. "I miss you! How much longer will you be over there?"

"Not sure. But it'll be a few years until I'm seasoned enough to run a kitchen in the States. You'll have to visit me."

I whipped off my shirt and attempted to get the halter top on. Nope. I needed help.

Cara was right there, lifting my hair. "You don't look super happy for the huge coup you just scored for LI."

"I'm thrilled."

"She says with no enthusiasm whatsoever," Cara said dryly.

She moved to stand in front of me and straightened the straps on my halter. Of course she noticed the necklace. "This is stunning."

"Thank you."

"It's from him?"

"Yes. I never wear it out. Tonight I felt . . . defiant."

Her eyes, such a unique mix of hazel and gray, locked on to mine. "I feel privileged that you told me about him, A." She paused. "No one out there knows about you two?"

"Just Dallas. Jensen knows because he caught us together." I groaned. "He and Axl are buddies now, which is weird. Axl's friends Martin and Verily, who live across the hall from him, know. The upside of that is I don't have to skulk around Axl's apartment building."

"All this sneaking around for months . . . it's been worth it?"

"He's worth it. I love him. I don't doubt his love for me."

"So how much longer does this sneaking around have to go on?"

"Not sure," I hedged. She didn't know the Haversman deal had been the holdup. Now that it wasn't an issue, I hadn't figured out a way to approach it with Axl. He seemed content with the way things were, and that scared me. But he was near the end of the season. He needed to focus on that. We'd waited this long; a few weeks more wouldn't matter. Would it?

She lifted up our margarita glasses for a toast. "You are a lucky pucker. *Skål*."

I laughed. "*Skål*."

The bus ride turned out to be wild fun. Cara led sing-alongs until we reached our destinations.

I had a few drinks but nothing like the rest of the crew, who were feeling no pain when we arrived at the fourth bar.

"Where are we?" Deanna asked.

"Flurry!" Dallas said, clapping her hands and directing the group off the bus like a chipper tour guide.

I hadn't been here in months. Since the Axl incident. This was not my favorite bar—it never had been—and I couldn't understand why Brady and Lennox loved it or why Dallas and Nolan were regulars. I suspected we were here so my brothers could spy on their wives.

Lennox had reserved the VIP section, so we all trooped upstairs. The music didn't suck for once. I'd checked the hockey score three times, finding out in the last update that the team had won and Axl had scored a goal. It boosted my good mood even further—he always had such inventive ways of us celebrating when he scored on the ice.

I tried to spread out and talk to everyone in our group, but I spent most of my time with Cara and Zosia. Guys were relentless in hitting on us. I hadn't missed that at all in the past few months of being exiled from the social scene with Axl.

I'd been nursing the same drink for an hour and tried not to yawn.

So I wandered around. Lola and Kiley were out in front of the dance floor leading a group dance. Deanna, Sydney and Betsy were entertaining yet another group of guys who were hitting on them. Lucy, Tiffany and Gen were in a serious discussion. I didn't see Lennox. Or Trinity. Or Dallas.

I turned down four guys asking, "Hey, baby, where you goin'?" on the way to the bathroom and decided to take my time before returning to the bar scene.

When I stepped out of the restroom, I felt immediately that the energy in the bar had changed. The entire upper level had filled with people. The bass from the music started vibrating the railings, the floors and the ceiling.

Oddly enough, I didn't usually get claustrophobia in crowd situations. But it seemed as if the room had become half the size and was crammed with five times as many people.

Then they dimmed the lights.

Breathe.

Don't move.

The room is not closing in.

The oxygen is not evaporating from all the extra body heat.

Then I remembered my necklace.

Any dark place, Annika. I'm always there with you.

My scalp tingled with a new sensation, and I opened my eyes to see what had changed.

At that moment I spotted Axl across the room from me.

Those knowing eyes assessed everything about me all at once.

The way I'd curled into myself.

My hand at my throat.

He probably could tell my respiration rate.

He started toward me.

Heaven help anyone who got in his way.

I wouldn't say the crowd parted for him, but it pretty much did.

Once he'd passed through the throng, no one turned around and gawked or paid him attention.

Not that Axl would've noticed. Not that Axl would've cared.

My beautiful man, the way you're coming at me, with that look on your face, puts the spectacle in spectacular.

Axl rested his hand at the base of my throat and covered my hand gently with his own. "How bad?"

"Better now that you're here." I swallowed hard. "*Why* are you here?"

"Not my choice. Jensen pulled some strings and got the whole team in."

"My brother is here? With this many people around and wearing a brace?"

"No. He just set it up." He leaned in. "I don't want to talk about Jens."

"Axl, I love you."

He froze—not from my declaration, because me confessing my love for him wasn't new, but it wasn't like me to blurt it out angrily like an accusation.

"I want everyone to know I love you. I want everyone to know you love me. And it sounds childish, but I would pay you a million dollars to take me out of here right now the way you do at home. When you pick me up, cuddle me against your chest and carry me to bed after I fall asleep on the couch."

"Annika—"

"Let her go, you piece of shit."

Jesus. Exactly what we didn't need right now, interference from my brother Walker.

I watched Axl debate on whether to stay in protective mode or go on the offensive.

Before Axl could react, Walker pushed Axl's right shoulder, trying to separate him from me. As soon as Axl turned, everything morphed into slow motion before my eyes.

Walker's arm coming forward, his fist headed straight toward Axl's face. The moment of impact, Axl's head snapping back, then his letting go of me as he staggered backward a step.

My brother's anger that he hadn't knocked Axl down completely had him moving in for another shot.

I stepped between them. "Walker. Stop."

"This is the fucker who caused all the problems for you and punched Jensen."

I looked over my shoulder.

Axl smiled nastily at Walker. He had blood all over his teeth. "Your little brother hits harder."

Oh my fucking god.

"Axl. Go home. Now! No goddamn scenes, remember? Keep it about hockey, remember?"

He retreated.

I didn't watch him leave. I didn't have to. I watched Walker watching him leave.

"Did he hurt you?" Walker said.

"What?"

"That asshole had his hand on your throat. Did he hurt you?"

"No. It wasn't what it looked like. And what are you doing here? You hate this place."

Walker scratched his cheek. "Tiffany is tired and I'm the backup bus driver."

"Then that's a sign to call it a night."

It was nearly an hour and a half later before I returned to my apartment.

The lamps were off in the living room, but bluish white shadows flickered in the hallway, so I knew Axl was watching TV.

He'd sprawled in the middle of the bed, naked, holding a can of soda to the left half of his mouth.

In silence I ditched my clothes and draped them across the back of the couch in the sitting area. After I finished my bedtime beauty care routine, I exited the bathroom with one thing in mind.

Axl watched me with wary eyes as I crawled across the bed and over his body. I curled my hand around the metal can. The thing was warm, which meant it wasn't doing him any good, so I set it aside. "So now you've met my brother Walker."

"No offense, but he kind of seems like an asshole."

I smiled. "Funny. He said the same thing about you." I pressed soft kisses to the swollen spot on his jaw. "Does it hurt?"

Axl pushed my hair over my shoulder. "Not as much as

you begging me to carry you out of the bar and offering to pay me a million dollars to do it."

I cringed. "I'm sorry. I was having a weepy day. A needy day. A missing-you day. A needing-validation day."

He touched my necklace. "I see that."

I refocused on kissing the swollen spot on his face. "I love you."

"Annika."

"I love everything about you and I hate that when all the women were talking about their conquests or their men tonight, I couldn't talk about you." I brushed my lips across the bruised spot one last time before I began to work my way down his neck. "I love your mind, your heart"—I left an openmouthed kiss on his pectoral—"and I don't even want to get into how much I love this wicked-hot, sexy body of yours."

Axl started to squirm because he was a smart man; he knew which direction I was headed.

When I reached my ultimate destination, I looked up at him, across his marvelously defined upper torso. I teased him a little because I could.

And then I stopped teasing. I showed him how much I loved this part of him too.

Afterward, I nestled my head on his chest and listened as his heart regained a normal beat, his fingers still twisted in my hair.

He said, "You have one more brother, right?"

"Yeah. Why?"

"If that's what I get when a member of your family takes a swing at me? I'll introduce myself to your other brother first thing tomorrow morning."

Thirty

AXL

I finally had an idea of something I could do to show Annika the lengths I'd always be willing to go to ensure her happiness. To assure her that she meant everything to me: more than hockey, more than my pride.

Just thinking about what I planned to do . . . I broke out in a cold sweat, my vision went wonky, my guts were tied in a million knots and I might actually pass out.

Dramatic much? Man the fuck up.

I made the first call. "I know what I need to do to prove it to her. Yes, I came up with it on my own, jackass. Sorry. I'm just"—*nervous as fuck.* I exhaled. "I'll need your help."

Then I placed the second call. "Would it be possible to meet with you privately sometime this week? It's important. It's . . . personal. Yes. I'll be there. Thank you."

To pull this off, I'd have to call in every favor and play the ultimate PR card.

But there was no doubt in my mind she was worth it. And if she needed an epic sign, I'd damn well give her one.

Thirty-one

ANNIKA

Maybe it made me a bad girlfriend, but I did not want to go to Axl's last home hockey game of the regular season.

I'd kept a super-low profile, tuning into the games at home. The advantage there? I could listen to the sportscaster's commentary, hit rewind, and watch what I'd missed. At a live game? I was so focused on my sexy beast whenever he took to the ice that I didn't pay attention to anything or anyone else.

But my man had actually nagged me about going to this game. "Princess, you haven't been to a home game in months. You don't have to sit in the group seats. I'll find you a single seat on the other side of the arena."

"Do I have to wear my Hammerquist jersey?"

He'd lifted that imperious brow. "Of course."

"What if someone recognizes me?"

He grinned. "Maybe you should wear the brown wig."

"You are *not* funny."

I ended up wearing a hoodie beneath the jersey, which was

better than a hat. Although I wasn't the only woman wearing HAMMERQUIST on my back, I thought to myself smugly how I would be the only woman wearing the *actual* Hammerquist on my front later.

Since I was alone and sort of bored, I snacked. Nachos, popcorn, licorice, cotton candy. I stuck with soda and skipped the beer. I'd shown solidarity with Axl and avoided booze when he did—the bonus orgasms I earned were way better and had zero calories.

I was about to sneak out during the break between the second and third periods when the announcer said they had a very special program planned and could everyone please remain seated.

The lights darkened for a moment, and then the words HAVE YOU SEEN THESE WOMEN? flashed across the TV screen. Followed by a picture of me. In the brown wig.

My heart stopped.

I blinked. I could not believe what I was seeing.

What the hell was going on? Was this some kind of joke? After a short pause, an image of blond me filled the screen. That started a rumbling through the arena.

I had the urge to slump deeper into my seat. Or slink out one of the exits.

Then a picture of me with red hair from last year's Halloween costume.

Louder rumbling. I actually heard someone shout my name.

Then all three pictures of me were put up at the same time.

It was obvious it was the same woman.

The next lines of text read:

BRUNETTE, BLONDE, REDHEAD—HAIR COLOR CHANGES
BUT THE HEART REMAINS THE SAME

The image changed again.

Axl kissing the brunette.

Axl kissing the blonde.

Axl kissing the redhead.

A gasp went through the arena.

THERE IS ONLY ONE WOMAN

THERE HAS ONLY EVER BEEN ONE WOMAN

FOR AXL HAMMERQUIST

AND SHE IS HERE TONIGHT

Oh god, what had he done? Maybe I should've waited to tell him about the Haversman contracts until after tonight's game like I'd originally planned instead of confessing all after girls' night out.

That was when the spotlight hit me.

"Annika Lund," a voice boomed over the arena's sound system, "could you please come down to the ice?"

I think I might've shaken my head *no* in a totally panicked WTF? moment—to the crowd's amusement—but Axl hadn't left anything to chance.

The next thing I knew, I was being helped out of my seat—by Brady and Walker.

"What is going on?" I hissed as they escorted me down the steps.

"You'll see," Walker said.

"I cannot believe you guys are in on this!"

"Forget about us. Enjoy every second of this," Brady said.

My heart was pounding so hard I thought I might pass out.

Jensen grinned at me and bowed as he opened the gate to the ice.

A chair waited for me. Not a posh, lush chair fit for a queen.

But something that resembled the iron throne from *Game of Thrones*.

Igor and Kazakov stood on each side and helped me in.

I had to be dreaming.

Had to.

Axl would laugh his ass off when I told him about this . . .

That was when the music started. When the voices kicked in to "Endless Love," the spotlight zoomed in on a lone hockey player at the other end of the ice.

Then he was speed-skating straight toward me.

The crowd went insane.

But I barely heard them.

My god. I loved this man so much. What might've looked absolutely ridiculous or cheesy to everyone else in the arena didn't matter a bit to me. I knew this wasn't a joke. Or a publicity ploy. I knew exactly what it was costing Axl to ditch his pride and make a public spectacle of himself for me.

The music cut off.

He skated to a stop in front of the chair, sending the spray of ice off to the side instead of all over me because he was thoughtful that way.

He slowly took off his hockey helmet and shook out his hair.

I clapped my hand over my mouth. He'd remembered that request I'd made early on in our "just PR" days. He'd dismissed it as hokey, embarrassing and lame. Vain and cartoonish. Treating it as a joke, even when he'd understood I thought it would be sexy and I hadn't been joking. But here he was, giving me that dream scenario I wanted. I didn't even mind that he'd skipped the part about taking off his shirt—all those glorious muscles of his were mine to admire, no one else's.

And it was far more romantic than I'd ever imagined.

Because even though he was fully clothed, he'd bared himself—heart and soul—to me for everyone to see.

He stood before me—my own Prince Charming in hockey gear.

Big heart.

Really big balls.

I saw the wariness in his eyes.

He was breathing hard. His face glistened with nervous sweat. I'd never seen a more beautiful and welcome sight in my life. I offered him my hand, and that calmed him.

Then Axl dropped to one knee.

The crowd lost their minds at that point.

I sort of did too. I'd started sobbing because I couldn't believe this was truly happening to me.

He grabbed a microphone beside my feet that I hadn't noticed. "Annika."

He swallowed with difficulty and I could scarcely breathe because I knew how hard this was for him. I leaned forward and touched his face, locking my gaze to his. I whispered, "Focus on me. Just me."

He nodded and kissed the inside of my wrist before he continued. "For months we've kept our relationship private, but it's time for the world to know we're a couple. This is the end of one hockey season, but I want it to be the beginning of our life together. Will you please marry me?"

I couldn't speak. I just nodded. Then I launched myself at him and it was a very good thing he was so steady on skates or he would've fallen on his ass.

I whispered, "I love you, Axl."

Then he kissed me—a lingering press of his lips to mine. Nothing more.

The spotlight cut out, leaving us alone in the dark on the ice. Around us the crowd was still cheering.

Axl stood and set me on my feet. "The team only gave me three minutes, so I have to go. But we'll finish this when the game is over, yah?"

"Yah."

The Lund Collective ambushed me when I entered the sky-box, still in a daze. Hugs first from Mom and Dad. Some tears too. Then hugs from my aunts and uncles. Then Ash and Nolan. And Lennox and Trinity. Dallas and I squealed together—probably less than we would have if we'd been by ourselves. Everyone seemed happy for me, which was great, given the fact that half of my brothers had punched my future husband in the face.

Peter had stopped me immediately after the on-ice event and congratulated me. He was impressed that Axl and I had pulled off a secret romance. He promised to deal with the press—neither Axl nor I had anything more to say tonight—and he assured me that this time I'd have full control of content.

We were sitting in the box, drinking a celebratory Grain Belt beer, when Jensen said to me, "So, how soon can Axl be out of his apartment now that you guys are official?"

Weird question. "I don't know. Why?"

"Because I called dibs on it. I've already found a new couch I wanna put in the living room."

"Whoa." Ash held up his hand. "Where does Axl live?"

"Snow Village."

"He lives in a snow globe?" Uncle Archer said.

Brady and Walker both choked on their beer.

"No, Dad, it's a—"

I could tell Nolan wanted to say *hippie commune*, but he smirked at me and amended it to "It's a place for athletes."

"Then it'd be good for Jens." He clapped him on the

shoulder. "I never liked that drafty loft of yours. Over a million and a half bucks for a one-bedroom without walls? You got snookered, boy."

"So I guess you won't be putting a bid in on it," Ash said to Nolan.

Nolan flipped him off.

"Spread the word: furniture, artwork and everything goes with it," Jensen said.

Walker and I exchanged a look. Jensen had been not a total dickhead since his injury, especially since his fate was still up in the air on whether it was a *career*-ending injury. He hadn't complained about physical therapy. He hadn't grown impatient or irritable with his progress or lack of progress, because he never mentioned it. He hadn't closed himself off from the family, which was what we all expected, sadly. Since Jensen practically lived at Axl's place, I'd spent more time with him than either Walker or Brady had in recent months. Something had happened after his injury that served as a life reboot of sorts. I didn't know what it meant or how long it'd last, but I was grateful to have my "old" little brother back.

Nolan said, "Okay, show of hands: how many of you knew that Annika and Axl were sneaking around?"

Dallas raised her hand, which wasn't a surprise to anyone.

Jensen's hand was up.

Nolan said, "How?"

"I've been hanging out at Axl's place, but I knew before that. Man, he was a freakin' goner for her the first time I met him. I saw the way he looked at her."

I blushed. Jens had a funny way of showing it, oh, by punching Axl in the face.

"Then when I saw the picture of him with the brunette, I knew it was Annika."

"You did?" Brady said skeptically.

"Yeah. She and Dallas played dress-up like that all the time."

"Who else knew?" Nolan asked.

My dad raised his hand.

Mom whirled on him. "Ward Lund. You know of this secret love and you don't tell me?"

"Yep." He allowed a smug smile. "Axl called me and swore he'd never disrespect Annika by cheating on her. He said they were together, but they both preferred to keep it private."

While everyone chatted about that, Dad pulled me aside. "Just so you know . . . Axl asked for my permission to marry you. Then he said he'd sign a prenup because he doesn't want your money—he just wants you." He cleared his throat. "He's a good man, sweetheart. I'm happy for you."

And I thought I was done with tears.

While my mother took my father aside to "chew his fat," my aunt Priscilla and aunt Edie approached me with Dallas. Aunt P took my hand. "Annika, we're meddlers, honey. You know that. So I'll be up-front. Brady and Walker were the first two Lunds to get married. We adore Lennox and Trinity and are happy to have them in the family. But your brothers denied your mother a chance to host a reception that befits her social standing. We just want to make sure—"

"Oh, trust me, I want the wedding with all the bells and whistles, the princess dress, the beribboned doves, the moving vans packed with towering floral arrangements and glittery candles, the twenty-seven-layer cake, the dance party that goes on until dawn. However . . . you'll have to encourage Mom to plan fast because Axl isn't going to wait long." And I didn't want to either.

"That's all we needed to know. We will make anything you want to happen . . . happen, in the time frame you want it to happen in."

I didn't doubt that a bit. Those women wielded some serious power.

After they left, Dallas hugged me. "I feel like my aura is actually tickled pink for you."

I laughed.

"You'll let me help you with some of the wedding planning, right?"

"A lot of the planning. That's what a maid of honor does."

Dallas leaned back and whispered, "For reals? You want me to be your maid of honor?"

"For reals. You've been through the designing-doll-gowns-out-of-tissues-and-lace years, and the dress-up-and-pretend-we're-getting-married years. As far as I'm concerned, you have years of experience." I glanced over my shoulder. "And to be honest? I'm sort of afraid I'll turn into Bridezilla, so you'll have to be my reality check."

"There's your reality check," she whispered.

I turned around to see Axl—my gorgeous, sweet, loving, perfect dream man—paused in the doorway.

His cheeks flushed when my family cheered at his arrival. He beckoned to me. "We have one thing to do and then we'll celebrate."

When I reached him, he clasped my hand in his and towed me down the short, deserted hallway. Then he pulled me into an alcove and hauled me against him, fastening his mouth to mine for a kiss that went on and on and just . . . undid me completely.

Apparently I wasn't done bawling.

He wiped away my tears. "Why are you crying?"

"Because I'm happy and overwhelmed. Thank you for . . ." I couldn't finish. I got choked up just thinking about him putting himself on display for me.

"You're okay with that excessive PDA?"

"It was beautiful and perfect and so unexpected." I grinned. "Totally epic!"

He laughed. "And you haven't even seen the ring yet."

I said, "Where is it?" fully expecting he'd hedge and say he wanted that part of our engagement to be private.

"It's in my top drawer in the bedroom. I planned on filling the tub up with bubbles and drinking a bottle of champagne with you. Then, when we hit the sheets, I was going to spring the ring on you and spend the rest of the night proving how much I love my fiancée."

I whapped him on the chest. "Ax-hell, you're *not* supposed to tell me that! It ruins the surprise!"

"You've had enough surprises for one day, yah?" He kissed me again. "Besides, I didn't spoil the surprise of what the ring looks like, and that's all you care about anyway. Are you worried I picked something you'll hate?"

"No. You know me better than anyone and this is important, so I know it will be perfect."

"Good answer, Attila."

"Can we go home now so you can slip that ring on my finger and make it official?"

"Won't your family be upset we're leaving?"

I kissed him. "I'm pretty sure they think we already left."

"Then let's go." Axl took my hand and we walked to the elevator together.

"Are you happy with how your first season with the Wild played out?"

"I wish we would've made the playoffs, but there's always next year." He pressed a kiss to my temple. "Besides, I'm more proud that I won you—my love of a lifetime—than something as trivial as the Stanley Cup."

I stopped and faced him. "Did you really just call the Stanley Cup trivial?"

"Everything is trivial compared to the way I feel about you, Princess."

"Oh, good answer."

We walked out through the front doors, hand in hand . . . just because we could.

He gave me a slow, sexy blink and then he smiled.

Heaven help me. His dimples were deep enough his beard couldn't mask them. His perfect teeth gleamed in a stunning smile. His lips retained that full, pouty look even with his wide grin.

He brushed his mouth across mine and whispered, "Guess it's my lucky day."

My lips parted to say, "Mine too," but no sound came out.

"How about we have a drink and you can tell me the real reason you used your tongue to introduce yourself instead of a handshake?"

That broke the spell. I lowered my arms and stepped back. "I'm sitting over here." I turned and headed to the table.

Perky Waitress showed up immediately after we took our seats. "What can I get you?" she asked him.

"Grain Belt, if you've got it on tap."

"Coming right up."

As soon as she was gone, he set his elbows on the table and invaded my space. "As much as I'd like to call you Hot Lips"—he grinned—"what's your name?"

Just then Vance and Tommy walked by—each with an arm draped over one of the women from the back room. Vance said, "See ya 'round, Amelia."

Crap. Of course karma, that vicious bitch, had ensured that I had to start this conversation with my new hot crush with the fact that I'd lied to those guys about my name. That'd go over well. Then he'd wonder what else I lied about and this would be over before it began.

"So . . . Amelia," he said, sounding pleased he'd overheard my name.

Surely at some point I could explain and we'd have a great laugh about it, right? So I went with it. "Yes?"

"What's your last name?"

"Carlson. And you are . . . ?"

"Walker Lund." His gaze roamed over my face. "Seems we're both of Scandinavian descent."

"You seem surprised. Because I'm not a six-foot-tall, rail-thin blonde with cheekbones that could cut glass and piercing blue eyes?"

He lifted a brow. "You got something against tall blondes with blue eyes?"

Then I realized how snappish my retort had come across. "Sorry. No. I find tall, blue-eyed blondes incredibly attractive." I flashed him a quick smile. "Especially the bearded variety. I've been overlooked and occasionally dumped because I'm not a blond temptress, so it's a knee-jerk reaction."

"You're plenty tempting, trust me. And don't pretend you aren't aware that any guy in this bar would change places with me in a heartbeat."

"Because I marched up to you and kissed you like it was my right?"

"I ain't gonna lie—that was one hot 'Hello, baby. I wanna eat you alive' kind of kiss. It's especially sexy when you've got wide-eyed innocence. Yet that mouth of yours . . ." His gaze dropped to my lips. "It's the stuff fantasies are made of. Plus, you've got great hair and a fantastic ass."

"When were you looking at my ass?"

"As soon as your back was turned. I really wished your table had been farther away."

Oddly flattering.

"So, sweetheart, why don't you come clean about why you really kissed me?"

"You want the long version?"

He shook his head. "I don't care, just as long as it's the no-bullshit version."

The words tumbled out of me in a rush. "My friend dragged me here and within an hour she'd hooked the interest of a really hot rugby player and left with him. As I lamented my crappy day and the sad state of my life lately, my ex-boyfriend showed up with his new girlfriend. And through a very awkward conversation, I learned that he'd been with her *before* we broke up. So in trying to not look pathetic because I was sitting alone, I lied and said I was waiting for a date."

Walker assessed me with scary detachment for several long moments before he spoke. "So that knockout kiss was all for show to make your dickhead ex jealous?"

"No." I glanced down at my hands. "I mean, yes, I had a plan of sorts, but when you walked in—"

"When I walked in . . . what?" he said testily.

"My plan vanished. I wasn't thinking about my jerk of an ex at all because I was entirely focused on you." As embarrassing as that was to admit, I met his gaze again.

"Is your ex still here, watching us now?"

"I have no idea."

He frowned as if he didn't believe me.

"Look. I didn't come up with the date idea to make him jealous. It was a spur-of-the-moment decision to make sure he knew that I'd moved on. I moved on the day I found out he was cheating on me. And to hear that he'd been cheating on me longer than I'd been aware of? I considered kneeing him in the nuts and using her fake boobs as speed punching bags. But then I figured even a dive bar like this would frown on that behavior. And the person I'd call to bail me out of jail was on a date with a rugby player." Somehow I managed to stop the blast of words and took a breath.

Walker let loose a robust laugh that was as charming as it was sexy.

The waitress returned with his beer.

He tried to pay but I waved him off and sent our server on her way. He held his mug up for a toast. "To giving in to overwhelming urges. You made this crap day a hundred times better."

"Back atcha." I touched my half-empty glass to his and drank.

After he set his beer down, he leaned back and crossed his arms over his chest. "So tell me what you do when you're not randomly kissing strangers in a bar."

I played coy. "Why don't you *guess* how I make my living?"

"What do I win if I guess right?"

Ah. So he was the "What's in it for me?" type. "What do you want?"

"Your phone number."

"Okay."

He pulled out his phone and looked at me.

"Oh. You want it *now*?" I rattled off the number without thought, watching his thick fingers type the digits in, wondering what he did for a living to earn calluses like that.

After he slipped his phone into his front pocket, he studied my face before his gaze dipped to the lace camisole stretched across my cleavage. "You're a teacher cutting loose during summer vacation. Your recent ex was also a teacher and you caught him banging more than the erasers with his new student teacher."

I laughed. "I'll give you points for creativity, but I'm afraid I'll just deduct those points when I tell you that you're wrong."

He affected an expression of shock. "I'm wrong? Damn. I'm never wrong. But I get another chance, right?"

"I don't remember agreeing to those parameters."

"Aha. That answer gave you away."

"How so?"

"Only lawyers or cops phrase things that way."

"Strike two." I sipped my margarita and eyed him over the salted rim. "You confident your third guess is a charm? Or are you about to strike out?"

He ran his hand over his beard. "You sound like my brothers with the sport references."

"Which is totally out of character for me since I don't follow any sports."

That surprised him. "None?"

"Nope. I don't get men's fascination with all things ball related." Right after the words left my mouth, Walker grinned.

"I could try to explain it to you, but I don't know if a conversation about my balls is appropriate since we just met."

I nudged his knee with mine beneath the table. "Quit stalling. What's my occupation?"

"You're a hostage negotiator with the FBI."

I made a buzzer sound.

Walker leaned forward. "I give in. Tell me."

Part of me wanted to lie and tell him I was a flight attendant—that had been a favorite fake occupation of Amelia's during college. But I liked this guy. He seemed to appreciate my quirky sense of humor, instead of acting like he wanted to run for the door. "I'm an artist."

"Really? That's cool. What medium do you work in?"

"All of them. I couldn't decide on a specific discipline because I couldn't see myself doing the same thing over and over like Thomas Kinkade does." I always used him as a reference because everyone seemed to know his name.

"But he's mega-rich," he pointed out.

"Good for him that he's above the poverty line as a working artist," I said dryly. "But making money with my art hasn't been my priority. I'm not saying that from an elitist attitude. The art I create just usually doesn't fit any kind of commercial mold."

"Such as?"

"The commission I lost today—which was one thing that contributed to my crap day—was for a textile piece. A mixed-media wall hanging that Missus Art Patron deemed too . . . modern and edgy."

Walker frowned and reached for his beer. "Isn't the definition of mixed media . . . modern?"

"Apparently she didn't get the memo regarding the parameters of newfangled artistic mediums. So rather than working with me to find a compromise, Mister Art Patron canceled the entire project. Now I'll have to find a part-time gig to cover that chunk of lost income."

"That sucks. You said that was one thing. What's the other crappy thing that happened today?"

The situation with my family seemed too personal to share. I stirred my watered-down drink, trying to come up with something else.

Walker took my hand and swept his thumb across my knuckles. "Might make you feel better to talk about it."

My belly did a little flip from his touch. I glanced up at him. He appeared genuinely interested, so I let fly. "My grandma left me her pearls after she passed on. I was too young to take 'proper' care of them, according to my step-monster, so she put them away until I was older. Every time I've asked about them, I've been assured the necklace is in a safe place and I can have it once I'm settled. Except now, since my half sister has gotten herself engaged, there was an engagement party I wasn't invited to and she's getting the pearls to wear on her wedding day. I hate to sound like a petulant child, but that's not fair. My grandma did not put a stipulation on them that the first granddaughter to tie the knot gets the pearls. But I have no recourse. It was just so typical of my stepmonster to make me feel like even if 'first wed' had been a determining factor in who gets the pearls, everyone knows it wouldn't have been me anyway."

"Babe. I'm sorry. That *isn't* fair." He set his forearms on the table. "Maybe we oughta plan a heist."

I couldn't help but grin. "Can't you see the headline? 'The Case of the Purloined Pink Pearls.'"

He laughed.

"While I appreciate the offer, should I be worried that you're a professional cat burglar?"

"Nah. I'm more of a dog guy."

"Funny. But speaking of . . . what does Walker Lund do to fill up his weekday hours?"

He smirked and those damn dimples winked at me. "Guess."

"I should've seen that coming."

"Yep."

"You dress up like a Viking warrior and reenact famous battle scenes at the Shakopee Scandinavian Culture Center. You wear skintight leather breeches and a fur vest over your bare, glistening chest. Oh, and you have a big . . . sword and a kick-ass shield that you use to beat back all the wenches who stand in line to be pillaged by you."

"Nice try. Points for vivid imagery and the use of the word 'glistening' with a straight face. But no."

"Shoot. I so thought I'd nailed you." *Dammit, Trin. What is wrong with you?*

"And extra points for sexual innuendo."

"Unintentional," I retorted.

"Still counts. Quit stalling and guess."

He'd set his hand back on the table by his beer glass. I reached over and ran the tips of my fingers across his rough-skinned knuckles. "Workingman hands," I murmured. "Maybe you're a Viking longboat builder?" When I looked up at him, the heat in his eyes set my stomach into free fall.

"That. Right there," he said on a low growl.

Confused, I said, "What?"

"That innocent look in your big green eyes. Makes a man think about all sorts of things that aren't even close to innocent."